1 0 DEC 2022

2 5 JAN 2023

Please return/renew this item by the last
date shown. Books may also be renewed
by phone or internet.

 www.rbwm.gov.uk/home/leisure-and-
culture/libraries

☎ 01628 796969 (library hours)

☎ 0303 123 0035 (24 hours)

D0528058

95800000199441

ALSO BY ELENA GOROKHOVA

A Mountain of Crumbs: A Memoir

Russian Tattoo: A Memoir

A Train to Moscow

A Novel

Moscow

ELENA GOROKHOVA

LAKE UNION
PUBLISHING

Published by Lake Union Publishing, Seattle

www.apub.com

Amazon, the Amazon logo, and Lake Union Publishing are trademarks of Amazon.com, Inc., or its affiliates.

ISBN-13: 9781542033879 (hardcover)
ISBN-10: 154203387X (hardcover)
ISBN-13: 9781542033862 (paperback)
ISBN-10: 1542033861 (paperback)

Cover design by Holly Ovenden

Printed in the United States of America

First edition

For Marina Maltseva,
a great Russian actress

ACT 1

IVANOVO

1

She immediately knows something is wrong. The door to Marik's house is ajar, and there is a black car blocking the street just a few meters away. Not really a car—there aren't many cars in Ivanovo. It looks more like the wagon that plucks drunks off the sidewalks on holidays and deposits them at the sobering station in the town's center.

Who is this wagon waiting for? Not for her friend Marik, for sure. Marik is seven, like Sasha, and no driver would waste time plowing through snow all the way to the edge of Ivanovo to stand by while a first grader pulls on his itchy uniform and tosses his books into a schoolbag. Despite the dusk of early mornings, Sasha has always savored this hour before school, from the moment she plunges out of the clouds of frost and into the warmth of Marik's house to see his father leaf through *Pravda* over a glass of tea to the minute she curls her fingers around the piece of sucking candy his mother stuffs into her hand before they leave for class. But all those safe mornings, she can sense, are now in the past. Today, everything is different.

When Sasha slinks in through the open door, she doesn't see Marik right away. Instead, she sees an unfamiliar man in a black coat and *ushanka* hat ripping apart the bed, turning the mattress over, tearing off the sheet, and yanking the blanket out of its duvet cover. She sees another man shaking out every book from the shelves, cutting out the binding, and squinting down its spine, which must be taking a long time because

Marik's mother is a literature teacher and has a lot of books. Sasha sees her standing by the table, next to her husband, clutching the back of a chair with both hands as though she would collapse if she didn't. The veins on the backs of her hands are swollen, thick as ropes. No one speaks, and the only sounds in the room are of tearing and slashing, the sounds of destruction. When the contents of the entire bookcase have finally been violated, another man, short and stumpy as a fireplug, snatches the briefcase of Marik's father off a chair and rips it open. He scans the sheets of paper with mathematical formulas scrawled in a hurried handwriting, as if he could understand any of them. Then he lifts his eyes and stares at the wall.

"Citizen Garkovsky, you are under arrest," he announces.

This is when Sasha sees her friend. Marik is crouching in the corner behind an armchair where he and Sasha usually read together after school. His head is between his knees, his red hair sticking out in all directions like taut little springs, so Sasha cannot see his face.

"For what?" asks Marik's mother in a ragged voice.

"You'll find out," says the fireplug, avoiding her eyes.

Marik's mother gives him a hard stare, as though she were facing a student who had misbehaved the entire year and failed the course. "You were in my class a few years ago, weren't you?" she says. "I remember you. You were a good student. You liked Lermontov."

The guard turns away and bangs the briefcase with papers on the table, as if it were the papers' fault that in eighth grade, he liked Lermontov, that he was a good student, that now he is here to arrest his former teacher's husband.

"It's all a mistake, just a misunderstanding," Marik's father says. He tries to speak in his usual manner, but his voice is cracking. It is a voice Sasha hears every morning, a voice of a mathematician from the Academy of Sciences, a voice that has always made her feel secure. She wants him to be right; she wants it all to be a mistake. She is in first grade and hasn't read Lermontov yet, but how can someone who likes poetry, she wonders, arrest her best friend's father? How can a good student of literature arrest anyone?

The first policeman, a tall, gangling man, has finished ripping apart the slashed mattress and has turned to the pillows, unleashing a blizzard of feathers that rivals the snow falling behind the window. Having failed to find anything (Sasha can't imagine what anyone could possibly hide inside a pillow), he strides to the table and pushes Marik's father away from his wife and toward the door. It is a small push, but there is a pent-up force in it; while still restrained, it makes Sasha think that it may be a precursor to upcoming, less civilized shoves.

This is when her friend Marik storms out of the corner where he has been cowering and flattens himself against his father, his arms like a vise around his father's waist. For a moment, the taller guard freezes, uncertain of what to do, but then his features reassemble into the earlier official mask, and the moment of hesitation melts away, like snow on the roof of the police wagon outside. He grabs Marik and tries to wrench him off his father. But Marik doesn't let him. He dives under the guard's arms and punches him on his thighs and kicks him on his shins. "Leave my father alone, you scum, you asshole!" he yells at the top of his lungs, words that sound incompatible with Marik and his house, adult curses Sasha hears only from drunks behind the liquor store. That's when she, too, plunges between Marik and the guard and tries to grip her friend's arm to pry him away from the policeman, but the next moment, she and Marik are rolling on the floor, slammed against the wall. She hears Marik's mother scream and sees her pound the policeman with her fists, even though it is evident that he is oblivious of her, pushing Marik's father toward the front door, still open, as if the private life of her friend and his parents has already ceased to exist.

"Put on your coat, Citizen Garkovsky," says the former fan of Lermontov in a flat voice, trying to normalize what has just happened. He stuffs the briefcase with mathematical formulas under his arm, his eyes flickering from Sasha and Marik on the floor to the police wagon in the window, still unable to look at his teacher.

"Please don't worry," says Marik's father to his wife and son, but also to Sasha. He stands by the door, scrambling to get his arms through the sleeves of the coat Marik's mother holds out for him. "Go to school and make me proud," he says to the children, who are clutching on to each other on the floor, braving the bruises that are just beginning to throb. "They will straighten this out soon," he promises. "I will be back in a few days." He is trying to stay composed, but his voice is quivering. "All will be well," he says, even though his words sound hollow, lacking the weight required to ground them in Sasha's mind, maybe even in his own.

Should Sasha believe him? Despite the two policemen leading him out of the house, Marik's father still looks like the hero from a film about the first Five-Year Plan they saw at school, imperishable and proud. Whom can she believe if she doesn't believe him? She holds on to Marik to keep him from lunging after the guards, wishing that everything, as her grandma likes to say, would soon indeed turn out to be well.

2

Sasha stands next to Marik by the gate to the courtyard, checking that Grandma can't see her. Her house, like Marik's, sits on the outskirts of Ivanovo where the town streetcar ends its route behind a field, where every hour it crawls past Grandpa's garden to come to a standstill farther down the street, by the cluster of lilac bushes. But Sasha is not thinking about the lilacs now. She is thinking about the streetcar clanging along the track, with sparks bursting on the wires above. The best manifestation of defiance is to jump onto the back of the streetcar and straddle the long piece of iron protruding like a tail, gliding past the clumps of nettles, past the envious glances of their friends, until the streetcar screeches to a stop and its driver rolls a cigarette between his fingers and cups his hands around a lighted match. So far, nine-year-old Andrei, two years older than Marik and Sasha, is the only one who has had the guts to ride on the streetcar's metal tail, and he has been sauntering around with his hands in his pockets since, forgetting that the three of them are friends, whistling and gazing over their heads as if they've suddenly shrunk in size.

She looks back to check that Grandma's face has disappeared from the window and waits for the streetcar with thrill and trepidation, as if it were a final test at the end of school in May. She and Marik both wait, ready and determined, glancing back at Grandma's house, which Sasha has always known is full of secrets. Secrets that are stashed in letters tied with ribbons under Grandma's bed, tucked away into the upper shelves of the armoire Sasha cannot reach, hidden in the dusty space of the storage loft above the front door. They are secrets from the old life, the life before Sasha and Marik were born: before the country shuddered and convulsed into a new social order, before her mother's two younger brothers became engulfed by the war. They wait and wait for their defining moment, their hands sweaty, their stomachs growling in protest to the daring plan they have concocted. To shrink the waiting, they kick the dust, although they know they shouldn't, because it will ruin their shoes, and getting new ones is an event almost as big as overthrowing the tsar.

And then, from around the corner, they hear the approaching rumble. The rattling of windows becomes louder as the streetcar turns and heaves in their direction and for a moment swallows them in its enormous wake. They let it pass and then run behind it on the track so that the driver can't see them in his mirror. She sees Marik grab onto the iron tail and jump, straddling the metal bar, clutching its cold neck with both hands. She jumps, too, and the tracks begin to sail away from under her feet, just like she saw in a movie once, but she concentrates on holding on. Her hands are sweaty, and Marik's must be, too, because she can see him grasp at the metal as his fingers keep slipping off. Is he as frightened as she is? Is his heart beating as fast as hers? To keep her own balance, she focuses on his tense back in front of her. Then the car lurches forward and slows to a crawl. Suddenly she can see Andrei from the corner of her eye, frozen against the fence. He glides past and disappears, but neither Marik nor she looks back because they can't afford to lose their balance when the streetcar swings on another turn. Then, when the brown grass rolls into view and when they are both still on the back of the streetcar clattering past the lilac bushes, she knows that they have done it, that the two policemen didn't win, that Andrei will never again gaze over their heads or spit out sunflower shells in their direction.

~

When she opens the front door, she sees Grandma, who usually sails around the house, running from the kitchen with her mother's speed. Her face, normally soft and wrinkled, has become sharp and angular, and her eyes behind round glasses burn with an anger Sasha has never seen. Grandma locks the door behind her and orders her to sit down.

It turns out that Andrei was not the only one who witnessed her forbidden ride on the back of the streetcar. A neighbor saw it, too, probably peeping between the boards of the fence, and, being nosy as their neighbors are, ran to their house to tell Grandma. So now Sasha is forced to stay in until her mother and Grandpa come home, and then who knows what punishment such reckless disobedience will get her. Grandma shakes her head and walks up and down the room, wiping her hands on her apron.

"Do you know what could have happened?" she asks in a shrill, unfamiliar voice. "Do you understand how dangerous it is, to jump onto a moving streetcar?" The word *dangerous* hisses out of her mouth like an explosion.

Sasha knows she is guilty because she broke the rules, but she has also done something that made her fearless and proud, like her mother must have felt before she was born when, despite the military order that forbade treating civilians, she cut into the belly of a nine-year-old wounded boy with her surgeon's scalpel and pulled out pieces of shrapnel, one by one. She and Marik did it, a small revenge for the bruises from the guard who took away her friend's father, the bruises she never revealed to anyone at home.

"But nothing happened," she pleads. "The streetcar is so slow here, right before the end of the route. It's so slow, I can walk faster," she says, stretching the truth so Grandma's face will lose its sharpness and become soft and wrinkled again.

She wants to tell her about Andrei's admiring stare and about Marik's tense shoulders in front of her on the tail of the streetcar; she wants to brag about their accomplishment and newly earned respect, but Grandma paces back and forth, not listening to any of this. She blames herself and says she is an old fool who didn't see what was happening because she was too busy in the kitchen boiling buckets of water for a load of laundry and wasn't looking out the window as often as she should have been.

"Such a reckless thing to do," she keeps saying. "And what if Andrei decides to jump off a cliff. Will you follow him, too?" she demands. "Mama was right when she refused to let him into the house. And what about Marik?" she asks. "Did he ride on the back of the streetcar, too?"

"No," Sasha lies, wondering if the neighbor snitched on Marik, too, wondering if Grandma will save her from what awaits when her mother and Grandpa get home from work. She will never tell anyone about Marik riding the streetcar with her. They did it, and that's enough.

She is on a bench, facedown, on her stomach. The wood surface is hard, made harder by her mother's hands that are pressing on her legs and shoulders, holding her down. She turns her head and sees Grandpa pulling the belt out of his trousers, black and thick, with a round metal buckle. She tries to flail her arms and kick her legs, but her mother's grip is like a vise. She turns her head, the only part of her body she can move, and sees Grandma standing by the door, the light from the electric bulb glaring off her glasses so she can't see her eyes. The belt swishes above, and she hears it cut through the air before it lands on her behind and leaves a sting so painful, she wails. But she knows Grandpa won't stop with only one strike, so she keeps wailing and screaming and wiggling under her mother's hands as the belt does its swishing and stinging, as the tears on her face mix with snot and leave pathetic swirls of drool on the wood of the bench. "I won't do it anymore!" she howls to halt the belt. "I won't, I won't, I swear I won't!" she shrieks, in sync with its rhythm, and then there is no more swishing, and the air becomes whole again.

"Next time I'll spank you with nettles," says Grandpa and threads the belt through the loopholes on the waist of his pants.

Her mother's hands open so she can scramble off the bench, past Grandma, whose eyes she still cannot see, and run to her bed and crawl under the blanket to pity herself and her punished behind, to think about injustice and the meaning of life.

At dinner, her mother talks about dangers. The dangers she saw at the front, where she was a surgeon until Sasha was born, and the dangers they all read about in *Pravda* or hear about from babushkas who sit on benches near the shed and chew on sunflower seeds. Mines in the fields and unexploded shells under the forest loam, whirlpools in the river where they go to swim in the summer, gangs of hooligans who get drunk on moonshine and break windows at the school and rip apples off Grandpa's apple tree. There are already so many dangers lurking around that only an unthinking fool like Sasha would conjure up new ones.

"Do you understand what you did?" she asks, and Sasha nods silently because she can still feel the belt welts and doesn't want to provoke any more punishment.

"Eat your soup," says Grandma and pushes another slice of bread toward her.

Back in the under-the-blanket murk, Sasha decided she would not eat, so she shakes her head and presses her lips together to show she is serious.

"Eat," demands her mother.

She sits with her hands on her knees, listening to her ailing backside.

"Are you deaf?" asks Grandpa.

"Just a couple of spoonfuls," says Grandma in her regular soft voice. "Did you hear me?" asks her mother. "What did I just say?"

"When I eat, I'm deaf and mute," she answers, quoting one of Grandpa's house rules.

"Then I'll have to feed you like a baby," says her mother and gets up. She sits next to Sasha on the bench, lifts a spoonful of soup from her own plate, and pushes it against Sasha's lips. She tenses her mouth, but her mother pushes harder.

"Next time, it's nettles," says Grandpa and gives her a hard look from across the table. His eyes are blue, the color of the forget-me-nots he grows around the gate, with grooves of deep wrinkles radiating into his white hair. He was a peasant before the Revolution, but after 1917, when the people rose up with hammers and scythes to liberate themselves from the yoke of tsarist oppression, he became an engineer. Grandpa's peasant ancestry is the reason they have three rooms and a kitchen all to themselves. Before the Revolution, the entire house belonged to Grandma's father. He was a factory supervisor and because he hadn't been exploited like workers or peasants, he didn't deserve to keep the place where he lived. Now one half of the house is theirs, with three families of neighbors sharing the other half, one family in each room. Grandpa must have been a pretty important peasant because they have an indoor toilet on their side of the house, while the three other families all troop to the outhouse in the back. Sasha doesn't understand why Grandma's father deserved to be thrown out of his own house and then shot for supervising factory work, but she has a sense no one wants to talk about this, so she doesn't ask.

With her mother trying to feed her, Sasha can see she is at a disadvantage, just like when she was pinned to the bench, so she relaxes her lips and lets the spoon spill its contents into her mouth. She holds it there, warm, salty water with potato chunks and grains of barley, as her mother repeats the motion three times and then goes back to her seat. Maybe she realizes Sasha is not going to swallow it, or maybe she is simply tired and hungry after work and wants to finish her own food. When all the plates are emptied but Sasha's and she is finally released from the table, she goes outside and, her body still aching from the policeman's shove and her grandfather's belt, spits out the soup into Grandpa's gooseberry bush.

3

Marik is *intelligentny*, a word Sasha's mother uses to characterize people. It is a salad mix of education, culture, intelligence, and manners, and all their neighbors and acquaintances have been divided into *intelligentny* and not *intelligentny*. Somehow the first group always comes out much smaller than the second. Not *intelligentny*: the three families who live in the other half of their house; every saleswoman in every grocery store, including Aunt Dusya from the bakery, with her carbon-penciled eyebrows and a kitchen voice; Sasha's friend Andrei because his mother is a janitor who finished only the seven compulsory grades of secondary school and now wears a burlap apron over her cotton dress when she sweeps the yard with a bunch of twigs attached to a stick. *Intelligentny*: Irina Vasilievna, who gives piano lessons in her house two blocks away; Marik and his mother, pale and freckled and, as rumor has it, a Jew.

Sasha doesn't know what Jews are and how they are different from the rest of them, but from the way people lower their voices when they say *yevrey*, a word that is spat out like a wormy chunk of apple, she guesses Jews are worse than they themselves are in some dark and hidden way they cannot discuss in public. She knows only one other Jew—Moisey Davidovich Zlotnikov, the head of the anatomy department of her mother's medical institute and the adviser of her dissertation. Sasha has seen Dr. Zlotnikov only once, when her mother took her to work because Grandma's heart was hurting, and he didn't look different from any other person in Ivanovo. He had glasses and a goatee, and he rose from his desk and bent down to shake Sasha's hand as if she were an anatomy professor and not a first grader with two skinny braids.

Marik is marked by another scar everyone knows about, an event Sasha can still see in her mind as if it happened only yesterday. In addition to being a Jew, he is now the son of a prisoner. After that morning, Sasha thought that Marik's father had missed a bell and come late for work—solid grounds for an arrest, according to her mother—but then she heard her attach the word *politichesky* to his name. Her mother uttered the word in a low voice when they were all at the table slurping cabbage soup.

"They don't put innocent people in camps, Grandpa said. Stalin knows who is with us and who is against us. Stalin—our leader, our father, the successor of our great Lenin. The engineer of our thunderous victory over Germany."

Andrei expressed a similar view, only in less pompous words. "He must have done something if he got arrested," he muttered, sharpening a branch with his pocketknife as they sat on the roof of the shed after Marik's mother called him home.

Andrei's father is not here, either, but according to Grandpa, he has a better chance of coming home than Marik's father because he is not a *politichesky*. Maybe Andrei's mother, as she sweeps the yard, also turns her head at the creak of the gate, just like Grandma has done since the end of the war, still waiting for her son Kolya to come back from the Leningrad Front.

It is her grandpa's birthday, which means a samovar is puffing on the dining table and Grandma is standing over a frying pan, her hands white with flour, making pancakes. Marik and Sasha are under the table, where the old linoleum is torn, revealing boards worn through by many prewar and maybe even prerevolutionary feet. While the guests, all *intelligentny*, are busy eating boiled potatoes with pickled cabbage, the children are out of their sight, playing a game while waiting for tea, when they can load slices of bread with spoonfuls of strawberry and apple jam from the fruit in Grandpa's garden.

They are separated from real life by the linen tablecloth that almost touches the floor. The jagged tear in the linoleum, in their imagination, is a river, and the torn edges of plastic are its banks. They just finished reading a book of Andersen's fairy tales, and the story they are playing is about a one-legged tin soldier. The brave warrior survives a fall from a window and the raging waves of a waterfall, only to die in a fire at the end. He is silently in love with a paper ballerina, who, in the soldier's mind, has only one leg, too. She has a pretty tinsel rose pinned to her dress. Does she know about the soldier's love? The hole in the linoleum is the river that will rush forward and drag the tin soldier to its depths, the river that will sink his boat and deposit him into the stomach of a big fish.

Marik is the soldier, and Sasha is the paper ballerina. The soldier is terrified of the darkness inside the belly of the fish, but he is too proud to cry for help because he wears a uniform. Through the scraps of ripped linoleum, the river roars until it becomes a waterfall, the boat made from newspaper disintegrates, and the water finally closes over the soldier's head.

"Farewell, warrior! Ever brave,

"Drifting onward to thy grave," recites Marik from the book.

Marik is as brave and proud in real life as the tin soldier is in the story, and, Sasha knows, he doesn't really believe that he is drifting to his grave.

Then, beyond the tablecloth, the din of voices quiets and the piano chords burst into the air before Grandma's voice, trained in a prerevolutionary opera school and called a mezzo-soprano, begins to sing about fragrant bunches of white acacia flowers. The music swells, and

Grandma's voice does, too, soaring and then descending, the lyrics compelling her to remember her distant youth when she still naively believed in love.

Sasha now hears the clinking of dishes, which means the table is being cleared of the dinner plates to get it ready for tea and jam, so she knows she has to be fast. "And back in the same room, the soldier saw the ballerina, still balancing on one leg." She extends her leg, like the dancer in the story, although she has to crouch not to hit the top of the table. "And then the boy threw the soldier into the stove. And the ballerina, caught in the draft, fluttered into the fire, too." She pauses. "They both melted, by the flames or by their love, no one knew."

There is applause on the other side of the tablecloth curtain and requests for more songs, accompanied by the clinking of teacups against the saucers.

"The ballerina was made from paper," says Marik. "So there was nothing left of her."

"Not true!" Sasha cries out. "A tinsel rose from her dress the maid found in the ashes." Despite the approaching tea with sweets, she can't let the dancer disappear without a trace.

"All right, a tinsel rose," Marik concedes. He stares at the river of the torn linoleum, sniffling and wiping his nose with the back of his hand. "But the soldier did not die. He melted down into a lump in the shape of a little tin heart."

Sasha likes it that something remained of the soldier and the ballerina after they burned in the fire, but she is not sure about the little tin heart. Is it too sappy a finale for such a proud warrior? She doesn't know, yet she decides to accept it without an argument. Despite its lack of what her mother values most, grit, Marik's ending seems to be a good fit for the story of courage and love they have just played out on this make-believe stage of the linoleum-river setting. It makes her happy and lighthearted, and she feels her mouth stretch into a smile, all on its own.

4

"Stalin, our military glory," sings a voice above her head. The radio, a little brown box with a woolen front, is perched on a shelf beside a wood-burning stove, and even if Sasha could reach it and silence the Stalin song they all know by heart, she wouldn't dare. She is standing here because she is being punished. The offense didn't approach, in its severity, the ride on the back of a streetcar, so the payback doesn't rise to the height of a whipping.

This morning, Grandma decided to unfold the old newspapers piled on the porch and saw that they were all stained with grease. Each day before going outside, Sasha would hide a slice of black bread drenched in sunflower oil and sprinkled with salt inside the newspaper heap, and when Grandma's face disappeared from the window, she would unearth the treat and savor it on the street in all its rich and oily glory. The best part was taking turns with Andrei and Marik, all three of them biting into the thick rye delicacy so much tastier in the fields, amid clumps of tall grass and sorrel. She doesn't know what possessed Grandma to sort through the old papers, with three heads of cabbage wilting on the kitchen floor, waiting to be grated, layered with salt, and pressed into a bucket to be eaten in the winter.

She whined and whimpered as Grandma dragged her inside, up the creaky steps of the porch, across the dining room, and into the corner. "A fine thing for a girl to do," she said and turned Sasha around to face the peeling wallpaper with faded berries and vines that must have been red and green at some time she doesn't remember. "Nice girls eat inside, with their napkins tucked in the front and their elbows off the table." She said this in such a determined voice that Sasha could almost see those napkins Grandma spoke about, squares of white linen she kept in her closet, part of her dowry (such an old, prerevolutionary word), until she had to rip them up for diapers when Sasha's mother and her uncles were born. She hadn't lamented them; since there was nothing to eat, the need for napkins vanished right after the disappearance of food.

When the song praising Stalin ends with the bang of cymbals, the voice from the radio announces, "Tonight we perform Chekhov's *Three Sisters.*"

She doesn't know about Chekhov yet because she just finished the first grade, but this radio play doesn't sound like anything they ever get to hear: the anthem of the Soviet Union that wakes them up in the morning or news from the fields with rumbling tractors her mother turns on when she returns from work. Sasha always wonders about the destination of these tractors filled with wheat. Maybe they are all sent to Moscow or Leningrad, which she knows are much more important to their country than Ivanovo, but she is afraid to ask because Grandpa is always within earshot, and he wouldn't appreciate her questioning the news.

But no wheat can be important when a story so much like theirs is broadcast on the radio, a story of three sisters who seem to live their lives. As she faces the wallpaper, the sisters take over their house and their kitchen, with a pail of drinking water and a dipper floating on top, a table covered with a tablecloth Grandma has cross-stitched between frying onions for soup and turning up dirt for potatoes and dill, a wood-burning stove that looks like a checkerboard, since half the tiles have fallen off. The oldest sister, Olga, is Grandma; Masha is her mother; and Irina, the youngest of the three, is Sasha. They sit around a table where a samovar puffs out little clouds of steam, blow into saucers of hot tea, and talk about Moscow and another life.

What is this other, better life the sisters dream and speak about in urgent, breathless voices? "To leave for Moscow, end everything here," says Irina, and Sasha repeats it in the theatrical voice the actress uses, a voice full of drama and importance. The men from the play are all in the military, although there is no war going on, and they're called lieutenant and colonel and even baron—an ancient word, because all the barons were disposed of in 1917. "I'm so tired," says Irina in the third act as Sasha picks at the grains of cement where tiles fell off the side of the stove. "This work is without poetry, without thought. I dream of Moscow every night; I've almost lost my mind."

"I've almost lost my mind," Sasha repeats, trying to sound as desperate as the actress on the radio. "And why I am still alive, why I haven't killed myself, I don't understand."

She doesn't want Irina to kill herself. She wants her to go on acting.

Then there is a gunshot, sharp and dry as snapped kindling, and Sasha starts sniffling. It wasn't Irina, but the baron Irina was going to marry who just got killed in a duel, and that means she will never be able to leave this provincial town that is driving her toward insanity and desperation. She will never be able to move to Moscow and live that other life she's been dreaming about, a life full of poetry and happiness.

Sasha is standing in the corner, hoping that Grandma won't call her in for dinner yet. The words of the play lap around her like the ripples of the river, washing over every pore of her skin, every fiber of her soul. She is afraid to move, breathing very carefully because she knows there is something big happening right now, more important than the gunshot that killed Irina's fiancé, weightier than going to Moscow. Something even more significant than the ride on the back of the streetcar, the flogging, and the new respect in Andrei's eyes.

She imagines the three actresses playing the sisters, in long dresses and makeup, in front of an audience wrapped in prerevolutionary velvet and furs. They are tall and beautiful, and their big eyes, outlined in stage makeup, sparkle with tears. She admires them, but she envies them more. She imagines how they first read the play, repeating every word, committing them to memory the way her teacher tells the students to memorize Pushkin's poems in her Russian class. She imagines them practicing the scenes, pretending to live in a world she knows nothing about, a world of nobility and servants. A swarm of questions buzzes in her head. How do they know what it feels like to have your supper cooked by a servant, to give parties and live in a house big enough for all those guests?

Even if a miracle happened and the empty shelves of their store suddenly sprouted with bologna and cheese, if their half of the house stretched and doubled in size, whom would her mother ask to come to dinner? Would she invite anyone at all? Certainly not the three families on the other side of the wall, who bark at each other every morning because they can't figure out the order of the outhouse trips, and not Andrei's mother, because she is a janitor who sweeps the yard.

And what if the actresses who play the sisters are not pretending at all? What if they have stopped being themselves and turned into the Chekhov sisters? Sasha is so fascinated by this possibility—the possibility of becoming someone else—that her cheeks burn as hot as the sides of the stove. The possibility of becoming Irina and living a noble life so different from theirs, a life of guests and servants and longing for Moscow. She can relate to longing to live in Moscow better than she can relate to guests and servants. She has always wanted to go to the May Day parade in Red Square, and her mother said that she may even take her there one day, on an overnight train that whistles before it pulls into their platform, immersing the station in clouds of smoke and soot. It feels gratifying to find similarities between Chekhov's Irina and herself; it makes Sasha feel sophisticated and almost grown-up. Maybe she can be like Irina, dreaming and hopeful and giving orders about what she wants for dinner. Maybe she can become an actress.

She stands under the radio, struck by the simple realization of what her future is going to be. She is going to be an actress and live a thousand lives. Lives that her mother, or Grandpa, or even Grandma have never even heard about, lives they will never know.

Sasha stands under the radio, pitying her old self, who only yesterday wanted to be an ice cream vendor and the week before a streetcar driver—such small, pathetic dreams. She feels sorry for her previous self, who only three hours earlier didn't know anything about Theater. It's a frightening thought that had Grandma not discovered the oily newspaper on the porch, she would never have had a chance to hear this radio play and find out what she was meant to be.

By the end, when Irina realizes that she will never see Moscow, when the actress's voice becomes heavy and drained of hope, Sasha knows that no matter what happens, she is going to be an actress when she turns eighteen, and this feeling of certainty spreads around her chest like a cup of hot tea sweetened with two spoonfuls of Grandma's black currant jam. She will spend her life onstage, her voice projected and her soul transformed; she will live the lives of others, and shed their tears, and die their deaths.

She will stow this secret inside her like a treasure, away from the neighbors' inquisitive glances, away from her mother's teacher's voice and Grandpa's blue stare. She will hold this secret on the back shelf of her heart, and no one will suspect anything, not even Grandma, who must have felt the hot touch of Theater when her retrograde father prohibited her from singing opera in Moscow. Sasha will pretend she wants to be an engineer, like Grandpa, or a doctor, like her mother, so no one will suspect anything until she finishes tenth grade and then leaves for Moscow to study acting.

5

"If you behave," her mother says, "we'll see about going to Moscow for the May Day parade."

The *if you behave* phrase, she knows, is as deep as their drinking well, but for a few months, she can stay away from dangers and honor Grandpa's house rules. She will behave. She will be like the three sisters from the play, dreaming and hopeful, waiting for Moscow, with its promise of another life.

On April 28, Sasha and her mother finally board the train at the Ivanovo junction. They stare at the birches and firs running behind the window; they drink tea out of glasses in metal holders the conductor with brass buttons on her uniform brings before they go to sleep, and then she wakes up in Moscow. The train lurches and exhales a cloud of steam, and she panics, afraid that she has slept through Moscow and now it's too late. But her mother is folding up the blanket into a perfect square, and she realizes that her fear is silly, that Moscow is the last stop on the train route because there is nothing else beyond it.

They walk onto the platform in a crowd bristling with elbows. They walk past people sleeping on wooden benches, past a cistern with "beer" painted on its side and a woman in a white apron rinsing the only mug under a squirt of water, out into a street, as wide as a whole potato field but entirely paved.

Outside the station, Moscow explodes around her with stone facades that rise into the sky and block the sun; with rivers of asphalt that radiate in five different directions; with the whistle of a militiaman who wields a zebra baton to freeze the four lanes of traffic and then, like a magician, make them move again; with buses and trolleys circling around a statue of Lenin, as if performing a ritual dance, and then, on cue from the militiaman's baton, vanishing into the tunnels of streets. It stuns her with its energy and bustle; it invades her senses; it pumps into her ears a loud, brazen invitation to a different life.

They are staying with Grandma's cousin Baba Yulia, who is short and wide and has a puffy face. She lives with her son, Uncle Seryozha, and his twenty-year-old daughter, Katya. The apartment is a dark, long corridor with a kitchen attached to the one end and two rooms to the other. Instead of a pail and dipper, the kitchen has a faucet, and the stove blooms with the gentle petals of gas when her mother holds a lighted match to a burner. Their bed is set on a divan in the room where Baba Yulia and Katya sleep behind a yellow curtain that disperses dust and a smell of mothballs.

On the first day, they don't even see Uncle Seryozha. The door to his room is shut, and no one is allowed in. "It's his illness," says her mother, but her eyebrows are mashed together, and Sasha knows that this illness is not as simple as measles or the flu.

In the evening, Baba Yulia and Katya set the table, on which, like in a fairy tale, appear pink slices of bologna, a hunk of perforated cheese, and a loaf of bread so soft, it gives under the weight of the butter she slathers on.

Baba Yulia, in an apron over a housedress, speaks somberly, but Sasha can see that she is happy to have them as sympathetic listeners. She tells them about Uncle Seryozha, who was an engineer at the Moscow automobile factory before the war. He was more than an engineer, Baba Yulia says; he was an inventor. He was the author of something called a patent that advanced the Soviet auto industry.

"This is what did him in," says Baba Yulia. "His dedication. For a new car model he was building at home, he needed ten special screws." She chews on her lip, and Sasha notices that she has only four teeth, three on the top and one on the bottom, all brown as crumbling stumps. "Stores didn't have the screws. Stores didn't have anything, but we looked anyway. We looked everywhere. His wife, Lusya, may she rest in heaven, took a day off from work to go all the way to a department store in Luzhniki." Baba Yulia pauses and stares into space, as if she could see the heaven where Uncle Seryozha's wife may be resting.

"I told him, leave this project be—work on something else until we find the screws." Baba Yulia shakes her head. "But did he listen? He took the ten screws from the factory where he worked." She stabs her fork into the boiled potato on her plate and mashes it down ferociously, as if it were the potato's fault that Uncle Seryozha didn't listen to her. "All I can say is he was lucky they arrested him on criminal, not political, charges. Ten years in camps, a year for each screw."

"That's the only reason he was able to come back last year," Katya chimes in. "Had it been a political crime, he'd still be rotting in Magadan."

"Where is Magadan?" Sasha asks, but her mother frowns. Maybe she thinks that it is impolite to ask questions about a place that makes people rot.

"In Siberia, on the other side of the Urals," says Katya. She cuts off a slice of cheese and puts it on Sasha's plate. She likes Katya. Her tight curls tremble when she speaks, and her round cheeks with freckles look as if someone splashed muddy water onto her face. She likes the sound of Katya's job—*telefonistka*—an elegant and impressive title, a word that rolls off her tongue like a whistle.

"He'll sober up in a day or two," says Baba Yulia. "It's the damned holidays, with all those banners and balloons. It's all that cheer." The door to Uncle Seryozha's room is behind her, and Sasha can almost see him crouched by the keyhole, half-rotten, listening. Baba Yulia grabs their empty plates and, with a deliberate clatter, stacks them up on the oilcloth. "But what can you do?" she asks, addressing a ballerina in a porcelain tutu bending on the sideboard shelf. The ballerina doesn't answer, and Baba Yulia picks up the plates and shuffles out, mumbling something through her four brown teeth.

At night, lying on the divan next to her mother, Sasha thinks about the three sisters and the actresses who played them. She thinks about how they believed the words Chekhov had written, pretending to be Olga, Masha, and Irina. But it isn't the same as pretending to want to be a teacher or an engineer so that no one suspects that she really wants to be an actress. This is the true pretending. It is Theater, the real make-believe, exciting and magical, not at all like the everyday make-believe they all have to live by.

In the morning, Katya takes them to see Moscow by trolleybus, and they get off in front of the central food store. Inside, behind the heavy doors of glass and oak, it feels like the rooms of Ivanovo's only art gallery. But it doesn't have the odor of a museum. It smells of the flour that hangs in the air of the bakery department, where bricks of black bread and loaves of white *bulka* are stacked on shelves like firewood, of milk that an aproned saleswoman ladles into aluminum vats that people pass to her over the counter, of cookies with patterns of the Moscow spires embossed on the front. The glass displays show three different kinds of cheese: a dense brick called Soviet, an anemic-looking wheel of Russian, and a cube of punctured Swiss—all real, all for sale. In front of the glass, as if guarding all this treasure, are chocolate bars called Soviet Builder in paper sleeves with a picture of a muscular man brandishing a hammer.

Even Sasha's mother, who was a surgeon during the war and doesn't surprise easily, stops in front of a meat counter to gawk at the signs for beef and pork, at the bones piled in rows, at livers and kidneys, dark and glistening, perfect for the sour pickle soup they haven't had since Sasha was four.

But the most unbelievable thing of all is not how much they have in Moscow. It is how little they buy. In Ivanovo, when Grandma and Sasha have stood in line from noon until her mother returns from work, they always buy kilograms of whatever it is they are standing in line for. They buy as many kilograms as the store is willing to dispense, as many as they can carry home. That's why when Grandma goes to the store, she always takes Sasha and sometimes even Grandpa. Here a woman in a felt hat is frivolously asking for a hundred grams of ham, sliced, please. A hundred grams? If ham magically turned up on the counter of their Ivanovo store, Grandma would never think of buying only a hundred grams, and their saleswoman, Aunt Dusya, certainly wouldn't waste time slicing it.

"You have a good life here," concedes her mother, who doesn't usually have an opportunity to talk about good things. "All this food and no lines."

"No lines?" says Katya, laughter dimpling her cheeks. "I'll show you a line."

They meander along a narrow cobblestone street that deposits them next to a wall made of shining granite panels. A half a block away, where the granite turns a corner, a thick line of people hugs the wall and disappears into the next street. They join the line, which moves in slow thrusts, like a purple rainworm across their compost pile, and wait with everyone else.

"It's Lenin's mausoleum," says her mother. "You must behave."

She must have forgotten that Sasha has been behaving since December.

Two hours later, they reach the doors guarded by two soldiers with guns. The line heaves forward and around the platform on which lies Lenin, eternally alive. Only he doesn't look alive. He looks dried up, with the head and face of a bird. He looks eternally dead.

"His body was preserved with formaldehyde," her mother whispers into her ear, "the same way they preserve bodies in our anatomy department."

She thinks of the dissection room at her mother's medical institute, with its tall tables on which lie brown bodies—not at all frightening, full of revelations about what was previously hidden—with every nerve and capillary and membrane exposed by her mother's skillful hands.

When they pass the table where Lenin lies under glass, her mother pushes her through the crowd to the first row. At this close range, Lenin is as uninteresting as she saw from a distance, yellowish skin stretched over his bony head, dead and undissected. But she must display proper solemnity, like the rest of the people who wrinkle their brows and pleat their mouths into mourning lines, as if he died only yesterday and not in 1924, when her mother was only seven.

It is early morning on May 1, and they are walking toward the Moskva River, behind Red Square, where Katya's group from the telephone center is assembling before the demonstration. It is sunny and warm, perfect weather for International Workers' Day, and the streets have been washed by blue trucks that Sasha saw earlier spraying water in heavy, blazing arches. She is between her mother and Katya, holding their hands, jumping over the puddles left by trucks. They are wearing their best dresses—a sunflower cotton shirtwaist for her mother and red polka dots for Katya. Today they don't mind her jumping, and they hold hands and swing her over the wet pavement as long as she wants.

The people from Katya's telephone center look as confident and bold as the workers with thick muscles from the poster of a Five-Year Plan they passed on the way here. They unfurl red banners on long wooden sticks and hoist up huge portraits of stern, unsmiling men.

Then everyone starts walking: people with banners and portraits and red carnations made from construction paper swaying on long wire stems. Her mother hoists her up onto her shoulders, so now Sasha is above the people's heads, in the midst of a forest of swaying sticks with flags, banners, and portraits, of balloons and red carnations. She squints and peers to her left, where everyone else is peering. There, five columns of people away, a group of men stands on a granite platform against the Kremlin wall. In the center is a separate dark figure in what looks like a military uniform. She knows it is Stalin, their conscience and their revolutionary glory, as the radio reminds them every morning. He is the father to all of them marching in this square and gathered around radios from here to Kamchatka, across all their eleven time zones. Only he is so far away, she can barely see him. He looks tiny and ant-like, and there is nothing glorious about him.

Riding on her mother's shoulders, Sasha tries to lean forward to see him better through the forest of portraits and flags. She cranes her neck to peek under a rectangular slogan on two poles, and for a few seconds, the tiny, dark figure flickers between the squares of red. But all she feels is disappointment. He looks nothing like the father they all know, grand and loving and immortalized in oil.

Then the ant-like figure raises his hand, and the square explodes. Every mouth in every lane of every column splits open in one unified roar, and the forest of banners and portraits jolts and sways, as if struck by a blast of wind as strong as the one that snapped Grandpa's oldest apple tree in half last year. It is so terrifying that Sasha screams. But the May Day demonstrators are all safely below, and she is the only one trapped in the center of the storm. The poles of the slogan on her left are rattling by her ear; the sticks with portraits aim at her head from the right. Flags shake with crimson furor and hiss like flames, as if someone has plucked her by the skin of her neck and is about to toss her into the gut of a wood-burning stove. The roar peals over the square like thunder, the mouths fusing into one howling throat, one hungry set of jaws with rows of sticks for teeth, ready to crunch and chew and spit her out.

Sasha shrieks and sobs, all in vain, because her voice cannot be heard against the roaring square. She wails and hunches over and rubs tears around her face. With arms over her head, cowering and bawling, she rides to the side street, where her mother and Katya finally hear her cries and see the snot smeared all over her face.

Her mother pulls her down from her shoulders, takes out a handkerchief, and starts wiping Sasha's cheeks. "She's tired," she says to Katya, patting Sasha on the head. "Getting up at six and all that walking."

Katya opens her arms, and Sasha jumps up and wraps her legs around her, clutching at her shoulders and flattening herself against her polka-dot dress. Katya knows Sasha is not tired, and she rocks in rhythm with Katya's steps, still wailing. She thinks of the three sisters, who wouldn't be so desperate to get to Moscow if they could see the spectacle of the whole politburo shaking on sticks. She thinks of the tiny man against the granite wall, their father who could never be her father. She thinks about another life, at the only place where it is possible, Theater. She sobs on the trolley, in the courtyard, on the stairs; she sobs on the landing and in the apartment's long, murky hallway.

"Nu, nu," says her mother, but Sasha still clings to Katya, sniffling into her shoulder. As long as she is in Katya's arms, the Red Square teeth will not be able to get her. Katya is her shield because she is from Moscow and she knows what they, living in Ivanovo, are too far away to see.

Then an old man comes out of Uncle Seryozha's room, peels her off Katya, and carries her somewhere in his tobacco-smelling arms. She lets him because he is also from Moscow so he also knows. He puts her on the divan in Baba Yulia's room and sits next to her and brushes her head with his hard hands full of calluses. But they feel good, these hands, so she stops crying and for the first time looks into his face, unshaved and ravaged, into his colorless, unsmiling, frozen eyes. It seems strange, the difference between his hands, warm and alive, and his dead eyes, but it isn't stranger than the eternally dead, birdlike Lenin lying under glass or Stalin, their leader and revolutionary glory, who turned out to be an ant.

They sit like this for a long time, Uncle Seryozha and Sasha, not saying a word, not moving. His face is hard and pitted, like their roads in Ivanovo when there is no rain. She doesn't know what he is thinking. Maybe about this place Magadan, where he was lucky to have spent only ten years; maybe about his illness that makes him hate all holidays; maybe about the ten special screws that got him sick in the first place.

She is thinking about another life, a life in Theater. She is thinking about the true make-believe, the only pretending that makes sense. She wants to be part of it more than she has ever wanted anything, desperately, and she will dream about it every night. She will be stoic and patient, enduring their long days and long lines and gray streets with empty horse-drawn carts inching along through the dust. She will wait until she finishes school; she will live with Theater smoldering in the corner of her soul.

6

She climbs into the darkness of the storage loft in their Ivanovo house, a magic place filled with the secrets from another life. Sasha hasn't been here in a year, since her tenth birthday. It smells of dust and mice, an odor of abandonment and desolation, as if this corner of the extinguished world ceased to exist because of her absence. This is her hiding place, her safe place, and today she is hiding from the present.

She is hiding from Grandpa, from the thick leather belt he flogs her with when she breaks his strict house rules. She is hiding from the radio reports announcing the biggest-ever harvests that never reach their stores and from her mother's warnings about danger when she speaks about the war, when the word *front* rumbles out of her mouth, sputters on her lips, and detonates in Sasha's ears, ending with a dead *t*.

Her mother saw the front when she was a war surgeon. The front killed Sasha's father, who, she says to their neighbors, perished in the Great Patriotic War. There is a photo of him in the family album, a blond man in a uniform cinched with a belt. But from Grandma's sighs and the neighbors' smirks, Sasha senses that the noble war death is simply another story, another lie. She knows she is too young to be told the truth, but she is patient.

The front also killed both her mother's brothers. Sima was wounded in battle and died in the back room of their house. Kolya, an artist, who studied in Leningrad and whose paintings hang on their every wall, is still missing in action. They haven't heard anything from Kolya since the war began—not a letter, not a note, not a word from any of those who have already returned—but Grandma is still waiting for him, running outside at every creak of the garden gate, certain that Kolya has finally made his way home all the way from Berlin.

The war ended eight years ago, and even if Berlin were on the other side of the earth, Sasha doubts it would take Kolya this long to make his way back home. But she knows she can't say this to Grandma, who still sets a cup and saucer from her prerevolutionary tea service for Kolya every year on May 9, Victory Day.

The loft is packed with piles of old magazines full of pictures of elegant women in long dresses, holding open fans, parasols, and leashes attached to small dogs in their long, ringed fingers. The pages also show plump jars of cream to make your skin soft as velvet, right alongside elongated bottles of liquid guaranteed to turn your hair thick as a horse's mane. She sits straining her eyes in the scarce light that sifts from the entranceway, stooping over articles describing the best way to handle your maid's lack of sewing ability when you're invited to a ball or the least expensive menu for a formal Christmas dinner to hand to your cook. The words *maid* and *cook*, she knows, are bourgeois and retrograde, atavisms of the tsarist past that the Revolution extracted from their society, like a cancer. She couldn't hear her grandfather use these words without irony, but Grandma somehow seems to fit in with those parasols, hats, and long, flowing skirts, and Sasha often imagines her free of glasses and wrinkles, giving instructions to cooks and maids in her low, patient voice.

There are also poems in these magazines by writers whose names, although she is almost eleven, she has never heard before, names absent from their literature textbooks and even from the catalog of the entire Ivanovo library. It is, she knows, because those poets wrote about unsocialist things, devoting every line to feelings rather than the workers' accomplishments, which was clearly selfish and individualistic from the point of view of their new progressive communist collective.

Since they both learned how to read at five, Sasha has shared all these books and magazines with Marik in the loft, where the two of them have crouched for hours in the dusty murk. She often wishes she could share these hidden stories with Andrei, too, so that all three of them would play Robinson Crusoe or Mowgli or Don Quixote, but she knows this is only a dream, because Andrei, who does not come from an *intelligentny* family, is not allowed into their house.

Behind the books is a round box, upholstered in fabric that was shiny many years ago, but is now the color of muddied cream. She undoes the faded ribbon that is tied around the box and lifts the top, placing it on the pile of books. Inside there is a woman's wide-brimmed hat, white with a green ribbon and a small white rose, a hat from a time when women worried about their hair and gave their cooks instructions for formal Christmas dinners. She carefully places the hat on her head and sits for a few minutes in its soft prerevolutionary embrace, wishing that she had a mirror to see what young Grandma might have looked like. She imagines her stepping out of a carriage, holding up her skirt so that the hem wouldn't sweep against the wheel of the droshky covered with Ivanovo dust; she imagines her asking a maid to set up a samovar for family friends, thinking of a different life. Has she ever dreamed of a life other than the life she has lived in Ivanovo? Has Sasha's mother?

She puts the hat back into the box, closes the lid, and ties it with ribbon, as if she had never been here to let the tsarist past crammed with unnecessary luxuries invade their simple unaccessorized present.

Behind the hatbox with Grandma's prerevolutionary hat, she sees something else, something that looks like a school notebook. Its light-blue cover is faded and frayed, pocked by stains and streaks, as if it had been lying somewhere by the road in a ditch, splashed with mud by passing horse carriages and trucks. She weighs it in her palm: there is a lot of heft to these crinkled pages with their torn-off corners, which

look as though they had been dropped in water and dried more than
once, which look as though they had been scarred by fire. On the front
page, in an angular, masculine hand, are the words that almost stop her
heart, *Kolya Kuzmin*, her uncle missing in action.

She opens the notebook and begins to read.

January 9, 1942

*The first time I saw a German up close was three months ago, in
October. The five of us were retreating from the enemy advance-
ment when a band of our soldiers, the remnants of an artillery
battery, emerged from the woods after sunset. That's how I met
Seryoga. He took a sip from a flask with a Bronze Horseman
on the cap, and right then I knew he was from Leningrad. He'd
studied chemistry at the university, he said, a few steps away from
my art academy. Now, instead of walking along the Griboyedov
Canal, we were trudging through the woods loaded with a rifle, six
grenades, a handgun, two cans of sprats, ten slices of dried bread,
and a flask with water.*

*By dawn, we'd walked about ten kilometers. The road went up
a hill covered with rickety aspen and birch trees. On the other side
sat an empty armored car with a 45 mm cannon, and an artillery
lieutenant, who looked no older than twenty, announced that we
were going to set a trap for the advancing Germans. He was a professional soldier, not an NKVD officer, and his mind was attuned
to war. I had no doubt he had received high grades in his military
classes, too diligent to have allowed himself to receive anything less,
impatient to get to the real battle he had studied for in class. We
were all in the middle of a war, but we were amateurs, trying to
avoid a bullet or a land mine, trying to balance our weight on the
wire between life and death.*

Just beneath the road, there was an abandoned water pipe, and inside it, the soldiers stretched a cable all the way to the armored car behind which we all hid. The sun was rising, and there were columns of smoke on the horizon. Aside from the armored car and the cannon, it looked like any mushroom-hunting morning at the edge of the woods near our house in Ivanovo.

It was around six when we heard the engines, and out of the morning smoke emerged motorcycles with sidecars. They stopped now and then, and the riders peered into binoculars and shot at whatever they thought looked suspicious. The sidecars were carrying MG 34s. The Germans wore metal helmets and large glasses covering half their faces. Martians, I thought, they look just like Martians. Round metal heads, big glass circles for eyes, all black. An unpatriotic thought rose to the surface of my mind: This is the war of the worlds, just as in H. G. Wells's book, and our world is losing. *There was something invincible and mighty about the Germans' movements, in their bizarre, alien appearance, in the way they sliced through the damp air over the fields. There was an arrogance and a luxury in the way the machine guns occupied the sidecars as though they were passengers, as though those iron contraptions were human beings deserving to spread their weight across the black leather seats, hitching a ride along a dusty road of an alien country.*

Then in a desperate, teenage voice, the lieutenant shouted, "Fire!" and the road exploded into a mash of body parts and twisted steel.

Sasha stops reading and examines a drawing penciled in the middle of the page: a man with a long, thin neck, yelling.

Screams ripped through the air; clouds of smoke rose up and screened the rising sun; gasoline mixed with blood poured onto the ground. The explosions were so powerful that the fire blew into our faces and scorched our skin. The blast ushered in a familiar smell of heat from rusted radiators mixed with the alien stench of burned human flesh. Martians, Martians, Martians *was beating in my temple as the motorcycles in the back turned around to drive away.*

"That was lucky," said Seryoga and rubbed his singed eyebrow with the heel of his hand.

On the lieutenant's orders, some of us killed the wounded and others set fire to the undamaged motorcycles. I knew Seryoga saw that I was relieved when I was ordered to kill the motorcycles rather than the wounded Germans. He gave me a sideways look of disappointment, the look my sister, Galya, had when I walked out of the morgue at her medical school the first time I saw corpses floating in wooden tubs of formaldehyde. "This is what's required here," *Seryoga's eyes seemed to be saying.* "Our main objective is to kill people. Or those people will kill us."

7

She stops after the first entry, closes the notebook, and stares at its violated cover. Everything is quiet downstairs. She is relieved that no one is home, but Grandpa or her mother could be back from work any minute. Sasha holds her breath and listens.

She is not yet ready to confront her mother and fling her anger into her face, her slow-boiling indignation at the way her mother treated her brother's war journal. And what about Grandma? Does she even know that her son's notebook has been hidden in this loft full of junk, behind a box with her prerevolutionary hat?

Why isn't there a monument to Kolya in their house, Sasha thinks, the same way there is a monument to all those war heroes in Ivanovo's main square? Why don't they light candles to celebrate his courage, the way Grandma lights a candle by the icon in the corner of her room depicting the gaunt face of someone from the religious canon Sasha cannot even name?

She hides the notebook under her sweater and slips out of the empty house into the yard. A rooster the color of rust, marked across the neck with Grandpa's indelible pencil, struts under the clothing line full of their neighbors' underwear blowing in the wind. A neighbor is smoking on a bench by the shed, the visor of his cap over his eyes so that she can only see his nose swollen with purple veins.

She unhinges the gate and sees her mother at the end of the street, walking home from work. The notebook feels rough against her skin, urging Sasha to right the injustice of confining her uncle's war journal to a place with old shoes and mice, to right the dishonor, yet she knows that her mother could be the one who put it there.

She starts walking toward her, not ready to confront her yet. As the two of them approach each other, Sasha decides not to say anything about the war journal, to keep quiet. She pretends that she is simply strolling in her mother's direction to help her carry a string bag with potatoes because she is almost eleven, old enough to know what would happen if she pulled the notebook from under her sweater.

Her mother's smile would be instantly wiped off her face. "What is this?" she would ask, stopping and lowering the string bag to the ground.

"You know what it is," Sasha would say theatrically. "Why was it in the storage loft, behind all that forgotten junk?"

"Let's go home," her mother would respond in her teacher's voice, her eyes fixed on the notebook in Sasha's hand, as if she were trying to melt it down to nothing with her gaze, to make it disappear from the vision of the neighbors peeking through the openings in the fence.

In the house, her mother would shut the front door and double lock it behind them.

"Who asked you to climb into the storage loft and nose around there?" Her voice would be metallic, moving up the scales. "It's not for you or anyone else. There is a reason why it has been hidden." Her nostrils would flare, and her eyebrows would mash together, her ire approaching the thunderous heights of Grandpa's.

"You just don't understand how dangerous it would be if anyone read it. You have no idea what they could do to our family," her mother would shout.

"But this is what he saw at the front," Sasha would yell back. "This is what really happened. He didn't make it up. He was there. This is the truth!" She would stab the air with the notebook to punctuate her words.

Her mother, in Sasha's imagination, would shake her head, as if to rid her mind of the nonsense her daughter had just uttered. "This is what you don't understand," she would say, forcing each word into the air through tightened lips. "This is exactly why this journal is so dangerous for the family. The truth that Kolya saw."

In the kitchen, Sasha's mother, now real, dumps the potatoes into a copper pot she uses to make jams, ladles water from the bucket to rinse them, and snatches an apron off a nail on the wall.

"What's the NKVD?" Sasha asks, the ominous letters from the journal clanging on her tongue like sounds of a latching padlock.

"Where did you hear about the NKVD?" her mother asks suspiciously.

"From someone at school," Sasha lies.

"The People's Commissariat for Internal Affairs," her mother says, tossing the potato peels into a waste bucket. For a minute, she is silent. "Grandma's brother Volya used to live with us before the war," she says, having decided to bring the NKVD to life with her uncle's story. "In 1937, they arrested him for telling a joke. He lived in this house, with Aunt Lilya and their fifteen-year-old daughter." Her voice now is stern, as if she were delivering a lecture. "There was a knock on the door in the middle of the night. I can still hear it, the kind of knock that only comes at two or three in the morning. Two men in black coats announced that Uncle Volya was under arrest. They didn't bother to say why they were taking him away. Weeks later, Aunt Lilya learned that as part of his job in a propaganda agency, Uncle Volya had taken a stranger from Moscow to a restaurant. There, not knowing he was sitting next to a good citizen dispatched by the NKVD to listen to conversations with strangers, Uncle Volya told a joke. It wasn't even a political joke," she says and shakes her head. "But he should've been more careful around strangers. He shouldn't have babbled. Babbling is dangerous; it's only one step from treason." Sasha knows what her mother is referring to: they've all seen the poster of a woman in a red head kerchief with a finger across her lips and the caption NE BOLTAI in big red letters.

"But how could they arrest him for a joke?" Sasha asks, glad that she didn't tell her mother about the journal she found. "Even if he babbled." She thinks about the early morning when they took away Marik's father, almost four years ago. Did he also tell a joke? Did he babble? "I babble; my friends babble at school. We babble all the time. Babbling is just speaking. Does this mean that we can't speak? Should we all be deaf and mute, as Grandpa demands when we sit at the table to eat?"

Her mother opens the door of the kitchen stove and shoves the remaining kindling inside. She lights a match and holds it to the thinnest pieces until they catch fire. The flickering flames are dancing on her face, and Sasha sees the anger rising in her eyes.

"You're still a child, and you think like a child." She is stern, punctuating her phrase with a slam of the stove door after she flings a couple of logs into the flames. "This was an arrest Comrade Stalin didn't know about." She straightens and walks away from the stove. "Comrade Stalin would never have given the order to arrest an innocent man," she says, a coda to her Uncle Volya story.

Maybe Comrade Stalin didn't know about Marik's father, either. Is it possible, Sasha wonders, that Ivanovo is too far from Moscow for Comrade Stalin to sort out who gets sent to labor camps from here? Too remote to see who does or doesn't come back home?

Her mother lifts the pot with potatoes and lowers it onto the surface of the stove. Then she turns back to Sasha, pointing her finger at her daughter's chest. "You should be careful what you say to others."

She folds her hands on her stomach, pressing the notebook into her skin, and waits for her mother to make her usual trip to the shed for more wood when Sasha can quickly climb up to the storage loft and return the journal to its hiding place. She knows she did the right thing not to have told her mother about the discovery. She feels content. She now has her own secret.

Her mother stares into the pot, where the water is beginning to boil, the tendons in her neck tense, as if she were fighting an invisible fight.

"Uncle Volya never returned from the camps," she says. "He was shot attempting to escape. At least that's what they told Aunt Lilya."

It is difficult to imagine that Uncle Volya, soft-jowled and asthmatic, tried to crawl under three rows of barbed wire. His daughter, Nina, nineteen when the war started, volunteered for the front to avenge her father and was killed during her first week of service. When the mailwoman brought a gray letter announcing her death to their door, Aunt Lilya collapsed and never recovered. She died from the heart, Sasha's mother says. All Russian women, according to her mother, die from the heart.

8

Whenever no one can see her, Sasha climbs into the storage loft to read another page or two. She has chosen to believe that Grandma doesn't know where her missing son's journal has been hidden. No one who still startles at every creak of the gate, Sasha has decided, could have allowed this notebook to end up in such a dishonorable place.

January 15, 1942

With a pencil I keep in the driest corner of my backpack, I draw Seryoga and our sergeant, but they come out one-dimensional and static, lacking the dark anger we've all acquired in the trenches. The paralyzing fear of the first German bombing, when my bowels instantly turned to water, has by now retreated into the pit of my stomach, where it lies curled up like a diseased dog. I stood in shock amid craters and burned grass, as planes were speeding toward us, filling the sky over the field with a deafening roar—alien iron machines armed with death—and Seryoga had to slap me and pull me down and shove me into the trench, where I sat shivering in a warm, stinking mess inside my pants. I've become angry since then, and my heart has hardened around the edges. In two months, I've learned to curse and down vodka, both of which would make my mother clutch at her heart and wipe her dampened glasses with a handkerchief, both of which would make my father proud.

"Hey, Da Vinci," calls the sergeant, looking over my shoulder. "Make sure you finish that masterpiece before the next attack. The Hermitage can't wait."

The sergeant knows nothing about the Hermitage. He is from a small town on the other side of the Urals where he probably failed drawing in middle school because of his contempt for anything that isn't real, and I know he has never been to Leningrad.

"Never read any fiction," he boasts, picking his teeth with a finger and sucking down bread crumbs that got stuck there when we chewed on our rations.

"Come on," says Seryoga. "You never read Pushkin in school? They never made you read Turgenev's 'Mumu'?" He pleats his eyebrows into a pitiful wave as he says "Mumu," a story we all read in fourth grade about a heartless landlady who forces a poor peasant to drown his dog. I remember fighting back tears as I was approaching the end of the story when the peasant cuddles the little mutt for the last time before tossing it over the side of the boat.

The sergeant spits out a black glob; the soot from burning telephone cable we use to thaw the ice in the trench has sifted down and settled in our lungs. "Next time the Fritzes come with their tanks or their planes, they'll show you 'Mumu,'" he says and stabs his finger toward the Germans' positions. "This is what's real." He is a man of utter concreteness, and this time he is right. No Michelangelo or El Greco can shield you from machine guns. No Pushkin, or Turgenev, or even Tolstoy, who knew all about war, can protect you from a shell fragment piercing your back or a tank crawling over your trench. When the sergeant yells, "Attack!" we attack, even if we are ordered to run up a hill where a German machine gun sits buried in a cemented bunker, spewing fire we can't extinguish. We attack, and after the first waves of us are mowed down, there are always more bodies to throw into the maw, more amateur soldiers to be fed to the meat grinder of battle by the decisions of our military commanders. They yell, "Attack," and we attack. And those who don't, those who are afraid to die, those who retreat toward the rear, are mowed down by machine guns of our own domestic making. Our own troops stationed in the rear, shooting all of those with weak nerves, those whose minds are clouded by seeing too many human guts wound around tank turrets, too many bodies with heads blown off, a bloody mess instead of legs, too much death. For fleeing death, they get death. Traitors *is the word now attached to their corpses. What's real is the only thing that matters at the front.*

The words in the last sentence are smudged, and Sasha has difficulty making them out, but *traitors* is pressed into the paper. Was she also a traitor, she wonders, when she didn't feel upset, like everybody else, at the news of Stalin's death? Was she a traitor when she didn't cry, along with all the teachers and other students?

On March 5, 1953, when Marik and Sasha were both ten, Marik's mother interrupted her literature class and announced that everyone must proceed to the Pioneer meeting room without delay to listen to important news. She said "important," not "sad" news, but as Sasha shuffled down the stairs next to Marik, she saw their math teacher on the stair landing, leaning on the wall, her shoulders trembling, her hand wiping tears from her face with a checkered handkerchief. This looked strange because Sasha never imagined their math teacher capable of any emotion beyond an angry frown when one of them couldn't recite the multiplication table without tripping over 6 x 9.

In the meeting room called the Communist Auditorium, students filed in. There were whispers rustling across the aisles; there was an occasional chair scraping the floor, and she saw Andrei among the other sixth graders two rows behind her. Their gym teacher was rubbing her eyes with her fists, and their usually stern and erect principal, Natalia Petrovna, was plodding to the front of the room, her shoulders slumped. She stood silently, waiting for the last whisper to die down, and Sasha saw a tear rolling down her cheek that she didn't even attempt to dry.

"Today is a day of mourning for all of us," she began in a fragile voice unfitting for a principal. "Our great leader, our father, our genius, our dear Comrade Stalin has died." Her last words were barely audible, but everyone heard them in the absolute silence that now congealed the air in the room, in the whole school, in the entire town. It was so quiet that Sasha heard the steady dripping of water from a melting icicle hitting the sill outside the window. She was probably one of the very few people there who'd seen the real, live Stalin in Red Square three years earlier, which was still as clear in her memory as if she'd looked at it through the shiny glass of a newly washed window.

The principal covered her face with her hand because her mouth was trembling and she couldn't utter anything else. Their math teacher, whom Sasha had seen sniffling on the stair landing, sidled up to the principal with her conveniently unfolded checkered handkerchief. The steel-like Natalia Petrovna was now weeping openly, as if all her teachers and pupils had been lined up and executed by the Nazis right in front of her, a scene from a war film they'd recently watched in their history class.

Sasha looked around surreptitiously, because they had been told to keep their heads down, and saw Marik's mother's dry face across the aisle. Her head was down, and her fingers were braided under her chest as if she were praying, although they all knew that praying was a rudiment of their dark tsarist past, along with serfdom and unemancipated women. Sasha was the only one in her line of vision, with the exception of Marik and his mother, who wasn't crying or, at least, pretending to cry. She couldn't see Andrei, who was two rows behind her, but she was sure his eyes were also dry. She could not imagine twelve-year-old Andrei, with hair as black as tar and arms strong enough to lift her into the air when the three of them played, casting his eyes down and shedding tears over Comrade Stalin's sudden death.

She thought of her two friends, of Marik and Andrei and their constant competition, of how they exchanged punches and bragged about what one could do better than the other. Andrei could do a lot of things well, but Marik was good at something no one else was, not even Grandpa. Marik knew how to fish. "Where did you learn to be such a first-rate fisherman?" Grandpa had asked him when Marik brought home a pike big enough for a whole pot of soup. "My father taught me," Marik had mumbled, embarrassed by the attention from the commander himself. Now everyone, including Andrei, was envious of Marik's secret. The secret Marik had tried to teach Sasha last August, when they took an old rowboat out onto a small lake.

As the principal's funereal speech droned on, Sasha thought of the rod Marik had handed to her, with a round bobbin painted half-red and half-white, of how he'd hooked a worm for her because it had been wriggling in an inch of water on the bottom of the boat and she didn't want to impale it. He'd cast her line without getting up, without tipping the boat. The line had whistled in the air in a perfect arc and plunked down ten meters away. Then he'd hooked a worm on his own rod, his fingers black from digging in the compost pile, and cast it on the other side of the boat. They'd sat and waited, silently, because fish, as he'd explained, could hear the slightest sound you made, even your clearing your throat, even a dripping oar. The brown water around the boat had been swirling in small ripples, until the red half of her bobbin plunged beneath the surface and Marik whispered, "Pull." She had pulled, astonished by how heavy the rod had become, leaning back so far that the boat tipped and the oars grated against their metal casings.

He'd guided her arms until she could see the fish sparkle just a few centimeters below the surface. In a precise movement, he'd whipped the line, and the fish vaulted through the air and thumped to the bottom of the boat. It was small, too small for the force of the tug. She'd watched it thrashing against the boards, with a comb of spikes on its spine. Marik had grabbed the fish by the head, and she saw the hook in its open mouth as it gasped, gleaming down its perforated jaw. He'd yanked the hook down and out, and the fish stopped gasping and lay still. "A perch," Marik had said. "Your first catch." She'd picked up the perch and held it between her palms, its scales hard and glistening, its eyes like glass.

She stood with her head down, thinking of that fishing trip, staring at the back of a chair in front of her where "Igor + Tanya = love" was scratched with a nail into the wood. With almost all the teachers and students weeping, she felt a strange mix of fear and curiosity, as if something overpowering had just ended. The entire assembly was now waiting to see how life could possibly continue after this tragedy that had reduced their intrepid principal to tears. Or maybe it wasn't as tragic as the principal thought. Maybe the absence of Stalin from their lives would bring back Marik's father after the three years of absence and uncertainty. Maybe it would make Sasha's mother less anxious about Uncle Kolya's journal and curl her lips back into a smile that had been wiped off by the war, a smile Sasha only knew from the portrait on the wall of their room painted by her uncle before Sasha was born.

9

Andrei's father comes back in 1955. Short, with gray stubble sprouting through his cheeks and a nose like a wilted red potato forgotten in the cellar, he sits on a bench by the shed all day long, smoking unfiltered cigarettes that he rolls in his gnarled fingers before he lights them.

Where did he return from? The war ended ten years ago, and Sasha is old enough to know he didn't return from the war. Their neighbors who live in the other half of their house sometimes whisper the word *ugolovnik*, a convicted criminal, when they pass him on the way to the store.

She waits for Andrei to say something about his father, to tell her where he has been all this time, to let her know if his father's return has made her friend happy. Would she be happy if her own father came back? She is not sure. From the way Grandma pursed her mouth when Sasha asked about his photo in the album, she sensed that there was something disreputable about him, something not to be discussed around the dinner table, something slippery and shameful.

But Andrei doesn't talk about his father. He doesn't talk *to* him, either, at least outside: when his father smokes on the bench by the shed, Andrei is nowhere to be seen, although the shed has been the place for the three of them to meet for years. Maybe Andrei was expecting a different father, someone taller and shaved, someone less scary and more heroic. Maybe he thought that his father would immediately go to work and break all records, like those workers in street posters: coal miners with faces dusted in soot or steelmakers peering into a furnace, a red glow of liquid metal reflected in their goggles. Andrei's father's only occupation seems to be rolling cigarettes, smoking by the shed, and yelling curses at Andrei's mother, who every day beats the dirt of the courtyard with a broom, muttering to herself and whipping up clouds of dust as she nears the shed.

Sasha notices that Andrei is now a head taller than she is, and when he stands next to her, her eyes are at the level of his mouth. For some strange reason, she notices his mouth, the way it curls when he speaks or wraps around a cigarette he steals from his father and smokes behind the lilac bushes at the end of the streetcar route. She notices the thick, stubborn curl of hair that falls across his forehead and makes him jerk his head to get it out of his eyes, which makes him look cavalier and almost grown-up. She notices that when she grabs his arm or holds her hands around his neck in their old game of War, he tenses as if in pain, as if she stepped on his injured toe.

She notices that her other friend, Marik, no longer looks or sounds like the old Marik. His voice doesn't seem to know if it wants to remain at the height of hers or descend to the depth of Andrei's, and when it dips and soars in the course of a single sentence, Marik often tears his glasses off and starts wiping them in a nervous, angry movement. She also notices that Marik's forehead has erupted in pimples, and his bones seem to have grown too big for his skin, bulging at his ankles and his wrists. Thinking about the changes in her friends, Sasha wonders if they also notice changes in her.

More and more often, when no one is home, Sasha steals into the storage loft, where Kolya's journal is telling her about forbidden things, about what her mother and her teachers refuse to talk about.

February 7, 1942

I draw Nadia as I remember her: narrow hands with elongated fingers, a pianist's hands; high cheekbones, a drop of Tatar blood in everyone born in Russia; thick eyebrows, the right slightly higher than the left, which gave her face a surprised look, as though she were in constant wonder. She lived on Herzen Street in a three-room apartment that was not communal, an obvious luxury for a family of three. Her father, Naum Semenovich, taught physics at the University of Leningrad, and, in her words, she inherited none of his scientific mind. Only his nose, she used to say with a sigh.

Sasha pauses to look at the drawing on the bottom of the page, a girl's thin face marred by a burn on paper. Was it a cigarette that Kolya was smoking? Or a spark from the fire that kept him alive in a frozen trench?

We met on the Palace Bridge, the only place we could have met: she lived on the left bank of the Neva, and I lived on the right. It was the end of October, with winter making an early entrance that year, blowing black clouds into the city sky, churning the water around the pillars of the bridge. She stood by the banister leaning over the river, looking down at where the wind tossed a knitted yellow hat with a pom-pom in the waves, her face as unprotected as her head, stunned by the sudden force that so suddenly had ripped her hat from her. I stopped. I had to stop: there was too much fragility in her posture to pass her by, too much need. She looked at me and smiled a sad smile, accepting the loss of her hat, shrugging, pulling her scarf up to her ears. If I'd been a real man, I thought, a character from one of our heroic Soviet books, I would have torn off my coat and jumped into the waves. I would have snatched her hat out of the wind's jaws and fought my way against the current back to the granite steps where she would be waiting for me, awed by my bravery and physical strength, grateful. Instead I looked into her face, her eyes the color of tarnished gold, and said something foolish, the first thing that came to my mind. "It's gone," I said, and she nodded. "I know."

I draw Nadia's room, the room I know so well, with its oak armoire and heavy curtains that screened us from the outside with their gray and yellow squares of wool. Her mother, like my own, was simply a mother, defined only by her family rather than an outside job she never held. It was only during the rare blissful hours when Evgeniya Iosifovna took a streetcar to Vladimirsky Market or a bus to the garishly decorated turn-of-the-century Eliseyev delicatessen that we had the apartment all to ourselves. To avoid the rush-hour crowds, she went shopping in late morning or early afternoon, and that was when we would cut our classes (Nadia would make an excuse to slip out of a seminar on lexicology at the philology department of the university, and I would creep out of the lecture on ancient art) to meet on the Palace Bridge and hurry to Isaac's Square and her building on Herzen Street. We would run up the four flights of stairs and spend an hour on the leather divan behind the drawn window curtains that made the room humid and dark, where we were as naked as those prehistoric people on the walls of the ancient caves of my textbook. For an hour once or twice a week, Nadia's divan, with its lumpy surface and arms worn from wear, was ours, an accomplice to our transgression. We were too impatient to pull the sheets out of the armoire, and the old leather felt warm under our skin as if holding us in its embrace, as if watching over the clumsy reaches of our arms and legs, the fumbling delirium of our lips and fingers. Then we lay pressed into each other in the seam between the seat and the back as though we were one, locked inside each other's arms and taking almost no space at all, the brown leather stretching before our eyes like the carefully raked top layer of a plowed field. From that strange angle, with all that leather between us and what was beyond, Nadia's room was the microcosm of a world where life seemed full of wonder and promise.

Does one need love, Sasha wonders—the forbidden kind of love no one talks about, the fiery love, hot and ruthless as the tongues of flame in their stove—to see life as Kolya saw it, full of wonder and promise?

10

"Hey, kike," yells a boy from a stoop as Marik and Sasha are walking home from school. "If you weren't ugly enough before, you're certainly ugly now."

The boy is a year younger than they are, and Sasha has seen him in the hallways of their school, always with a runny nose and scabs on his elbows. She knows it is not a noble thing to strike someone younger than you, but this boy surely deserves it. She lunges to the stoop and pummels him with her schoolbag, on the head, right and left, and then a few more times on his shoulders and his chest. Luckily, the schoolbag is heavy, since they have a lot of homework today, and it thumps against the boy's head, two times for each of the *uglies* and some extra pounding for the *kike*.

From the boy's widened eyes, she knows that he did not expect this: he has heard and uttered the insult so many times before that to his ear, the word may have lost its pungency and now sounds just as bland as anything their principal may say in their monthly Pioneer meetings. After a little arm flailing, he scrambles up and escapes inside the house, but when he is out of her reach, when he knows she can no longer whack him, he yells "crazy bitch" and thrusts his arm in her direction, as if he were throwing a rock.

Sasha is not proud of beating up a seventh grader, but Marik is grateful. He looks at her with admiring eyes, as if she'd just single-handedly defeated a battalion of Germans. "You're a real friend," he whispers, blinking and squeezing her hand, not daring to trust his changing voice. "I don't know what I'd do without you."

She is not sure Marik is right that she is his real friend. More and more often, she finds herself being a buffer between Marik and Andrei, whose resentment of one another seems to be growing together with their muscles and bones. What happened to their games of Cossacks and Outlaws, when the three of them outwitted the other team of local kids and found the most unexpected places to hide, or to the game of War, where Marik and Sasha were heroic partisans, ready to withstand the most hideous threats from Andrei, the Nazi commandant? What happened to their Three Musketeers promise, the vow of "one for all and all for one" they took shortly after Marik's mother gave her the volume by Alexandre Dumas for her birthday?

She searches for answers in Kolya's journal.

February 21, 1942

Every day I think of Nadia, of the hollow of her collarbone where the skin seems almost transparent, where a web of tiny vessels is like a blueprint into a wondrous world inside her. I was glad she lived in Leningrad and not Ivanovo so I didn't have to bring her before my family yet. I knew Mama would embrace her, take her by the elbow, and lead her to the armchair in the corner of the dining room, an honorary place where she greeted all important guests. It wasn't Mama who darkened my mind when I thought of introducing Nadia as the woman I loved, my future wife. I thought of my father, who would only need one look at Nadia's curly hair and skinny arms to know she was Jewish, to know that his son could do much better than entwine his life with an offshoot of the rickety intelligentsia that the Revolution of 1917 had succeeded in deposing. My father has always been a man of concreteness, not unlike the sergeant who detested fiction, and his lack of elevation from the mundane, his self-proclaimed earthiness, is what grounded him as a Bolshevik. "Collectivization and industrialization are what has made this country great," my father would announce every time we sat down to dinner, as if reciting this slogan before a meal were his way of saying grace.

When my father learned I had applied to the art academy in Leningrad, his face contorted with fury. I thought he was going to hit me when I said I wanted to be an artist, and it was only Mama, by silently sliding into the leaden air between us, by standing in the middle of his wrath, who saved me from his blow. The knowledge that I would be studying painting—instead of engineering, like him, or medicine, like my sister—seemed to wound him almost physically. I have a suspicion that my father was pleased when I was mobilized into the army and sent to the front in September 1941, since in his eyes the war has plucked me out of the sissy world of art, the untrustworthy world of make-believe, and dropped me into the trenches, where everything is real.

On the day Nadia and I met, the day of her hat bobbing in the waves under the Palace Bridge, I walked her back to her apartment because I knew the moment I saw her that she was going to be part of my life, when she suddenly stopped before the Admiralty and said that I should know something right away, before it was too late. It was already too late, but what was the purpose of telling her? She put her schoolbag down on a bench under a naked poplar tree and lowered her scarf from her face down to her neck.

"There is something I have to tell you," she said. "I'm not very practical. I'm not like other women. I can't sew, and I'm a terrible cook. Even standing in lines is a skill I haven't fully mastered. Like my father, I was born without elbows. I feel more comfortable in a lecture on Cervantes than on a crowded bus."

I stroked her hair shining in the light of a streetlamp, and she leaned her head into my palm. I kissed her cheek, then her lips. She didn't resist.

"Maybe we are both misfits," I said, "because I have a warning for you, too." Her eyes were lowered, as if she were watching my mouth wrapping itself around the words. "I am not as strong and confident a man as you deserve. I'm only an artist. I can paint, but I can't beat people up."

"Why would you need to beat people up?" she asked.

"To protect you. So that they won't take you away from me."

She smiled and straightened my glasses. Then she lifted them off my nose, and her face lost focus and became blurry, similar to Dora Maar's in the portrait Picasso had just painted, the unsocialist portrait my professor recently showed our small class surreptitiously and without comment. Nadia's lips were cold and salty, like tears, like the Baltic water under the Palace Bridge.

Sasha lifts her eyes from the pages and takes a deep breath of the stale air of the storage loft. The dust of time, of war, of knotty love settles in her lungs. In their house and at school, where everything seems to be based on lies, is she a misfit, too?

It is December, and the three of them are at an ice field in the park behind the end of the streetcar route, tying skates to their *valenki* boots with ropes. "Tighter," she says to Marik, whose right skate wobbles when he steps on the ice. She doesn't have to say anything to Andrei: his knots are exacting, and he is the first to race to the other side of the field, his skates cutting through the ice with resolute lines. Marik and Sasha step onto the field with caution. It is their first outing of the season, and it feels as though they are trying to make sure that their grown arms and legs still remember the moves.

"Hey!" Andrei yells from the other side of the field. "Come over here and we'll have a race."

As she glides across the ice, her feet do their work, and her arms hold the balance just as they did the previous year. She's not sure Marik is as confident. She hears him gouge the ice with the point of his skate behind her; she hears Andrei shouting, *"Slabak!"* from where he waits, calling Marik a weakling. But when she looks back, Marik has already leveled himself off, and all she sees are his cheeks red with cold and his eyes white with determination.

On the other side of the ice field, they get in positions: Marik on the right, Andrei next to him, and Sasha to the left of Andrei. She doesn't care if she doesn't win. It is Grandma's superstition that if you keep your fists clenched so tightly that your fingernails dig into your palms, your wish will come true. She keeps her fingers clenched, wishing for Marik to keep up with Andrei, wishing for him not to stumble.

"On your mark, set, go!" yells Andrei, and they tear forward through the wind, all the way to the other end. She skews her eyes and gets a glimpse of Marik panting and rushing forward, moving ahead of Andrei, who is stabbing the air with his elbows in mad, desperate kicks. And then, a few seconds into this ferocious race, she hears a thump: a body padded with the wool and cotton of a winter coat hits the ice.

She grates to a stop and so does Andrei. They both stare at Marik curled by the edge of the field, stroking the ice around him and squinting, feeling for his glasses with his fingers.

"You pushed me," he spits out as she hands him the glasses. "I was winning, and you pushed me."

"No, I didn't," says Andrei. "You stumbled and fell. You always stumble and fall."

"I didn't stumble!" Marik shouts, but his voice betrays him, and the words come out in a thin falsetto, a mockery of his intended message.

"He pushed me," he whispers as he looks at her, a whisper that comes out as a hiss.

She wants to believe Marik, who is sitting on the ice, wiping his bloodied lip with the sleeve of his coat. She saw him winning, and then she saw him fall. She also wants to believe Andrei, who is standing and whistling, his hat in his hands, his black hair blown across his forehead. They are her friends, and she wants to believe them both, but Marik acts as if he wants her to make a choice. He keeps peering at her, tight springs of red hair framing his face, his eyes as liquid as they were when she beat up a stupid sixth grader. His eyes want to know if she believes him, if she is still as noble as that girl who avenged his dignity with a schoolbag full of homework.

"Be a man and face your defeat," says Andrei, a phrase he undoubtedly lifted straight from *The Three Musketeers* Sasha gave him last summer so that the three of them could play the story out together. "And don't whimper on *devchonka*'s shoulder." He adds a sliver of his own wisdom. "Maybe you can catch a fish, but you skate like a girl."

After a fifth grader with skinny braids bangs a Tchaikovsky étude on the keys of the school's untuned piano, after a seventh-grade ballet group stomps around the stage in a Ukrainian folk dance, it is Sasha's turn. She can feel her armpits drip with sweat and her stomach contract with cramps. The audience of students is noisy and resentful: they were detained after classes, herded into the auditorium to hear the principal's speech about the achievements of the 20th Congress of the Communist Party. The concert is a perk, but at this point, no one cares. They all want to escape into the frosty sunshine of December, into the brilliant winter day that is already dimming into evening. None of them has a shred of interest in her acting, and except for first graders, all have seen the proverbial scene from Act 2 of *Romeo and Juliet* performed by the previous crop of the school's drama club, the scene staged every year without fail. The only person who wants to see her act, she knows, is Marik.

She concentrates hard on being Juliet. As she speaks the lines, immersing herself in the text, a new sensation brushes against her, a feeling of lightness, of escaping the confines of her body. This new sensation is intoxicating, and she tries to capture it and gently hold it in her hand like a bird. The words she speaks—the words she believes—seem to weaken the pull between her body and the floor, making her feel weightless, as if she could defy gravity and float above the stage and soar. Becoming someone else has emptied her body of fear and pain; she no longer feels stomach cramps. The students' whispers, the shuffling of resentful feet, the bursts of snickers in the audience have now stopped.

"Well, do not swear," she orders her acting partner, Vova, to the auditorium's dead silence. She doesn't see the rows of chairs, or the windows pasted with garlands of frost, or the eyes aimed at her. She only sees the boy she loves standing beneath the balcony; she only tries to grapple with the passion that is pushing her toward him, overwhelming and conflicting. "It is too rash, too unadvised, too sudden. Too like the lightning," she confides to the audience frozen in rapt silence.

Approaching the end of the scene, she has yet to understand what has thrust the room full of her impatient schoolmates into this quiet focus. But she can sense this force, even though she doesn't know how to attach words to what is swirling inside her. She knows one thing: she has connected with the audience and made them watch her, made them listen. She has convinced her schoolmates to follow her despite their boredom, despite the sun slanting its last rays into the dirty windowpanes. She doesn't yet comprehend the nature of this new power, but it feels like magic.

11

The three of them are in the forest that starts behind the end of the streetcar route, and both Marik and Andrei are wearing *ushanka* hats with flaps hanging down to the shoulders of their cotton-padded coats. It is the dawn of March, when the winter still insists that it is in charge despite the signs of receding snow wherever the sun can reach down through the canopy of firs. They are sitting around a campfire Andrei has built with branches and twigs they found sticking out of the snow, patches of dead grass and brown leaves radiating from their burning pile of sticks.

As they were searching for wood, Andrei had stumbled onto an unexploded shell, small and darkened by the years that had passed since the front turned west. From the tense curve of his back, as he was digging in the loam, Sasha knew that he had come upon something prized, something she and Marik would never find no matter how painstakingly they trained their eyes to search the porous snow. Why was it always Andrei who found forbidden things, who explored any place he wanted without curfews or rules, who was always the first one riding on the back of the streetcar? She stares at his open palm, red and blotchy, where the shell now sits covered in old dirt, pretending to be no more dangerous than an ordinary stone. Andrei carefully lifts and examines it before he offers it to Marik in an apparent show of sudden generosity.

She knows Marik shouldn't lift the shell from Andrei's palm, but he does, and now it's his. Now he owns it. His fingers, swollen from the cold, embrace and welcome it, accepting Andrei's risky find, now putting Marik in charge.

"Come on—throw it into the fire!" Andrei yells, whirling his arms as if he were a windmill. "Let's see the fireworks." The flames from the fire reflect in his eyes, like little dancing darts of orange on green.

She knows, of course, that throwing an unexploded shell into a fire is a dangerous thing to do. Her mother has told her about local boys with missing fingers and feet, stupid children who didn't use their brains to think about the consequences of their actions, and she wishes her mother were here now to tell Marik what to do.

Sasha sees Marik standing on the edge of the fire, his hand extended, every freckle on his face lit orange by the flames. He just stands there, scared to move, as if he were a statue. But in addition to fear, she sees a flicker of pride in his eyes, the pride of being able to hold a live shell, of being as tough as Andrei, of being a man.

"Don't be a fool," she screams as loudly as she can, hoping the force of her voice can influence Marik's next move.

"You don't have the guts!" Andrei shouts at the top of his lungs, and his words overpower hers. His *ushanka* hat is clutched in his hand, and she sees his eyes wild with excitement, a black curl of hair dancing on his forehead. "You're a coward!" he yells. "You're like a little girl. You can't even throw a shell into the fire." Andrei takes a breath and reaches for the sharpest argument of all. "Your father's *politichesky*, and he is never coming back."

"Leave him alone!" she yells at Andrei, whose mouth is a thin, straight line, as if carved in stone and who now almost looks like his father.

"Don't!" she yells at Marik, who is clasping his fingers around the shell, his eyes white with rage, just as they were at the ice-skating pond last year. The piece of metal in his hand is dark and filled with death, but Marik doesn't seem scared. He is cuddling it as if it were an egg, as if what he did with the shell might bring his father back.

She knows she shouldn't be here. Whatever is going to happen belongs to the realm of danger her mother invokes so vividly when Grandpa pins her to the bench and flogs her. She's not afraid of another flogging, even if it is with nettles. What she's afraid of is being where she shouldn't be, within the reach of danger. But she also knows something else, viscerally. She can smell it the same way she can smell Marik's anger and Andrei's contempt. She can feel in her bones that Andrei has dug his boots into the marshy ground and Marik is closing his fingers around the shell for the same reason, the reason she refuses to acknowledge, even to herself. She knows why they are fighting, but knowing the cause of this clash doesn't help her know what to do.

"Stop!" she yells, but they don't seem to hear her. They are frozen in their bitterness and in their battle. She knows she can't make them stop because they have already abandoned the safe perimeter of common sense and crossed into a place from which they cannot turn back, so she starts running toward home, as fast as she can. Her felt *valenki* sink in the wet snow, and as she runs, snow gets into her boots and melts inside them. She tenses her feet to keep her *valenki* from falling off as her heels make slurping sounds inside the soaked felt, as fir branches whip her in the face. She runs and runs, with every second adding to the distance between rage and reason, between her and danger.

Then from the forest behind her, there is an explosion. The sound bounces off the trees and then hollows out. The explosion freezes her heart and she knows, even without her mother having to tell her, that she did the right thing by running away from danger. But all she feels is the opposite of right. Would Uncle Kolya have left his fellow soldiers to be killed or captured by the Germans because they were in danger? Would he have abandoned his friends when they needed him?

She turns around and runs back, following her own footsteps in the snow. The road back to danger seems much shorter than the road away from it, and a few minutes later, she is where the fire they built sputters little ribbons of flame, tired and spent, wheezing like an old smoker.

She sees Andrei pressing his hands to his ears, walking around in circles, stumbling like their neighbor Semyon when he is drunk. She sees Marik lying on his side, as if he were smelling the snow, a stupid thing to do, since everyone knows that snow has no smell.

"Marik!" she shouts, but he continues to smell the snow as if he hasn't heard her, and there is a trickle of blood coming from his mouth.

"Andrei!" she shouts, but he is oblivious to her yelling, too. He is hitting his ears and jumping, as if his feet were on fire.

At least Andrei is moving, but Marik is not. She kneels next to him to do what her mother does when someone is sick, to wrap her fingers around his wrist and feel for a pulse. But the fire is still hissing, so she can't feel any pulse, and she can't hear anything, either, when she opens Marik's coat and presses her ear to his chest.

"We have to get him to a hospital," she yells as she gets up, but Andrei keeps lifting his legs in a frantic dance, rubbing his ears, as though trying to knead the sound back in. She thinks of a sled Grandpa made for her a few years ago, a sled still hanging on the wall of their shed back home, and she pulls Andrei by the sleeve of his coat toward a big fir tree, not far from where Marik lies on the snow. Together they tug at the lowest bough, up and down and right and left until it becomes loose and crunches off the trunk. The bough is thick and long, a little bigger than Marik's height, and they pull him onto this fir sled, Andrei and Sasha, because Marik is heavy and limp and doesn't help them at all.

It is no use asking Andrei what has happened. He has stopped jumping and beating his ears, and now he does nothing but twitch his shoulders in rhythmic shrugs.

They pull Marik out of the woods on this makeshift sled, trudging silently through the snow, like the tired dogs tugging at their load in a grainy film about the Arctic they all saw at school. When the forest ends, they walk across the field and onto a road that leads to the hospital where her mother works. It is harder to pull Marik over the rough surface of iced pebbles and frozen dirt, and Andrei is not much help, slapping his head as if he'd forgotten something, his shoulders still twitching. Sasha's winter coat padded with cotton feels as hot on the inside as their black stove, and she unbuttons it, letting the wind gush onto her chest, something Grandma would be horrified to see, certain that Sasha will get pneumonia. They pass the tracks where the streetcar turns around to go back to town; they drag Marik past wooden houses squatting on the outskirts of town under roofs that have been ravaged by the winter; and finally, as her arms begin to quiver and she is afraid she won't be able to take one more step, the hospital arranges itself in front of her, as if magically lowered from the pewter sky.

Two women in white gowns run out of the door from behind a counter and carefully transfer Marik onto a stretcher. They wave for Andrei and Sasha to follow them into the bowels of the hospital, into a room where a doctor with a thin neck and a pimply face plugs a stethoscope into his ears and bends over Marik. He pulls apart Marik's eyelids, wraps his fingers around Marik's wrist, and then tells the two women with the stretcher to take Sasha and Andrei out of the room and close the door.

"So what did you hooligans do?" demands the older woman, as thick and round as the pot warmer Grandma pulls over their teakettle.

"I didn't do anything. And I'm not a hooligan," she says, knowing that this makes Andrei the hooligan. As hooligans do, he crossed the threshold into danger, and now Marik is lying behind this door, and her mother is probably already on her way here because she works on the hospital ambulance on Sundays, and her medical institute is only two blocks away.

Andrei slaps his hands over his ears to show that he can't hear what the pot-warmer woman is saying. She looks at him suspiciously, fists on her hips. "Sit here and wait," she says and points to a bench.

They don't even have time to sit down before she sees her mother running down the hallway, scooping her in her arms, moving her fingers over her head and shoulders as though checking to see that she is in one piece.

On the way home, they pass a babushka with a baked-apple face who is weeping on a bench next to a house made from brown logs, dabbing a white handkerchief at her eyes, and a stubbled man in a wool hat wiping his nose with his sleeve behind the liquor store where he usually waits for a drinking companion. They should indeed both be crying, Sasha thinks, although she doesn't know how they could have found out that Marik is dead. *No vital signs.* This is what the doctor with the thin neck, who had probably been her mother's student, said when she opened the door they were not allowed to open. *No vital signs,* he said, as if he were still in her class and this was a test. Sasha has been to the morgue before, so she knows what this means. It means that the shell Andrei handed to Marik exploded with such ferocious force that its fragments pierced Marik's padded coat and made little holes in his belly and intestines. Only this time, her mother couldn't save him, as she had saved the boy at the frontline hospital, because it took them too long to drag Marik through the woods back to town. Would Marik still be alive if she hadn't left the two of them by the bonfire? Would he be alive if her heart hadn't raced each time Andrei's sleeve inadvertently brushed against hers?

Since the word *war* first sputtered on her mother's lips, death has been all around them. Her uncle Volya, who was arrested in 1937 for telling a joke. Uncle Volya's daughter Nina, who volunteered for the front in 1942, a futile attempt to avenge her father's death. Uncle Sima, who had been stationed on their border with Poland when German troops crossed into Russia on June 22, 1941, and was buried in Ivanovo a few weeks before she was born. Her father. Probably her uncle Kolya, who is still missing in action twelve years after the war.

But all these deaths had no lives attached to them. Sasha didn't know them when they walked to work, or waited in lines, or stood with a fishing rod by the river. She only knew them dead. Marik is the first person who stopped existing right in front of her eyes. The person who told her she was good at acting, who made her smile. For fourteen years, they played the same games; for ten years, they read the same books; for eight years, they went to the same school and practiced the same piano pieces. And only a day before that Sunday, behind their shed, did he take Sasha's hand in his, in a different way than they'd held hands before. She tensed the moment his fingers met hers. His touch was clammy and shaky, and there were drops of sweat on his forehead despite the cold outside. For a few seconds, he held her hand as if trying to decide what to do with it; then he took a breath and asked if he could kiss her.

And now Sasha wishes she'd said yes.

12

How do people fall in love, one of Turgenev's characters asks in *A Nest of Nobles*, which they are reading at school. The moral conflict of Turgenev's novel is between personal happiness and duty, says her teacher. A year has passed since Marik's death, a long year full of struggle between personal happiness and duty inside her. The teacher, a chinless woman with graying hair and a squirrel face, is lecturing about *lishnie lyudi*, or useless people. There is a whole gallery of such people in Russian literature. Today it is Turgenev's Lavretsky, who failed to challenge the serf-owning nobility because he couldn't find enough willpower to tear himself away from the spoiled society that produced him. Must Sasha make a choice between her own personal happiness and duty, between Andrei and Marik's memory?

Sasha imagines herself as Lisa and Andrei as Lavretsky. It is nighttime, and they are in the orchard—all classical Russian novels have an orchard as vast and dense as a forest—and Andrei is kneeling at her feet. Her shoulders begin to twitch, and the fingers of her pale hands press even closer to her face. Andrei, of course, understands what these twitching shoulders and tears mean. *"Is it possible that you love me?"* he whispers. *"I am frightened,"* she says, looking at him with moist eyes. *"I love you,"* he says. *"I'm ready to give up my life for you."* She trembles and lowers her eyes; he quietly stands and pulls her toward him, and her head falls on his shoulder. He moves his head away and kisses her pale lips.

How do people fall in love? Maybe she was never attracted to Marik because they were too alike: he was *intelligentny*, he took piano lessons, and his mother was a teacher. He read the same books. Andrei, on the other hand, was always from a different group of blood, as her mother calls him. Is it his otherness that feels so thrilling, his green eyes that regard her with admiration, his hair the color of tar, innocent of barber conventions, his arms strong enough to lift heavy sacks of sugar or whatever else the freight train brings every afternoon to the railroad station where, after finishing school, Andrei unloads train cars for a ruble a day? Or is it her mother's disdainful sighs at the mention of Andrei's name that fuel the attraction?

She is only sixteen, almost two years after Marik's death, when she can no longer resist Andrei. Does she trust him more than she trusts her mother? She is under the spell of literary trysts in moonlit orchards, and she needs a pledge that will demonstrate her love, a gift that will unite the two of them forever. What is the biggest, most sacred secret she can lay down at his feet?

She finds Andrei on the riverbank, standing on the little dirt beach, skipping stones into the brown water. He is as good at skipping stones as he is at skating, making fires, and just about everything else. She looks at his silhouette etched against the darkening sky, a body that fits so well into the perfect frame of nature, a body that intrigues and frightens her. She wishes that they could still play War, but in her soul, she knows those days are over.

He turns around and peers at her, his eyes all black because he stands against the light.

"It's my uncle Kolya's war journal," she says, handing him the notebook. "The uncle who was an artist, whose paintings hang all over our house. The one still missing in action."

She doesn't know how Andrei will feel when he reads the journal. It is not the heroic war they learned about in history class, with soldiers humming patriotic songs and attacking under a red banner with a hammer and sickle to overwhelm the Fascists with the sheer willpower of their belief in the approaching future. What she hands to him is the opposite of myths concocted by the state to make them feel better when they leaf through history textbooks and read about the millions who died at the front or starved to death in besieged cities. The war narrative they learn in school, she now knows, is crammed with as many fairy tales as the stories in Grandma's prerevolutionary book about saints they no longer believe in.

"Tell me about it," Andrei says.

She can't do justice to the story by retelling it, but Andrei listens intently as the words tumble down her tongue, just as she knew he would, as only a soul mate would listen. She pauses and looks at him: he is serious and pensive, his eyes deep and dark, his hand curling around her wrist and making her breathing fast and shallow.

She tells him about Nadia, and as she speaks the words, she sees herself standing on the bridge across the Neva the way she imagines it to be, the color of zinc, wind tossing the water against the stone pillars, snatching her yellow wool hat off her head and blowing its cold breath through her hair. She sees the water churning under the bridge, her hat bobbing on the spines of the waves. She sees the pale building of the University of Leningrad's philology department on the embankment on the right and a little farther, the yellow facade of the Leningrad Academy of Arts. The wind dives and soars and shrieks in her ears, so she raises the collar of her coat and winds the scarf tighter around her neck. The iron bridge railing is cold, so she leans on her forearms and stuffs her hands inside the coat sleeves. Although Sasha has never been to Leningrad, she sees what Nadia saw on that October night, like frames of a movie rolling before her eyes, making the story alive, acting it out for Andrei, making it theirs.

She tells him about Uncle Kolya's paintings hanging in their house, the paintings Andrei has never seen because he is not allowed inside. A portrait of Sasha's young mother, her lips curled in an ironic smile, the way she used to be before the war wiped all the joy off her face and made her serious and orderly. A portrait of her grandparents in their dining room: Grandma in an armchair, her face turned slightly toward Grandpa, who stands with his hand clasping her shoulder. His blue-eyed stare is straight and resolute, as though if he weren't holding her down, the armchair would float up into the air and out the window—over the lilac bushes, over the birches of the park and the firs of the woods that stretch as far as her eyes can see—sailing with Grandma into the gray-blue palette of the Ivanovo sky.

She tells him about two later works, painted when Kolya came from Leningrad, during a break between semesters at the art academy, the time when the word *front* had already begun to gather strength during the war with Finland: a painting called *Ration*, a slice of black bread and a small dried fish, scaly and parched, lying on an open page from *Pravda* and an oil painting of a soldier throwing a grenade at a tank, the soldier's back tense and determined, the tank halted by yellow flames waving at the sky.

She tells him about a painting that used to frighten her when she was little. A tiny skeleton of an unborn child her mother brought from her anatomy museum stands next to a mirror where Kolya's face is reflected, a violin leaning against the mirror's frame. She was afraid to enter her grandparents' room when she first saw it, until Grandma said she shouldn't be. The strange painting, she explained, showed Kolya as he saw himself, between the violin that was art and the skeleton that was death. As soon as she said it, the picture snapped into focus in Sasha's mind, and she felt stupid that she hadn't seen it herself. It became transparent, but it didn't stop being eerie. With his pencil and his brush and his own proximity to death, Uncle Kolya infused it with power, as dark and insidious as the word *front.*

She tries to imagine Leningrad, where Kolya studied painting, with the Neva flowing through its center, the river shackled in its granite embankments. She tries to imagine the Winter Palace, the home of the tsars who, by their staggering opulence and their indifference toward the workers, had oppressed the country for centuries before they were deposed as a result of the workers' revolutionary intervention. *Dictatorship of the proletariat,* Grandpa says in a deep, proud voice, although she is not sure, since he used to be a peasant, how he fits into this dictatorial plan.

She can't see Kolya talking proudly about the dictatorship of the proletariat, or about any other dictatorship. She knows this from her mother's portrait, from the light in her eyes and her ironic smile she sees only on Kolya's canvas. She knows this from Grandma's effervescence in the family painting, where her grandfather needed to hold her down so that she wouldn't sail into the sky. Kolya was an artist and could see things others couldn't see. His soul, his *dusha*—the word Sasha learned from Grandma—was exposed, unprotected by the things they all wrap around themselves like winter clothes. This is what probably killed him: the war and his naked soul.

There is no doubt in her mind that Kolya knew about the life of make-believe, the life of art. Sasha is convinced he would not question her desire to go to Moscow and apply to the best drama school in the country, a plan she has harbored in her soul since she was seven and hasn't mentioned to anyone yet, a plan that will undoubtedly cause a seismic tremor when her mother and Grandpa hear about it. As she stares at the pages of the journal, she sees Kolya's face, as round and soft as Grandma's, his eyes smiling from behind the glasses, looking at her from a photograph in the family album, from the depth of time. She wishes she had been born a few years earlier, before the war, when he was still here. She wishes she had a father like him—not like the blond man in the photograph no one wants to talk about; not like Dr. Zlotnikov, who fixes her mother with his eyes behind a pince-nez when she talks to him about her dissertation; and certainly not like Andrei's father. She wishes Kolya were here now to tell her about the life of make-believe, the life he understood because he lived it.

To give Andrei a sense of the real Kolya, she opens the journal and reads a few pages.

March 22, 1942

Seryoga and I are pulling a cannon, harnessed like the horses in Ivanovo that used to pull loaded carts along the main road when I lived there. Only here, the ground is maimed with bomb craters and pocked with shrapnel, and no horse would be able to make its way forward. The whistle of mines and the louder roar of artillery shells rip through the air, and we roll into a trench, into something viscous on the bottom. From the explosions, we are almost buried by the falling dirt, but we are still alive. I try to move my arms and legs, still there. I can see Seryoga digging himself out, spitting out dirt, wiping his eyes of the muck from the bottom of the trench. We've survived this time. We get up.

The sticky stuff on the bottom of the trench is someone's guts and blood, but it isn't ours. The wind rains shrapnel, and we bend to get back into our harness when the lieutenant crawls out of a bomb crater next to us. His face is black from dirt, the fringe of his coat is burned over his knees, but he is brandishing a handgun.

"Attack!" he yells, pointing forward, like the statue of Lenin in front of the Finland railway station. We both look at where he

is aiming. Three German tanks are crawling from behind a grove of trees, rattling over the maimed earth, their clatter filling the air.

"Move fucking forward!" the lieutenant screams, and for a few seconds, I stand there questioning the order to attack with guns and grenades the roaring tons of steel with turrets of fire aimed in our direction. I hear the blood rushing through my veins, protesting, with each pump of my heart, my oncoming death, demanding to preserve this unaccomplished, short-lived life.

But Seryoga and I know better now than to question the commander's order, no matter how reckless or futile. So we clutch grenades in our sweaty fists, and we attack. There are four of us, four human decoys in the tank shooting gallery. The lieutenant stays behind, and if any of us survives, he knows that he may get a bullet in his back the next time he leads an attack himself. The tanks are creeping forward slowly, as if amused by this pathetic sight: four men walking toward three advancing bunkers of steel.

Then there is a series of explosions and flashes of flames, and I can no longer see Seryoga. I can no longer see anyone. The tank turrets are moving, focusing on those of us who remain standing. I'm still standing, so I pull the pin and toss the grenade. The detonation hits so close that the wave of heat throws me back, into one of the trenches that crisscross the field.

I am not alone in the trench. There is a soldier, one of the four of us, slumped on the bottom against the wall, his chin touching what used to be his chest and is now just a red porridge of flesh and bone. His eyes stare straight ahead, and his hand sits in the middle of the crater in his chest, as if he were trying to stop the bleeding in his last few seconds of life. Only an hour earlier, I saw him reading a letter from home. There is a smell of gunpowder and warm blood, a stench that makes me retch. I am on my knees, vomiting the vile mess onto what's left of the soldier's body. Vile on top of vile.

Then there is screeching and roaring, more deafening with every second, and the tank's caterpillar tracks are hanging over the trench, over the man with a funnel in his chest, ironing him into his grave in the trench wall, a half a meter away from where I crouch, trying to become invisible, trying to flatten myself into the mutilated earth.

This is death, *I think.* This is the end. *I think of Nadia as the sliver of gray sky disappears above my head. I crawl another meter to the left, where the trench ends, to keep the sky visible, as if the sight of the torn edge of a rain cloud over the mangled earth could save me. Sweat pours into my eyes, but I can't wipe it off because every part of me is shaking from the racket and the stench, from the metal heat and the terror beating inside my chest, from not wanting to die yet. As the tank swivels right and left over the trench, pulverizing the dead soldier into a mash, I press into the sticky muck on the bottom and lie there like a wet rat, suffocating, mortified, and already half-dead.*

And then it becomes light, and I can see the sky again. The tank has moved forward. I dig out, spitting out fetid dirt, bumping into the sole of a crushed boot, and peek out. The tank is clattering away; the other two are far ahead, all but disappearing behind the grove. I remember what Seryoga told me: When all you see is its back, it can't hurt you. This is when the tank, with all its crew, all those who were safe and untouchable only minutes earlier, is yours. Strike their motor in the back, *Seryoga instructed,* and when they start to climb out, shoot them, one by one.

I have one more grenade. I wait until the tank clatters about ten meters forward, then pull the pin and throw. The explosion shakes the air and flings me back onto the bottom of the trench. Seryoga was right. Two figures clamber out of the tank hatch. There is desperation in their jerky movements, in their arms and legs that twitch as if pulled by strings. I wait until they jump on the ground, and then I shoot each of them with a handgun, one after the other, one bullet for each. That's all they're worth, two bullets. "This is for you, Seryoga," I want to say, but I don't, because the words refuse to leave my throat. They are caught inside, together with the taste of trench dirt, together with the smell of warm blood; they almost gag me. I no longer have words.

When I stumble back to our position, caked with foul soil and blood that isn't mine, Seryoga is in the trench, and seeing him alive makes my legs turn to jelly. He is sitting up, scraping dirt from under his fingernails with a knife. Dirt and someone else's blood, probably, but that doesn't matter. What matters is that I didn't leave him to die on the battlefield with the three Nazi tanks and no cover.

He is glad to see me, too, and he points to the vodka left in his tin cup, the ration dispensed by our commander who sent us to fight the German tanks. "There's more," says Seryoga and waves in the direction of the commander's dugout.

I down what was left in his cup. The vodka burns its way to my stomach, warming every centimeter of my gut on its way, then shoots up to my head and makes it light. Seryoga hands me a chunk of bread and stands up to bring more.

We drink and get drunk because there is nothing to eat except for two hundred grams of bread and because we want to erase what we've seen from our memory.

"I did what you told me," I say.

"What?" Seryoga asks and hiccups.

"You told me to toss a grenade into the ass of the tank," I say. "Remember?"

Seryoga looks at me with glazed eyes and shakes his head.

*"And then I shot the two Fritzes when they scrambled out."
The words feel heavy in my mouth, and it takes extra time to send
them into the air. "The one on the right first, then the one on the
left."*

Seryoga nods. "Molodets. Good for you."

*We drink more, which isn't nearly enough. I still remember
the two figures jerking when my bullets hit them, then going limp
and collapsing on the field.*

*"They didn't kill you, so you killed them," Seryoga says. "It's
war."*

*Seryoga is right. It is that simple: we won because they died
and we didn't. I take another gulp from the mug, but it still does
not convince me that I won. I don't feel like a winner. The vodka
may have cleansed my insides, but on the outside, I reek of exploded
guts, shattered bones, and dried blood. I feel like a butcher.*

When she finishes reading and the images fade, Andrei enfolds her,
pressing her face into his neck, her shoulders twitching and her pale lips
trembling, just like Turgenev's Lisa in Lavretsky's arms. Their embrace
smells of damp soil and Andrei's father's filter-less tobacco. Her face is
so close to Andrei's that his features have blurred, but he lets her know
where his mouth is when she feels it on her lips. He tastes like the bit-
tersweet cough medicine Sasha had to swallow when she had bronchitis,
one gulp of which made her feel delirious and silly.

She slides her fingers over Andrei's face, and he slides his fingers
over hers, as if they needed to add another sense to what they already
know about each other: a sense of touch, without which, from now on,
no understanding could be possible between them.

13

It was utter stupidity to kiss on the riverbank where anyone in Ivanovo could have seen them, so Andrei now meets her on the edge of the park where it begins to turn into the forest. This is where they are: on the edge between the delineated pathways of the park and the wild, unchartered danger of the woods.

They meet in the evening, when Andrei comes back from work and before she has to go home for supper. For half an hour, they lie in the grass and talk and kiss and stare into the sky. Although it isn't even six, the air becomes grainy with gathering dusk. Or maybe it only feels like twilight in their bed fringed by tall grass: sturdy stems of chamomile flowers and thick, oily leaves of yellow cups everyone calls "chicken blindness." They are in their own space now, screened out from the sun, darkened and hushed. The space determines how much light reaches the roots of the plants around them and how willing the field is to accept their intrusion into its midst. Sasha looks to her left and sees the bluish band of the forest lit by the fading sun, as it stood watching the three of them, Marik, Andrei, and her, on that Sunday in March, collecting dead branches and then watching a fire consume them.

Andrei and Sasha never talk about that day in the woods, about the moment that changed everything. Does Andrei wake up and stare into the night, as she does, wishing he could make things go back to the way they were? Does he mourn the loss of his rival as much as she mourns the loss of her friend? But there is a darker question that Sasha would never ask anyone: Was Marik's death necessary for the two of them to be lying in this field, the required conduit to their growing affection? What they don't talk about is as dangerous as the forest itself, a secret they have kept out of sight, on the lowest shelf of their hearts.

Instead, they talk about Sasha's school drama club and Andrei's new job, safe topics unlikely to shake the earth on which they lie. She knows she has to tell him, sooner or later, that she is going to go to Moscow to study acting, and she has even tried to devise in her mind what she will say, but the words always seem to get stuck on their way out, as if caged by an invisible force inside her head.

"What is it like working for the Young Communist League?" she asks instead. After delivering mail and unloading freight trains, Andrei now has a respectable job, working in the center of Ivanovo, where he takes a streetcar every morning six days a week. This new job makes Grandpa, for the first time in his life, greet Andrei when he crosses paths with him outside. "Good morning, young man," he says, looking up from an apple tree branch he is dusting with DDT and nodding, but barely, not to let Andrei think he is too special. But Andrei is special. He now wears a navy sports jacket he bought at the secondhand store near the bus station, which sharpens his shoulders and makes him look handsome and important.

"Much better than carrying sacks. I shuffle papers and sometimes the phone rings, so I answer it. Sometimes I go to meetings. Not a bad job overall." He fumbles in his jacket pocket and shakes a cigarette out of the pack. It is a filtered cigarette, not like the rough filter-less Belomor that hangs on the lip of every Ivanovo man. He strikes a match and blows out the smoke, letting her breathe in its vaguely pleasant, adult smell. "They have accepted me, just as you did. It didn't matter where I came from, as long as I believed in them."

Sasha thinks of Grandpa, who believes all the news he hears on the radio, and of her mother, who believes that the war was all heroism and valor. Or maybe she doesn't completely believe it. After all, she worked in a hospital one kilometer from the front, and she must have seen what Kolya saw. But she is no longer sure what Andrei believes in. He has become a mystery, and maybe this is precisely why she is here, lying in the grass next to him. He is like a tough equation she has to solve in math class. She knows she has to unravel the variables that will allow her to learn who he really is, to get down to the X he harbors at his core.

He looks down, shakes the cigarette ash into the grass. "The Young Communist League has saved my life. I was going nowhere, and they gave me a sense of purpose; they made me one of them." He pauses and peers down into the grass teeming with grasshoppers and ants. "My whole life, people have been looking at me and smirking. I'm not stupid; I know what they whisper behind my back: There goes the loser, the son of a street cleaner. The one who is likely to end up in jail, just like his alcoholic father. But with them, for the first time in my life, I have a future."

He looks away, toward the forest, considering the heft of what he has just said. When he turns back to her, his face has lightened. "And they also tell me I look a lot like Mayakovsky," he says and chuckles.

He does look like Mayakovsky, whose poems they were all made to memorize in eighth grade, a high-cheekboned poet who glared down from the wall of every literature classroom, with his piercing eyes and a square chin, handsome in his seriousness about the Revolution. She cups her hands over Andrei's ears and peers into his face. "You have his coal-like eyes," she whispers, drawing so close that she has no choice but to kiss him. They stay immersed in this tobacco-scented kiss until he pulls away, takes her by the shoulders, and separates their bodies carefully and deliberately, as if his was a stick of dynamite and hers a lighted match.

"And there is one more thing about my job," says Andrei, as if to certify that he has changed the subject. "We have a special store with decent food."

She doesn't know why the Komsomol town committee workers have access to decent food when the rest of them stand in lines for bread and milk, but this is when Andrei unwraps a newspaper parcel he brought and pulls out a sweet roll. She has never seen a sweet roll so gleaming with glaze and studded with poppy seeds and raisins, so plump in its freshly baked glory. He orders her to take a bite, and she obeys with pleasure. The only sweets she has at home are cubes of sugar they drop into their cups of tea and a little glass vase with sucking candy Grandma keeps on the bottom shelf of the buffet. The roll melts in her mouth, warm from the sun, decadent and sweet, magnificent in its special Komsomol deliciousness.

She is grateful to Andrei for the poppy seed roll, for wrapping it in newspaper and bringing it here. She kisses his salty eyelids to thank him. She runs her fingers through his black hair; she presses her cheek into his damp neck. This is all she is ready for; this is all she wants so far. She knows this is all he wants right now, too. He is happy to tolerate her touch because he says he loves her.

No one has ever said they loved her before, either outside her family or within it. In their house, they don't talk about love. Days are filled with more pressing matters: sheets needing to be boiled, chickens needing to be fed, wood needing to be split for their furnace. Every day, they stand in lines for milk and bread and carry buckets of water to Grandpa's beds of potatoes and dill. In July, they make jams from strawberries and currants; in September, they shred head after head of cabbage and layer them with salt and cranberries to fill a barrel for the winter. There is no time for talking about love. So she feels guilty lying with Andrei in this field swarming with grasshoppers and ants, talking about love, instead of digging up radishes for salad or lugging water from the well for Grandma's nettle soup.

She feels guilty because she loves Andrei's love. It feels good being loved by an older boy, being admired and touched reverentially, as if she were an ancient Greek vase on display in the Hermitage. It feels a lot like Turgenev's orchard scene or Nina's part in Chekhov's *Seagull* she is rehearsing in the school drama club. But even though she loves Andrei, she also loves Theater. The one thing she knows for certain is that she must go to Moscow, and it is time to tell Andrei about this, even if it makes his coal-like Mayakovsky eyes turn white with anger. She takes a breath and tries to release what has been stuck inside her for too long, but the words still refuse to clothe themselves in sound. She sits with her mouth open, silent. She knows that what she is not able to utter yet will catch him as off guard as an expert solar plexus strike and will be just as devastating. She also knows that soon—despite the pain it is bound to inflict on both of them—she will have no choice but to tell him she is leaving.

Andrei peers into the wall of grass before him, as though the ants crawling up and down the thick blades hold the key to what he senses she cannot yet say, as though if he stares long enough into the yellowish thicket, their future would reveal itself in its entirety. Yet their future is still opaque; she is not ready to say what she has to say.

She turns away from him. From the angle of the sun above the forest, she knows that Grandma has already started to prepare for supper, so she has a perfect excuse to extract herself from the thicket of this uncomfortable silence. "It's getting late," she says. "I have to go home."

As she gets up to leave, she looks down and sees Andrei grab a lime-green grasshopper pulsing on its spindly legs by the stem of a bluebell flower and crush it between his fingers.

14

At home, Sasha steels herself for the announcement that she wasn't able to utter in the field. She waits for everyone to be sitting around the table, for Grandma to stop running into the kitchen and lower herself into her chair. She ignores Grandpa's dictum "when I eat, I am deaf and mute" because she knows that the severity of what she is about to say will overshadow the prohibition against speaking during the meal.

She takes a deep breath and focuses all her strength on the words, as if she were about to go onstage. "I want to be an actress," she utters in what she thinks sounds like a Theater voice. "When I finish school this summer, I am leaving for Moscow to take the entrance exam to drama school," she continues, even as her resolve is leaking out, making her look down into her plate, into the puddle of cabbage soup.

This is the first time she has wrapped words around this desire that has been burning inside her for almost ten years. Spoken out loud, her intent is now serious and real, validated by the fact of having been announced.

When she lifts her eyes, she thinks of the mute scene at the end of Gogol's *The Inspector General.* Grandpa is sitting with his mouth gaping open, his hand with a spoon full of soup frozen in the air. Her mother is staring at her with her most serious frown, the one she saves for talk of war and other dangers. Grandma is looking down into her plate, her hand covering her mouth, as if she is afraid she will accidentally say something positive about Theater and acting.

Her mother is the one to break the silence. "And afterward, what will you do?" she demands. "Will you spend your life in some provincial theater so you can come out at the end of the first act to announce, 'Dinner is served'? Will you end up in Vladivostok or Pinsk, with the rejects who can barely make it through a plumbing course?" Her voice is her teaching voice, and this is a lecture. "You wanted to be a lot of things when you were growing up. You wanted to be a streetcar driver. Do you remember that?"

"Yes, I remember," Sasha says. "I was six!" It makes her furious that her mother would compare Theater to streetcars.

"And what is acting, anyway? You don't treat the ill; you don't teach; you don't produce anything. You aren't doing anything of value. It's all frivolous and chaotic, an unworthy job for a serious citizen."

"You know nothing about acting! It's not unworthy and it's not frivolous," Sasha says angrily, challenging her mother and her worship of the practical. "I will be producing something, but it's something you can't touch. Something you and Grandpa will never understand."

"It's time to grow up, Sasha." Her mother takes a deep breath, a sign that she has heard enough arguments she considers senseless. "You're not going anywhere," she announces in a voice swollen with anger. "I'm your mother and I'm not letting you go. You will stay here and go to college and get a decent job. And that's that."

Sasha doesn't know how her mother or Grandpa can stop her from leaving, unless they bar the windows and double-lock the front door. The thought that they are powerless makes her sit up and pull her shoulders back.

It hasn't gone unnoticed, this gesture of defiance, and she sees her mother pause, but it's a pause before a storm.

"Why can't you be normal, like everyone else?" Her mother's voice is both authoritative and pleading. "Can't you see that acting will take you nowhere? That all you'll be doing is wasting your life?"

"I'm wasting my life now!" Sasha spits out.

Her mother gasps. "Better than an actress, why don't you join a circus and become a clown! You're certainly acting like one."

"An actress?" roars Grandpa, who has been uncharacteristically silent. He throws his spoon to the table and fixes his blue-eyed stare on Sasha. "I won't allow you to make this house into the laughingstock of the entire town. Do you hear me?"

His ridicule of Theater makes Sasha livid. "If I want to be a clown, I'll be a clown!" she cries out in what remains of her stage voice. "I'll be anything I want to be! Even a circus is better than this pretense of life."

"Don't you dare yell at us!" her mother shouts. "What makes you believe they will even look at you in Moscow? You think those plays you put on in your drama club were so great? They weren't. They were pathetic. Pathetic plays in a pathetic theater in a pathetic little town. You're nothing but a fool, like all the other young fools from all over the country who race to Moscow like flies to sugar, all wanting to be stars, all thinking they're the next Sarah Bernhardt."

Sasha cringes because she fears her mother may turn out to be right. The best drama school in Moscow, the one where she wants to go, admits only twenty-five applicants a year from all over the country, and there must be thousands of people like her who have been infected with the germ of Theater and who will do anything to have a life of real make-believe. The thought that she may fail makes her anger blaze even hotter.

"I will go to Moscow and I will become an actress!" she screams. "I'm not you and I won't live like you've lived. I won't spend my life in this house being ordered around by him." She thrusts her finger in Grandpa's direction.

Grandpa scrapes his chair back and stands up. "I've had enough. I'll tell you what you will do," he rumbles. "You will listen to me, that's what you will do. You'll go to school right here in Ivanovo. You'll learn something useful. How to build a house or treat a disease, like your mother did when she was your age." Sasha sees that Grandpa's hands are shaking, as if he is about to hit her. "You will respect your family!" he shouts. "You will be like your uncle Sima, who died right here, in this house. He was a hero who made me proud. You make me sick. Your mother is right: you're nothing but a clown. A disgrace."

Then Grandma gets up and whispers something into his ear. She strokes his arm, hoping that his rage will dissipate. She is the only one who hasn't condemned acting. From her abbreviated experience singing opera, she knows what it feels like to escape and have another life, even if only in her imagination. *"Vsyo budet khorosho,"* she says, her favorite saying. "All will be well."

But all is not well.

"No one in this house is going to Moscow," declares Grandpa and takes a step toward the door. He walks out into the yard, where the neighbors' sheets fluttering on a line quickly hide him from their view. A few minutes later, he is back, a bunch of nettles clutched in his right fist. With his left hand, he grabs Sasha by the back of her neck, like he grabs blind kittens to be drowned in a ditch, and drags her onto the porch. There he locks her waist in the vise of his elbow and whips her bare calves until they become swollen and red, until blood begins to rise to the surface of her skin.

The nettles' sting makes her clench her teeth, but she doesn't wail, as she did when she was younger. Never again will she reveal her pain in front of him. She will remain silent, just as his dictum demands, deaf and mute.

∽

She wonders if all will ever be well, as Grandma promises. She feels like Nina from Chekhov's *Seagull*, bathing in Konstantin's love yet yearning to leave her small town and go to Moscow to become an actress. And what then? Will she, like Nina, turn out to be naive and simple-minded, deceived by a famous man, one of the scores of heartbreakers who undoubtedly prowl the drama schools in Moscow? Will she, like Nina, end up performing in stuffy provincial theaters, riding crowded trains whose cars reek of beer and urine, from one dilapidated stage to the next?

The enormity of Moscow's possibilities is as thrilling as it is terrifying. In the night, terrible dreams return again and again. She bends over the ledge of their drinking well and falls in. She is flailing in icy black water, the logs of the walls closing over her head, as a tiny figure etched against a square of light high above watches her scrape the slime off the walls. "Help!" she cries, but no sound comes out. She takes a breath and shouts again, but she can only hear splashing water. She has no voice. She is thrashing desperately, mute, the figure above a dark silhouette of someone she doesn't know. In her dream, she always wakes up before she drowns so that she could fall into the well again, the next night and the next.

Yet she knows she must go to Moscow and study acting. Even if she ends up in provincial theater, even if she has to announce that dinner is served. The need to leave this place gnaws at her bones like a hungry dog, poisoning her dreams, making her wake up in a cold sweat.

15

Sasha does not see the fire. Only when she comes back from school, their last day of the last grade, a day of farewells, does she see what is left of Andrei's house. It has always been more of a shed than a house, with a wood-burning stove in the front corner and two tiny rooms separated by a door with a missing upper hinge that always made it hang at an angle. But now there is no house; there is no shed. There is a heap of charred, broken ribs jutting out of the smoldering pile of crumbling boards.

No one saw how the fire started, her mother tells her, but once it did, it spread fiercely and fast, devouring the house.

"Andrei's mother was inside when we heard a boom, like an explosion. I ran out into the courtyard and saw the house ablaze. His father was wobbling around, drunk, with a broken vodka bottle in his hand. So drunk he could barely stand. So when he lost his balance and fell, the jagged glass must have knifed straight into his stomach." Her mother nods her head, whether to drive in the irony or to affirm the outcome, Sasha doesn't know.

The courtyard is filled with the bitter smell of wet ash, and Andrei is slouched on the ground next to the fence, streaks of black across his face. Sasha kneels down next to him.

"Tell me what happened."

He doesn't move and doesn't say anything, as if he didn't hear her. And maybe he didn't.

~

For about a week after the fire, Sasha cannot find Andrei. He is not in any of their usual haunts; he has completely disappeared. Asking her mother would only provoke another tirade on danger. Two years ago, Sasha would have asked Marik, but all that is left of her friend is a heavy stone of guilt in the pit of her stomach. And now there is more guilt staring her in the face: the approaching date for her Moscow drama school exam, the knowledge that she must leave her life in Ivanovo, the nauseating feeling that she must leave Andrei, in spite of what he has lost.

What would Andrei do if her house burned down, her mother, Grandma and Grandpa, and every one of Kolya's paintings she knows by heart, gone? If she were alone and the only thing she had left was a charred carcass of what used to be her home spreading the reek of damp ash all over the courtyard? Would Andrei leave her for Moscow?

~

She stands at the streetcar stop when Andrei appears in the opening door, ready to get off. He freezes when he sees her. A wiry woman pushes him in the back with a string bag full of turnips, but he doesn't move. He doesn't seem to notice the impatient passenger behind him. All he sees is Sasha, her face naked in its trust, open to him and no one else.

He steps forward and embraces her. For a moment, Sasha doesn't know what to do with her arms, but then they rise and wrap themselves around him. The two of them stand like this, buried in each other, for how long she doesn't know. Inside her, the love for Andrei pulsates with such intensity that it nearly burns, catapulting her back to the memory of a ball of lightning she saw when she was six.

She remembers she was at the river with Grandma, rinsing a load of laundry, when a thunderstorm came out of nowhere, and they hid in a shack where someone, long dead, had kept his rowboat, now all crumbly and rotten through, a dark skeleton from old times. They stood inside the shack and waited for the storm to end as a ball of lightning heaved through an empty window cut out of the wall but never enclosed with glass. Afraid to move, she looked at Grandma, her frozen profile, her stiff vertebrae, the corner of her petrified eye. The ball of lightning sailed across the room and lingered over the boat, sighing and glowing, like an enormous egg yolk suspended in the air. They flattened themselves into the splintery wood of the wall, afraid to stir, watching it crackle with electricity. Then the ball of fire dipped, almost touching the bottom of the boat; heaved its glowing mass to the windowsill, as if it had seen enough of what it came to see; and rolled out.

Sasha still remembers the feeling of overwhelming powerlessness, of being at the mercy of that fireball, of knowing what would have happened had it decided to veer a few centimeters off its path. She still holds in her bones the feeling of being paralyzed by the lightning's lethal intensity, of being held captive, just as she is now, in Andrei's embrace.

When they separate, Andrei holds her at arm's length and peers into her face.

"Where have you been?" she asks.

"Staying at my boss's house until I can get back on my feet." He pauses, as if unsure whether he should say anything else.

"I didn't know where to look for you," she says. "There was no one I could ask." She notices that his features have hardened, marks of grief gouged into his face, making him look several years older.

"Let's get out of here." He points to the street where they met after her piano lessons.

They walk past the neighbors' houses, past the lilacs struggling to escape from behind the fences.

"Why are you staying with your boss?" she asks.

For a moment, he is silent, as though thinking about how much he should reveal.

"I don't know why Vadim has been so good to me. He feeds me; he shares his home with me. He talks to me and promises me a good future." Andrei stops but then decides to continue. "We drink vodka at night after work. Just the two men, *hozyaeva*, as Vadim calls us, the masters. The masters of his apartment, of Ivanovo, and, by the time the bottle is empty, the masters of the entire world. The masters who will soon build this glorious dream, he says, an idea so grand that it will make our skin crawl."

He pauses as they walk past a house with two *babkas* on the bench, whispering. "I'm not a master of anything yet," he says, "but the glorious dream and the shining future—what Vadim promises—sound good to me. Wouldn't you want to live in the shining future? Not like my father, who only lived in the rotten past."

Sasha feels odd jealousy rising inside her, a jealousy toward Andrei's boss she has never met, the person who has been next to him after the fire, soothing his grief with vodka, helping him heal. This is something she should have done, without the vodka part. All she can give Andrei now, it seems, is sympathy.

"I am so sorry about your mother," she says. "And your father. You must feel so much pain . . . I'm terribly sorry."

"Don't feel sorry for my father." Andrei's face suddenly cringes with hatred. "He didn't deserve your sympathy. He was a drunk and a criminal, and I wish he'd stayed in the camps where he belonged. I wish he'd never come back." They turn onto a footpath leading to the river, and as they walk on the hardened dirt, the expanse of still water opens before their eyes. "All my father ever did was spout stories about his time in the camps, about the savagery and atrocities, stories I never believed even for a moment."

Andrei falls silent. She watches his jaw tense as he swipes his hair off his forehead. They are now standing at the bank of the Uvod' River, over the little beach carved by the water from the thicket of reeds and tall grass.

"Do you want to hear any of this?" he asks. "It's gruesome, like some of your uncle's war journal."

Sasha nods. She is not sure she wants to hear it, but she knows Andrei is entrusting her with something he won't share with anyone else. Probably not even with his boss. This may be Andrei's response, she thinks, to her entrusting him with Kolya's journal.

They sit down on the grass and stare into the water, black from peat.

"My father came back from the camps with no teeth and no forgiveness. He boiled with hate, and he unleashed that hate on us, but mostly on my mother. It was as if it were her fault that a quarter of his life had been stolen from him, as if she didn't try hard enough to glue together the pieces of the wreck he had become. He said he told me those stories to teach me a life lesson. *There is no friendship in the camps,* he said. *It's always you against them.* As if I needed a lesson from a thug. As if I was going to end up behind barbed wire, like him."

Andrei picks up a small stone and tosses it into the water. She watches as the stone skips three times and disappears under the oilskin of the river.

"Imagine this if you can: once in June, he told me, he saw a prisoner tied to a tree, naked. He knew the man, an engineer from Moscow, Igor. They'd driven shovels into the rocky earth together. From the moment Igor arrived, my father knew he wouldn't survive. Too civilized. That day, when the guards tied him to a tree, my father saw the glare of insanity in Igor's eyes; he heard the threats bubbling up on his lips. But what would have been my father's reward had he stopped Igor from lunging at the guard? Not a day off from digging, not even an extra ration that night. The next evening, they passed the tree on their way back from work. All that remained of Igor were flaps of skin hanging off a skeleton. The man had been eaten alive by gnats. *Better him than me,* my father said.

"But winter, he said, was far worse. Prisoners who failed to fulfill the daily quota of work were tied to trees and doused with water. From November to April, dozens of ice statues loomed about the campgrounds. Reminders to others not to question anything. Reminders to fear those with power, to follow the rules. And for those who didn't, he said, there were so many ways to be tortured and killed. My father was a common criminal, so his life was easier, but he saw what they did to political prisoners, to traitors. They were forced to sleep on the lower bunks, the coldest place in the barracks. Kirill from the bunk below my father's was always scribbling in a notebook and was accused of insubordination. They beat him with iron pipes and left him outside to freeze. The white-haired man everyone called 'the scientist' had his hands tied behind his back before they pushed his face into a bucket full of shit and urine. That was his punishment for treason and subversion, a punishment that served him right, my father said."

For a minute, they sit quietly, watching the figure of a lone fisherman with his rod, motionless, on the opposite bank.

"How could I believe him? This was the stuff of Auschwitz, not our own Vorkuta or Magadan. This is what the Nazis did in their camps. My father had become everything we were fighting against, his cruelty toward my mother, his drunkenness. That's why I went to work for the Komsomol Committee, because of him. To get away from him, to take revenge on anyone like him. To build a world in which he wouldn't exist."

Andrei's mouth tenses, and he looks away. "I hated my father, and I still hate him. Not a single tear for him from me." He turns to Sasha and cups her hand between his palms. "Except for you, Sashenka, from now on, not a single tear for anyone."

16

In their field, she hardens herself to tell Andrei that she must go to Moscow, that she has already bought a one-way ticket and hidden it on the bottom of her suitcase. A one-way ticket, a brazen purchase, as if she knows for certain that she will pass the three rounds of auditions required to get accepted.

She has been putting off the announcement long enough, and for that she is punished: the enormity of Andrei's recent losses has drained the certainty of her intent to leave and allowed doubts to seep into her soul. Her leaving will clearly announce her priorities: acting and Theater are more important than life and love, more important than Andrei, even after the fire has robbed him of his family.

She is prepared to say, as a preface, that long ago, she and Andrei made a promise not to hurt each other, when there was so much hurting happening after the war. Then she would admit that she has been keeping something from him, something that she knows is going to hurt him. She has prepared all those words, neatly arranged, but not one of them is now breaking from its mooring to float to the surface.

"There is no easy way to say what I have to, so I'll just say it." She cringes at her own awkwardness. "I'm going to Moscow to take an entrance exam to a drama school. I leave in two weeks," she utters, unsure of whether she can keep up her resolve and not disintegrate into tears because the mere thought of leaving makes her nauseous.

She is afraid to look at him, and when she does, his face has lost focus as it blurs when it is next to hers, but now there is at least a meter of space between them, space charged with the smell of gathering rain and betrayal. She has never seen Andrei look so unguarded, so fragile.

"Why?" he asks. His voice is heavy, swollen with pain. "Why are you leaving? Have I said something? I don't understand . . ." His voice trails off, and he peers into the grass, breathing hard. "What have I done to make you leave?" His eyes are now searching hers, not finding any answers.

Should she say that she might be back next month, one of the scores of high school hopefuls who didn't get accepted, humiliation lapping around her like a foul smell? Or would the possibility of such an inglorious return mark the end of everything for her, even though Andrei might see in it a glimpse of hope?

"Ever since I was seven," she says, "I've wanted to study acting. If I don't try, if I don't go to Moscow and at least try, I will never forgive myself." She knows there is another reason for going to Moscow, something that has been percolating through her mind ever since she heard *Three Sisters* on the radio, something that she decides not to tell Andrei. There has to be more than Ivanovo. She needs to see Moscow, to experience a different kind of life.

She says the words she has prepared, but all she hears in response is silence, and all she sees is Andrei's wounded face. She never knew she could possess the power to hurt someone so deeply, to inject such anguish into someone's eyes. The power she will learn to wield in Moscow, the power that ten years earlier made her believe that the actors in the radio play were really desperate to leave their provincial town, the power that will make her audiences laugh or cry. Was her mother right when she called her an *egoistka*? An egomaniac basking in her freshly discovered power while plunging a knife into the heart of someone she purports to love.

Her body suddenly feels ungrounded, because she knows that whatever she says now will only hurt him more. There are no words that will wipe the grimace of suffering off his face and allow her to do what she must. In vain, she fumbles for a reason that will extract her from this uncomfortable silence.

"It's late." She begins to get up from the grass, but Andrei doesn't let her. He pins her to the ground with his body, his mouth clamped on hers, the taste of cigarettes as harsh as his forced kiss. His left hand is pressing on her shoulder, pushing her into the grass, and his right hand is fumbling beneath her shirt, his fingers hurrying into places that have up to now been forbidden by their unspoken understanding. His body is heavy and insistent as she wriggles and thrashes to get him off her, to arrest his hands that are now groping under her skirt, pulling at her underwear. Almost instinctively, she closes her teeth around his lip and bites hard. He releases his grip and pulls back, leaving a taste of blood in her mouth. She pushes him off her and quickly gets to her feet.

As she straightens her dress and brushes off whatever may have stuck to it, her heart still racing, she glances at him sitting in the grass. His head is hung, and his shoulders are stooped, her closest friend who has just hurt her. Or was it she who hurt him first?

"I'm sorry, Sashenka; I'm so sorry," he says in a hollow voice, as if there is nothing left inside him. "Forgive me. I don't know what came over me.

"I'm sorry," he repeats over and over again, to which she says nothing, turns, and walks away without looking back.

～

On Sasha's bed is an open suitcase, and she has just told her mother that two weeks earlier, she bought a one-way train ticket to Moscow for June 16, eight days from today.

"This is nothing but a stupid childish whim," her mother says sternly. "You're too young to know what's good for you. I won't allow you to leave."

Sasha straightens her spine. Her posture makes her feel that she is looking down at her mother, and she realizes that in the past year, she must have grown taller.

She is wise, her mother, so she turns away and takes a few breaths, swallowing the furor bubbling up on her tongue.

"Do you know how fierce the competition is?" she asks, switching to a different strategy. "You must have extraordinary connections to get accepted. You must be related to the Minister of Culture. No one gets in, especially not a girl from the provinces."

Her mother knows what to say to make Sasha feel even more frightened than she already feels. *You know she is right,* a little voice inside her whispers; *you're nothing but a provincial girl with no connections.* She feels a gnawing sensation in her gut, as if a determined hand were trying to unravel her intestines.

"I'm not saying you don't have talent," her mother adds in a conciliatory gesture, sensing Sasha's dread. "But with all those hordes of youth with connections, whose names are already on the list of the admission board—honestly"—she pauses and gives Sasha a sorrowful smile—"you don't stand a chance."

17

Every night leading to her scheduled departure, as she packs the note-book into which she has copied Uncle Kolya's journal by hand, along with a few skirts and dresses Grandma sewed for her, she hears her mother and Grandma whisper in the kitchen. Her mother's voice is sibilant and injured; her grandma's—reassuring and calm. She hears Grandpa at his drafting table pressing thick, angry lines into yet another plan for a movie theater or a music school that will remain unbuilt.

Her hands feel unsteady, and her stomach churns, but she cannot show anyone, even Grandma, that she is terrified. She cannot admit, even to herself, that this is the end of everything she knows, that, just like Andrei's house, her Ivanovo life is about to go up in flames.

$\sim$

The train station is a wooden structure with "Ivanovo" written in big brown letters on its facade. A leak under a second-floor window has reduced the final *o* to a dirty smudge, so her town's name is now the same as Chekhov's play.

"Ivanov," she whispers, looking at the station facade, taking it as a good omen for the start of her acting career, then reciting in her mind Lermontov's "The Sail," which she prepared for the Moscow drama school audition:

A silver sail, the ocean loner
Is lurking in the azure mist.
What has she lost in foreign corners?
What in her homeland did she miss?

Her mast is clattering and bending
Midst whistling wind and raging wave.
Alas, she seeks no happy ending,
Nor runs from happiness away.

Beneath—the crystal torrent tempteth,
Above—the golden rays caress,
Yet she, rebellious, longs for tempests,
As though a tempest granted rest.

They are two hours early for her train to Moscow, so the three of them sit on the hard bench and wait. Grandpa, still furious at her for defying his orders and at her mother and Grandma for *walking on a leash of the child's foolishness*, has refused to come to the station with them. Even with all the windows open, the room smells of stale beer and soot, and the air is permeated with the acrid melancholy of leaving mixed with the pungent anticipation of travel.

Sasha looks around at what she is about to give up. Across from them sits a skinny man with a red mustache and watery eyes, as if he has already started to lament his own exit from the life of Ivanovo. A few meters away is a family of five, the youngest child still an infant in the arms of a bovine-looking mother, the oldest a boy with scabbed knees and shifty eyes who is nine or ten and who wipes his runny nose with the sleeve of his shirt.

There is a suitcase by the feet of the father, a small man with curly black hair and a cigarette that hangs off his lip as if it had become a permanent feature of his face. He holds on his lap a whining girl of about three, who is trying to wiggle her way out of her father's arms, wailing and rubbing her eyes with her clenched fists. Holding the baby with her left arm, the mother bends her right elbow, not a muscle twitching in her face, and slaps the girl on the back of her head. The girl stops wriggling and becomes quiet for a few seconds, then explodes into a new, louder wail. The mother whacks her again, and the girl swallows her sobs, curls into a ball on the man's lap, and begins to whimper softly, like a beaten dog.

Sasha sees the girl's brother, now by the station's food kiosk, watching a stocky woman in a sleeveless dress eat a fried turnover, eyeing the grease the woman licks off her fingers when she finishes the last bite. The woman's arms are as plump as loaves of white bread in the Ivanovo bakery where every morning, Grandma and Sasha stand in line for a brick of black bread and three rolls of white.

From now on, she will save every image she sees and set it onto the innermost shelf of her memory, next to everything else she has experienced and observed in her nearly seventeen years in Ivanovo. She is going to save it all—every glance, every head movement, every scene, and every face she sees—and she will store it all inside her until she needs to pull it out for the roles she will be playing when she becomes an actress.

"This is for you," says Grandma and hands her a handkerchief tied at the corners. "Open it."

Inside is a ring with a green stone, gold and delicate, a treasure worth more than everything she has ever owned.

Grandma lifts the ring and puts it on Sasha's finger. "Fits you, just as I thought. This used to be my lucky ring. An actor's stone." They both stare at her hand, which now looks as if it belonged to someone else, someone talented and noble, someone who could easily fit into the life of hats and banned poetry, someone who could get accepted, even without connections, to the best Moscow drama school.

"Be careful when you get out of the station in Moscow," her mother says. "Don't stop and don't talk to anyone; God knows what hoodlums hang out there in the middle of all that transit bedlam." She has already warned Sasha several times, but she wants the message to remain fresh in Sasha's mind, her proverbial message about dangers. "Cross the square in front of the station and wait for trolleybus number eighty-seven. The fourteenth stop is yours." For the two weeks of auditions, she will be staying with Baba Yulia and Katya, whom they visited for the May Day parade when she was seven, and then, as her mother hopes, Sasha will come back to Ivanovo *to start a normal, serious life.*

She wishes she could convince her mother, the same way she has been trying to convince herself, that in two weeks, she will not be coming back. But what if her mother turns out to be right? What if Sasha's readings from Lermontov and Chekhov make the judges yawn? What if she is too immature to understand what adults already seem to know—that everyday survival always beats art, that the material invariably trumps the intangible? What if, ever since she heard *Three Sisters* on the radio, she has been chasing after a phantom; what if life is indeed all utilitarian and tethered to the ground, like the spindly goat of one of their neighbors, circling the pole, day after day, over the dusty grass of the yard?

Her mother looks at her watch and gets up. They walk outside, onto the platform where passengers are already waiting, about forty people, the size of Sasha's drama club. The family from the waiting room is already there, the mother rocking her infant on her left arm and holding her daughter with the same hand she slapped her with, the father clutching a suitcase and fumbling through his pocket in search of something to give to the boy, who leans forward in a stiff, pleading way.

The train will arrive from around a curve where the forest begins its dark expanse behind a meadow dotted with fresh haystacks on the left, and everyone stands swiveled in that direction, waiting for a whiff of smoke to appear above the trees.

Sasha throws her arms around Grandma's neck. She smells of kitchen and soft cotton, and Sasha presses against her warmth. She knows that Grandma doesn't believe Sasha will return in two weeks, and this knowledge fortifies her resolve and brings back her strength, at least for the last few minutes. She tells herself that she can't fall apart in front of everyone on the platform. She can't allow tears to overwhelm her; she can't let her mother think that she has been right all along. She looks away, at what she is leaving: everything.

With a whistle, in a cloud of smoke, the train appears from around the curve, and her mother now hugs her as Sasha snuggles into her wet cheek. *"Vsyo budet khorosho,"* her mother whispers. "All will be well." This is her usual refrain—although Sasha knows that her *well* is very different from Sasha's—which drowns in the hot steam of the train sighing its way to a stop.

They have two minutes until it whistles again, until the platform begins to sail away, until Sasha gets, with every moment, farther from life in Ivanovo and closer to Moscow. As she looks over her mother's shoulder, she sees Andrei standing at the end of the platform. He appears and then vanishes in the clouds of steam rolling from the engine, almost a vision, if she believed in visions. She blinks to see if he is real, but from the stern look on her mother's face, from the way she resolutely swipes a finger under her eyes and frowns, she knows that he is.

ACT 2

Moscow

18

Sasha does not see her name on the admitted list at the Vakhtangov Drama School, and everything inside her begins to loosen and dissolve, her legs refusing to support her weight. She leans against the wall and breathes in and out, as her drama club leader has taught them, to keep upright, to keep thinking, to keep going on, but tears are already rising in her throat, choking her and drowning any protest to this hideous injustice. What does she do now? The question, like a hammer, strikes against her skull, reverberating with all the shameful and appalling answers. Will she now have to trudge back to Ivanovo, humiliated and defeated, just as her mother and grandfather hoped, the word *talentless* tattooed onto her forehead?

Sasha takes a deep breath and turns back to the two pages with twenty-five typed names clipped to the board. Her vision is blurry, but she stiffens her back and focuses on the middle part of the list, between the *L*s and the *N*s, where her name should be, willing with every fiber inside her to coax it out of nothingness and force it onto the page of the admitted. Then she closes her eyes and exhales. When she looks again, her name is on the list, between the *L*s and the *N*s. She screws her eyes shut again and presses her palms over her face in an effort to test the reality she seems to have warped, but every time she looks back, her name is still there, among the twenty-four others. Why didn't she see it right away? A temporary blindness, most likely, the product of anxiety, a few nauseating minutes of stomach-churning dread.

She runs to the post office and sends a telegram to Ivanovo. At ten kopecks a word, she must be brief: "Accepted," she writes. "Kisses. Sasha." She imagines her mother's face when she receives it. At first, her mother may feel angry to read the judgment that instantly shatters her plans for Sasha and legitimizes such an unworthy profession as acting. But at the same time, Sasha knows, her mother won't be able to deny feeling something that resembles pride. For a minute, as her mother stares at the words of the telegram, Sasha imagines the anger and the pride bumping against each other, with pride, at least in her mind, unexpectedly taking the upper hand.

She knows that Grandma will smile and Grandpa will glare. She knows that Grandma will busy herself in the kitchen, smiling furtively as she rolls the dough for *pirozhki*, while Grandpa will storm out into the yard and furiously start pulling dandelions out of a bed full of blooming strawberries. Sasha sees her telegram spreading the word to their street, to their neighbors in the other half of the house, as they munch on the news that the girl who used to run barefoot around the yard chasing chickens is now in the country's capital, just steps from Red Square, learning to become an actress.

She sees Andrei, or maybe she doesn't see Andrei. He is elusive: what he says does not always match what is reflected in his eyes or what may be brewing in his heart. She knows how badly she has hurt him, but instead of brooding, she also knows she must focus on the enormity of the task before her. It is only by an act of sheer will that she can push aside, albeit temporarily, the guilt that presses on her heart.

~

She sits in her dorm room, a mirror propped up on the desk against a stack of textbooks. There is nothing interesting about her face that she can see: big gray eyes her acting teacher calls photogenic, a pudgy nose that her roommate Sveta says will always typecast her into character roles, bangs that fall down to her curved eyebrows Sasha has recently plucked with tweezers. *This is what art demands,* said Sveta, who has already starred in a movie, so Sasha believes her. She sits before a mirror, ruthlessly yanking little hairs out of her face, biting her lip with each tug.

During the month of September, like college students all over the country from Kaliningrad to Kamchatka, they pay for their free education by working on a collective farm, where there is a perpetual shortage of hands to harvest the vegetables planted in May. Every morning, they climb into a creaky bus and for eight hours bend over rows of potatoes, onions, and turnips, raking through the dirt soaked from recent rains in search of produce that hasn't yet rotted in the ground. Sasha doesn't know where all the collective farmers are, the workers who have tended to these crops they are now told to harvest, but as she lifts her head, all she sees are drama students up to their ankles in mud. Every day, practical as ever, Sveta stuffs the best-looking vegetables into a bag to take back and store in the bottom of the armoire in their dorm room. At the end of the month, they have a pile of food that will last them until New Year's.

Sveta is inventive in other ways, too. She is a year older than Sasha and, in her own words, she has already seen life. She sends Lara, their third roommate, to buy a few meters of cheap upholstery fabric and instructs Sasha to sew them skirts with big pockets. "For crib sheets," Sveta says. "For history and philosophy, when we have our first final exams in January." With a blonde braid down to her waist, Sveta has the slight build and pure blue-eyed stare of an ingenue. Sasha had to look up the word *ingenue* in a French-Russian dictionary—"an innocent, unworldly young woman"—and she thought it was ironic that the real Sveta was the complete opposite of the Sveta she would portray onstage.

The only classes they would never dream of approaching in their devious skirts with crib-sheet pockets are the classes they came here for, the reason they left their homes and endured three brutal rounds of auditions. These are the classes of stage movement, dance, voice, and, the most frightening, the most important class of all—acting. Acting is sacred, and they all know that the first two years are when some of them will be expelled for what their dean calls "professional inadequacy," or simply a lack of the acting gift.

During the first year, no one is allowed to speak in acting class. For two semesters, they drink from imaginary glasses and eat with nonexistent forks and knives, diligently screw in light bulbs, feel the wind standing on the bow of a ship, thread needles and sew up holes. For her first final exam in acting, Sasha picks up imaginary clamps and scalpels and hands them to the surgeon played by Lara. She has learned to do this by observing a nurse during surgeries at Central Clinical Hospital, four operations a week, for two months. The rest in their class silently slice apples, bang make-believe keys of typewriters, sway in crowded buses, knit scarves, chew on lemon wedges, embrace illusory lovers, wait in lines, walk pretend dogs, uncork wine bottles, wash underwear in the sink, stand on the observation deck of the highest building in Moscow and look down at the sprawling city laid out below—all on the small stage of their freshman studio.

By the end of the first semester, three students are dismissed for professional inadequacy, and Sasha feels a rush of overpowering relief that she is not among them. Their dean calls it "the first wave of attrition," and the word *first* sends a cold shiver down her spine.

There are twenty-two of them left, ten girls and twelve boys. "My girls and boys" is what their artistic director Vera Konstantinovna calls them, and a smile spreads wrinkles across her face as she surveys her students before their History of Theater class. Vera, as they call her when she is not within earshot, is short and small-boned, and Sasha wonders if she, too, was an ingenue when she was young. When she speaks, she waves her ringed fingers as if conducting an orchestra, and her sharp nose and a green shawl around her shoulders make her look like an exotic bird.

Vera tells them that they are now actors and will always live on this side of the curtain, the stage side. From the time they walked through these doors, she says, the world has split in two: one half is Theater, where everyone is one of them, *svoi*; the other half is the audience, *chuzhoi*. Among the audience is a world they are told to observe, full of situations they will use onstage and characters they will inhabit when they are finally allowed to speak. They are different, those people; they lead normal, ordinary lives; they are *civilians*, as Sasha's teacher calls them. By the end of the first year, they must learn to become them.

But what about Sasha's mother and grandma? Are they also on the audience side of the curtain, among the ordinary people, or are they with Sasha, on the stage side? Does Theater allow those close to you into the space where acting happens? And where is Andrei in this new scheme of things? Which side is he on?

She hasn't written to him, not a single letter. She feels that acting, like distance, is building walls to separate them even further.

Moscow is full of things Sasha has never seen: hard salami and chocolate candies in bright wrappers, silk scarves and cakes adorned with pink cream roses, nylon see-through stockings and whimsical bottles of bitter-smelling perfume. There are also open exhibits of modern art labeled "cosmopolitan," which were banned only a few years earlier. There are unofficial concerts by a young bard Volodya Vysotsky, who often comes to their dorm to sing about struggle, angst, and love while they sit on the kitchen floor, mesmerized and quiet, drinking teakettles of young sour wine Georgians sell at the nearby railroad station. There is a film called *The Magnificent Seven* playing in two central theaters, the first movie from America that ever made it across their borders.

Sveta, Lara, and Sasha sink into their seats as the galloping horses on the screen deliver American recklessness straight into their waiting hearts. After the movie ends, they walk out silently, filled with the joy of color and the thrill of danger, so different from the monochrome monotony of their own films. Although only three of the magnificent seven survive at the end, Sasha feels relieved that one of them, Chico, goes back to the village and the girl who loves him. The night air of the Moscow streets seems charged with energy, filling her chest with a lightness, transporting her back to the innocent times of her life in Ivanovo when she felt safe, loved, and protected by Andrei.

It is 1960, and to afford the benefits of what their teachers call "the political thaw," Sveta, Lara, and Sasha participate in the mass scenes at the Vakhtangov Theatre, where they are paid seven rubles and fifty kopecks a performance. They can always count on Gorky's *Summerfolk* and *The Lower Depths*, and Sasha's singing voice gets her into a Gypsy choir in Tolstoy's *The Living Corpse*, but they know that the mass scenes in movies pay considerably more. They also know that their school strictly prohibits first-year students from working in film, since their professors see motion pictures as a detrimental influence on the students' stage training.

The three of them hold a discussion about the possible repercussions of challenging the ban, which ends with Sveta's decree that *The Magnificent Seven*, which they have already seen three times, as well as the cosmopolitan art exhibits and Vysotsky unofficial concerts, are sufficient reasons to break the school rules. Sveta gives them permission to sign up for the crowd scenes at the Mosfilm studio and tells them to hide in the back so as not to be caught on-screen.

19

On those evenings when they do not participate in mass scenes at the theater, Sasha and her roommate Lara sit on her bed and talk. Lara is from Pskov, a town to the northeast of Ivanovo, a place as small as Sasha's hometown, a place often paired with the adjective *provincial*. They are the same age, both children of the war, both fatherless. Lara's father was killed in Poland in 1944, when the tide of the war had already turned and Russian troops were advancing west, when the word *victory* had already begun to form on people's lips. "1944, when no one should have been killed," Lara whispers, looking down as she straightens the corner of the duvet cover with her hand.

Does she feel a connection to Lara because they both grew up in small towns in the provinces and both left for the capital? Did the two of them sense that Ivanovo and Pskov were too suffocating, that both wanted more than their homes could offer? Is Sasha's search for a different life in Moscow simply an extension of her looking for a father, someone noble and heroic, someone whose name wouldn't make Grandma frown? Has Lara, all this time, been looking for a father, too? It is probably to fortify the growing bond between them that Sasha tells her the story from her childhood.

Sasha's mother, who told her that her father died during the war, never specified how he died, and this vagueness created a vacuum that, in her seven-year-old mind, gradually filled with plots of nobility and valor. Some men in her fantasies turned out more heroic, tossing a grenade at a tank and dying in an explosion of flames, while others perished more slowly, like partisans living in the woods in the middle of winter, sleeping in log-reinforced trenches below the ground, hidden under a meter of snow.

She doesn't remember when she realized it was useless to wait for her father to return, but at seven, Sasha knew one thing: if she wanted a father, she had to take matters into her own hands and find him.

So the next time her mother took her to the town park on Sunday, Sasha didn't waste time on the sandbox or the swing. Leaving her mother on a bench under a tree, she ran around the park looking for a handsome, brave man to be her father. It took her only ten minutes to discover that there weren't many handsome men around. Another few minutes revealed that there weren't many men of any kind.

She took a path that ran past a kiosk where a round woman in a stained apron and henna hair presided behind cones with fruit drinks, and that was when she saw him. He stood by the kiosk with a glass of golden liquid in his hand, his resplendent uniform cinched by a belt with a shining buckle, his black boots reflecting the sun. Two women on a nearby bench undoubtedly saw him, too; they whispered to each other, covering their faces with their hands as they spoke, and each gave him a quick, furtive glance. But Sasha had an advantage: she was already on the path, skipping toward him, pretending to be drawn to the multicolored drinks sparkling in their vats.

When she was about a meter away, she stopped. Out of the corner of her eye, she saw that the women ceased whispering; they were now silent, their hands sternly in their laps, their eyes latched onto her—cold and hostile, like the eyes of behind-the-wall neighbors who didn't have an indoor toilet.

"Zdravstvuite," she said politely, as if he were her teacher. The man swallowed what was left in the glass, and she saw the sharp bone in the front of his neck move up and down. He looked at her, and his eyes

crinkled, golden and liquid, as if the juice he'd just swallowed, instead of going down his throat, went up and lit his eyes from within.

"Do you want to be my father?" she asked, and from the way his smile spread across his face, she knew he did, even before he could open his mouth. "Come," she said and grabbed him by the hand. "I'll take you to Mama."

They walked past the two women on the bench, stiff and silent, past the empty-sleeved invalid and the drunk sleeping under a tree. She saw her mother on a bench near the sandbox, where a bunch of nursery-school girls in berets were digging a ditch that looked like a war trench.

She clasped her mother's hand and set it down onto the man's broad palm. Her mother's face was open and unprotected, lit by surprise. "Here," Sasha told her. "I want him to be my father."

The next few weeks were light and breathless, like the anticipation of a New Year's Eve. The man's name was Alexei, Lyosha for short, and he was a military pilot. On his first visit, he came to their door dressed in his uniform, which temporarily melted the icy blue stare of Grandpa, who didn't trust strangers. His word for strangers was *chuzhoi*, as opposed to *svoi*, our own. The same words Vera in their drama school uses to separate actors from those on the other side of the curtain. You can only trust *svoi*, said Grandpa, a small bunch that included their immediate family here and Grandma's sister who lived in Kineshma, ninety kilometers away. Sasha was not sure she liked Grandpa's philosophy. If what he said was true, she couldn't trust Marik, or Andrei, or Marik's mother, who taught them about Pushkin. If they couldn't trust anyone but their family, how could they even get on a streetcar without risking their lives? And what about those radio reports of tons of grain they never saw? When it came to the radio, did Grandpa not trust the news, either?

The reason he wasn't sure if he could trust Lyosha, she thought, was the melting gaze in her mother's eyes when Lyosha looked in her direction. That was when she forgot about Grandpa, which instantly stripped him of his command status because, as they all knew, a commander could never be ignored.

Sasha liked Lyosha's strong arms that lifted her onto his shoulders, from where everything seemed smaller. Surveying the familiar from above, she sailed over their yard, past the envious eyes of Andrei and Marik sitting on the roof over the garbage dump; past the babushkas on a bench, who stopped chewing on sunflower seeds and burst into furious whispers; past the fences bleached gray by the winter and the rain that had recently turned their street into an alley of mud. Even at seven, she knew that what drove the babushkas to flap their arms and fuse together into what looked like a murder of crows was envy. Lyosha was not an invalid and not a drunk, with arms and legs intact, and that made him a rare commodity in postwar Ivanovo. He could have been the only man with extremities and a smile to roam their streets in the last five years.

But after four months of this privileged, man-infused existence, something happened. Her mother's eyes were no longer liquid, because Lyosha only stopped by once a week and was not there long enough to lift Sasha onto his shoulders so she could parade around the yard. He smoked by the porch, taking long and deliberate breaths so he didn't have to say anything. Her mother stood next to him, waiting for something other than a nicotine cloud to emerge from his mouth, her eyes surveying the ground around her feet.

Then one week, he was not there at all, and her mother announced at dinner that Lyosha had been sent with his air squadron to an overseas military mission. She said this staring into her borscht, and from Grandma's deep and silent sigh, Sasha knew that she didn't believe her.

$\sim$

The war aftermath is what Sasha and Lara both remember, not the war itself. The time of women, children, and old men; the time of nettle soup in the summer and cabbage soup in the winter; the time of waiting for fathers, sons, and brothers to return. The time of the gradual realization of how many wouldn't.

One evening, when Sasha searches for words to bandage around their postwar wounds, words she cannot find, she turns to Kolya's journal and reads to Lara what she herself doesn't know how to express. She is still astonished, after all these years, by the grace of his sentences written in the trenches.

February 19, 1942

It's the end of February, eight months since the beginning of the war, and our division is hobbling toward the front, which has been recently pushed half a kilometer west by a few hundred men from the provinces. Bowlegged, sinewy, and short, they threw themselves over the German machine-gun bunkers with the same irrational abandon that propelled them, in the steam of a peaceful bathhouse, to down tin cups full of undiluted spirits and then jump naked into the snow. A platoon of sharpshooters followed over their bodies, and now it is our heavy artillery division, with six cannons pulled by tractors, which has been tossed into the maw of battle.

We step out of the woods to cross the railroad tracks, which are still under bombardment—no longer from machine guns but from heavy artillery—farther away. The forest on the other side of the tracks looks like a broken comb, with sharp, uneven teeth of splintered tree trunks against the sky.

"Run over the tracks, don't walk," Seryoga instructs. "Hurry."

But it's impossible to run. There are corpses everywhere, frozen in piles covered by the recent snow. Some are still fighting a fight that has now become eternal. A Russian soldier is clutching at the throat of a German whose hand still holds a knife dug into his ene-my's back. A sailor who was struck as he was throwing a grenade, frozen, like a monument to himself, towering with his raised arm, rooted into the ice, the copper buttons on his black jacket sparkling in the sun. An infantryman, already wounded, started bandaging his leg and froze forever, struck by a bullet he never saw. It won't be until April when the snow melts and reveals what is below these winter corpses—more dead. Layers of the dead: at the bottom are soldiers in summer uniforms; on top of them are sailors in black jackets and flared pants; then lie Siberians in sheepskin jackets and felt valenki *boots who died in the December attacks of 1941. On top of them are fighters in cotton-filled jackets and cloth hats that had been distributed in the besieged Leningrad. Layer upon layer of corpses: a monstrous, bottomless layer cake of death.*

"Let's go, move," yells Seryoga and pulls me over the tracks, over the mountains of frozen bodies that keep rising before us. As I stumble into the woods on the other side, I think of Borodino, of Tolstoy's Volume III of War and Peace *we had to read in art school. Imagine this picture, the professor said: tens of thousands of bodies strewn across the battlefield, the ground soaked with blood, half the Russian Army killed in one day. And the most surreal thing of all is that we claimed victory. I still remember the image: the vast field under the murk of dampness and smoke, dark clouds spitting drizzle at the dead, the wounded, the frightened and exhausted survivors, as though nature were warning people to look around, take inventory of the carnage, and think of what they had done.*

How many have been murdered here, on the Leningrad Front? Could this be half of our present army Seryoga and I are walking on right now, stumbling on its soldiers' frozen heads and arms? But even if it were, our army has always been bottomless, like a magic lake in a Russian fairy tale. It is promptly replenished with fresh arms and legs and newly shaved heads mobilized from republic

capitals and small villages, from factory towns and collective farms,
dressed in new uniforms and thrown into the foul cauldron of new
battles.

~

Like Sasha, Lara has seen her father only in photographs, but she mourns him nevertheless. "Had he been there, he would have protected me," she says quietly, staring at the blanket. "He wouldn't have let *that* happen." *That* is a secret she hasn't told anyone in Pskov, but now she is far enough from home to have the courage to uncage it. It is as dark as that Sunday in Ivanovo, the day Sasha and Andrei don't talk about, either.

"It was my mother's fortieth birthday," Lara says and as she speaks, Sasha can see her friend's apartment crowded with at least twenty guests: her mother's coworkers from the local cafeteria, all women; and their neighbors, three war widows from the first and second floors; and a married couple, Zina and Oleg, from across the hallway. Oleg is the only man they know who returned from the front. He drags his left foot, which was struck by shrapnel, and he yells and flings things when he gets drunk, but his wife is grateful that he is back home, alive.

The night before the party, Lara says, Gennadii, her older brother who just graduated from high school, lugged in a case of vodka and a case of wine, stacking them up in the corner of the kitchen. A half a bottle of vodka per person, the standard calculation for any celebration.

After all the potatoes, beets, and carrots were boiled, chopped, and drowned in mayonnaise, after trays of *pirozhki* were pulled out of the oven, brushed with milk, and covered with towels to soften— just as they were in celebrations in Sasha's house—Lara teased her hair and outlined her eyes with coal. She was still in ninth grade, but that night, she remembers she was feeling very grown-up. The sounds of the doorbell announcing guests buzzed joy into her heart. The two tables were pushed together, the eating surface extended with several boards propped on boxes. Every guest had to stand up and deliver a toast—to her mother's health, to success in work and private life, to happiness, which seemed to everybody abstract and elusive—and Lara quickly drank two glasses of wine, or was it three? After two hours of toasts and chasers, of vodka and *pirozhki*, the tables were pushed against the wall, and someone put on a record of a popular song Lara liked.

"Remember the Rio Rita?" Lara asks. The popular song wailed from the record player, and Oleg, as one of the two men in the room, extended his hand to Lara's mother and ceremoniously dragged her onto the dance floor. The rest of the women danced with one another, stumbling into the sultry rhythm, shuffling their tipsy feet on the linoleum, shouting over the music and laughing. Lara's brother grabbed her by the shoulders and pulled her into the gyrating flux of bodies, into the delirious heat. His arms locked around her waist, and his face, hot and damp, pressed to her cheek. It was an important birthday, after all, and everyone was getting drunk. The women from the cafeteria were now in a circle, telling lurid jokes in loud, uncontrolled voices, bursting into fits of intoxicated laughter. Oleg, having tried to dance with every woman, was now propped against the wall by his wife, who gave him fierce looks, holding in check his inclination to yell and fling glasses at the guests.

"My brother poured me another glass of wine and spilled half of it on the floor. I don't remember how I got into my mother's bedroom." All she remembers is the walls spinning and the ceiling pulsing above her head. All she remembers is her brother's weight pressing her into the cover of her mother's bed, his vodka breath smearing her face, his unyielding grip that left black marks pressed into her shoulders. All she remembers is the shame.

"I never told my mother," Lara whispers. "I never told anyone." She stares at her clenched hands and begins to pull at the skin around her fingernails. "After that, home was poisoned. I stayed late at school;

I found every pretext to sleep over at my friends'. I flunked my classes, almost every one of them, except music." She smiles faintly, still staring down. "That's why I am here, in Moscow. I couldn't stay, despite my mother's pleas. I had to leave, even though I knew that no college would accept me. I wasn't good at anything. The only place where I stood a chance, I thought, was drama school." She shifts on the blanket, straightening her back. "It's still raw, like an abscess I've tried to squeeze out of my mind. I knew it was my fault. I was drunk. I am the one to blame."

Sasha wraps her arms around Lara to hold her, but Lara stiffens, resisting her embrace. She has been trying to erase *that* from her memory, as if it had never happened. She thinks that if she empties her mind of that day, the event will disappear. She believes that pity will only cement it into her memory.

The last thing Sasha wants is for Lara to relive that day, so she releases her from the hug, and Lara slides away, relieved not to be held, not to be touched. To get her mind off that day, it is now Sasha's turn to unleash her secret, so she tells Lara about Andrei and Marik, about that day in the forest everyone still calls *an accident in the woods*. She tells Lara about the guilt she feels for leaving Andrei. She tells her how he begged her to stay and how she refused, even after the fire, even after his parents both died and his whole life went up in flames. She feels she betrayed him, she tells Lara. She is grateful to her friend for listening, for not holding her hand, and for not saying she is sorry. Like Lara, Sasha doesn't want to be held. Unlike Lara, she is guilty.

Yet in her bones, Sasha knows how fortunate they are to be here, in this city and this school. She knows that acting will endow them with power, the power Lara lacked when she was in ninth grade. When they master its secrets of becoming someone else, Sasha says, Lara will be as liberated from her past as she is when she inhabits the characters in classic plays, strong yet conflicted, but always in control of their lives.

20

Despite her school faculty's disdain for movies, the Mosfilm studio regularly scouts their hallways for fresh talent. Studio agents, unshaved men in denim and loose-haired women dressed in clothes they don't see in stores, catch students between classes to invite them to screen tests, enticing them with fees only the studio can pay. During the spring semester, Sveta is offered the lead part in a film set in contemporary Moscow, and Sasha is invited for a supporting role in Rimsky-Korsakov's film opera *The Tsar's Bride*.

The studio sends its emissary to their dean, who has starred in many Mosfilm studio films himself, to plead for both of them. Sasha hopes the emissary is a green-eyed beauty in a peasant dress and no makeup, a look the dean is rumored to favor. But all that Sveta and Sasha can do to influence a favorable outcome is to sit on her bed and curse each other with the foulest epithets they can fish out of memory, a superstition for good luck Grandma and her mother both believe in. It turns out Sveta knows many more despicable obscenities, so for Sasha, this cursing session has become a learning opportunity.

Sveta is lucky. The dean allows her to accept the role, since all the shooting will be completed in the summer, during their vacation. Fortunately for her, the filming of her movie will not interfere with her education. Sasha's case is more complicated. *The Tsar's Bride* will film all the outdoor scenes in the summer, just like Sveta's movie, but the indoor shooting in Riga is scheduled during her first semester of the second year, throughout the fall.

She imagines the dean sitting behind his massive desk, weighing her future in his hands. His dark hair is chafing like a storm around his unsmiling face as he tears up the letter from Mosfilm in the same fit of splendid anger he recently exhibited in his own on-screen performance in *The Idiot*. This image makes hope leak out of her, drop by drop, like hot water from the broken radiator in their dorm room. Sasha knows he is not going to allow a second-year student to miss the whole fall semester, with classes in literature, political economy, and history of art, not to mention the new sophomore classes of ballet and fencing. With regret, she thinks of Riga, the capital of Latvia, where the indoor filming will be done, the Soviet Union's most western city she will never see.

When their artistic director Vera relays the dean's decision, Sasha is stunned.

"We've taken your good grades into consideration," says Vera, blowing out a cloud of tobacco smoke. "You will study the required general subjects on your own and take exams in January. The film will be counted as a pass for all the other classes that have to do with acting."

Sasha doesn't know what has swayed the long odds in her favor. Was it the classic opera contained in *The Tsar's Bride* or perhaps the white beard and serious gaze of the revered composer Rimsky-Korsakov? Was it the stunning emissary from the film studio who showed up in a flowery dress and no makeup? Or maybe it was something else entirely, a recollection that floated unexpectedly to the surface of the dean's mind: his own first film role when he was still a student—unrecognizable now, with bony arms, short hair, and surprised eyes—the role that forty years ago silenced his venerable teachers into consternation and inducted his name into the esteemed columns of the national movie magazine, *Screen.*

Sasha is triumphant and relieved. She will spend the summer in the old town of Suzdal, which she imagines to be a lot like Ivanovo, only full of ancient churches. Then, in the fall, when her classmates move on to improvisations with words, she will be living in a real hotel in Riga, as foreign as any city abroad, getting paid a salary exponentially greater than any Moscow mass scene could offer.

Sometimes she wakes up at night and listens to Lara's mumbling when she has a bad dream and Sveta's even breathing on the bed across from hers. If she keeps her eyes open for a few minutes, the contours of things slowly step out of the darkness, like a developing photograph: the doors of the armoire materialize into a grainy image in the corner of the room, and the table covered with oilcloth gathers into a familiar outline next to what she knows is the doorframe. It is three or four in the morning because it is completely dark and silent: all the buses, trolleys, and streetcars are parked for the night in their depots, and the red neon sign for a Georgian restaurant they can't afford has been switched off since midnight.

This is the time when guilt, a nocturnal predator, crawls out of its lair. She feels guilty for sauntering around Moscow as though she was born here, for singing on the oldest theater stage in the capital as though she were a professional actress. She feels guilty for living so close to Red Square and not wanting to admire the Kremlin wall or the Lenin Mausoleum. She feels guilty for not wanting to go back to Ivanovo.

She feels guilty about Marik. She sees him the way she last saw him, his eyes white with rage, his fingers clasped around the shell. This is the time she knows she could have stopped him. She could have averted his death, but instead, she ran away. This is the time of night when the tape of that day in the woods spins in her mind, the ruthless tape with no stop and no fast-forward button. Could she have asked Marik in a calm, mature voice to hand her the shell? *"Give it to me right now,"* she hears herself say four years too late, knowing that he would have done what she asked because he would have done anything for her. It seems so simple now, putting herself in control of a split second before everything changed, before everything slid off its base and collapsed.

She lies with her eyes open, wondering if Andrei is as racked with guilt as she is, hoping he is also awake in his house in Ivanovo, staring into the night. Hoping but far from certain, since this is the time of night her hope often turns to doubt. Did Andrei's face ever darken over Marik's death? She never heard him lament placing the shell into Marik's hand. Shouldn't Andrei have known that what he drove Marik to do was within the realm of danger? Shouldn't he wake up at least as often as she does, the weight of Marik's death constricting his chest? The thought takes her places that only emerge late at night, when everyone is asleep, when the layer of everyday life is stripped away and there is nothing, not a glimmer of light, to detract from the darkness. Terrifying places that she is not ready to acknowledge. To escape from them, she thinks of what happened after Marik died.

She saw Marik's mother only once after the accident in the woods, as Marik's death was referred to in their family, when her mother, Grandma, and Sasha went to his funeral at the same cemetery where Uncle Sima had been lying for fifteen years. The new section, with a freshly dug grave awaiting Marik's coffin, was at least a kilometer from Uncle Sima's; so many had died since then that the cemetery had swollen past its original fence and spilled onto the field leading toward the underbrush that marked the edge of the forest.

As they walked along the alleys of the dead, she thought it was ironic that Marik's grave would overlook, for all eternity, as Grandma whispered in her under-the-breath prayer, the woods that killed him. Or was it the remnants of the war that killed him? Or was it Andrei, with his goading and mocking? Or maybe—a thought that still stings—what killed him was her abandoning them by the fire, two stubborn boys who wouldn't budge, two friends who for a moment became blinded by rage and who had no one to shake them back into their own truth. Maybe what killed Marik was her betrayal.

Marik's mother stood by the open grave, in a black coat and black fur hat, her hands clutching the edge of the coffin above Marik's head, as if this were her only support, as if without holding on to it, she would lose her balance and fall.

She had been sick, they were told by their substitute teacher after Marik's funeral, and no one knew when she was going to come back. "She can't get out of bed," Sasha heard her mother say to Grandma when she thought Sasha was out of earshot. She couldn't imagine what kind of illness could shackle Marik's mother to bed for so long, the same teacher who read the last chapter of *Yevgeniy Onegin* to them without interruption, forty students rapt and silent, impatient to hear if Tatyana would leave her old husband to be with the man she had loved her whole life.

Then, one day, a month later, Marik's mother got out of bed and made her way to where the river settled into a small lake, a little dirt beach for sunbathing and swimming in the summer. It was the end of April, and no one understood how it could have happened that she found herself in the water. No one understood how the placid Uvod' River, even at its April fullest, could have turned into a stormy sea and drawn someone to its pebbly bottom.

An accident at the lake was what their principal called her death at a school meeting. But Sasha was not sure it was an accident, the same way she knew Marik's death was not an accident. What was it, then? Did she die because her son died? Did this mean that Andrei was complicit in her death as well? Was Sasha complicit, too?

Her mother, Grandma, and Sasha went to Marik's mother's funeral. Her grave was next to Marik's, which meant, Sasha wanted to think, that March and April were relatively happy months for Ivanovo because no one else had died.

21

In August, she is in Suzdal, filming *The Tsar's Bride*. It is an opera, with the Bolshoi stars singing on tape as they act the scenes, so the experience is not unlike what they have been doing during the first year in drama school: living and acting but remaining speechless. The film's director, Sergey Vladimirovich, gives her thoughtful notes at the end of each day, and she is grateful he treats her just like all the other actors. Or maybe not quite. Maybe he is a little too involved in her scenes, a little too attentive in his instructions to her. She closes her mind to this. He is married and middle-aged and besides, back in Ivanovo, there is Andrei. Or at least she hopes there is still Andrei.

Her character, Lyubasha, smolders with anguish and anger. She begs the man she loves, the man who has already laid eyes on someone else, not to abandon her, not to crush her life. Night and day, she thinks of him. Night and day, only him, she sings. Lyubasha, short for Lyubov, love. She is despondent, feverish, losing hope, as the Bolshoi orchestra echoes from a tape recorder with music as restless as her mood. Lyubasha is so desperate to keep her lover that she decides to buy poison to exile her rival from life. Poison that will extinguish her rival's eyes, drain color from her cheeks, make her hair fall out, strand by strand; poison that will bring her lover back. "I will give you everything I have, all my pearls and all my precious stones." She sings Rimsky-Korsakov's lines to the chemist who has promised the deadly potion. "And if that's not enough, I'll borrow or steal. I'm not afraid of servitude or debt." The orchestra reverberates in heavy chords throbbing with a premonition of tragedy. But the chemist doesn't want her necklaces or her rings. He wants only her honor. Her honor she has already given to the man who is about to leave her.

"Night and day," she sings, "I think of him. I have forgotten my father and my mother for him," she laments, holding the procured poison, shadowing the harmonies that pulse with dread. "I have abandoned all my family. I've given him everything I have. And now he wants to leave me for a girl whose eyes are brighter, whose braids are longer. A girl who doesn't love him, who is innocent of his desire, who is betrothed to someone else." A French horn enters with a throaty solo. "What have I come to?" cries Lyubasha, brokenhearted, bitter, inconsolable, the violins of the orchestra weeping from the Bolshoi Theatre tape.

They are almost done with the outdoor shots, and at the end of this week, after a banquet thrown by the local government office, the film crew will pack up and take the train to Riga.

This is Sasha's first banquet, and she has been looking forward to it for weeks. Back in drama school, when they have extra money, Sveta and her other classmates mark the end of exams at Café Leningradskoe, where they pool their rubles together for a bottle of wine and a few cheap *zakuski*, but she has never been to a celebration that is designed to honor artists. The local Communist Party Committee has invited them all—the actors and the crew—to the biggest restaurant in Suzdal, Bely Lebed, or the White Swan.

She watches Raisa, who plays her on-screen rival, Marfa, the woman Ivan the Terrible chooses as his bride, the woman Lyubasha poisons, spend half an hour teasing her hair and pinning up a shirt that in two months of work has become too wide at the waist. Sasha watches

127

her thread a needle as she stretches out her arm that underscores the length of bone expected for a heroine. She is shorter than Raisa, and her Ivanovo bones boast in breadth rather than length. In the movie, Marfa, innocent of Lyubasha's rivalry, doesn't want to marry the tsar because she loves another man, and only a few days ago, in one of the ancient monasteries Suzdal is famous for—white stone walls covered with dark icons lit by candles—Raisa filmed the final scene where, after five takes, she goes insane and dies. As Raisa is finishing pinning her shirt, Sasha ties her hair back into a ponytail, makes up her face using the tricks she has learned from Sveta and their makeup class, and puts on her only good dress, stitched together from black cotton dotted with tiny daisies.

The White Swan is the size of a gymnasium, with one long table stretching the length of the room covered with dishes, glasses, and platters of food worthy of the tsarist feast they just finished shooting. There are crystal vases brimming with Olivier salad; bowls with rainbow herring under a fur coat sheathed in layers of carrots, potatoes, and beets; plates with pickles, salami, and cheese; and smaller dishes glistening with red and black caviar. Sasha thinks of the sweet roll Andrei brought her from his special Komsomol store last year, a roll full of poppy seeds and raisins that caused her to salivate just as all these delicacies spread in front of her now.

For no reason at all, she turns to the door and sees a handsome man in a suit and tie shaking everyone's hand. She knows it has to be a mirage, but even after she shuts her eyes and opens them again, Andrei is still there. She looks away, but her head turns back, like a ball of iron attracted by a magnet, and the tugging pain of the year without him suddenly swells inside her and makes her walk in his direction, as if hypnotized.

He takes her by the shoulders and kisses her on the cheeks, three times, an old-fashioned custom Grandma favors. There is a different air about him, the way he carries himself, the way he moves—an air of gravity and importance. Maybe he is no longer Andrei but Andrei

Stepanovich, a man she knows yet does not know. In this byzantine room of so much excess, he seems completely at ease, introducing himself to the crew members and kissing Raisa's hand as if she were a real tsarina. Sasha sees all this in snatches—discarded frames on the floor of a film editing room. When they are invited to sit at the table, Andrei is next to her on her right. Sasha's first banquet is foggy, experienced through the delirium of his presence.

Someone in a gray suit makes a toast, and they all drink what has been poured into their glasses. First it's vodka; then it's either cognac or wine. She chooses wine. It is red and sweet, the wine from Georgia called Khvanchkara, the favorite wine of Stalin, the toastmaster proclaims. Sasha has her doubts about this claim, for whoever knew what Stalin favored has probably been dead for at least a decade, arrested and shot for knowing too much, but sitting next to Andrei makes her skepticism melt away. Despite a line of waitresses snaking through the room carrying trays of hot dishes followed by a whole roasted baby pig on a platter, she cannot but feel heat radiating from him. Neither the pig's baked eyes nor the signature dish of Bely Lebed, a whole roasted swan, with its curved neck and a charred beak, distract her from Andrei's hypnotizing presence.

He piles up their plates with meat and raises his glass. "To your first film role," he says. "Drink to the bottom."

She drinks to the bottom. She is thrilled to sit next to Andrei, their sleeves touching, their legs pressed together under the table. She feels liberated to be with him, without her mother's condemning looks and warnings about danger, without the whole town of Ivanovo gossiping on benches about the daughter of an anatomy professor seen walking around with the janitor's son. She doesn't know how Andrei found out about the filming in Suzdal, but she is glad he did. She is glad she can be alone with him in this town that has been turned into a huge movie set. She is glad she is nearly eighteen, an acting student doing real acting. Today is a perfect day to celebrate all this.

She also knows what being alone with Andrei means, how this banquet is likely to end, and knowing it makes the hours of sitting at the table even more intoxicating. They eat the pig and the swan until only their carcasses are left, devouring their flesh made succulent by spices she doesn't know, sucking on the bones when there is no meat left. They are insatiable and hungry, as if they haven't eaten in a year, as if this first meal together is also their last. She feels conflicted, not wanting this gorging frenzy to be over and counting the minutes until it ends.

22

He now tastes of the aged Armenian cognac he toasted her with, no longer of the sweet cough medicine that made Sasha dizzy a year ago. He unzips and unbuttons her, carefully, and he doesn't seem to notice what she wears underneath her dress. She wishes she had worn something prettier, something that only exists in her imagination, but he doesn't seem to care. His eyes are black, all pupils, and he smells of cigarettes and roasted meat. *"Kra-sa-vi-tsa,"* he spells in little puffs of air on her shoulder, "a beauty."

The only light in the room is a narrow streak that reflects on the wood boards of the floor, a streetlamp sifting a yellowish glow through the slit between the curtains. This hotel room undoubtedly belongs to the Party Committee; the curtains are thick, and the sheets are crisp. She has never been certain of what she's been aching for, but being with Andrei in this room has sharpened the focus and honed it down to this moment, reckless and electric. After almost two years of tiptoeing around, this is the moment they have yearned for, the moment that will bind them forever by blood. She is not afraid of blood or pain, a small price to pay for the intoxication of the two of them finally becoming one. She knows what she wants: his mouth and his hands, his weight on her, the taste of his sweat. This is the beginning of her adult life, and they are writing its first chapter together—in this town full of white churches and dark saints—with their hands and their lips. They are both stripped of clothing, stripped of their shells, exposed to each other. She wants him to keep saying "I love you" in his new voice, a voice that makes him as vulnerable as she is now, a voice that forces the familiar pain that has churned inside her for a year to boil and explode, making her feel certain she is going to die.

～

"Are you all right?" Andrei asks, pulling the blanket over them. "Did I hurt you?"

She still feels the echo of the ache, but it is dormant now, all gathered in one place, no longer demanding attention. "No," she says. "I feel good, for the first time."

He seems unhappy with her answer, and she senses a current of tension run between them. She sees the struggle in his eyes, as if he were not sure whether he could believe what she just said, as if he wanted to be guilty. It is the same struggle she sensed in him when she announced she was going to Moscow, a struggle to believe what she was saying. Or maybe it is much simpler than that. Maybe, as all provincial men, he thinks that a proper virgin should whimper in pain or squirm in shame, instead of feeling satisfied and happy. She wants to tell him that she is certain she could reach into the place where she stores other people's emotions and find the requisite pain. But she knows it would be someone else's pain, not hers. She wants to feel what she feels, to be content for the first time, to prop herself up on the Party pillow with a smile on her face, the smile that makes his face tense.

She rolls to the edge of the bed and lifts the blanket. There is no blood on the sheet, not even a drop. She has no idea what this means, and she wishes she could ask her anatomist mother later, but she knows, of course, she can't.

"It is my first time," she says, her voice already defensive. "You are my first." She wants to say *"my first man,"* but that would sound as if she were putting him into some grotesque line with men she hasn't yet met who are going to queue up to have sex with her next.

He draws his arm around her and presses her face into his neck. It smells like marzipan she tasted once, a gift from a Georgian student in her dorm, a sweet and sweaty smell. "I love you," he says, "no matter what."

"No matter *what*?" she asks.

He doesn't answer. He has already closed up, retreated into himself. He strokes her hair, then winds it around his hand. "Let's go to sleep, *krasavitsa*," he says. "It's late." He kisses her on the cheek and turns away.

She wants to object, to clear the air between them, but when she turns to Andrei, he is already asleep.

Sasha opens her eyes and sees the streak of light on the floor, only now instead of the pale yellow, it is bright saffron. Andrei, dressed, is packing his suitcase. She sits up in bed, rubbing open her eyes to face the first day of her new life.

"Do you have to leave so soon?" she asks as he pushes the clasps on the suitcase closed.

After a minute of silence, he speaks reluctantly. "I have to go back to my life. And you must go back to yours."

There is a shadow now that dims everything in the room, as if the curtains were suddenly pulled closed. The street below is empty except for a blue Moskvitch parked at the curb below their window, probably an official Party Committee car waiting for Andrei. "Why did you come here," she asks, "if you only intended to stay for a night and run out at the crack of dawn?" He straightens up but doesn't turn to her and doesn't answer. "Why did you go to all the trouble to find me? There are other women, I'm sure, women you could've had with much less effort."

From his tense shoulders, she knows he is back to being as closed as he was in Ivanovo, as guarded as the borders of their motherland. Sensing her anger, he turns and sits in an armchair by the bed. With morning light flooding into the room, he is no longer Andrei. He is Andrei Stepanovich, a Party functionary.

"Is that car downstairs one of the Party perks?" she asks, sharpening her voice to counter his silence. "Am I just a perk, too?"

"Leave the Party out of it," he snaps. "There are things about the Party you'll never understand. The Party isn't a concept; it's made up of people, flesh and blood. And these people trust me. You might even say they love me. They were my family when I no longer had a family."

She walks around the bed and sits on the arm of his chair, hoping that he will stop talking about the Party and pull her into his embrace. For a moment, he hesitates but then holds her tight.

"I saw you at the train station when I was leaving Ivanovo," she whispers into his neck. She can't see his face, but she can hear a sharp exhale.

"I wanted to say goodbye to you before I left. The real you, not a mirage hovering at a distance I could only see through a cloud of smoke."

"You always expect too much of me, Sashenka." He releases her from his embrace. "You—more than anyone else—know who I am. My father was a criminal, and my mother swept the streets. I live in the provinces. I have provincial blood running through my veins." He looks down, searching for words. "I didn't say goodbye to you at the train station because I was confused and scared. Because I did something I'm ashamed of. Something I couldn't tell you about."

She puts her hand on his sleeve. "We have always been close," she says. "You understand me better than anyone else. I wouldn't have told you so much about my life, I wouldn't have told you about my uncle's journal, I wouldn't be here in this room with you if I didn't think I could trust you."

He pulls her in again, and she presses herself against him. They stay in this tight embrace for a minute, or maybe several minutes, just as they did when she last saw him in Ivanovo before she told him that she had to leave.

"What happened that you couldn't tell me?" she asks when their bodies separate.

He looks away. "I still can't tell you. I don't know if I'll ever be able to tell you."

She feels that the air in the room has lost its charge; it is already a room that belongs to the past, a room waiting for its next encounter, a room to be forgotten.

He leans forward, his elbows on his knees, and stares into the space in front of him. "You left."

"I left to go to acting school," she says. "You know I had to leave. I had no choice."

He doesn't move, and in the silence, she hears the blood simmering in her ears. "Things are changing in my life, and I have decisions to make," he finally says and gets up. He stops by the window to peer outside and then turns to her. He is standing in a parallelogram of sunshine, and his face is dark because all the light is pooled behind him.

"I cannot marry an actress," he says, looking at the floor. "It's one of the Party's strictest rules."

This is so sudden, she is rendered mute. His words feel like a gut punch that has left her trying to catch a breath and find her balance.

"How do you know I would even consider marrying you?" she spits out when she is finally able to speak, a question that makes him wince. "How do you know I would consider marrying anyone?"

There is a sharp intake of breath, his mouth tensing around what he decides not to say. Instead he steps toward her and pulls her into his arms again. "I love you, Sashenka," he mutters into her ear. "But there are things happening in my life that I cannot talk about, at least not now. Please try to understand."

"I'm going to Riga in two days," she whispers. "To film the rest of the movie." She is glad he can't see her face, her constricted mouth. They are at the door, still on this side, the side of what happened last night.

"I'll write," says Andrei and kisses her on the lips, a goodbye kiss. He opens the door, a suitcase in hand. "Do you need a ride back?"

She doesn't.

"I love you," he says and starts running down the stairs.

"I love you, too," she says, but he is already two flights down.

23

For nearly three months, she clings to a foolish hope that Andrei will write to her. He doesn't write in September, when she runs to the main Riga post office every day. By the second week of her visits, the old spindly woman behind the general delivery counter shakes her head even before Sasha can utter a word. He doesn't write in October, when she cuts her post office detours to twice a week. By mid-November, the post office with its general delivery counter is completely off her route.

When her scenes are not on the schedule, she walks on Riga's narrow streets, past its cathedrals, so gothic and un-Russian, the antipodes of Suzdal's churches. In her mind, she rewinds their Suzdal night again and again, looking for clues. He cannot marry an actress: what an absurd, insulting declaration. It reeks of the medieval stupor of old times when actors could not be buried inside a Christian cemetery, when their bodies were laid to rest behind the cemetery walls, away from all the decent, sinless souls. And who said she is ready to talk about marriage? Who said that Theater does not have its own requirements, just as severe as the Party does?

She walks and thinks about Andrei. She tries to remember how old she was when the two of them—young but no longer children—despite her family's prohibition against it, snuck into his house. His father was still safely in Siberia, so was she twelve? And what were they planning to do there in his tiny kitchen? When his mother caught them that afternoon, she poured them milk, placing her glass on a doily embroidered with elaborate roses she had cross-stitched. It seemed impossible that her gnarled hands, big and full of calluses, could have produced the tiny filigree stitches on the doily, but that was the heart of Andrei's house—and maybe of Andrei himself—roughness stitched into beauty.

She thinks of her character's death at the end of *The Tsar's Bride*. In the final scene, Lyubasha admits that she has poisoned her rival, who has just been chosen as the tsar's bride. Her lover is furious, grief-stricken, desperate. He knows they are both doomed, and he plunges a knife into Lyubasha's chest. A quick death, for which she is grateful. "Thank you." She sings Rimsky-Korsakov's words in a pale voice to the mournful wail of cellos. "Straight into my heart." Lyubasha dies first— to a coda of tragic chords—just before her poisoned rival goes mad and expires, just before her lover is dragged away to be beheaded.

Why is it, Sasha wonders, that she was able to intuit such tragic, crushing love? What made the director so satisfied with the way she acted in the scene? How was she able to get it right so that the camera believed her? She has so many questions she would like to ask, although she knows she would never dare pose those questions to the director or to anyone else. Why did she have to die? Is death Lyubasha's punishment for her intense, unbending passion? Does death stalk under the murky vaults of medieval and contemporary mores, her punishment for sex?

Sasha walks past the dark buildings, wallowing in sadness, as despondent as Irina from *Three Sisters*. She walks and walks, burnishing her sadness with every step into the ancient cobblestones of Riga's streets, and Chekhov, she thinks, would be proud of her angst.

∾

In the beginning of November, the film director, Sergey Vladimirovich, calls her into a scene that isn't hers, and as she sits in the corner knitting another sweater for the winter, she feels his gaze on her. If she is honest with herself, she doesn't dislike this gaze. It is inviting and admiring, and it emanates from someone who—while not as good-looking as her acting partner who plays her lover—is still attractive, with his dark curly hair and thin-rimmed glasses pinched low on his nose. She doesn't dislike his medium height and build, the solidity of him. Sergey Vladimirovich is also twenty years older than she is and, technically, he could be her father.

As she sits there, dipping her knitting needles, she fumbles inside herself for feelings toward Sergey Vladimirovich, itemizing in her mind all the pros and cons. He has been kind and generous to her, an acting student, although he is a film director with two major motion pictures to his credit. He is older and more established than anyone who has been interested in her before, but he is also married to an opera singer who is voicing over the main part of the film, which is a definite con. She should be grateful it isn't her part, which would be utterly ironic. She thinks of having raced to the post office for three months, and she almost hopes that the director decides to keep his eyes on her a little longer. Besides, shouldn't she be grateful to him for teaching her how to act on camera, a lesson her drama school has deliberately denied its students? Shouldn't she thank him for showing her how to make the camera caress her face with radiance and light?

Sasha looks back at the director and smiles, letting him know that his attention hasn't gone unnoticed, telling him with her eyes that she is almost ready.

24

Sasha returns to the Vakhtangov Drama School in January, with full credit for all the courses she missed during the fall semester. In a year and a half, she has learned to observe. She has learned to watch what people do, how they move, and how they speak, how they squint their eyes, tighten their jaws, and knead their hands. She remembers every character she sees and every emotion she feels and stores them in a little box inside her, like photos in an album, where they will wait until she will need to pull them out for a role. She has also learned about heartbreak, thanks to Andrei and Rimsky-Korsakov, the opera composer.

In acting classes, they have moved to scenes. Yet they rarely see themselves onstage the way their acting teachers see them, and their stage personalities don't even hint at their real ones. Why does the most stunning woman in their class, Zhanna, with raven-wing eyebrows over dark-blue eyes, become average and boring onstage, while her roommate Lara, quiet and unnoticed in life, suddenly grows ten centimeters taller, her face illuminated from within? "Stage charm," their teacher Vera says, the term she has just introduced in their new class, Manners.

"You don't lose your stage charm when you're angry," Vera tells Sasha. "You have a rare quality: your charm is in your anger."

Of course, Sasha doesn't want to hear this. And who would? She wants her charm to be in her heroism and beauty, not her anger. She wants to play tragic lovers, not character sidekicks and irate bullies.

They all do. But Vera stands in front of their class, her fingers firmly wrapped around a cigarette, letting them know the rules: "Next year, when you are allowed to choose your own scenes, you can play whatever characters you like, but right now, be so kind as to play the roles you are assigned and work within the *emploi* we see you in." She flicks off the ash at the new word *emploi*, the role archetype. Their school has told them what their archetypes are from now on: Sveta is an ingenue, Zhanna is a Soviet heroine, and Sasha is a character role catchall: a funny klutz, a peasant bully, or a heroine's sharp-elbowed friend.

She doesn't go back to Ivanovo in the summer. She, Sveta, and Lara are free from classes for almost a month, and they have Moscow, sunny and breathless thanks to Khrushchev's political thaw, to themselves. With the extra income from film, they live like they imagine artists should live, recklessly and freely. They feast on bowls of *pelmeni* dumplings and bottles of Georgian wine in a café two blocks away from their dorm and dive into the Moskva River with a bunch of schoolboys who are not afraid of swimming in the shadow of the Kremlin. They race one another on merry-go-round horses in Gorky Park, their faces whipped by the wind and their hearts brimming with happiness at their utterly un-Russian independence from their families and their pasts. Sasha begins to think there may be a slight possibility that Andrei no longer matters.

She asks herself whether she would go back home if she was not afraid to see him, if she was sure she could kiss him on the cheek without bursting into flames, if she could engage in insincere talk about her neighbors' potato field and the Party's progress. Would she have given up holding Grandma's soft cotton shoulders in her embrace if Andrei wasn't there? She only knows that forcing herself to say something meaningless to him would empty her body of breath and curdle the edges of her heart.

Instead, she accepts the director's invitation to see his apartment. Why couldn't Sasha shed her *emploi*, her funny-peasant archetype, and plunge into a magnificent love affair, the kind only a drama heroine can have?

❧

"Please come in and feel at home," says Sergey Vladimirovich, pointing to a couch.

It is the biggest apartment she has ever seen, cavernous and full of light, warm air hovering somewhere around the intricate ceiling molding four meters high, an apartment where the excessive space hypnotizes and intimidates.

"I want to show you a book on acting by Vakhtangov, a first edition," he says, fumbling through the book spines on the shelf behind the couch. Vakhtangov was the founder of Sasha's drama school, an indisputable object of her interest. The director's wife is on tour with the Bolshoi Theatre, and Sasha knows what this book viewing invitation means. She has learned many things since her night with Andrei in Suzdal, and she tries to suppress the gnawing feeling in her gut that she will end up doing something she is not sure she wants to do.

But she also knows that Sergey Vladimirovich has been mindful of the difference in their ages, and his courtship since November has been considerate and kind. Just last week, in one of their late-night conversations, Lara told her that she is lucky her suitor is courteous and gentle, that she is not the object of interest of their school's assistant dean, as Lara was when they started school. "He didn't bother to invite me anywhere," she says, trying to keep her voice from clotting. "He didn't even bother to pour me a glass of water. He just pointed to my clothes when he was through and said I could leave. He treated me like I wasn't even human. Like a dog."

They all know that the assistant dean, a balding man with a paunch, who used to be a decent actor before he found teaching more rewarding, is known for summoning female students *to read for him* in his office. When his secretary sent for Sasha a few months ago with an *audition call,* she scribbled a note full of the medical jargon she'd heard at her mother's hospital that certified she had promptly come down with a bad case of strep throat. To make it look official, she stamped the phony paper with a doctor's stamp she had long ago stolen from her mother's anatomy department. Had Sasha known the assistant dean had set his eyes on Lara first, she would have used that pilfered stamp to produce a fake note for her, too. The only thing she could do now was to sit and listen and try not to show how sorry she felt for her friend. She hoped Lara would find the strength to rip the memory out of her mind and fling it to the mental garbage pile where it belonged.

In the director's apartment, Sasha finds herself sinking into the plush upholstery as he pours her a glass of golden wine from a bottle that she has never seen in the stores. She knows she is fortunate that the director is patient, but she can sense that his patience is wearing thin.

He sits next to her and hands her a filled glass. "To the end of our work together," he says and clinks his glass against hers. "And the beginning of something brand-new."

Sasha knows it is new, this post-filming territory where Sergey Vladimirovich can no longer give her orders to be more happy or less happy than she already is. *The Tsar's Bride* is over, and so is their work together. Is she happy in this vast place where everything pleases the eyesight: big windows, half-opened, letting in the jingles of a streetcar; dark bookshelves filled with first editions of tomes by theater titans; a glass coffee table, a piece of furniture she has never seen before? Is she happy to feel the director's hands on her shoulders? Is she, at least, not terribly unhappy?

~

Every time Sergey runs his hand across her back, she thinks of Andrei. She thinks of how much she misses him, of all the sadness she has hidden away in the darkest corner of her soul's storage loft, where no one can find it unless they crouch and rake through years of discarded junk.

Everything is so much simpler with Sergey. He has the soft chest of an older man, and he enfolds her in his arms, grateful that she has agreed to come to his apartment, that she is almost twenty, that she listens with attention when he speaks about himself and the Theater. Every time they meet, he buys her a pastry filled with whipped cream from the best bakery in Moscow and watches reverentially as she bites into it and then licks the sweet cream off her lips. In addition to good cognac, he introduces her to the Hungarian Tokaji in round bottles with elongated necks you can't find behind the counters of Soviet wine stores. He is always there, leaving messages with Aunt Sonya at the entrance to her dorm, and if he suddenly disappears for a week or two, she knows that his opera singer wife is back home from a Bolshoi tour.

But there are two quintessential Russian questions she asks herself: *Who is to blame?* and *What is to be done?* Raised in the nineteenth century by classical writers Herzen and Chernyshevsky, these questions were flung at all of them by her eighth-grade teacher, the one with the squirrel face and admiration for books with simple answers to questions fraught with infinitives.

Eighth grade, when everything was simple, when Marik was still alive, when Moscow was only a dream. Is it her fault that she is in the capital and Andrei is still in the provinces, that he has chosen to work for the Party, that he cannot marry an actress? Is she the cause of her own misery?

Having to consign Andrei to the emotional storage loft fills her with the same despair she felt when she found Kolya's journal. Yet, in the absence of letters from Andrei, the war journal is the only tangible connection she has to him. She rereads the story of Kolya and Nadia they read together, the story of a happier love Sasha envies, as though

144

her uncle's words could rebuild the bond between the two of them, bring Andrei closer, make him open up to her and no one else. As though her uncle's journal could shed a glimmer of light on Andrei's baffling betrayal.

February 13, 1942

I saw Nadia only cry once, when she told me about her father's arrest. There was a knock on the door of their apartment, a loud, demanding knock. A knock that always comes at three in the morning because this is the time when a person is in bed, undressed and most vulnerable.

After the arrest, I came to her apartment almost every day, and what I saw was a different house. It looked bigger and emptier, a place where every noise seemed to echo against the high ceilings as if there were nothing soft left in the apartment to absorb the sound, as if all that was left amounted to stone. Evgeniya Iosifovna's face also seemed to have turned to stone, and so did Nadia's. They sat in the kitchen in front of cups with tea that had turned cold, staring at the pattern of the oilcloth on the table, sunflowers smudged from wear. I think I was the only one who came to visit Nadia and her mother after Naum Semenovich's arrest. Her house might as well have been stricken by the plague, and their friends and neighbors, those who were not informers, were afraid to catch the deadly infection.

It was April 1941, and to distract Nadia, I took her to look at the melting ice on the Neva, at the gray slabs being thinned and weakened by the zinc water whirling below. We stood on the Palace Bridge, the place where we met eighteen months earlier, staring at the funnels of whirlpools around the stone pillars of the bridge, pulling our wool hats over our ears to protect them from the icy gusts of Baltic wind.

"What would you do if something happened to me?" she asked, her voice so soft that I could barely make out the words, almost as though she didn't want me to hear them.

But I did hear her, and I knew exactly what she was asking. I wanted to tell her that nothing bad was going to happen to her, that I would kill any bastard who would so much as attempt to touch her, that I would always be there to protect her. But we both knew that if the NKVD came for her and her mother, the same way they came for Naum Semenovich, there would be nothing I could do to stop them. We both knew what I would never tell her, what could not be acknowledged if we wanted to stay sane and go on with our lives.

"Nothing bad will happen to you," I said. "I promise."

She didn't respond, still looking down into the water raging under the bridge.

I took her by the shoulders and made her look at me. "I promise. Do you hear me? I promise." Her eyes seemed dark and set deeper in her head, eyes of an older person full of sad wisdom. "I will always be here to protect you."

She nodded and looked left, where for a minute the sun blazed into the windows of the Hermitage from under the clouds torn by the wind.

"I know," she said.

Sasha closes the notebook with a sigh, wishing that Andrei, too, were always there to protect her.

25

In the spring of her last year at the drama school, there is the most important exam of all, the scene that will determine whether they will spend their lives playing important roles on the Moscow stage or huddling in mass scenes in provincial theaters. "You'd better be ready to show everything you've learned," their artistic director Vera tells them, "or you'll get a failing *dvoika* in acting, and they'll ship you straight to Pinsk to organize an acting club for janitors in their local House of Culture."

For this exam, they are allowed to choose their own scenes, and what Sasha chooses makes Vera light up a cigarette and silently gaze into the distance.

"This is not your role," she finally says and exhales a puff of smoke.

"But this is what I want to play," Sasha insists. Like everyone else, she wants to play a heroine.

"Child," says Vera, calling her what she calls all her fellow students. To her, they are all naive and silly children, and she is here to guide them through the maze of Theater, lighting their way with an acting master's torch of wisdom. "Listen to what I tell you. We know you, as an actress, better than you know yourself."

"You only know what you allow me to play!" This sounds brazen, but if Sasha doesn't say this now, she will never get another chance. She has to prove—to Vera, to her school, and to herself—that she can be more than just a heroine's funny friend, or a rude saleswoman, or a clumsy cousin from the provinces.

She breathes in and out, just as Vera taught them. "I want to play Dostoyevsky's Grushenka." The beautiful, conflicted, and infinitely flawed femme fatale Grushenka in *Brothers Karamazov*. The tall, curvaceous twenty-two-year-old, a local seductress with feline movements, who is in love with the tempestuous Dmitri. A role that wouldn't be assigned to her by anyone but her.

"It's outside your *emploi*," says Vera. She doesn't have to say this, because Sasha already knows it. She is a character actress, and Grushenka is a seductive heroine. She can't make Andrei write her even one love letter, while Grushenka has so many men buzzing around her that she has to swat them off like flies. But under the sheath of paralyzing fear that Vera may be right, there is a hot nerve of obsession that links Sasha to this woman, a character who seems to have risen from the pages of the novel and beckoned Sasha with her plump hand to embody her. She wants to feel her, to become her, to get into her skin.

She is also, as her mother often says, stubborn as a goat. "I don't care about my *emploi*," she says quietly, dizzy with her own audacity and disrespect. "I know Grushenka, and I want to play her."

For a minute, Vera considers her silently, exhaling rings of smoke. Her face is an impenetrable mask, and Sasha doesn't know what she sees.

"As you wish, then," she says finally. "But you will regret this. Maybe for the rest of your life."

～

She doesn't tell Sergey about the Grushenka battle with the acting department of her school because she suspects that he would agree with her mentors. The person she wants to tell about Grushenka is Andrei, someone who knows the viral labyrinth of small-town gossip and passion unhampered by reason, the fabric of *Brothers Karamazov* set in a small town not unlike Ivanovo. Someone who is familiar with the fiery temper and injured pride Dostoyevsky was so fond of dredging out of his characters. Someone who has infected her with the constant longing of *toska* and fits of senseless gazing into the distance that Sveta berates her for, as her mother would if Sasha were ever to open up to her about Andrei, or anything else.

But is it possible that all this brooding about provinces and Dostoyevsky is nothing more than a distraction? Is she in such desperate need of Andrei simply because he has placed himself out of her reach, having exited the stage?

For her Dostoyevsky scene, the school provides a mentor whose name makes Sasha breathless, the legend of Russian theater Elena Aleksandrovna Polevitskaya. They all know about her from classes on the history of Theater, where their professor lauded her famous interpretations of classical roles on Russian and European stages. How someone could have performed both in Russia and Europe, Sasha cannot fathom. True, Polevitskaya began her acting career in tsarist Russia, leaving the country shortly after the Revolution, but then she chose to return to her motherland, which was by then Soviet, and to spend the rest of her life acting and later teaching at the Vakhtangov Theatre. They only hear about people leaving for the West; they never hear about anyone coming back.

But there is no time to ponder such nonacting questions. Sasha can't believe she is going to work with the actress who played Dostoyevsky's Grushenka for Russian and European audiences, to critical acclaim. She can't believe her own impudence and gall, her foolish insistence on a role that the renowned actress will immediately know isn't Sasha's. "You're chopping off the branch you're sitting on," said Vera coldly after she informed her of the rehearsal arrangements, a phrase Sasha pretended not to hear so she didn't have to fumble for a response.

Her partners are her classmates. She casts reedy Slava, whose name means *fame* and who was born in a small town on the Caspian Sea, to play Alyosha, her beloved Dmitri's younger brother; she casts Lara, her closest friend and roommate at the dorm, to be the noble Katerina, her rival in the fight for Dmitri's heart. Their mentor is in her eighties, so the rehearsals, Vera says, will take place in her apartment. When the door to Polevitskaya's apartment opens, they see a fragile woman with the depthless blue eyes of a silent-film star, her silvery hair pulled back in a bun, her skin like crumpled silk. She bows her head slightly and invites them in.

They all sit down in a tiny living room, mortified yet ready to start reading, notebooks with their lines on their laps. But Elena Aleksandrovna is in no hurry.

"Sasha," she says, "tell me about yourself."

The words baffle her. "What do you want me to tell you?" Sasha asks, wondering what her story has to do with Dostoyevsky and how this storytelling detour will prevent the looming disaster of her failure.

"Everything. From the very beginning."

She talks about growing up in Ivanovo, about leaving, about her years in Moscow. About Grandpa and her mother. She even tells her about Andrei, just a couple of things. For a moment, she considers mentioning Kolya's journal, but she doesn't. With her story ends the first rehearsal. Their notebooks never get opened.

The next rehearsal is for Lara's story. The following is for Slava's. At the fourth rehearsal, Elena Aleksandrovna talks about herself and her sixty years in the Theater. It is, surprisingly, a story of doubt, pain, and anguish rather than the story of success they read in their history book. Speaking about her constant struggle and a litany of losses, their mentor no longer seems an icon or a star. She sounds more like them, beginners, with her insecurity and apprehension and jokes betraying an ironic view of their craft.

"Do you want to know what acting really is?" she says as she describes her work in prerevolutionary Moscow. "Imagine you are bathing in a tub, with all your favorite oils and scrubs, and suddenly a tour group walks in."

They giggle at the image of a tour group barging into a bathing ritual, and Sasha notes to herself that she would like to learn, although she'd never dare ask, about the un-Soviet oils and scrubs.

By the time their mentor is finished, her face darkens. She pauses and looks around, stopping her gaze at each one of them.

"Do you understand, children, where you are heading?" she asks in a grave voice. They don't know if this is a rhetorical question, so the three of them remain silent. "Well, do you?"

Sasha thought she knew where she was heading—although lately she hasn't been sure if she would end up on a stage in Moscow or an auditorium in Pinsk—but she senses that what Polevitskaya is about to utter is not what she wants to hear.

"Theater will rob you of everything," she says. "Everything." She looks at Lara and Sasha as if their faces were open books with their life stories, where she could already read the future. "You, girls, will never have a family. It will be replaced by Theater, which will always control you, like a jealous husband. Nothing else will ever matter to you but Theater. And then, in the end, when you're old and sick, it will chew you up and spit you out. You will end up all alone, and there will be no one to so much as bring you a glass of water on your deathbed." She gets up and walks toward the window, where her small figure is outlined by the last streaks of pale spring light. What she has just said, despite her conviction, sounds so melodramatic that Sasha has a suspicion she has just recited lines from one of her many roles.

For a few minutes, they sit in silence, and then they know their fourth rehearsal is over. The three of them get up and leave, quietly closing the door behind them because any sound would seem to devalue this bleak pronouncement of their future.

Did Polevitskaya say this about Theater to test their dedication? Or did she want to warn them, before it was too late? Was this a probe of their resilience or a desperate call for a last chance at a normal life?

· The three of them run down the stairs, the sound of their boots springing off the walls like dry peas. Out in the street, life boils in the steam of early frost, and Sasha is twenty, and dying is so nebulous and far away that she expects Polevitskaya's words to evaporate from her head like little clouds of winter breath. But they don't. Instead, they lodge in her brain like splinters of doubt: about her stupid choice of role, about her acting gift, about choosing Theater as her life. A question scratches in the back of her mind like an ungrateful cat: What will she tell her mother and Grandpa when she fails? What if they were right all along? What if Grandma, the only one who ever believed in her, turns out to be wrong?

26

As Sasha reads her first line at their next meeting, Elena Aleksandrovna looks out the window, as if she hadn't heard a word she said. "What do you think Grushenka was doing before her meeting with Katerina and Alyosha?" she asks. "What was she doing from the time she got up that morning?"

Sasha didn't expect to be stopped so soon, and she certainly didn't anticipate this question, so for a few moments, she sits there in a silent stupor.

"What time did she get up?"

"Not too early, probably." Sasha has no idea what this is about. "She got up, and she ate breakfast."

"What did she eat?"

She feels at a loss, not knowing what to say.

"Well," Polevitskaya says as she rises to her feet. "For our next rehearsal, you will come alone. Read the novel again. Read it very carefully. You'll find everything you need to know."

≈

During the next month, they each visit Elena Aleksandrovna separately. Sasha doesn't know what happens with Lara and Slava, but they walk around with a tome of *Brothers Karamazov*, just as she does. When she asks them about their rehearsals, they both say that they simply talked. At her rehearsals, she does more than talk. She draws the plan of the house where Grushenka lived, complete with the view from her window, all based on the descriptions in the novel and on her memories of her grandparents' house in Ivanovo. By the end of that month, she knows not only her role from the beginning of the novel to its end, but also the complete novel itself, almost by heart. And what she can't find in the novel, she creates: every event and every character, no matter how small, now has a story that precedes their appearance on the page. She knows every person's routines and habits; she knows what they crave to eat and what hides behind the doors of their armoires. She sees their wrinkled foreheads and pursed lips; their hair, carefully arranged or disheveled and unwashed; their stooped shoulders, their straight backs, their striding or mincing steps. She knows what makes their hearts swell and their blood run cold.

The next three weeks go to researching hundred-year-old paintings and photographs from Elena Aleksandrovna's collections and the archives of several Moscow libraries. They examine every piece of furniture and silverware, every hat and hairstyle, every necklace and scarf. No detail is too small. On their teacher's order, Lara and Sasha spend evenings walking around the dorm with dinner plates balanced on their heads, their waists constricted by thick strips of rubber so that they can feel corsets from the previous century on their own skin. Every day it takes a few tries before they learn to align their necks and spines so that the plates don't tilt, threatening to crash onto the hallway floor.

~

After they untie the rubber strips and release their waists, Lara and Sasha huddle on the bed in their room with the overhead light out and only a desk lamp throwing a cone of yellow light onto the floor. On these evenings, all kinds of things get released and spill out into the dusk. She sits and rants, and Lara sits and listens. Sasha is grateful to her friend for being there, for being quiet, for letting her purge the crippling, vomit-tasting poison of doubt and guilt.

"My mother was right when she tried to force me to stay in Ivanovo," she says. She is not sure she really believes this, but she knows she needs to dress the idea in words. "I should've listened to her and gone to study at the medical institute." There she would never fail or get dismissed for professional inadequacy. And then she would become a doctor, just like Chekhov. Noble and safe, with no doubts and no guilt. Her mother saw the truth: following in her steps was the only thing Sasha was good for. "But did I listen to her? And now I'm going to fail abysmally, to fall on my face in front of the whole Moscow drama school, in front of the entire city." This is what she deserves, failure and torment. She shouldn't be studying acting in the capital; she doesn't deserve to stand on a Moscow stage. She doesn't deserve to approach any classic, let alone Dostoyevsky. "What possessed me to choose a scene from *Brothers Karamazov*? Didn't Vera warn me more than once? Didn't everyone warn me? Was I overpowered by the demons of temporary insanity, and now it is too late, and now the only possible ending for me is disgrace and shame?"

She works herself into sniffling and wailing, rubbing the tears around her cheeks. "Everything I've ever dreamed of, everything I've worked for is hinging on this scene," she whimpers. "And it's the wrong scene. And I am in the wrong role."

Lara has already presented her archetype-appropriate scene and received an A, so Sasha is not sure her friend can understand her turmoil. She is now a professional actor, just as is Slava, and they are both going to star on the Moscow stage because they both have talent. They deserve to be here. What she deserves is nothing. She is nothing. Why did she think she had a gift? Why did she think she had enough strength for *this*?

27

Ten days before the acting exam, the three of them first recite the lines of their scene. They do their best; they try to be persuasive and organic. They try to please their teacher who has invested months of time in their nineteenth-century immersion.

Polevitskaya is quiet throughout the scene. She is quiet after the scene ends. "Well," she finally says and rises from her chair, ending the rehearsal.

On Sasha's way back, she tries to decipher her *well*. The optimistic possibility that her mentor feels she could make something out of the scene swims to the surface of Sasha's mind, sparkles like a small fish, and promptly goes under. She is hardly an optimist. She has to presume that her mentor's *well* is the verdict of Sasha's total hopelessness.

The next morning, Sasha wakes up determined to go into the rehearsals full throttle, ready to accept her legendary mentor's criticisms and follow her direction. She knows this is her only chance to survive the ordeal.

But the day begins with a bombshell. Vera calls the three of them into a classroom to announce that Polevitskaya has fallen ill and will no longer be able to work with them. Sasha stands there dumbfounded, unable to digest what Vera has just said. Could their reading have been so disastrous that it made her mentor's soul revolt against it? Could it have made her so sick that she cannot now get out of bed? She feels the walls of the room close in and collapse silently around her, but she sees Vera's mouth moving. "If you are unable to finish the scene on your own," she says, turning to Sasha, "we will still credit you for having tried. A credit, not a grade. It doesn't guarantee your chances after graduation." She pauses. "It's up to you to decide what to do."

Sasha is in such shock that she simply stands there, paralyzed, after the door shuts. Polevitskaya's illness is undoubtedly a sign of fate, a clear harbinger of her looming failure. She feels she has already fallen into an abyss, and from the bottom of the canyon, she hears Lara's faint voice.

"So . . . ?" Lara squeezes out after a gap of leaden silence.

"We can't! We simply can't!" Sasha shrieks, her voice on the verge of breaking. "I'll mess up and they'll kick me out and they will be right."

"Calm down," Slava orders in a new voice edged with steel, a man from the Caspian Sea taking charge of the Dostoyevsky territory. "We are going to stage this scene ourselves. It's a piece of cake."

"It may be a piece of cake to you!" Sasha yells, raising her voice to stage heights. "You only sit in the corner while the two of us do all the heavy lifting."

"Then I will direct the scene," Slava says in his new commander voice. "I've been watching the two of you for almost six months, and I know you can pull it off. The committee knows our mentor became ill and couldn't work with us. So what do we have to lose?"

Sasha thinks that they have everything to lose. She has everything to lose. She will lose the respect of her acting teachers, of everyone in her school, and maybe even of the entire Moscow acting community. For the rest of her life, she will be known as a failure, as a talentless impostor, as professionally inept. She can almost hear hushed voices snickering behind her back, her acting career now undoubtedly somewhere in the depth of Siberia. The pathetic handout of a credit Vera has offered will get her nowhere but into mass scenes of theaters in the provinces from which she will never again emerge. And back in Ivanovo, her mother will shake her head, unsurprised, and her grandfather will glare with expected satisfaction.

Yet if she doesn't finish this scene, her failure will be irrevocable and instant. If she doesn't prove that she belongs in the world of Theater, she might as well pack up and take the first train to Ivanovo, where for the rest of her life she will be like everyone else, building their bright socialist future, one red brick at a time.

These ifs are hanging in the air, and she is in their midst, grateful that Slava has taken charge. He is their director now, and he tells them that they are going to reserve time for three rehearsals in the student theater.

"Today we'll block the scene, and then we'll run through it twice," he decrees. Sasha is glad someone has made a decision, and she forces herself to concentrate on what Slava is saying. "Remember your objective," he tells her. "You want to humiliate your rival. You promised Lara's Katerina, who wants to marry Dmitri, to give him up, and she believed you. She invited you to her house to thank you. But you love Dmitri and have no intention of giving him up. You play with Lara, the way a cat plays with a mouse before devouring it. You let Lara praise you; you let her kiss your hand in gratitude and adoration, and then you strike. You tell her you'll never give up Dmitri. What you want is to keep your lover and to humiliate your rival. This is your objective in the scene. Remember this and everything will work."

The next three days slouch by like the heavy fog of this cold, late spring. Lara bounces around their dorm room, tense as a drum. Slava has become quiet and pensive, just like Dostoyevsky's Alyosha, watching them from the corner of the stage as they go through the scene. Sasha wallows in a strange cloud of calm, as if nothing matters anymore.

On the night before the exam, Lara and Sasha use their student IDs to see a performance at the Vakhtangov Theatre. Ironically, it is *Crime and Punishment* by Dostoyevsky. Sasha is certain this is another sign that she should stay away from material she is not ready to handle, but she knows it is much too late to change anything. For three hours, they stand in one of the loges (as always, there are no empty seats) and then walk back to the dorm under a cold drizzle without uttering a word. More than ever, she is resigned to never playing Dostoyevsky, or any other classic, on a Moscow stage.

The next morning, she takes Grandma's ring with the green actor's stone out of the small box where she keeps her most important things and puts it on her finger, the way she did for the three admission rounds of auditions. What is she hoping for? That a miracle will happen and it will protect her now as it did three years ago? That it will conjure up Grushenka, in all her flesh and blood, and plunge her down into Sasha's heart?

On the way to the exam, she thinks of the scene, and images begin to roll before her eyes. She sees the dusty streets of Ivanovo where she grew up, bird-cherry and lilac bushes with the white and purple froth of flowers, a window with lace curtains looking out into a small garden, a horse harnessed to a carriage by the gate into a courtyard. She is Grushenka, restless and willful; her movements are tender and her steps are soft; she blooms with the kind of beauty that will lose harmony by the time she is thirty: the beauty of the moment, a flighty beauty. She walks noiselessly, like a cat, and she speaks slowly, stretching the vowels to bring significance to every word. Her right hand is small and plump, the hand that Katerina, with all her nobility and wealth, will hold and kiss three times with strange ecstatic adoration, an act of reverence and revenge Sasha is about to stage for the kindhearted Alyosha, the brother of her beloved Dmitri. The passionate and proud Dmitri, who she knows will choose her over the noble, beautiful, and rich Katerina. The Dmitri she has always loved, her soul mate Dmitri, who now in her mind has Andrei's face. She loves him maddeningly, madly—him alone and only him, Dmitri-Andrei, engraved on her heart for as long as she lives.

She doesn't remember the exam itself. She remembers only the silence in the room after the curtain falls. She remembers only the complete emptiness inside her.

There are two scenes left on the schedule, other students' scenes, but Lara and Sasha are finished, spent. Silently, they creep downstairs and sit on the porch steps at the entrance to their school. Tears roll down Lara's face as they sit there quietly, with no need to say a word. A trolleybus rolls by, its wires like the antennae of a gigantic insect. A knot of girls in uniforms and red pioneer scarves bustles past on their way from school. Sasha registers it all automatically, as if watching everything from behind glass because nothing matters anymore. A strange calm binds her like a bandage. She fears that she has failed on an unprecedented and profound level, that this school has never seen such a colossal flop, that her entire future has just tumbled into the abyss of professional unfitness.

When they are called, they slink inside to hear and accept the verdict. Sasha knows she is the only one to blame for this abominable journey, from the cursed moment when the name Grushenka floated into her brain warped by egoism and grandeur, to this disgraceful finale open to the eyes and ears of everyone she knows. The curtain is down, the committee is in the first row, and they quietly slide into the two seats next to the door. From here, it will be easier to escape the shame.

"*Brothers Karamazov*," Vera announces. The title, with Sasha's name attached to it, scrapes her ears, emphasizing the incongruity between the two, exposing her impudence to the entire school. Vera pauses and looks up. Sasha's heart stops.

"The opinion of this committee is that in your scene, you have persuaded the audience by masterfully portraying the atmosphere of Dostoyevsky. Aleksandra Maltseva will receive the highest grade and credit with distinction. The scene is judged outstanding and will serve as proof of high professionalism in her acting diploma."

This is when Sasha feels that something has cinched her throat, and she knows she is crying. She heaves with sobs as if a dam has broken, releasing all that has been stored inside since she first read the Grushenka scene. A few friends jump up from their seats, but Vera stops them. "Let her cry," she says, waving her hand. "She needs to let it out."

Sasha is grateful to Vera for allowing her to cry in public. She sits there rubbing the tears around her face and weeps as spasms keep rising from her chest. The more she cries, the more she needs to, as if these tears are cleansing some grime inside her, as if they could deliver some kind of understanding of what has just happened. Or maybe she simply feels sorry for herself because she has just given away the most valuable part of her, something visceral and deep without which her life will no longer be the same. For six months she has kept it all inside, these fragile, intertwined images of Grushenka's and her own life, and now they are gone, released into the wings of the theater, into the hearts of the audience. And now she is completely empty. Empty of everything she has learned, everything she has stored inside her, everything she has created. Yet she knows that this emptiness is fertile; it is the blank canvas to draw her future roles, the soil from which her characters will grow. One thing is obvious: something significant has just come to an end, and she is standing at a threshold. From this moment on, she will have to start everything anew.

She cries because her former life is over. She cries because what lies before her is daunting and unknown. Or maybe she cries because her drama school ordeal has ended, and she has prevailed. She, not Grandpa and her mother, who have been waiting for her to crawl back, humiliated by her lack of an acting gift. She cries to sear into memory the moment she heard *Three Sisters* on the radio, the moment she realized that Theater would be her destiny. She now knows she was right. She and Grandma, and no one else.

161

ACT 3

Leningrad

28

Leningrad is more dignified than Moscow, its low skyline letting the winds from the Baltic Sea bloat the Neva in the fall when the water rises and floods the streets, closing schools but never canceling performances at her theater. The Bolshoi Drama Theatre is in the center of the city, on the Fontanka embankment, an imposing building with white columns along the facade. It is this theater that Sasha, Lara, and Slava have been invited to join upon graduation.

She could have stayed at her school's Vakhtangov Theatre, along with Sveta, but after years of studies, Moscow felt too familiar, too provincial, too much like Ivanovo. She knew exactly what roles she would be playing, all Russian classics; she knew her future acting partners, all her former classmates. She also knew she would be expected to come to Sergey's apartment every time his wife went on tour; she even knew what pastries he would carefully arrange for her on a dish with the lily-of-the-valley border.

Leningrad, on the other hand, is an enigma, and the Bolshoi Drama Theatre, a legend. She has always wanted to live in Russia's only European city where art graces every street with the curved facades sculpted by architects from Italy and France who reinvented their designs for this northern climate, where the air is grainy with the afternoon twilight in winter and the milky nightglow in June. Besides, she has wanted to live in the place where Kolya studied art; she has wanted to stand on the bridge where he met Nadia. She has wanted to see with her eyes what she has only pictured in her mind: the building on Herzen Street where Nadia lived with her parents, Leningrad University on the Neva embankment where she studied philology and, not far from it, the Academy of Arts where Kolya learned to draw and paint.

She now has her own place to live. After the first six months of work, when she lived in the dormitory, her theater gave her a one-room apartment, perhaps to offset the dismal salary of all stage actors in repertory theaters dictated by the state.

A week after Sasha moved to her new apartment, Aunt Luba, who guards the stage-door entrance, yells for her to come to the phone. When Sasha mutters a tentative "hallo" into the receiver—no one has ever called her there—it takes a few moments to recognize Sergey's voice. He is in Leningrad, for a meeting with a screenwriter, he says, but the introductory pleasantries sweep past her ear.

The following evening, she is free, and they meet at the lobby of the hotel where he is staying. When he sees her, he gets up and beams and stretches out his arms, so she has no choice but to hug him, even though she doesn't want to. He holds her in his embrace for a long time, too long it seems, before she can free herself and sit down in an armchair across from him. In the time they haven't seen each other, he seems to have aged: his glasses magnify the bags under his eyes, and his hair is longer and more tangled than she remembers, with little sprigs of salt and pepper, all white around the temples.

After a few compulsory questions about her work in Leningrad, he grows silent for a minute, as though contemplating something important. When they said their goodbyes in Moscow, a month or so after her graduation, she thought it was a farewell. Their meetings in his apartment lasted as long as they did, and Sasha never planned to see him again, so sitting across from him in Leningrad now seems odd and out of place. His being two bus stops away from where she is working seems inappropriate, or maybe it is she who is inappropriate sitting in this hotel lobby, so close to a man for whom she is no longer able to muster even a semblance of affection, not one little tingle in her veins.

Sergey takes off his glasses and starts deliberately wiping them with a handkerchief, as if a great deal of what he is about to say depends on his clarity of vision. Without his glasses, his face appears even older and somehow more vulnerable; he looks like he is planning to reveal something she doesn't know about him, something fragile that will make her want to protect him.

"I've realized something," he begins in a small voice, as though afraid to warp the words with sound. "I hope you understand. It's quite simple, really, so I hope . . ." His voice trails off, and he pauses to take a breath to start again.

"In these six months—and I counted each day—I've realized how much I miss you. I've realized that seeing you, being with you, was my happiest time."

A nauseating sensation stirs in the pit of her stomach. The words Sergey is saying, is about to say, are beautiful and delicate, but to her, they only sound objectionable and distressing. They are the words that should be directed at someone else, someone who would appreciate their generosity, someone who would love this upcoming revelation and, by extension, love him. They are words completely wasted on her thick, impermeable skin.

Sergey must sense her tense posture implying rejection, but she guesses he wants to be certain, so he continues, racing to the crux of this encounter and the objective of his speech. "I've separated from my wife," he says and swallows so hard, she can see his Adam's apple move. "So now you and I can be together."

Sasha can no longer look at him, his exposed face, his naked eyes. She lowers her gaze and peers at the red carpet under their feet, her head shaking slightly, delivering her answer.

He leans back, his body suddenly slackening and turning pliant, like a rag doll's.

"I'm sorry," she whispers and gets up. What else can she say? "I'm so sorry."

His hand with a handkerchief rises to his face, and for the first time in the two years she's known him, she sees tears glisten in his eyes.

Her first role in real Theater is as a cleaning woman who has two silent entrances in the first and second acts. She walks around the set, swiping a rag at typewriters and blowing dust off the office desks. It is a Soviet comedy, and her speechless performance makes the audience laugh. Since Soviet comedies make up a big chunk of their repertory, Sasha has to think that this is the genre the audiences prefer, the genre that doesn't seem to demand much acting. She suddenly feels nostalgic for the classics her drama school required. She feels that her friends Lara and Slava, who make up her *kompaniya*, are more interesting and complex than the characters they play onstage.

Their small *kompaniya*—three like-minded friends with shared interests—is the microcosm of Theater, a tiny extension of the dictum they were taught in drama school that Theater was the microcosm of the world. The three of them don't usually go home after rehearsals like everyone else. They sit in the backstage café and talk about the plays in their repertory and the roles they would like to play.

"Masha in *The Seagull*," Lara says, not hesitating even for a second. "I've always wanted to be in mourning for my life." What she has told Sasha about the secret pain of damage and debasement, about her older brother back home and then their assistant dean, may indeed require mourning. When she looks at Lara, her own anxieties and guilt tend to shrink, and that's when she feels lighthearted and unencumbered, upbeat enough to want to play Irina from *Three Sisters*, at least Irina in acts 1 and 2, when there is still a featherlight measure of hope.

The three of them come to the theater hours before their scheduled plays, the time when they own all this empty space. The backstage is almost as vast as the eight-hundred-seat theater itself: several dozen dressing rooms, along the maze of wide hallways winding around a resting area for actors, with couches and a scattering of armchairs, like a living room in an enormous apartment, if Russian apartments had living rooms. On the second and third floors, Ira and Tamara, the theater seamstresses, preside over a workshop filled with racks of costumes and bales of fabric; Uncle Tolya and Uncle Moishe hammer nails into newly cobbled shoes; and their makeup artist, Lida, upholstered in a blue lab coat and layers of cheerful plumpness, takes care of trays of greasepaint, arrays of brushes, and at least a hundred wigs. On the top floor, in a suite of four high-ceilinged rooms wallpapered with the posters of its century-long history, are copies of plays that have been performed here over the years, along with other exhibits of their theater's museum. The Bolshoi Theatre is like a medieval fortress, and if they decided to reside here and never return home, every requirement of their life, from food to clothes to books, would be easily sustained within these walls.

They gossip about the latest liaisons and scandals and try to figure out the identity of the current KGB informer, because there is always an informer in the theater, listening in on their conversations, pretending to be one of them. "There is an informer in every workplace in our vast motherland," Sveta warned them back in drama school, "but Theater is always in the avant-garde of Soviet spying," she insisted, "because plays have the power to influence so many people all at once. 'Theater is a very dangerous weapon,'" she quoted the legendary director Meyerhold. Sasha wasn't sure she believed Sveta back then, but in the few months working here, she has learned this much: trust is an exotic fruit that doesn't grow in this semiarctic zone of freezing winters and rainy, mosquito-infested summers. Aside from their small *kompaniya* of three friends, they can trust no one in their Bolshoi Theatre.

"Do you remember the exercise we did in drama school called Contact?" says Slava when Sasha asks about the informers in their theater. She remembers. You had to stand back-to-back with a partner and feel his pressure as you both squatted simultaneously and then slowly lifted yourself up again. It only worked if both did the equal amount of work, if you could give your partner a feeling of support and trust and, as a result, receive the same trust in return. It worked back then, when *The Magnificent Seven* from America was playing in Moscow theaters, when life was all in the future tense, when she could be—despite what her acting teachers thought—a Dostoyevsky heroine.

She trusts Lara and Slava unequivocally. The person she doesn't trust is herself. She is still not sure she has acting talent. She is not sure if her final Dostoyevsky scene wasn't simply a fluke, a lucky outcome of being coached by a master teacher.

She knows one thing: she longs to be other people, not to be herself. A role—any role, even that of a Soviet janitor—is a mask, a costume she is compelled to wear, a disguise that turns her into someone else.

29

After Sasha's first year in Bolshoi Theatre, her mother is offered a job teaching anatomy at Leningrad Medical School, packs up the forty-nine years of her Ivanovo life, and takes a train a thousand kilometers northwest to live with her daughter. Sasha has become accustomed to living alone, and the prospect of living with her mother, again, stirs up anxiety and conflict. Is she still going to try to control Sasha's life, the way she did in Ivanovo? Will she be capable of understanding that Sasha is now an adult? That she will be living in Sasha's apartment, no longer in the provinces?

It is the end of July, and the rains have already washed the summer dust off the city streets when Sasha meets her at the Central railway station. They heave her two suitcases past the bust of Lenin presiding over the waiting hall and take bus 22 to her new apartment on the sixth floor of the corner building everyone calls by its prerevolutionary name of the Fairy Tale House. In a book on Leningrad history, her new place of residence is decorated with exquisite tiles picturing scenes from Russian fairy tales. There is no trace of those tiles left. The building was badly damaged during the siege of Leningrad in 1941, and the massive postwar restoration could not afford to focus on the aesthetic. Her mother and Sasha haul the suitcases through the front door only to discover that the elevator is out of order, and it takes them twenty minutes of tugging and resting between floors to hoist them up the six endless flights of stairs. When they reach the top, her mother, red-faced and breathless, dubs Sasha's building the Reality House, and from that day on, the name will stick with both of them.

When Sasha switches on the lights in her new apartment, she watches her mother's face as she looks around the hallway and into the open doors to the bedroom and the kitchen. Wrinkles gather around her eyes, and her mouth softens: she is clearly impressed.

"Good for you, Sashenka," she says, stroking the rounded door of the refrigerator in the corner of the hallway. "Your theater must like you."

Although Sasha can't deny a rush of pleasure at hearing the words she has hoped for since drama school, she is not quite sure what they mean. Has her mother finally accepted Sasha's choice? This is the first time she has attached words of praise to *theater*, but what exactly is she praising? Sasha's acting career or the apartment that came with it?

Sasha lifts her suitcases onto the divan and helps her mother unpack. She has brought her good dress, white with a red apple print; her photo album with pictures of Sasha in a white apron on the first day of school, of Grandma and Grandpa staring into the photographer's camera on their fiftieth wedding anniversary, and of her pressing stethoscopes to the bare chests of eight-year-olds at her first job in the summer camp called the Dawn of Socialism.

She has also brought Kolya's original journal.

March 14, 1942

I don't know why I am writing all this, and for whom. I suppose I am still clutching at the hope that this war will end before I get killed, that these pages will somehow find their way to my mother and sister even though no censor will let them pass through. But if I don't write and if I don't draw, I will become like my sergeant. I would invalidate every painting on the walls of the Hermitage. I would betray the milky air of Leningrad's streets, and the softness of Nadia's arms, and her foolish trust in my promise to save her.

A hunk of sealing wax with a round stamp across their front lock, a stamp that branded Nadia's apartment the property of the state.

I stood in front of that sealed door, in a state of shock so complete that I could see myself from the outside: my frozen limbs, my jaw hanging open in a stupor, my eyes squinting to make out the letters stamped on the wax. I stood there, helpless and defeated. Then I began banging on the door with my fists and then with my feet, as if those who took away Nadia and her mother might still be inside, waiting for an accomplice to whatever crime they have concocted.

Just then, the door to a neighboring apartment opened a crack, held by a chain from the inside, and a young woman in an apron glared out. I had seen her before: we collided at the front door to the building a few times in the past when she clicked her way down the stairs on high heels in red lipstick and teased hair. "What's all this racket?" she demanded. Her hair was peroxide blonde, and there was something waspish in her demeanor that warned me not to ask any questions. "No one lives there anymore; can't you see that?" she said and gave me a long, scathing look to make sure that the message had sunk in. It had. "And if I were you, I wouldn't hang around this place too long," she added and banged the door shut.

I stared at the wax seal on Nadia's apartment again. The landing smelled of old cigarette butts and yesterday's soup. That was the moment when I realized, with horror, that I didn't know any of Nadia's family or friends. Her mother had a sister, Nadia's aunt, living somewhere in Sverdlovsk; Naum Semenovich had no siblings. If Nadia had any grandparents left alive, she never talked about them. She and I were so wrapped up in our own world, we were reluctant to open its doors to anyone from the outside. We didn't need anyone else, she used to say; all we needed was each other.

At the university, the secretary at the philology department where Nadia was studying leafed through the students' files, and I watched as her fingers with short, bitten-off nails reluctantly walked through sheets of paper in the drawer. She finally stopped at one folder, stared at it for a while, then lifted her eyes to look at me. I held her gaze, suspicion mixed with disdain.

"She left school," said the secretary curtly and looked down at the file to avoid my gaze.

I knew what this meant but wanted to press this bureaucrat further, to make her uncomfortable, as if she were complicit in Nadia's disappearance. "When did she leave the school?" I asked. "And why?"

It was as useful as Evgeniya Iosifovna asking the men arresting her husband about the reason for his arrest.

"Recently," said the woman, letting me know with her frown that the second half of my question was out-of-bounds. She pushed the filing drawer shut and straightened her spine, signaling that our conversation had come to an end.

I don't remember going down the stairs and walking out of the university, but I must have walked over the Palace Bridge because soon I was on Nevsky Prospekt. The day was mercilessly long—in a couple of weeks, the sun would barely bother to touch the horizon before springing back up. Fog hung over the oily surface of the Griboyedov Canal, mixing with the low gray clouds, obliterating the sky.

I walked because I had to walk, cursing the secretary of the philology department, cursing the two men who had arrested Nadia's father. I cursed the neighbor and the vigilant friend who ratted on Naum Semenovich for something he didn't say. I cursed everyone who denounced Nadia and her mother because they were Jews or because—as a reward for being vigilant—they hoped to get their apartment that was so brazenly better than their own communal hovels.

If I believed in God, like Raphael or Michelangelo, I would have cursed God. In the absence of God, I cursed my motherland. It was supposed to nurture and protect us, the people it had inspired to its revolutionary ideals of a meager life and hard work, and while we had been busy keeping our end of the bargain, our motherland, like a courtyard thug, had turned around, pulled out a switchblade, and stuck it under our ribs.

I walked past the peeling facades of French classicism and Italian baroque draped with the red banners of our bright future. I thought of those in the stratosphere of the Kremlin, dressed in generals' uniforms and party suits, puffing on pipes at their desks, debating the fate of our lives between sips of cognac, issuing search warrants, signing decrees of death. Sitting like judges at their engineered trials, pounding gavels with their meaty hands: death, death, death. What made their hearts beat, what pushed through their veins instead of blood was the sludge of paranoia and betrayal. Who is not with us is against us, *their eyes instruct us from the portraits hanging in every office.* We do not arrest good people, *they say.* We're simply protecting our motherland from its enemies with the help of other good people, all those neighbors with properly attuned ears, insufficient living space, and healthy socialist envy.

I thought of the night when they came for Nadia. How terrified she must have been, how desperate and lost. I saw the two men stalking around their apartment, picking out things they liked, packing them into their bags. "You won't be needing this anymore," *one may have said, lifting a bronze writing set off her father's desk.* "And this," *said the other thug, taking off the wall* an old pendulum clock that belonged to Nadia's grandmother. They had probably cut the pillows open, as they always do, so feathers must have been flying everywhere in a surreal blizzard in early May.

And where was Nadia now? In a stone coffin of a solitary confinement cell? On the third tier of plank beds among fifty other suspected traitors and spies? Being interrogated by a sadist in an NKVD uniform, who is shouting that she is automatically guilty because she didn't inform on her father?

I had to blot those thoughts out of my mind, for they spawned monstrous images of humiliation and medieval torture, of fingers broken in doorjambs, of nipples stabbed with sharpened pencils, of hot irons sizzling the skin. Had I allowed my mind to wander along this path, I know I would have gone mad. So I kept trudging along the streets and circling whole blocks in a pointless search for answers. My thoughts were racing; I couldn't focus; my mind was a toxic tangle of awful possibilities.

I thought of Volya, my uncle arrested in 1937 for telling a joke. I thought of the poet Osip Mandelstam, who died in the camps for doing his job, writing poetry. I thought of my art professor, the one who showed us Picasso's work that seemed to challenge the laws of socialist realism yet was so charged with life, who one day simply failed to show up to teach our seminar. "Do not try to investigate his disappearance," cautioned the dean, a dire warning to my class of twelve that we obediently followed.

I thought of my mother: of her round glasses, her hair pulled back in a bun, her soft cotton dress. She wasn't at all as steely and tough as our motherland; she was, in fact, the opposite—forgiving and kind. She was someone I would die for, without hesitation. She and Nadia.

I turned and walked along the canal embankment, cutting through the fog that began to feel like drizzle. On the other side *of the street, the door leading to a store was open. I crossed and walked inside.*

On the shelf to my right, a few candlesticks made of jade and brass stood next to a lamp with a flowery cloth shade. In a cabinet of dark wood with glass shelves, a tea service with round cups and a teapot boasted its cobalt net of classic imperial design. A pile of spoons glimmered beside the saucers. Bigger pieces occupied the space in the back of the store: a set of four chairs with curved legs stacked up before a round dining table, a couple of mismatched stools, two nightstands with the surface of polished wood. The secondhand shop, selling the contents of people's former lives.

Behind the first room was another, to the left, and I made my way there without thinking, as if someone had grabbed me by the elbow and pulled me forward. I stepped inside and froze in place. Against the wall, between two lamps with hideous curlicues, stood a divan I remembered so well. I hoped that the vision would disappear, but there it was still, an object whose pattern of wear was forever imprinted in my brain, whose scratches and bumps I knew with every fiber of my body—our divan, Nadia's and mine.

I stood in front of it, emptied of feeling, numb. Before me was Nadia's past, for sale, her family's past turned to merchandise in a secondhand shop. It only confirmed the worst scenarios hurtling through my mind, the dark scenes I'd been trying to banish so I wouldn't go mad. It only validated the toxic fear that there were no more Goldbergs. It only pressed into my brain the monstrous, vomit-tasting probability that there was no more Nadia.

30

"So after that," Sasha asks, pointing to Kolya's scorched notebook, "what do we do?"

"After that, soup with cat," her mother says, a saying she invokes when the future presents itself as nebulous and murky, as opposed to the unclouded version offered by the *Pravda*, or when she doesn't even want to think about the future. She has just lumbered in with a load of wet laundry that she begins to pin on two clotheslines that crisscross the room.

"I have to tell you something," Sasha says. "I've read all this already. I found this journal in Ivanovo, when I was eleven, stuffed into the storage loft, behind Grandma's prerevolutionary hat."

Her mother unbends from the aluminum tub with the heap of laundry and for a minute stands there silently, looking at her, waiting for an explanation.

"Our house was full of secrets." *"Full of lies,"* Sasha wants to say but doesn't. "And this journal was just one of them. A secret, I knew, you didn't want me to know." She walks over to the wall and tightens the sagging clothesline around the nail. "I hated you and Grandpa when I found it. You hid the truth Kolya saw at the front, and that was another lie added to a mountain of lies about our glorious past. It made me feel complicit, this adult secret I had to carry all those years. It almost felt like an initiation, a required rite of passage into our life of lying and pretending. The guilt that we pass down from one generation to the next."

Her mother is bent over the laundry, taking a long time to unwind the nightshirts from the towels.

"Why did you keep it *there*, with all that old, discarded junk?" Sasha asks, watching her mother's deliberately slow movements, watching her straighten a towel to fit over the rope.

"You still don't understand," her mother says and sighs. "It was the only safe place in the house. It was the only place they didn't turn upside down in 1937, when they arrested Uncle Volya."

Sasha had to know this: the storage loft was not a place of disgrace but safety. The only place to hide prerevolutionary and unpatriotic things. She is chagrined by her unnecessary question, yet there is still more she needs to know. "But how did this journal get to you in Ivanovo? All the way from the Leningrad Front?"

For a few moments, her mother pats the hanging towel, ironing the wrinkles. "A man came to our door in 1943. He may have been in the same platoon with Kolya; I don't know. The man was demobilized; he had been wounded in the head. He could barely remember his own name, but he had our address written with indelible pencil on the inside of his shirt. *Kolya Kuzmin asked me to give this to you,* he said and handed me the notebook. Of course, we immediately brought him into the house, Grandma boiled tea, pulled out every scrap of food we had. He didn't touch a thing. He didn't even sit down. He paced the room from corner to corner, shaking, his teeth clattering, as if he had a high fever. Then he would suddenly stop and look around. We asked him where he had been; we asked about Kolya. He didn't answer any questions. He only mumbled about some peasants from a tiny village he'd been ordered to shoot in the woods."

"What was his name?" Sasha asks.

"Anton, he said, after we repeated the question five times at least." It wasn't Kolya's pal Seryoga. No easy coincidences here, no missing pieces conveniently fitting into an unfinished puzzle. "His shoes were all torn, and his feet were bloody. I tried to clean and bandage them, but he pushed me away. He gave us his address, somewhere on the other end of the town, but when I went there a month later, there wasn't a trace of him. A family, evacuated from Kalinin, had just moved in, a woman with two children and a sharp-elbowed mother-in-law. They hadn't heard of a wounded man who returned from the war. They had their own two men still fighting, the woman's husband and brother, and they didn't want to hear anything about someone who had just been demobilized and sent home." Her mother pauses. "After that, we sent Kolya several letters addressed to the Leningrad Front. I don't know if they ever reached him. We wrote that his brother Sima had died. We wrote that you were born. But we never received anything from him again."

Her mother picks up a duvet cover twisted like a rope and begins to unwind it.

"So what do we do now?" Sasha asks. "After we both know what Kolya went through at the front, after what they did to Nadia's family, after all those arrests and murders? How many? Thousands? Millions? And for what?"

"Don't be so dramatic," says her mother. "This isn't the theater." She shakes out the duvet and adjusts it over the rope. "Mistakes were made; we all know that. There was an abuse of power, a cult of personality. But look what we've built: a country that the whole world respects." She hangs the pillowcase over the rope and clips it with a wooden clothespin. "And they admitted their mistakes," she says. "Don't you remember Khrushchev's speech in 1956? They admitted they were wrong, and they released political prisoners. That was a start."

Sasha smirks, but she feels the anger tightening her chest. "This is laughable. Uncle Volya, Marik's father, Nadia and her parents. I'm twenty-one, and I know of five people who were murdered by the state.

And Uncle Seryozha. He survived, but he might as well have died. It was all in his face, the camps. He had the face of a corpse."

"You have to have patience," her mother says, her usual refrain. "This is what Russia has survived on, century after century—patience and perseverance. We work, we wait, and we hope. And we believe. We have to believe in something. Before the Revolution, there was God. Now it's our better future."

She has heard all this before—from everyone in Ivanovo, even from Grandma—a pitiful excuse that absolves nothing.

"I work hard, but I don't know what I'm waiting for." Sasha wants to show her mother that she is wrong, to let her know that she now lives in Leningrad, where such views are as provincial as chickens in a courtyard or piles of firewood stacked under the roof of a shed. "I swear, it's no different from the pretending I learned from Aunt Polya at the lunch counter in first grade." Aunt Polya is still as clear in her memory as she was fifteen years ago, pouring milk and dispensing soup, ordering them to chew and swallow and not waste a single crumb. Sasha remembers how she watched them to make sure they finished the bread and the milk and the soup. "I knew she was watching me, and she knew that I knew, and I knew that she knew that I knew. We played this little game every day: she would give me an unexpected glance, and I would chew diligently, pretending I didn't know she was looking."

Sasha shakes out a few pillowcases, which make a loud slurping noise. "I never know if the play we're rehearsing will be closed by the Ministry of Culture because someone high up thinks that the playwright's words are aimed directly at those in power." She pauses to help her mother spread the sheet over the rope, so there is now a wall of wet laundry between them. "Look, I know it's probably better now than it was under Stalin, but this is not enough," she says, her words addressed into a barrier of wet cotton. "How am I supposed to live in a country where everything is based on lies? Our national game isn't hockey. It is lying and pretending."

"You've said enough to get yourself ten years in the camps, back under Stalin," says her mother from the other side of the sheet, and Sasha can hear that she has a rueful smile on her face. "But these are vegetarian times, thank God," she adds. Neither of them believes in God, but they both know that the vegetarian times of Khrushchev are the times of milder, less brutal repressions than the carnivorous times of Stalin. She bends over the tub, moving slowly, as if trying to avoid what she is going to say next.

"Do you remember the head of the Ivanovo anatomy department, Moisey Davidovich Zlotnikov?" she asks.

Sasha remembers. She was a little afraid of him when her mother took her to her institute, where she sat among jars with organs floating in formaldehyde, copying a diagram of lungs with blue-and-red vessels tangled up inside a faceless man's chest. Dr. Zlotnikov always greeted her with a handshake, as if she were an adult. He had a small, graying beard, a balding forehead, and a pince-nez, too old to be anyone's father, too unsmiling, too stern.

"After the war, when you were nine or ten, I was summoned to the Ivanovo NKVD headquarters," her mother says from the other side of the sheet. "He was my PhD adviser, and they demanded that I inform on him." Sasha hears a sharp intake of breath. "Every month, I would come to this secret apartment and write the most mundane, innocuous things I could think of: a conversation about the percentage of enlarged thyroids at the Ivanovo textile factory, a shortage of scalpels at a dissection class, a lab assistant's alcoholic son." She pauses, and Sasha waits. "Those were still Stalin times, carnivorous times. I couldn't refuse. Once a month, I came to that apartment, as though to an illicit, sordid rendezvous that had to be kept secret from the honest world. A young, plain-clothed man sat there, on the other side of the room, and watched me write. He always smiled when he saw me, a wide, open smile that dimpled his cheeks. But even though what I wrote was harmless and benign, I was always afraid that something I wrote would be twisted and used against Dr. Zlotnikov. Every day at work, I waited for them to come and arrest him, and then he would only need to take one look at me and he would know who was to blame." She pins the last nightshirt on the rope and wipes her wet hands on the apron she is wearing. "This lasted for one year. Then Stalin died."

Sasha follows her mother to the kitchen, her hefty figure leading the way through the hallway, past the refrigerator and the coatrack. She has always led the way, but Sasha hasn't always followed. She has escaped from Ivanovo, and for all these years, she has wanted to think that its provincialism had not left a permanent mark on her soul, that the air of Moscow and Leningrad allowed her to draw a clear line between truth and pretense, between the heroic textbook story of the war and what Kolya lived through at the front.

In the kitchen, her mother boils water for tea and spoons out of a jar the strawberry jam from Grandpa's Ivanovo garden. Frankly, Sasha doesn't know how to react to her mother's story. She thinks she would feel better if she hadn't told her, if she didn't know that her mother was an informer. She wonders if having this knowledge makes her a coconspirator, if she is now complicit in the deed. This knowledge has raised more questions than she knows how to answer. If she were in her mother's place, would she have done the same thing? Would she have come to an NKVD apartment every month and concocted reports about her teacher, no matter how benign? And although she wants to think that she would never succumb to spying, how can she know this for certain? And if she refused—if her mother had refused—what would have happened then, to her and to Sasha?

Her mother drops two cubes of sugar into her cup and slowly circles her spoon around until they dissolve. Kolya's journal is between them at the center of the table, a stark reminder of their past, marking the gap between their ways of thinking.

"We wrote to Leningrad to find out about Kolya," her mother says. "Right after the war and then again, at least three more times. It was always the same answer: *not listed among the dead or the living.*" She takes a sip of the tea from her spoon, then pours it into the saucer because it is too hot to drink from the cup. "I even went to the island of Valaam soon after Stalin died. There was a holding pen for war invalids in the old monastery there, men without arms or legs, some without both arms and legs—they called them *samovars.* I don't know how those people got there. There was a rumor they were rounded up at night in the streets and railroad stations of the cities where many of them begged for a living. They put them in cattle cars, the rumor went, and brought them to this faraway island on Lake Ladoga so people wouldn't have to see their deformities and be reminded of the war. Anyway, that's what we heard." She lifts the saucer to her lips and takes several sips of the tea. "And then there were some who chose to go there because they didn't want to be a burden on their families after the war." She pauses. "This is what Kolya would've done, I thought, if he'd been badly wounded. So I took a train to Leningrad and boarded a boat—they had excursion boats going to Valaam once a day. It's a serene island, with a striking northern nature, stark and beautiful. I knew they didn't let tourists visit the invalid home, and even giving someone directions could cost you your job. So I'd packed my white doctor's coat and hat. The monastery wasn't difficult to find—it was the tallest structure on the island. The white coat worked: the nurses and doctors all wore white gowns, as I knew they would."

Sasha sits over her cup of tea and listens: today seems to be a day for revelations. She can't imagine Uncle Kolya maimed, with missing arms or legs or with his face burned away—disfigurements that would make him unrecognizable to her. She doesn't want to think of him ending up in such an inglorious place as this invalid repository on some remote island.

"It was a day in August, unusually warm, and everyone who could get outdoors was outside, on the grounds of the monastery. The men without legs rode on boards with little wheels, and those without arms, who could walk on their own, sat on benches. The *samovars* with no legs and no arms were hanging in baskets suspended on tree branches, brought there by the nurses." Her mother stares into her cup, as if trying to see once again what she saw on Valaam island back then. "They were hanging off the tree branches, talking to each other, arguing, laughing. With their war decorations displayed on their chests. I walked around and peered into their faces. They were young, most of them, but they all looked older than me. One man Kolya's age, with four medals and the familiar softness of the chin, called to me as I was walking by. *"Sestrichka,"* he said, "can you help me?" He called me *little sister* and asked me to carry him inside and put him on top of a bucket so he could relieve himself. I did, even though he wasn't Kolya. Even though not one of the invalids was Kolya."

31

"They trained us on classics and then graduated us into the world of socialist realism and gray Soviet plays," she says to Lara.

At the drama school, they played characters from Tolstoy and Chekhov, from Brecht and Pirandello. Slava and Sveta even did a scene from *The Catcher in the Rye* by an author from America, where *Pravda* tells them capitalism is in a state of deep, permanent rot.

Lara nods but says nothing. Maybe she thinks that the drama school's lack of warning to its graduates about the paucity of their future repertory is not as serious a crime as allowing its assistant dean to routinely rape its students. Maybe she is waiting for their artistic director to decide to stage *The Seagull* so that she can finally declare onstage that she is in mourning for her own life.

A week after their talk, almost as though the director heard Sasha's rant, he announces the next play to add to their repertory, *Twelfth Night* by William Shakespeare. A classic at last. He casts Lara as Viola, a young shipwrecked woman who disguises herself as a man, and Sasha as the servant Maria, sharp-witted and daring, the engine that fuels all the tricks concocted by her own small *kompaniya* of friends.

Although Sasha feels happy, she is also anxious. What's going to happen if she fails, if this classic finally reveals her professional inadequacy? She reads *Twelfth Night* the way her mentor taught her to read *Brothers Karamazov*, assiduously and with the utmost attention. She goes to all the rehearsals, even those where they work on scenes that aren't hers, and writes down the director's every word.

Before rehearsals, in their dressing room, Lara is her savior, insisting that they begin with an exercise from drama school: Sasha becomes a rusty engine in need of lubrication, and Lara presses her palm to her friend's and makes believe that she pours oil into her creaky system. Sasha feels the revitalizing oil run through her veins, making the joints rotate smoothly, pumping energy through to her limbs. Maria's every word filters through the nerve fibers of Sasha's body, and when the rehearsal is over, she feels emptied of emotion. For a few hours afterward, she feels so hollow inside that she can't think of anything, even Andrei.

~

She doesn't see Andrei until the entire cast comes out for a curtain call. They were all at their best that evening—Vladimir Ivanovich, who plays her earthy partner Sir Toby Belch; Lara, the willful Viola in men's clothes; Viola's twin brother, Sebastian, played by Maksim, just out of drama school; and the rich and ravishing Olivia, played by the director's wife. For two and a half hours, she was Maria, and they lived inside a mesh of golden light charged with the energy they have created, which has left them all breathless. As she smiles and curtsies in front of the curtain, adrenaline still pumping through her veins, something forces her to look down into the third row of the audience, as if the stage lights have instantly reversed direction and plucked Andrei's face out of the crowd.

When she fits the key into her apartment door, glad that her mother is on a visit to Ivanovo, they don't even bother to turn on the hallway light or hang their coats on the coatrack in front of the refrigerator. The coats drop onto the floor, followed by her sweater and his jacket, layer after layer of clothing, a trail of selfishness and frivolity leading to a finale to which no Party Committee would ever give its stamp of approval.

During her last two years in Moscow and her first year in Leningrad, she has yearned for Andrei every single minute she was not onstage, despite her promise after their night in Suzdal that she would not allow him to enter her life again. But the moment his face shone out of the crowd, the smoldering pain exploded into a fire, reminding her how much she still longs for him, tossing all her promises out the window. In the darkness, with their fingers on the buttons of each other's coats, desire bumps against resentment, challenging it to a brief duel where desire promptly fires a fatal shot straight into resentment's heart. It is fast and simple, and it is the only thing that matters. They are together again, fused by a force that seems bigger than anything they could control, a force that flows from Andrei's eyes and enters her directly, without words, which penetrates her every nerve fiber, as if he'd never left her on the threshold of that Komsomol hotel room, as if he'd never promised to write and then failed to do so, as if she were still in the provinces, still innocent of life.

Afterward, Andrei sits across from her in her Leningrad kitchen, in her mother's chair, his hands folded on the yellow oilcloth worn out to patches of dirty white. It is two in the morning, and the January darkness outside is like tar, the light in their window on this Wednesday a challenge to the decency and order of all those who, like her mother, hold serious jobs. Sasha is glad she is away, or else she would deliberately shuffle to the bathroom, her hair, mussed by sleep, slithering down her back in a skinny braid, to remind her that she shouldn't be with Andrei, or anyone else, at this hour, that it is the middle of the night when all decent people are asleep in their beds.

They are drinking the Armenian cognac Andrei has brought, five stars imprinted on the label, the best cognac that never reaches their store counters. He has also brought a stick of hard salami called *servilat* she has seen only on the tables of theater banquets. They are slathering butter on slices of white bread, gluing to it the glistening dark-red circles pocked with white to make open sandwiches, which they devour in three bites because they are both starving. If her mother were here, shuffling down the hallway, she wouldn't like what her senses would reveal: Sasha is wearing Andrei's shirt over her naked body, and they both reek of the sweet, sweaty smell of sex. They chew on *servilat* and reminisce about Ivanovo, the only chunk of life they still have in common, the life when they were innocent, the life whose scenes still roll before her eyes like an old, beloved film.

"Do you remember the orchard at the end of our street, with those lilac bushes?" she says. "When I walked home from my piano lesson, twice a week, I always bumped into you at that turn where the fence was coming down in waves. Do you remember that?"

"*Bump* isn't the exact word I'd use." He laughs. "I waited there for you, deliberately, every Monday and Wednesday, from four to five, because I was never sure when your lesson would end."

"Even in the rain?" she asks with a foolish smile she is unable to suppress. She knows the answer, of course, but she wants to hear it from him.

He knows this is not a real question. This is a silly postcoital game they are playing, and he knows to oblige. "Especially in the rain."

"And then we could walk for five minutes next to each other before we turned onto the street where that scary house stood, behind a rotting fence. I always hated that we had to say goodbye there, by that black fence, before we went in different directions, so that Grandpa wouldn't spot us together."

They are smoking Andrei's cigarettes, filtered and mild, much better than the harsh Cuban tobacco she buys for herself at Leningrad kiosks.

"When your father came back, I was so envious," she says. "I wanted my father—not my real father but my imagined one, who looked like Kolya—to walk through the gate of our courtyard, just like that, and claim me. I often saw him in my mind, in a uniform cinched by a belt

189

with a shiny buckle. He opens the gate and immediately walks toward me, then picks me up and hoists me onto his shoulders. And then, in my mind, I sail across the courtyard, taking it all in: the black roof of the shed, the backs of waddling chickens with their necks marked in Grandpa's indelible pencil, the highest branches of apple trees I never got to see that aim straight into the sky. I so much wanted Kolya to return and claim me as a father would."

"I know, but you didn't want my father. He was a convict and a drunk. And anyway, by the time he showed up, I didn't need a father. And even if I did, I certainly didn't need him."

How unfair it all seemed. Of all the fathers for whom so many sons and daughters had been waiting, the only father who returned was the unwanted one.

What she really wants to convey to him is the sadness that fills her about leaving him so shortly after his parents died. She should have been there to protect him, instead of choosing to save herself. The words don't come, making her turn to a safer subject. "You used to walk around reciting Mayakovsky, remember?"

"I remember." Andrei gives a little chuckle and takes a sip of the cognac glowing in his glass like honey.

She recites the lines they all had to learn by heart:

> "Of Grandfatherly gentleness I'm devoid,
> There's not a single gray hair in my soul!
> Thundering the world with the might of my
> voice,
> I go by—handsome,
> Twenty-two-year-old."

"Back then, I thought I could've written it myself," says Andrei. "To be handsome and twenty-two, with not one gray hair in your soul— that was the dream. No, it was even more than a dream: it was a goal, a manifesto." His eyes grasp hers for a moment, then return to his glass, to their Ivanovo past. "Back then, I wanted to be a fighter, too. A revolutionary. Rising above the muck of that courtyard, the outhouse and the chickenshit, the moonshine my father brewed behind the shed so he could muster enough courage to hit my mother. To make a better life." The honey depths of cognac must hold a great deal of Andrei's Ivanovo childhood for him to stare into his glass as long as he does. "Mayakovsky was like a *mayak*—a lighthouse. He was everything I wanted to be." Andrei pauses. "And everything I'm not."

They take sips of the cognac and chew on *servilat*, the bitter and salty tastes mixing on her tongue.

"To fight, that was the goal. It sounded so heroic, the opposite of the filth we all waded through. Remember the poem Mayak wrote when Yesenin killed himself?

"In this life
It's not difficult to die.
To make life
Is more difficult by far."

She remembers. They all read it in Marik's mother's literature class, Andrei two years prior to her. Their teacher ranked Yesenin's poetry higher than Mayakovsky's, maybe because her son preferred it or maybe because Yesenin's writing was more lyrical and less confrontational, a bandage for a woman's heart, as Grandpa used to call it.

"Do you ever think about Marik?" she asks, because she knows that mentioning Yesenin has brought Marik up in his mind, too.

For a minute or so, Andrei doesn't answer, frozen over his glass.

"I think of him all the time." She answers her own question. "Of that day, of how if I had stopped him, he would still be here. That day still haunts me. I've blamed myself; I've blamed you. I've even blamed

Marik. But maybe it was just the war, those shells buried under the loam, I don't know. Or maybe it was all of our faults."

The tar of the night seems to press harder on the windowpane, as if it wanted to enter the room and warm its black gut with their cognac, or maybe to ooze through the cracks and flood the kitchen, crushing them into the walls and squeezing all the air out of their lungs. She sees Andrei take a breath, sees his chest rise in what she hopes is preparation for letting out the words she wants to hear. She needs him to feel as guilty as she feels about Marik's death, a guilt that will somehow unite them, solidify their love by sharing the moment that defines them.

"I can never forgive myself," he says, and she empties her lungs of air, as though all the time he was silent, she has been holding her breath, waiting for something significant to announce itself. "I was stupid and young, but I should've known better even back then." Andrei pauses. "I was so jealous of him. Of your bond with him, of those books you both read. Even of your piano lessons." He drives the butt of his cigarette into the saucer they are using for an ashtray. "There were two of us and only one of you. It was as simple as that."

Two of them and one of her. But was it really that simple? The one of her had chosen Andrei, even back then. The one of her walked away and allowed the unexploded shell to blow up the lives of all three of them, forever. Maybe the cognac is to blame, but everything has loosened up inside her, and when she presses her hand over her eyes to keep the tears from bursting out, it is of no help at all. She sniffles and whimpers into her palm. Then she feels Andrei's hands on her shoulders, and she is grateful for his touch and the smell of his skin, for being able to cry into the hollow of his neck, for hearing him stifle his own sobs.

∽

"I didn't know you were so good onstage," Andrei whispers into her ear after their tears have begun to dry up. The night is still pushing against the windows, but she knows it will soon begin to dissolve into streaks of gray and then pink, so she is no longer afraid of it pressing its heft into the kitchen and suffocating them. "I completely believed it wasn't you," he adds, a statement that would have compelled her teacher to give her an A for acting. *I believed it wasn't you* is the highest praise Andrei could give her.

So maybe she didn't spend three years in Moscow for nothing after all, learning the art of real make-believe, as opposed to the phony pretense of their history books with their heroic valor and pretend radio broadcasts Grandpa probably still listens to every morning. Maybe she has actually learned something: maybe she has learned to act by pretending to be someone else, and this pretending, paradoxically, has become more truth-telling than their real life.

In the three years they haven't seen each other, Sasha has learned a lot about make-believe and Andrei has learned a lot about real life, or is it the other way around?

He pours what's left in the bottle, and it fills their glasses one more time. After the performance, after reuniting with Andrei, after reliving the fateful day in the woods, there is an emptiness inside her, just like after every performance, and she is grateful they have cognac to fill it. The alcohol, now warm, oozes down her throat, makes her dizzy, and fills the void. She is in her kitchen with Andrei, who smells just as he did back in Ivanovo, who has just allowed her a glimpse of his pain.

They drink, and then there is silence, but not the easy silence of the past few hours. This new silence makes her tense because it has become deliberate, with a strained presence of something heavy and unsaid hovering in the air.

"There is something I need to tell you," Andrei says before he gets up and walks to the entrance hallway, where she hears him fumble through his clothes. He returns with a new pack of Bulgarian cigarettes called Stewardess, shakes one out, and reaches for a box of matches on the ledge of the stove. He motions the pack toward her, but something makes her shake her head, as if she cannot afford a distraction, no matter how small, as if she needed all her senses focused on what he is about to tell her.

"This is difficult," he says, shaking his head, and from the pause that follows, she knows to expect the worst. It is indeed the worst, the most devastating news, an atomic bomb dropped out of the sky.

"I got married a few months ago," he says, staring at the radiator under the window, deeply inhaling the cigarette and breathing out a cloud of smoke as though he wished it to spread over the kitchen so that he could hide inside it.

His words slam her forehead with the force of a truncheon; they make her heart stop; they empty her lungs of air. They make her as sober as she was when only hours earlier they fumbled for each other in the hallway, when she thought, like an idiot who never learns, that the pain of longing was over and they would finally be back together again.

She gulps down the cognac that is left in her glass because she no longer wants to be sober. Being sober means she must feel the hurt of this stunning announcement by erupting in anger or disintegrating into tears. She must say something in response to the words that have just crushed her windpipe and left her speechless.

"You have to understand," he says. "I had to. I couldn't not . . ." He doesn't finish the sentence, doesn't want to repeat the words for what he has done. His eyes are downcast, evading hers.

"You couldn't not?" she repeats. "What does this mean?" The cognac she has just swallowed instantly makes her drunk again.

Andrei gets up and paces to the wall and then back. "I had no choice. It was a requirement from the ministry." He pauses. "No. It was my father-in-law's requirement," he says. "I can't explain." He shakes his head. "It would make no sense to you."

She doesn't want to hear how he was forced to marry someone else. "Fuck you and fuck the ministry and fuck your father-in-law," she says, the drunken words sticking to her upper palate. What she really wants to say is, *"Why did you do it? If you had to marry someone, why didn't you ask me? You know I would have said yes. Why didn't you come here and ask me to marry you? Why did you marry someone else, someone who knows nothing about Ivanovo, who never rode on the back of a streetcar, who doesn't share with you the dark secrets hidden in the most remote corner of your soul? Why did you marry her and not me?"*

Suddenly she knows why. The words swim up to the surface, struggling through the thick, slow current of her drunken mind. *You told me why when I was filming* The Tsar's Bride. *The Party told you that you couldn't marry an actress. And, like a good Party member, you had to do what the Party ordered.*

"Why did you come here tonight?" she asks. "To tell me *this*? To tell me one more time that you couldn't marry an actress?"

Andrei stands with his head down, silent.

"You are only good at suddenly appearing," she says, anger bubbling up from the dark cauldron inside her. "And then suddenly disappearing." After what he has just told her, she no longer wants to love him, not even a little bit. She wants to hurt him and make him suffer like she is suffering. She wants to punch him straight in the pit of his stomach, a blow that will bend him in half and force him to whimper in pain. "You're no different from any other man. You pretend that you care; you fold me into your arms as if you loved me; you get inside me, all the way down to my soul; and then you exit and abandon me again. And then, in case you hadn't done enough damage, you get married." She spits the word *married* out of her mouth as if it were a moldy crust of bread.

He sees the fury in her eyes and turns away, not able to face her.

"I know I hurt you." He stares at the floor, and Sasha stares at his profile. "Honestly, if we could be together, you would be so disappointed. I've always wanted to be the man you wanted me to be, but I can't. I never could. I came here to tell you that I hate myself for what I did. I hate myself as much as you hate me."

"So why, then?" she shouts. "Why did you do it?" *Why did you have to marry someone else, with me right here, waiting for you all these years, like a fool, like the Ivanovo idiot Grishka, always clinging to our shed in the rain, always begging.* She doesn't say anything about clinging or begging aloud, but somehow, Andrei hears her silent question.

"You know I love you, and I've always wanted to be with you. Only you," he says, although she knows, of course, the proverbial *"but"* will follow next, already chomping at the bit, ready to gallop out of his mouth. "But I simply couldn't. I made a deal with the Devil. I had to. I can't tell you more than this. It was beyond my control."

So here it is, his explanation, as murky as this January night. There is always something beyond his control, always something he cannot tell her.

"So you came to my theater and then to my apartment only to let me know that you got married." The fire in her gut triggered by the alcohol has died down now, and she no longer wants to hurt him. She simply wants him out. Out of her apartment and out of her life. But there still remains an urge to lunge at him, to reassemble the shards of her self-respect, a desperation one feels clutching at the last straw of dignity. "What did you hope to get from this?" she says, even though she doesn't want to hear his answers. She only knows one thing: she must harden her heart against him, now and for the rest of her life.

He is fully dressed now, wrapping a scarf around his throat, and she averts her eyes because looking at him seems to hollow her stomach.

"I came here to repent," he says. "I wanted you to taste my guilt and my humiliation." He starts to open the front door and then turns back for the last time. His sentences are measured, delivered as one might hand over an unexpected gift. "My whole life, I have only loved you. What I did has crippled me. It has flayed off my skin, strip by strip. I cannot look at what I've become." He pauses, and when she peers into his face, she sees hopelessness and torment, but she also sees grief. She has to avert her eyes because she, too, cannot look at what he has become. He raises his hand and runs a finger over her cheek, a tender goodbye touch. "I needed to tell you. I'm not asking for forgiveness. I know there can't be any. I simply wanted you to know." He pulls open the front door, then pauses and turns to her. "I need you to know that I love you."

32

She is at the theater, at the shoemakers' lair, a room full of broken and newly mended shoes, and she is weeping. She came here with a pair of pumps that needed repair, and when Uncle Tolya asked, "What happened?" her throat closed, and she burst into tears. She is holding a shoe in each hand, wiping her eyes and nose with her forearm, wailing so loudly that the senior shoemaker, Uncle Moishe, bent over a piece of leather when she entered, now clucks his tongue and shakes his head and peers at her from above his glasses. "*Nu, nu,*" he says and pats her head with his gnarled hand. "Sit, little girl, and let me bring you some tea." Uncle Tolya, bony and long-jawed, stops hammering a nail into the bottom of a shoe and looks at Uncle Moishe, who waves his wrist to send him on a tea quest. Uncle Moishe's hands smell of old leather and shoe polish, a comfortable smell that makes her calm down, go from weeping to sniffling. Then Uncle Tolya returns with a kettle and pours steamy, strong tea into a glass. The tea has the color of cognac, which makes her start weeping again, and her tears leave stains on the broken shoes she is still holding in her hands.

When she leaves the shoemakers' workshop, she is empty inside, as hollowed by the crying as she usually is by a performance. She walks along the endless hallway to her dressing room, when she passes the open door and sees Vladimir Ivanovich, her partner Sir Toby Belch in *Twelfth Night*, who waves her in. She likes Vladimir Ivanovich, although he is in his fifties, almost thirty years her elder, and is married. He has a deep, fatherly voice; he is dependable and strong. His face is too idiosyncratic for him to be cast as a hero, even when he was younger—a fleshy nose; dark eyes, set a little too close apart; an imperious chin with a cleft—so he is a character actor, like Sasha.

"When leaving the stage, don't forget to leave your character's skin behind," says Vladimir Ivanovich, who thinks that she just came out of a rehearsal and hasn't had a chance to disconnect from her role. He is an inexhaustible source of these little sayings, small scatterings of acting wisdom that make her laugh even when she doesn't feel like laughing. *Behind every peacock tail, there is a chicken's ass,* he told her when Olivia, the director's wife, tried to upstage her in their scene in *Twelfth Night*. Sasha attempts a smile and shakes her head, letting him know that her distress has nothing to do with acting.

On the other side of the room is Yuri, the assistant director, with an opened bottle of vodka in his hand. "Do we have an extra glass?" asks Vladimir Ivanovich, which is a rhetorical question in the theater. "You are our third," he says, laughing his humid laugh of a smoker, pouring vodka.

"The problem with this world," he announces as Yuri pours, "is that you're three glasses more sober than I am." She smiles because it is true that she is still sober and because she thinks it is an insightful way of looking at the problems of the world. "To our Maria!" Vladimir Ivanovich proclaims, and they empty their glasses. The vodka flows down where the tears had erupted from, warming up her chest and making the image of Andrei smudge at the edges, as if she were looking at him through clouds of smoke from a departing train.

33

"Again! Drunk as a plumber!" her mother wails. "What did I do to deserve this?" Every night, she listens to the elevator door bang shut and to a key scratching around the keyhole of their apartment, Sasha's key. She claims that she knows when Sasha is drunk even before she opens the front door, just from hearing the key jiggling tentatively in the lock, trying to figure out the right way to turn. Then she stands by the door, waiting for Sasha to slump into the hallway, ready to pull off her coat, lifting her arms as if she were a rag doll, ready to lead her to the divan and throw a blanket at her, like a stone.

The next morning, six months after Andrei's visit, she is hungover and humble. Now it is her mother's chance to say what she can't say when Sasha is drunk. She drives her fists into her hips and delivers her lecture about the dangers of *zelyoniy zmei*, the green serpent—the color of the bottle—wringing its coils around Sasha's neck. She rattles the silverware in the drawer and bangs the lid over a pot of soup to punctuate her statements because this is just what she predicted back in Ivanovo: Theater is too toxic, too unstable, and the love for *zelyoniy zmei* is what happens to everyone who comes under its corrosive influence.

"There are so many normal jobs," she says, knowing that after last night, Sasha has no choice but to listen. "Look at Valya from the fourth floor—she's just got a position at the district library around the corner. Look at Irina Petrovna's daughter. Your age and already a chief engineer." These are the jobs her mother understands, practical and safe, unlike the chaos and frivolity of Theater.

Last night, they celebrated the opening of a new play until four in the morning, so today her mother is more upset than usual, trotting out a longer list of toxic outcomes that await Sasha, leaping a full meter further than usual in her condemnation.

"When are you going to get married?" she demands as she cranks the handle of the meat grinder to make *kotlety* for dinner. "Look at yourself: no family, no children. Everyone your age is married, and some are even divorced by now. Not that I am promoting divorce," she adds prudently, so that Sasha doesn't get any wrong ideas in her head.

She has poked at the topic before by bringing up various young men she knows: heaping praise on a young anatomy professor at her medical institute, lionizing the engineer son of their neighbor on the third floor. Sasha doesn't want to discuss with her mother the possibility of marriage, especially now. She doesn't want to give her mother the advantage of being privy to what is swirling in her daughter's heart, of sighing and pitying Sasha for not getting the man she wants. She keeps it all inside her, away from everyone's eyes, because, as Grandma told her, what's inside you, no one can touch.

"I'm married to the Theater," she says, pushing back a headache.

"Don't be so ironic with me," her mother warns, letting her know that she is engaged in a serious conversation.

"I'm not being ironic. This is what my teachers told us at the drama school." She thinks of her Dostoyevsky scene mentor, Polevitskaya, who warned them that Theater would take over their lives and bring them to ruin. As a spasm of nausea begins to creep up her throat, she is willing to admit that Polevitskaya may have been right. All of this—clouded in the bank of fog her mind has become—seems like a century ago.

"You need a normal life," her mother says. "You need order. You need a family. Not a married man thirty years older than you."

Her mother has expressed her critical disdain for Vladimir Ivanovich many times, in pursed lips, silences, and frowns, but this is the first time she has verbalized the accusation. Sasha has never told her anything about him so that her mother wouldn't feel sorry for her, or worry about her, or give Sasha unwanted advice. She can't explain to her mother, an optimistic patron of order, anything about such hopeless and messy things as men or love. She can't explain to her, for instance, that Vladimir Ivanovich has become her safety net. Without him, she would have quit the theater last year, when the new director, after watching all of their repertory, gathered the actors and slammed them with a scathing condemnation for their flat performances, singling Sasha out with a torrent of special scorn for her role of a village divorcée from a new contemporary play. Had Sasha quit then, when her humiliation was at its peak, where would her mother be living now? She can't explain to her how many of Sasha's anti-Soviet outbursts he has kept from spilling into earshot of their regular informers and, by extension, of their theater's administration. Her mother wouldn't understand that he is the most important actor, after Polevitskaya in her drama school, who was able to drive through Sasha's head how ruthless Theater really is. *To survive in a big company like this one,* he said when she had just arrived from Moscow, *you need teeth, horns, and hooves, and I'll teach you how to grow them.* Her mother would not understand the sad humor of his favorite sayings that, for her, encapsulate the essence of their work. *Keep in mind,* he told her after her debut in *Twelfth Night, success is never forgiven,* a piece of wisdom she has never forgotten.

But the most important thing she can't even begin to explain to her mother is how much he feels like a father to Sasha. He is someone who keeps her safe, who protects her from other men always on the prowl, who steers her along the perilous maze of life in the theater. On their recent tour in Baku, Azerbaijan, when one of the local bazaar vendors cupped his hands over her breasts, he locked the man's head in the vise of his elbow and made him whimper for mercy, begging forgiveness for what the man thought was a gesture of admiration toward the Russian buyer's daughter.

Sasha takes a breath before she strikes back as a headache pulses through her temples and coaxes angry words out of their deep lair. "Maybe if I'd had a father to protect me all these years," she says, "I wouldn't look for older men."

Her mother gives out a little gasp, then tightens her mouth. She hasn't expected opposition in such close proximity to the time Sasha's key scratched around the lock and didn't find the keyhole. She is usually the one doing the lecturing; she is the master of dispensing guilt-provoking tirades and unsought advice.

"Your father perished in the Great Patriotic War," she says in a wounded voice. "You know that."

Sasha knows. His sepia photograph is on the first page of their family album in Ivanovo. Until she was seven or eight, she had been hopelessly waiting for him to walk through their gate, despite his "perished in the war" status, but then something snapped her waiting vigil. Was it her mother's reluctance to share any memory of him, or was it Grandma's inevitable sigh at the rare mention of his name? Or maybe it was an old neighbor, one of those who had to line up to use the outhouse, a *babka* with sharp eyes and a bent spine that made her look like a question mark, who one day coughed up the real story of Sasha's father to her neighbor on their courtyard bench, making sure Sasha was close enough to hear every word.

"He didn't perish in the war," Sasha says. "He died of TB, two years after the war ended, in the town of Atkarsk, where he lived with his common-law wife and a ten-year-old daughter." She sees her mother swallow hard, her face tightening. She remembers that afternoon in their Ivanovo courtyard, the *babka's* coarse voice marking the moment when her mother's heroic war-perishing story turned out to be nothing but another lie. Lying, their way of life, the stubborn abscess oozing into the cells of their system, infecting everyone.

Strangely, Sasha feels removed from this whole scene, watching the action from the wings, like a director during a performance. Her mother, the tragic heroine of the second act, admonishing her prodigal daughter who, in turn, admonishes an untruthful mother.

"I wanted to protect you," her mother says, sniffling. "I only wanted to keep you safe. That's all I ever tried to do."

She wishes her mother would stop protecting her from danger, from experience, from life itself. She wishes she would stop protecting her from Theater.

Her mother wipes her eyes before she cranks the handle of the meat grinder, and its iron face erupts in red twists of meat squeezing out into a bowl underneath.

"I only want you to have a normal life," she says. "To have a family of your own, like everyone else. Not to be alone." She takes two slices of bread soaking in milk and with her hands kneads them into the ground meat. "These older men will never marry you. They will never leave their wives," she declares, as if she were drawing a verdict, as if this were something she has learned from personal experience. "Anyone is better than an older, married man."

"You still don't understand," Sasha says. "I don't want to marry Vladimir Ivanovich. He's done good things for me, but I see him mostly for sex." The word hisses out of her mouth, sibilant and harsh, a shocking word never used in public, as noxious as a curse. It has produced the planned effect, draining blood from her mother's face, turning it white.

Her mother turns away and begins to shape the pile of meat into oblong *kotlety* between her palms, her tense back a reproach to Sasha for wrapping such a scandalous topic in words.

"There is only one man I'd even consider marrying," Sasha says. "Someone you've never approved of. Someone who is married to another woman because he is not allowed to marry an actress."

What she has just uttered slaps her like a whip across her face. She feels blood rush to the wound; she feels her cheeks burn. Her thoughts shoot back to this very kitchen months ago, to Andrei sitting on the other side of this table.

Her mother turns and gives her one of her long, drilling looks. She may have heard Sasha mumble Andrei's name when she is drunk. What does she say when her tongue is so heavy that it refuses to wrap around the sounds and form coherent sentences? Does she curse him, threaten him, or does she pledge eternal love? She would like to know, but she can't approach her mother with this question.

"And do you know what else?" Sasha says. "All my life, I could feel that you never believed in me. Not when I lived in Ivanovo, not when I was in Moscow, and not now. You always told me I'd never make it as an actress. But here I am, in the Leningrad Bolshoi Drama Theatre. I did make it. And it must kill you and Grandpa that I've succeeded, that you turned out to be wrong. But you were right about one thing: Theater is toxic and corrosive. It has cost me plenty. It has cost me the only man I've ever wanted."

Her mother looks at Sasha, her eyes like broken glass. "You're wrong. I am proud of you," she says quietly. "I've always been proud." She swipes under her eyes, stifling tears. "It's just that theater is so chaotic, so unruly. I've always wanted you to have an easy life, not like mine or Grandma's. A warless life, a life of peace we didn't have. A life of order."

She waits for Sasha's response, for some indication that she is open to normalcy, her sunny, righteous mother, as down-to-earth as Grandpa, who still believes what he hears on the radio, who refuses to look out the window and see there is no bright dawn on the horizon.

"I don't want order, and I don't want a peaceful life," Sasha snarls back. "Let Andrei and his wife live this life of regiment and calm and hope for a bright tomorrow. I don't want any more lies, any more pretense." She knows her voice is on a steady ascent to shouting heights, but she does nothing to restrain the anger rising in her throat.

"Then tell me, what do you want?" her mother asks.

"I want you to leave me alone!" she yells. "Stop lecturing me. I'm not your student. I want you to stop waving flags for a minute and look around. I want you to stop pretending that everything is fine, stop making excuses for the mess we're in." She sharpens her voice like a knife. "This isn't Ivanovo. We live in a country full of hypocrites and bandits, and of people like Grandpa and you, true believers, who have survived Stalin only because he was too busy murdering the other twenty million." She pauses to take a breath, to ready herself for the final blow. "If you can't empty yourself of this crap, of this toxic provincial thinking, you may as well go back to Ivanovo and tend to the chickens."

Out of the corner of her eye, she sees her mother hunched over the table.

"I have a rehearsal to go to," she says and gets up, leaving her mother alone with the anguish and pain and the newly made *kotlety*.

34

The new play is called *The Dawns Here Are Quiet*, five women comman-
deered by a young male sergeant, a tiny regiment operating near the
front line during the Great Patriotic War. Although it's a Soviet play,
Sasha can relate to the material better than any other contemporary play
so far. Lara is the tall, acerbic Zhenya who comes from Moscow, and she
is Liza, the daughter of a peasant from a small village.

In *Quiet Dawns*, she is on a reconnaissance mission, making her
way through the swamp, carefully stepping from one mound of earth to
the next, feeling the ground before her with a pole made from a thick
birch branch. The swamp is vast, several kilometers in any direction, but
from the sun that is beating into her right cheek, she knows she is going
north. When her sergeant gave her this assignment, she felt terrified of
walking alone across the swamp that is rumored to have claimed many
lives, but the war has taught her a shifting sense of danger: what seems
frightening at first is often recalled later as safe as your Ivanovo home.

She is in cold water up to her ankles, but she knows she is safe as
long as she is standing on firm ground. The birch pole is her guide.
When it sinks, there is nothing in front of her except the bottomless
sludge of death; when it meets resistance, she pokes around for a minute
to make sure the ground is solid and takes the next step. There are trees
and spindly bushes rising from the mud, and between them are the cold
cauldrons of the bog, with bubbles floating up from their black depths.

She tries to imagine those who drowned here, sucked into this abyss. She thinks about all who were killed in the war, all who died in the camps, millions of snapped, diminished lives. She thinks of the totality of death. She thinks about Uncle Kolya, who is not listed among the dead or alive, and Uncle Sima, who died in their Ivanovo house three weeks before she was born. She thinks, reluctantly, about her father.

Sima, the youngest in the family, had been stationed on the border with Poland before the war began, writing only one letter home when the post delivery still functioned, a triangle of gray paper Grandma still keeps in the bottom of a drawer. "They feed us well here, thick soup and boiled potatoes," he wrote for Grandma's sake. "Yesterday the sergeant said they might soon issue us guns." Her mother says she could never understand why soldiers on the Polish border, right before the German blitzkrieg into Russia, did not have guns.

Unarmed and dazed by the sudden invasion of German planes and tanks on June 22, 1941, Sima, unlike most of his comrades, managed to survive. Six months later, he was wounded at the Belorussian Front and made his way back home to Ivanovo in 1942. This is how her mother remembers that day: It was January, and there was a knock on the door. When Grandma opened the latch, there stood Sima—in a military coat with burned bullet holes, on crutches, a torn *ushanka* hat tied under his chin. The hospital could no longer do anything, so they released him. Sima decided not to write home because he wanted to surprise everyone with his arrival. Grandma, wiping under her eyes and making sniffling noises, boiled water for him to wash, as Grandpa ordered Sima to take off his clothes immediately—everything down to the rags inside his boots—so he could throw the dirty heap outside, where it was minus twenty degrees Celsius, to save the rest of them from typhus and lice.

A piece of metal lodged in Sima's lung had created an abscess and was beginning to cause an infection in his brain. It made her mother furious to think that a doctor at a front hospital had failed to operate properly, leaving a shard of a grenade in her brother's body. Although Grandma spoke of his recovery, her mother was a doctor and knew he wouldn't survive. But she had to pretend for the sake of her parents, and as Sima, blind and delirious, lay in the room where Sasha would grow up, she sat by his bed, with her big belly resting on her knees, taking his temperature and peering into his throat, making believe that whatever small medical procedures she performed could make a difference.

Was Sasha's father lying in bed in their house, too, with his wet cough rolling in his chest like the cannonade they heard at least once a day? And when he began spitting up blood, was he admitted into the Ivanovo hospital, her mother's alma mater? She must have consulted the head of the TB clinic, her former professor, who probably told her that after his release from the hospital, her father must leave, since he could not stay in the house with a newborn. Was her father relieved to leave Ivanovo and go back to his other daughter and his other wife? Or did he try to fool the doctors into letting him stay to see the arrival of his new daughter? And then, after he left, did he ever wonder about her?

Day after day, her mother sat by Sima's bed thinking about her brother and her husband, both dying. She couldn't cure them, so she concentrated on doing what she could do. She sold her ration of four hundred grams of bread and with that money bought fifty grams of butter, which, she hoped, might boost her brother's and her husband's chance for health.

Sima died at home on November 1, 1942. Her mother washed him and shaved him and dressed him for the funeral. Since she was eight months pregnant, Grandma and Grandpa decided that she should not go to the funeral, an invitation to premature labor. Her mother stood on the porch, watching Grandpa crack a whip, watching the horse snort and jerk forward as the cart with Grandma, slumped against Sima's coffin, slowly bumped onto the road, rutted by recent rain.

Sasha's father left soon after Sima's funeral, probably on November 7—three weeks before she was born—on the day of the Great October Socialist Revolution, which in peaceful times is an occasion for a citizens' parade, for people marching in rows and banners flapping in the wind. But before he left, he took both the butter and the bread, added a few bars of soap from Grandma's closet, and sold them to buy himself a jar of moonshine. In the gray air pocked with drizzle, Sasha sees her parents walk through the ruins of the town and stand waiting for the train, her big-bellied mother and her husband, who would die of TB in his hometown on the other side of the Urals five years later, never having seen his daughter. When a plume of smoke billows out of the train's stack and a spasm lurches through the cars, her mother takes a step toward the clattering wheels and raises her arm in a last goodbye. She waits until the train shrinks to toy size, until the only smoke she can see is a streak of soot rising from an apartment building bombed the day before.

Sasha feels affection for Liza and the *Quiet Dawns* story, but Liza, so far, is reluctant to let her close, to grant her the proximity she requires to become her. Sasha knows she hasn't earned this closeness yet; she needs to do more work. The work unspools images from her Ivanovo childhood, from war descriptions in Kolya's journal, the scarred pages that she hopes will help her find some solid ground underneath her feet.

January 31, 1942

A low-flying German plane chugs over the treetops, and our sergeant sinks to his knees, clutching at his throat. His eyes are desperate, but they are still the eyes of a living man. I've already bandaged several wounded—a skill I probably acquired from my older sister—and I know the glassy look in the eyes of the dying. The sergeant isn't dying. "Those fucking Fritzes," he whispers. A shard of iron must have pierced his throat without severing anything vital, a piece of luck every soldier hopes for. Being wounded means spending time at the hospital, which comes with the almost impossible perk of getting away from the front, from the Martians with their alien weapons, from the cold, from the hunger, from shitting in your pants. I press a cotton pad to the sergeant's wound and wrap a bandage around his throat. Then I haul him up to his feet, and with most of his weight on my shoulders, we set off hobbling to the makeshift hospital about three kilometers away.

What a strange place it is, this road between the rear and the front, between life and death. It is as wide and crowded as an avenue, the Nevsky Prospekt of war. We are walking away from the front, along with other wounded, drawn on sleds or piled onto an occasional truck. Toward the front crawl tanks, horse-drawn carts, and trucks filled with weapons and food. The new soldiers marching past are wearing military capes over their shoulders that make them look like hunchbacks, as if they had already been damaged.

We lumber past the everyday life teeming on the sidewalks of this avenue. The sergeant's embrace is suffocating, but I know I am the one without the shrapnel wound, so I don't complain. It is so cold that your spit turns into an icicle in the air before it hits the ground with a ping. We pass two soldiers sitting on a military cape spread across the snow, sawing a frozen loaf of bread into pieces with a two-handled saw. I can taste that frozen bread in my mouth, a piece of hard candy you have to roll on your tongue until it thaws. They scoop up the sawdust of bread crumbs and divide them equally.

Suddenly there are several explosions: first in the distance, then closer, then only a few meters away. On the ground, I see a soldier crouching in a puddle of blood, but all I feel is relief that it isn't me. An older man who was walking in front of us is now on his knees, clutching his thigh. Next to him is a nurse, a girl who looks no older than sixteen, helpless, dribbles of tears streaking down her dirty face unwashed for days. She doesn't know what to do, and I see that her hands are shaking. The older man lowers his pants, plugs the bloody hole in his thigh with a bandage, and tries to console the girl. "Don't be afraid, dochka, *don't cry."* Dochka, *he calls her, my little daughter.*

We reach the hospital at dusk. The bandage around the sergeant's throat is all red now, but he is still hanging on to my shoulders, dragging his feet in the dirty snow. The hospital is not really a hospital; it is a train parked on an auxiliary track. There are scattered bloodstained rags and too many men to count. The young doctor with a face drained of color and short chestnut hair has lost her voice. She looks as if she could faint at any minute, but she tries to project authority. She looks a little like my older sister, Galya, who is also a surgeon at the front line, near Kalinin. I carefully lower the sergeant to wait in line with the other wounded sitting on the floor of what used to be a corridor when this train was a train, when there was no war. Then I turn around to take the road back to the front. This is the closest to Nevsky Prospekt I'm going to get for a while.

And what if I didn't go back to our trench carved in the frozen flesh of the field? What if I stayed right here and got lost among the scraps of life swarming along the war road? A seductive thought, a dangerous thought. A thought that has crossed my mind more than once, that has crossed the mind of every private who wanted to survive. A desperate attempt to stay alive that usually fails.

You clench your teeth and shoot your foot through a loaf of bread. You turn your head away and fire at your wrist through the arm of a soldier with a funnel in place of where his stomach had been only a few minutes earlier. You are desperate enough to jump into a bomb crater and detonate a grenade that will rip off your arm at the elbow. And then what? Then there is an NKVD officer with a heavy jowl from extra rations and an unflinching communist gaze who has seen all this before and who can tell in an instant a real wound from a self-inflicted one. There is no hesitation in his eyes because the front allows no benefit of the doubt for the cowardly and the weak, for those who have to think about whether they are ready to die for their motherland. If you are weak, you are killed like a rabid dog, like a horse infected with anthrax, to keep other dogs and other horses healthy and in working order. The verdict is quick: you are a deserter, so you stand in front of your platoon, your belt taken away, your pants falling down, the commissar aiming his gun at your head.

I walk along the road back to the front, back to Seryoga, into the rapidly descending winter night.

Sasha is at the rehearsal for *Quiet Dawns*, and she is feeling the swampy water before her with her birch-tree pole, trying to distinguish land from morass, life from death. Everything is absolute: if you make a mistake, there is no second chance. One wrong step is your destiny. You have one moment to make a decision that will define your life, whatever is left of it. A single moment can either leave you balanced on ten centimeters of firm land or open a void under your feet, a bottomless quagmire of cold muck ready to suck you in and swallow you whole. One moment Marik was standing by the fire, his feet dug into the mud, and the next thing she saw was blood from the corner of his mouth leaving a red stain on the snow.

She doesn't want to think about the quivering depths beneath her feet, so she thinks of their sergeant, Gleb Petrovich. He is young, and giving the five of them orders makes him uncomfortable: he looks away and rubs his forehead under his military cap when he has to tell them what to do next. She has a suspicion no one has ever called him Gleb Petrovich, and every time Zhenya or Liza shape their mouths around the sounds of his patronymic, he blinks in surprise, as though the more formal name they use for those in charge should be addressed to someone else, someone worthy of command. In her thoughts, she calls him simply Gleb, and sometimes even the diminutive Glebushka when she thinks of his blue eyes and his hair the color of straw, when she admits to herself that she likes him, the way she liked Andrei when Marik was still alive: longing, not yet desire, the small, unopened bud of future love. Gleb is from a tiny village, like her, and she can tell from the pink hue that floods his freckled cheeks that he likes her, too. He doesn't blush when the tall and beautiful Zhenya-Lara sings "Katyusha" in her deep, seductive voice or when the other three girls whisper into each other's ears and stifle giggles.

As she takes careful steps onstage, she is thinking about Kolya's fears at the front, of Uncle Sima's, and sometimes even her father's. She should be grateful that at least it isn't winter, when Kolya said the insides of your nostrils stick together and when your teeth ache from the cold. It is June 1942, one year since the invasion spilled east from their borders, toward the Volga and beyond, a chilly June when even the weather doesn't feel like warming up, when the sun remains hidden behind the gray haze, refusing to shine light onto this ravaged land. She is as scared as Kolya was when he first saw Germans roaring across the countryside on motorcycles, in helmets and big glasses; as scared as Sima must have been when he ran in retreat, deafened by the blitzkrieg of tanks and planes on June 22, 1941; as frightened as her father when he first saw droplets of blood on the handkerchief he pressed to his mouth to cover his cough. Her fear is uncontrollable and primal, like a small animal with razor-sharp teeth and viselike claws that has gripped her insides and will not let go of them until they turn liquid, just like this swamp under her feet. The fear is that at any moment, despite your best effort to survive, you can be shredded by a grenade; or minced to a bloody pulp by a bomb; or burned to a cinder in a locked barn; or hoisted aloft with your hands tied behind your back so that your arms, with a splintering crack, dislocate from their sockets at the shoulders; or sucked under the oilskin of this bog. This is the fear of dying she now knows all too well—despite her youth and strength and all the joy and love she hasn't yet had a chance to taste.

"How is *Quiet Dawns* going?" asks her mother. Sasha is in a hurry before a rehearsal, slurping soup in the kitchen, their usual place of conversation.

"I think I've got it," Sasha says. "I think I've got Liza." She says this for her mother's sake, but she is not at all sure that she has mastered the role. The knot of insecurity and fear tightens under her ribs every day, and she knows that the nauseating feeling of failure won't let go until opening night, if all goes well. She forces herself to finish the last spoonful of barley soup and gets up to gouge a little leftover macaroni from the pot on the stove. She knows she must eat, although her stomach aches and contracts in protest. "I've reread Kolya's journal, and it helped."

For a minute, her mother is silent, clinking the silverware in the sink. Then she turns and takes a breath. "Maybe he was too bitter, Kolya. Too disdainful about the country, about our way of life. Too negative."

They have had this conversation before, an argument that never ends well.

"Too negative?" Sasha says, hearing her voice rise in tone. "He wasn't negative enough! He wrote what he saw around him. He didn't make anything up."

"But maybe—and I've been thinking about this—maybe he had this pessimistic view because the one he loved had just been arrested. If they hadn't arrested her, things would've been different for Kolya. Nadia's arrest made him see everything through this dark lens."

"So what are you saying?" Sasha hears irritation in her voice but does nothing to rein it in. "That he saw everything through a dark lens while in reality everything was rosy and light?"

"No," says her mother and shakes her head, getting defensive. "What I'm saying is that maybe this personal trauma blurred his vision, so he wasn't able to see reality the way it was."

Sasha is already late for a rehearsal, and her anxiety about the role is only fueling her anger. "He was there; he was the only one who saw reality the way it was!" she shouts. "*He* was at the front, not our leaders. He fought for the motherland against the enemy, while they sent people to rot in camps."

"Don't boil over," her mother says, her usual warning, but Sasha is already past the boiling-over point.

"You know what I think? After rereading his journal and after rehearsing *Dawns*? I think that all those ancient men in Moscow have simply usurped the war. They have wrestled the war, the heroism and the death, out of the hands of those who lived it, and now they are the ones who own it. And now they wave it like a red banner on Victory Day. After all, they think they are the ones who made the victory happen, the Party and the KGB, and not the tens of millions who were murdered, by the Germans and by our own."

She bangs her plate and fork into the sink, angry because she is in a hurry and doesn't have time to fight with her mother; angry because no matter how hard she tries, she can't drive this simple understanding into her mother's head; angry at another looming proof of her professional unfitness.

"I don't have the time now," she spits out, "to argue. And you know what?" She pauses for a second, glancing at her mother's fallen face, but the words have already formed in her mouth, ready to bubble out. "You're hopeless, as hopeless and retrograde as Grandpa. As blindly patriotic. That's why it was so easy for the Party to hijack the war and the victory from those who had fought for it. That's why we live the way we live, wallowing in lies, like pigs in mud. Because of fools like you."

35

It's opening night for *Quiet Dawns*, and Sasha is onstage, flying through the forest as if she had wings, on an assignment from Sergeant Gleb to go back to their base and report that a regiment of Germans is laying mines around the lake. Gleb and Liza had a little time to talk after he told her how to retrace her steps back to the base: first through the forest, then through the swamp (make sure you take the birch pole we left by the big pine on the way here), and then across the field just before the base where they came from. There was a song they sang in their village, he said, a song Liza started to hum because she knew it well. Gleb pressed his hand to her mouth to silence her because the Germans were getting close, and for a few moments, he kept his palm on her face before he pulled it back. This is all that she is thinking of right now: his hand, the smell of it, tobacco and warm skin, the smell that is now propelling her through the forest.

Thinking of that moment, she flies past the tall pine where they left the birch pole, not realizing it until it's too late to go back. There are scores of big, dead branches scattered in the puddles on the brink of the swamp, and she quickly chooses one. Then she takes off her skirt, ties it to the top of the pole, and steps into the swamp.

At first, the swamp is not very deep, and Sasha even calms down a bit as she waddles along the sloshy path. She thinks of her mother breaking the military order when she operated on a civilian at the front, a nine-year-old boy, before she was born. It took her mother a second to evaluate the alternative between the military rule and a child's life before she chose life. She didn't hesitate to disobey the commissar and do what she knew was right. So why does she apologize for the heartlessness of their motherland, for the long shadow of that commissar today?

Onstage, she walks, connecting the firm hillocks with her feet, until there is only the last few hundred meters of dirty ooze left before her, the most difficult stretch. The quivering depths of all her insecurity and fears, of all her losses and guilt. How does she locate firm ground to support her and lend her some understanding? How can she fight back the feeling that she is standing on nothing at all?

Suddenly a huge brown bubble burps out of the swamp's gut right in front of her, so loudly and unexpectedly that without thinking, instinctively, she swerves off her path. Just one step sideways, but her feet instantly lose support, as if someone yanked the road from under her boots. With all her weight, she leans onto the pole, but the dead wood cracks and splinters and—face forward—she falls into the cold liquid mud. The path is close, a step away from her, maybe a half a step. But it is a step she can no longer make.

Russian women die from the heart, Grandma used to say. This is what Liza-Sasha has always thought would happen to her: like all Russian women, she would die from the heart. Not from the cold burp of a bottomless muck that is pulling her under and beginning to leak into her lungs, extinguishing hope for any understanding.

She hears herself scream, an awful, lonely scream that rings over the rusty swamp, over the stage, and into the audience, then soars to the tops of the pines, gets tangled in the leaves of young aspens, and falls again. The sun sails from above the trees, and for the last time she sees its white light, as brilliant and warm as the promise of tomorrow.

～

Vladimir Ivanovich is waiting for her in the wings. Sasha doesn't know why he is here: he is not in the *Quiet Dawns* cast and should probably be home with his wife watching the nine o'clock news. She sees him, but she doesn't see him. She still holds Liza inside her, her short-lived love, her crushing fear, her unfaltering if rueful hope, her staunch surprise at her cruel, and utterly un-Russian, death. Or maybe every death, no matter how senseless, is fundamentally, at heart, a Russian death. She has been emptied by two onstage hours of Liza's life, and she takes a breath before she can fill the void.

She knows there is time to decompress. Since her character has just died, she won't be in the second act, but she has to wait another hour for curtain call.

"No curtain call tonight," Vladimir Ivanovich says, his eyebrows mashed together into one bristling line above his eyes. "We got a call from the hospital." He pauses, giving time for all the blood to drain from her body, and she knows what he's going to say next. She closes her eyes and shakes her head, but he says it anyway. "It's your mother."

"When?" she asks as though it might make a difference.

"Seven o'clock, half an hour before curtain."

She opens her mouth to say something, but he quickly adds, "They ordered me not to tell you until the end of the performance. That's the protocol, the chief administrator said. I had to fight with him to even let you leave before curtain call."

Her legs feel like cotton, and she sits down on a rolled-up rug, the green field of the last act, the field that Liza didn't have a chance to see.

"I'll take you to the hospital if you want to go," says Vladimir Ivanovich.

"If I want to go?" she asks.

"They called just before you finished the scene," he says. "The doctor at the hospital."

"I thought they called before I went onstage."

"They did," says Vladimir Ivanovich. "Then they called again just now."

He doesn't need to explain why they called the second time. There can only be one reason. He pulls her into his arms and holds her, as if otherwise she would fall apart into a thousand pieces at his feet, and she knows what he is going to say, and he knows that she knows, so he doesn't say it. Instead, he strokes her hair and kisses her forehead and holds her tight to keep her together, like a father would, to prevent her from breaking apart.

～

The funeral is a blur; the days before and after are a blur. There are cars, and heaps of flowers with a sickly sweet smell, and people with somber faces Sasha should know but cannot remember. There is Grandma and Grandpa standing in the door of her apartment, wearing black. A Volga bumps along Leningrad's center, crosses the bridge into the city outskirts, and takes them to the cemetery where two men with unshaven, veiny faces loom near a freshly dug grave. They are always the same men, in Leningrad or Ivanovo, two drunks earning a few rubles for another bottle. Grandma bends down; scoops a handful of wet, heavy dirt; and tosses it into the grave—it hits the lid of the coffin with a thump. Grandpa circles his arms around her shoulders and leads her back, since she can't see where she is going, tears clouding her glasses. She leans on Grandpa's arm, blindly following his lead, wondering why there are any tears left in her at all.

Someone has arranged everything: her theater? Vladimir Ivanovich? Her mother's medical institute? Feeling numb, Sasha throws a handful of dirt into the grave, just as Grandma did, because this seems what a funeral requires. She cannot remember the custom from Marik's funeral back in Ivanovo. She must not have been paying attention, just as she is not paying attention now. Her insides feel as quivery as the swamp that claimed Liza's life, its rancid ooze rising in her throat, making her take a few steps and hide behind a thick linden tree as she fights the spasms of nausea that bring tears to her eyes. Or have the tears been there all along? She rubs her eyes with her fists, and when she opens them again, she sees Andrei standing in the distance between two birches. She blinks to make him disappear, but he still stands there, black suit and black hair, as beloved as ever, until he realizes that she sees him, and then he raises his hand slightly and walks away.

She is back in her apartment, with the dining table open to its maximum length and lined on either side by the bed and the couch turned into seats. The table is filled with the usual *zakuski*: pickled mushrooms and cucumbers, baked *pirozhki* filled with egg and scallions, potato and beet salads bathed in mayonnaise. She can't eat; everything inside her feels parched. Instead, she drinks. There is a bottle of vodka on her right, and the man next to her, probably a professor from her mother's medical institute—maybe even the one she hoped Sasha would meet and marry—is attentive and generous in keeping her glass filled. Maybe her mother was right, after all, and Sasha should have met him. Maybe if she had, they wouldn't be sitting at this table now, drinking toasts to her mother's heroic life, bemoaning her death.

Then she is on a stool in the bathroom, leaning against the washing machine, a cold towel on her forehead. How did she get here? She doesn't remember. She opens her eyes and sees Grandma fanning her with an old copy of *Pravda*.

"*Nu, nu,*" Grandma says, dabbing Sasha's face with the wet towel. The room is spinning, but Grandma's hands fix it in place. "Mama loved you," she says in her soft, cottony voice. "She knew you loved her, too."

She knows Grandma says this to calm her down, but she is not at all certain she is right. Did Sasha love her mother as much as her mother loved her? Did she love her enough for her mother to know? She searches inside herself, but she is not sure it was enough to keep her heart going, enough for her to put up more of a fight against death and survive. Grandma's hands are as soothing as her voice, wiping away the tears—for Mama, for herself—and Sasha needs to feel her warm palms pressing damp fabric to her cheeks.

~

When she wakes up in the middle of the night, she stares into the darkness, alone in her apartment now, the enormity of loss pressing on her heart. This loss on top of other losses is keeping her awake, allowing the armoire to step out of the corner and cast an eerie shadow on her bed. This loss is the most raw and bitter of them all, the heaviest, the most brutal. This loss is as thick as glue, sticking to all the other losses scattered on the bottom of her soul, dragging them up, pulling off all the scabs.

There is always Andrei, who now comes to her in nightmares that wake her up drenched in icy sweat, dreams of her life collapsing quietly and suddenly, like a bank of sand. And there is always Theater, the cruel master of all actors, whip in hand, who didn't even tell her that Mama had been taken to the hospital because she had a performance to deliver. Yet had they told her, would her being there have changed anything? She doesn't know the answer, but she blames Theater for being the culprit in this death. Had Sasha been at the hospital, the knowledge that Mama was not alone to face the chasm opening before her may have soothed her heart and made it beat again.

She was a Russian mother, with a very Russian daughter. A daughter who didn't accept her for who she always was—a methodical, ferocious survivor. She had survived the famine, Stalin's terror, Grandpa, and a frontline hospital during the Great Patriotic War. She had survived losing Sasha's father. For nearly twenty-four years, she had survived Sasha.

223

Was Sasha blind to fail to see all this, or was it merely convenient for her to look away? It was so much simpler to wish her mother had been more sophisticated and less concrete, to wish that Sasha could attach the word *intelligentsia* to her weighty figure in a polyester dress made by the "Bolshevik Woman" factory, to wish that she had come from Leningrad and not Ivanovo, from the world of Pushkin and the tsars, of granite embankments and lace ironwork, of pearly domes buttressing the low sky. It was simpler not to see her life as it had really been, an every-minute battle. In addition to teaching at the medical institute, on Sundays, she worked in an ambulance at the Ivanovo hospital, and during the summer, she treated fractured wrists and sick stomachs at a pioneer camp on a lake so that Sasha could stay there, too, and *breathe some fresh air*, as Grandma liked to say. So why wasn't she kinder to her? Why did she need to be harsh and critical of everything she said, constantly aiming her stage voice at her chest, like a knife?

She lies awake and stares into the ink of the night, with darkness gathered all around her and not a single drop of light able to glimmer through.

36

She is in a new play, a work by Alexander Ostrovsky, a classical playwright whose bearded portrait hangs in the literature classroom of every secondary school. This is the reason she gets out of bed, instead of huddling under a blanket and wallowing in the soupy dusk of an October morning. She is Matryona, a wealthy merchant's wife. Her stepdaughter Parasha is the main character in *An Ardent Heart*, "a ray of light in the dark kingdom" of merchants, a world of hidden grief, gnawing pain, and deadly silence, as their eighth-grade literature textbook taught them. The famous literary critic Dobrolyubov called Ostrovsky's works "the plays of life," a phrase they all memorized to quote on an eighth-grade test. To Sasha, Ostrovsky always seemed preachy, so she used to doodle on her desk, pretending to listen to her teacher lecturing them about *An Ardent Heart* and its moral conflict between duty and personal happiness, which seemed to be the moral conflict of every work in their textbook, with duty, by the last few pages, always taking the upper hand.

Only now, her director is doing something very different from what they were taught in eighth grade. The merchant's wife and daughter, in their production, are practically the same age, both abused, both locked up in the courtyard of the merchant's house, behind three rows of fences, away from life and any chance of personal happiness. Her character Matryona, always played by middle-aged actresses as a petty tyrant, in their production is as much of a victim as her stepdaughter, who, in turn, is as far from being "a ray of light in the dark kingdom" as any of the play's despotic merchants.

They rehearse every day, and this routine—getting up, making coffee in a small copper pot she brought from Georgia where her theater went on tour last summer, when her mother was still alive, getting dressed and waiting for a bus under her windows—makes life purposeful and gives shape to the quiet, empty mornings. She wakes up to the silence in the kitchen and the silence in the room where her mother slept. Silence, despite the streetcars screeching on the turn under her windows and the neighbor behind the wall adjusting the volume of their radio to listen to the morning news. Silence in her apartment, silence in her soul, silence hand in hand with guilt. She gets up, pulls on a sweater and pants she wore the day before, and walks downstairs to the bus stop, almost sleepwalking, as if she'd been enmeshed in cobwebs, so every step requires effort to push through the sticky binding. Even the smallest task—taking her coat off the hook, for instance, or lifting a scarf out of a drawer—seems like a colossal endeavor that requires might and concentration almost beyond her power.

Vladimir Ivanovich, who is her merchant husband in the play, watches her during rehearsals, senses the cobwebs, and tries to pick them off with remarks that would normally make her laugh. Sasha doesn't know what he sees when he looks at her. What she saw this morning when she glanced at the mirror was distressing: a pyramid of bones upholstered in sallow skin, exhausted eyes, the face of a stranger. "The problem with young people is that I am no longer among them," he says, trying to make her smile, and her mouth smiles, but he can see that her eyes don't. In spite of having a wife and two grown children, he cares about her, Sasha knows; once in a while, he even says he loves her.

She calls him by his name and patronymic, the way you would address someone else's father.

After the rehearsals are over, she works with the director, who also senses that something is off in her, that she is not all there. They go over her words and add a subtext of what Matryona would think as she lashes out at her permanently drunken husband and her self-righteous stepdaughter conniving to take the reins of the house away from her. The subtext mostly comes out as *mut*, the lowest of the sordid jargon of obscenity, the mother tongue of construction sites and lines to beer kiosks. Sasha is grateful to the director for helping her with the Matryona role and for keeping her in the rehearsal room, away from the silent emptiness of her apartment, from the guilt, from a bottle of vodka always stashed in someone's dressing room.

They are already six weeks into rehearsals, but Matryona doesn't come to her. She hovers close but refuses to invade her. She is still a specter, a fleshless apparition, devoid of blood and bones, of meat and skin. Sasha senses her presence, but she does not feel her heft and cannot smell her breath. They are already at the stage in the production where the set designer has completed the layout of the scenery and brought it to one of their rehearsals. The stage set is the courtyard of her husband's house, surrounded by three rows of tall fences, with a stump in the middle. Matryona and her stepdaughter live locked inside this courtyard, but the stepdaughter, at least, has a chance of getting married and breaking out of here. For Matryona, this courtyard will be her life until she dies, and she is only twenty-three. Her husband, more than twice her age, drinks all night and sleeps all day while she goes to the market, and when he wakes up late in the afternoon, he lumbers down the porch and lifts his eyes to the sky, certain that it has cracked in half and is about to fall. That's when he screams for her to hold him upright and assure him that he is only hallucinating, that the sky is still whole, at least for tonight. That's when he takes his first swig of vodka, crunches down the steps of the porch in his boots, and yanks her to the ground behind the stump. Then, with his filthy, callused hands, he tears at her dress, rips open her skirt, and rapes her.

~

Sasha has decided not to take a bus to the opening night. What point is there in clinging to a routine when she knows it's all going to end in a colossal shipwreck? She is going to falter and fail and take the whole production down with her. In two hours, she is to play Matryona, who is still remote and intangible, a bunch of lines Ostrovsky wrote, which they have backed with some crude layers of *mut*, all in vain. Tomorrow, after reading the abysmal reviews in every paper, their administrative director will call her to his office and inform her that she has been fired for professional inadequacy, her apartment taken away from her. At least her mother is not here to witness her failure.

It is the middle of November, and she is leaning into the wind on Dekabristov Street, walking toward Theatre Square, where the green and white building of the Kirov Opera and Ballet Theatre looks pearly in the distance through the blustery air pregnant with rain. As she looks up, she sees low gray clouds rushing across the sky, across the narrow space between the roofs. They race overhead with decisiveness and deliberation, scurrying from one side of the roofs framing the street to the other, chased by more clouds blown in by the wind. There is always wind, blowing from somewhere far away, trapped between the fences, swirling dirt around the stump, then flying away. This is all she can see: the bustle of rain clouds above her head, the three rows of fences, and the low sky clamped over her head like a lid. This is her life, every single day until she dies—the towering fences, the courtyard with its racing clouds above, and the stump behind which her drunken husband rapes her. Suddenly something clicks, and it all comes together: two months of rehearsals, the text and the subtext, her dead-end youth and her own old age she can already see peering from the face of her perpetually inebriated husband. Twenty more years of this revolting dead-end life is what she has to look forward to, if she survives that long.

This is the moment Matryona enters her and Sasha shapes her body around her soul. The moment every line she utters is carved into Sasha's heart. The moment Matryona's pulse begins to beat in sync with Sasha's, the moment her blood begins to course through Sasha's veins.

37

"They are going to close the play," Andrei says.

They are walking along Nevsky Prospekt, away from Sasha's theater, away from the three hours of intense magic at their seventh performance of *An Ardent Heart*. Nearly three years have passed since he told Sasha he was married and she hoped that if she ever saw him again, her heart would remain as frigid as this November night with snowflakes floating through the air. He was waiting outside the theater, away from the stage door, on the periphery of her vision, as she was signing programs for a small crowd of fans. Her heart lurched and then plunged when she registered his silhouette as she handed the last program back and said something she doesn't remember to a handsome man with ears red from the cold.

They are walking toward the Neva, through the darkness diffused by the few neon signs still lit at this hour, breathing in the icy dampness that numbs the throat and metes frost into the lungs. Sasha opens her mouth to ask him how he knows the play will be closed, but she catches herself. Of course he knows. He works at the department that decides things like that—which plays to close and what books to ban—the Ministry of Culture of the Municipal Committee of the Communist Party. It is located in the Smolny, a former institute that prior to the Revolution housed a school for young maidens of noble birth. They no longer have nobles, and there are far too few maidens left among them.

"Why must they close the play?" she asks instead. It is an unnecessary question, but she wants to hear his explanation, feeling anger constricting her chest. She is angry at his official look, at his surprise late-night visit to tell her that the role she has just created will soon be relegated to the archives of the Bolshoi Theatre museum. She asks why they are closing her play, because she wants to hear him confirm his complicity.

"The public wants optimism, a positive hero," he says, his voice flat. "They need something to believe in."

Of course she knows this—one of many Party slogans—but the need to challenge him is itching in her throat. "How do you know what they want?" she says, refusing to continue this argument along Party lines they've both known from birth. She wants to hear what he really thinks, what is hidden behind the facade of his official face, although she doubts he will ever reveal it. "They buy tickets, those who are lucky enough to get tickets. They give us a standing ovation every night. They love the absence of light. They identify with the darkness. They applaud all our characters, and none of them are positive heroes the public can believe in. Why can't your bosses ever allow the people to see life as it really is?"

She glances at his profile, waiting for him to answer. His hair is completely black in the dappled red neon from the Kavkazsky restaurant sign, still open.

"This only tells me that we still have a lot of work to do," he says, and she can't tell if he is being sarcastic. He doesn't smile, so she must allow for the possibility that he believes what he has just said, even though it sounds too suspiciously close to what he would say to someone at work. How is it possible that she detests him as much as she does at this moment, and at the same time is searching for a pretext to stroke his hair?

"We all live surrounded by three rows of fences, in a courtyard with a stump behind which you get fucked," she says. "Just like the characters in this play you're closing."

They both know that the scene from Ostrovsky is a metaphor not only for life in their motherland but also for the dead end of their own nonlife together. Maybe she should tell him she no longer believes in the sentimental nonsense about connected souls and unbreakable bonds. Several years of working in repertory theater have successfully wiped out all vestiges of that hope.

He stops to peer into her face, and they stand there for a few moments, bathed in red, searching for a trace of something in each other that may still be there. Then he lowers his eyes and reaches for a pack of cigarettes in his coat pocket. They are Marlboros, the American brand they hear about only from jammed broadcasts of the BBC, and it occurs to Sasha that he must be climbing the Party ladder. He offers her one, and for a few minutes, they walk silently, inhaling capitalist tobacco so scandalously better than their own.

"Maybe you were right to leave Ivanovo when you did after all," he says, stopping in front of a courtyard that seems to shimmer under an ordinary-looking archway, so painfully beautiful that for an instant, Sasha wonders if she has been blessed with a mirage. A wrought-iron bench glistens under a tree, and a marble statue, white and seemingly glowing, stretches its arm in their direction, in a puzzling gesture of either invitation or forbiddance. "Are you happy?" he asks. "Now that you've become an actress?"

She doesn't know if he wants her to answer the first, existential, question or to attach the second, qualifying, half to it, but she knows that it is safer to remain within the confines of acting. The answers to these two questions, if she is honest, are diametric opposites: no, she's not happy without him and yes, she is happy when she is onstage. She is happy to be breathing in the damp smell of wool from his coat. She is unhappy that they can't go to her apartment, tear off their clothes, as they did three years ago, and ravage each other until they both melt and start coursing through each other's veins like lifeblood.

"Acting is freedom. It's searching for what's real," she says. "Every performance is different. Together with the other actors onstage and with the audience, I search for the truth—we all do—and sometimes we almost find it. That's the essence of acting: looking for the truth. There is nothing fake about it. There is no pretending."

They walk inside the courtyard and sit on the bench, which is freezing cold and damp from wet snow.

"So it is the opposite of our life here."

"It's the opposite of your job," she says. "The opposite of banning plays that fail to lead the audience into the shining future. It is allowing people to think, to examine their failings and their faults, to peek into the dark corners of the soul. To see human beings as they are, not as we think they should be. Maybe that's the reason Theater is so dangerous."

He smirks, or maybe she only thinks she sees him smirk.

"Last time I saw you," he says, and she hears an intake of breath, "I came to tell you what I'd done. I wanted to confess to you. I hated myself and wanted to tell you the truth. My truth."

They are both silent for a minute.

"My wife is a good woman," he says, fumbling inside his pockets, as if he were looking for something and not finding it. "I only wish she'd found someone better than me, someone more deserving. I don't love her, and I never did." He plays with a pack of matches he has fished out of his pocket. "She fell in love with me the first time we met, the daughter of my boss, someone to whom I owed everything. He took a big chance on me when I had nothing, not even a pair of shoes to wear to the office. Anyway, she begged him to do whatever he could to get me to marry her, even if it meant twisting my arm. She sensed that I was in love with someone else, but that didn't stop her. She just refused to feel humiliated. She wanted me, and nothing else mattered."

Andrei lights a cigarette he finally finds in his pocket, inhales, and lets the smoke extinguish a whirl of snowflakes. "A pathetic story, isn't it?"

He pauses, and from the corner of her eye, Sasha sees him bite his lower lip, as if getting ready to tell her something. For a few seconds, he seems on the verge of letting the words out, but then he looks away. She sees his hand with the cigarette tremble, or maybe he is simply shaking off the ashes. "My father-in-law has been diagnosed with cancer," he finally says. "He needs surgery and then radiation. My wife is devastated. If she didn't have me, she would fall apart."

Sasha tries to imagine a woman who had to beg her father to make someone marry her against the man's will. Or was it really against the man's will, after all, if the man agreed to the marriage?

"But you allowed your arm to be twisted. You did what they wanted you to do."

"It wasn't that simple." She hears him shift on the bench, as if with his weight he could substantiate this claim. "There were things done that couldn't be undone. There were things said and choices made. It's always about choices, dead ends and mistakes." She hears him inhale as if he were preparing to say more. "Do you want to hear a little story about my father-in-law's choices? The story he told me a couple of weeks ago when I visited him at his dacha. Maybe it was his cancer diagnosis that helped loosen his tongue about his past, but once he set the vodka down and started talking, my only job was to sit back and listen."

She is too tense to sit back, but she is willing to listen.

Andrei leans forward, staring at his shoes. "Toward the end of the war, they chose Vadim to work at the NKVD. The Party trusted him to do important work, he said, as important as killing Germans at the front. He hated Germans. They were the enemy who had to be killed. And when he killed them, they screamed in German, in their foul language of bandits and invaders. But his prisoners, the ones he interrogated in the NKVD cellars, screamed and begged in Russian. Not in that alien language he couldn't understand. The language he was speaking to me, our mother tongue." Andrei speaks evenly, almost monotonously, not allowing any opening for an interjection.

"Every day by noon, he was covered in blood. He reeked of blood, despite a bucket of cologne they brought in at the end of the day. Even his dog refused to come near him at home. He had to wipe his hands on his hair to keep the gun from slipping out of his grip. But that was his work. That was his duty, he said, and he was a soldier. They told him to serve, and he served. They told him to execute, and he executed.

"Every day, by the end of the shift, he had pulled the trigger so many times that his index finger became numb. It hung limp as a whip, completely useless. But they had a monthly plan, like any factory, a plan that had to be fulfilled. So they brought medical experts to advise them what to do. Physicians in white coats armed with notepads sauntered along the hallways, furrowing their brows and watching them inter-rogate the prisoners. The result? Twice a week, each of them was to get a massage of the right hand. A massage of his trigger finger, as my father-in-law called it. So after that, on Tuesdays and Thursdays, during lunch hour, a terrified-looking woman slinked into his office. A new one every time. I'll spare you the details. But at the end of the month, the quotas were met. The NKVD even gave him a plaque for 'living up to the special task of the Party.' He has a cabinet full of those plaques."

Andrei stops, and she sees he isn't going to say more.

They both remain silent for a minute or so. What is Sasha going to do with this story? What is she going to do with the fact that Andrei did not walk away from that conversation, from his father-in-law and his dacha, from that life? What kept him there, drinking and listening?

"Congratulations on being related to someone who can brag about such a glorious Soviet past," Sasha says. But what she really wants is something much more selfish than this grand moral condemnation. "So you allowed yourself to be bought for a cushy job and a pair of nice shoes," she says.

He turns to her, his face contorted with sudden anger. "You weren't around, remember? I was alone, with nobody there. You left. My parents were dead, my house burned to the ground, and all you could think of was yourself and the theater." He gets up and strides out of the courtyard. She follows, trying to catch his words. "I told my father-in-law things he could use against me. Things he could put me in the camps for. Stuff I did."

Sasha grabs his elbow to prevent him from walking away. "What did you do?"

He struggles out of her grasp but stops. For a minute or so, they stand under the arch, silently, and she can hear him breathe hard. "What I did is too late to fix. Years too late. There is nothing anyone can do now." He starts walking back to Nevsky Prospekt.

Without saying a word, they walk toward the blustery Neva that lets them know it is close as they tense against the heavy gusts of wind. They walk past rows of darkened windows, on the sidewalk that is already a gruel of dirty snow until the spire of the Admiralty becomes visible against the sky, until the Hermitage steps out of the dark like a photographic image floating in developing solution. They make their way to the river through the grip of an early winter, contemplating what has just transpired between them, thinking of their ruined lives.

"Did you arrange for my mother's funeral?" she finally asks.

"Your theater arranged most of it. I only helped." She thinks of Andrei at the cemetery standing at a distance, just as he did in Ivanovo, in the cloud of train smoke.

"So you've been watching me from your Party perch at the Smolny," she says, "like the NKVD watched Kolya's Nadia and her family. Like they watched everyone." The words come out metallic and harsh, as if she wanted to hammer them into his temples, and maybe she does. Maybe she wants to grab him by the hair and dunk his face into what he does for a living, to force him to suck in the toxic sludge and choke. Maybe she was as wrong to tell him about Kolya's journal as she was to love him in Ivanovo and Suzdal and Moscow, as wrong as she is still to love him now.

"Why don't you ban *me* from existence, along with the play?" she asks. "I have no doubt you can make me disappear. I've said lots of subversive things. Enough to get me ten years under Stalin, according to my mother."

He stops and shakes his head, as though he were a patient teacher and Sasha, a brazen student bent on challenging authority. "I would never do anything to hurt you, Sashenka," he says, peering into her face. "Remember that." She stares back, and as he looks away, he adds, under his breath, almost as if he wasn't the one uttering the words, "Although I could."

He didn't have to say this. She knows he could, and she is as grateful for his assurance of her safety as she is revolted by the sheer stretch of his power. They have reached the Palace Bridge, and the wind makes her stop and grasp the wrought-iron railing, forcing her to pull her hat down over her ears and hold it from being blown away.

"This is where they met, Kolya and Nadia, isn't it?" says Andrei.

Sasha looks down at the black water hissing around the pillars of the bridge, seeing in her mind Nadia's yellow hat bobbing on the waves. This is where they met. Right here, where they are now standing, probably on the same spot. This is the railing Nadia grasped a quarter century ago, looking down on the same angry waves charging at the granite below. Sasha wishes she could feel as unequivocally about Andrei as Nadia felt about Kolya. What if her mother was right about him after all? What if he is indeed of *a different group of blood*?

"I'm sorry about the play closing." Andrei runs his fingers across her cheek and steps back. "I just wanted to let you know, before you heard about it from the theater administration."

"Thank you. That was very helpful. Now, with *An Ardent Heart* closed, I won't have to yank my guts out to play Matryona and scatter the bloody mess across the stage for the audience to applaud. At least there's comfort in that."

He doesn't answer. A streetcar clangs across the bridge, probably the last one for the night, a small firework of sparks sizzling around its wire above. Andrei knows nothing about acting, so she is not sure he understands what she meant about scattering her blood and guts onstage.

"Do you still read Mayakovsky?" she asks.

He leans on his forearms and looks down into the water, then quietly, just so she can barely hear him, recites a few lines of the poem they memorized in Marik's mother's class in Ivanovo. Most of them learned it by heart simply because this poem was about love, hopelessness, and disappointment, unrevolutionary things that excluded it from the required reading list.

> "My love is
> an arduous weight,
> hanging on you
> wherever you flee."

He stops and waves his hand, as if waving away bad memories. She knows the line that precedes it, "Let's part tonight and end this madness," and he knows that Sasha knows, but they both remain quiet; they don't say a word. She knows Mayakovsky has always been his hero, but she also knows—a stinging thought—that now, working at the Ministry of Culture and banning plays, Andrei has crossed into a place that doesn't care about literary heroes. A place beyond truth, a place beyond art.

Are they parting at last? A minute passes in silence, or maybe five minutes, before he stirs a little, as if words were bubbling up on his tongue, but no sound emerges from his mouth.

"I have a matinee tomorrow," she utters after a stretch of silence. *The Twelve Months*, a fairy tale for children, where she is a stupid, unkind sister with a lisp. "I have to go home."

"I'll get you a taxi," he says, although she knows that no cab, even if you're lucky enough to see one, will ever stop at this hour in the middle of the Palace Bridge. They begin to walk back toward Palace Square, and when a car magically appears, he flags it down with a V sign—the sign for double fare—and the taxi obediently brakes where he is standing. Andrei's figure is etched against the light-green car as he hands a small collection of bills to the driver—shoulders leaning forward, hair tossed by a wet, briny wind.

He turns to Sasha and holds her by the shoulders. "I will be watching you from the Smolny, my Party perch," he says and makes big eyes, trying to imitate what she said, trying to sound funny. "But really, if you ever need anything, anything at all, just let me know. Here is my number." He slips a small card into her coat pocket.

She says goodbye and kisses him on the cheek and for a few moments stays pressed to his face, with its still-familiar smell of skin and tobacco. She thinks of their meetings in the field, of their bed in the Ivanovo grass, of the vast expanse of future, stretching before them, when everything was still possible. Then she does what she has wanted to do since she saw him by the theater door a few hours earlier: she gives him a kiss on the lips, salty and raw—the taste of their Ivanovo afternoons, the taste of this blustery night.

ACT 4

Ivanovo-Leningrad

38

She is back in Ivanovo, the town she has stayed away from for all these years, the memories she has hidden in the most remote corner of her soul. Everything is so much smaller than she remembers: the houses seem to squat under black tar roofs, the streets that she holds in her mind as avenues are alleys, and the trees whose branches blocked the entire sky now barely reach to the lines of the electric wires. The only thing that is still the same in Ivanovo is the dust. The silky dust of the summer covering the roads—its ubiquity, its warmth.

She is not here because she chose to come. A late-morning telegram is fate's way of punishing her long absence; she is certain. It is fate's way of letting her know that once you leave home, you become an outsider, and there is no way back.

In the telegram, her grandfather wrote that Grandma had been taken to the hospital. It was her heart. What else would it be? She got another telegram five days later with the date for the funeral. She didn't go to the funeral. She had two performances of *Twelve Months*, Saturday and Sunday, and the understudy was on maternity leave, so the administrative director didn't allow her to go to Ivanovo, either to say goodbye to Grandma or to bury her. She played *Twelve Months* and then *Quiet Dawns*, and then there was a week off, a rare break when no performance of hers was on the schedule. Every night before the break, she drank in Vladimir Ivanovich's dressing room, to fill the emptiness left where Grandma's image—her tender way of speaking, her cotton dress permeated with the smell of their armoire, her soft fingers on the piano keys—had rested next to Sasha's heart. Every night, they emptied a bottle of vodka, and then she had a crying fit in front of his makeup mirror. A little less drunk than she was, he tried to hold her, but this only made her wail louder and slap her own face. Each time she sobbed and beat herself, Vladimir Ivanovich waited patiently until she calmed down, wiped her face clean of running makeup, and took her home in a taxi. This is what he told her; she doesn't remember any of this. In the morning after the last performance, she went to the administrative director and told him she was leaving for Ivanovo.

Grandpa met her at the train station. Sasha saw him even before the train pulled to a stop, from her compartment, through the haze of the locomotive smoke and window grime. She saw him standing in the middle of the platform, trying to gauge where her car would pull to a stop, his white hair long and wispy, tangled by the breeze, his shoulders stooped. It suddenly became clear to her that Grandma was the one who cultivated his image of a commander. The power he projected, his weight, his authority Sasha was so intimidated by, his permanent seat at the head of the table—all existed because of Grandma. Like a sculptor, she molded him into a stern father and grandfather, a protector, the hard-edged face of the family everyone feared and respected, maybe so that she herself could remain gentle and kind and still survive in the heartland of their heartless motherland. And now, with her no longer there, he simply disintegrated down to his essence: an old man, lost to the point of being extinct, squinting at the numbers on the train cars, hobbling up the platform as the train chugged and clattered forward and sighed its last breath.

It only took seconds, as the front door gave a familiar creak and Sasha stepped over the threshold of the house, for memories to spill over and flood the senses. She had to prop herself up against the cupboard made from dark wood that only turned darker over the years. It was where Grandma kept the everyday plates on the lower shelf and the tea service with red roses they used for holidays—her family's gift for their wedding—on top. The plates were all there, neatly stacked up, the holiday service probably not touched since May 9, Victory Day, when she always pulled out the cups and saucers with roses, two extra sets on the table for Sima and Kolya.

Sasha thinks of a day when she was six or seven, when Grandma took her to get their bread rations and look for lines. If there was a line, she said, you must always join it because there is food at the other end.

They walked along the tracks, away from the loop where the streetcar ended its route, past the gray wooden houses lining their street, past the fences hiding black currant and gooseberry bushes next to what in the summer would be beds with beets, carrots, and dill.

Near the center of the town, behind rows of barbed wire, a group of men in faded military uniforms was clearing debris from a square of wasteland that used to be a school or a store; Sasha was too young to remember. They were German soldiers, prisoners of war, those enemies who had invaded their land. Only they didn't look like enemies or invaders; they looked like the rest of them: sharp-faced and hungry, exhausted by the war.

Grandma stopped by the barbed-wire fence where several men were driving shovels into a pile of dirt spiked with jagged pieces of cement. Their movements were mechanical, as if under their coats, they all had hidden creaky motors that lifted their arms and bent their legs. The German closest to the fence looked up and met her eye. Grandma dipped her hand into her bag, unfolded her ration of bread carefully wrapped in a handkerchief, and fit her arm between the rows of wire, a small brown cube in her open palm. For a moment, the German hesitated, looking around furtively, as if accepting the bread could result in being saddled with more digging, then took it with his muddy fingers, as gnarled as the claws of an ancient bird from Sasha's book of folktales.

His eyes were the color of the frozen ditch on the side of the road, surprised and bewildered.

"Why did you give him your ration?" she asked as the German hastily stuffed the bread into his mouth.

Grandma rewrapped what remained in the handkerchief and put it back into her bag. The words came out gently, as soft as her wrinkles, as sad as her eyes. "He is someone's son, too," she said and motioned for Sasha to move on, probably thinking of her own son Kolya, the one still missing in action, hoping that he was alive somewhere in a foreign land, hoping that someone would offer him a piece of bread.

39

It is three days past Grandma's name day—Elena's day, the day her name saint was born and the day Grandma was buried. This is always the time when lilacs burst into bloom, and through the kitchen window, Sasha can see a bush frothed in purple, branches swaying in the breeze. The kitchen now has a faucet—when did they lay down pipes for running water? An old nylon stocking used to wash dishes, crisscrossed by runs beyond repair, sits on the lip of the sink next to a bar of laundry soap, just as it did when she was a girl. She picks it up and closes her hand around it to feel the greasy silkiness Grandma felt only days earlier. Is she hoping that some of her warmth has remained in this rag that touched her hands daily, for decades, more often than anything else in the house?

The dining room table is littered with issues of *Pravda* and a scattering of handwritten receipts, a sight Grandma would never have allowed in her house. Sasha looks up at the wall with Kolya's paintings she remembers so well. One of them, *The War Ration*—a slice of black bread and a small fish, as dark and dry as the bread—is hanging at an angle, revealing a patch of blue wallpaper underneath, bright as a cornflower, not discolored by light. She straightens the frame, and the original deeper blue of the wallpaper disappears. It is back to its washed-out color, the wear of time. It's back to order now, as Mama would say.

Mama and Grandma are both gone. And how many are left of those who used to inhabit this house? Sima is buried in Ivanovo; Grandma is there, as well, although on the other end of the cemetery that burst beyond its original boundaries decades ago; Kolya, most likely, under layers of mud and other bodies at the Leningrad Front; Mama in Leningrad. Besides Grandpa, she is the only one left.

The door to her grandparents' room is open, and she walks in as she used to when she was a child and wanted to play under Grandpa's drafting table that is still jostling for space with the armoire. The bed is in the corner, its hand-crocheted cover Grandma knitted pulled on hastily and crumpled in places. Sasha straightens it, ironing out the white lace with her hand, just as Grandma would have done. Then she steps to the armoire and opens its heavy door, something she has never done before, something she was never allowed to do. She feels she is allowed now. Grandma's dress is still hanging inside, the dark-blue cotton dress with little white stars and a white collar she remembers so well, the one that always gave her the woody smell of home. Sasha holds the soft fabric between her fingers, then buries her face in it, sniffs the smell out of the collar and the sleeves, inhales whatever is left of Grandma, now all ephemeral, all fleeting. All gone.

The shelves on the left are filled with packs of aspirin and tetracycline, with rolls of bandages and cotton, with knitting needles and a rainbow of crocheting thread, the same things Mama kept in their Leningrad armoire. The top shelf seems to be empty, and for no reason whatsoever, she stands on tiptoe and shoves her hand up to swipe around its bottom. Her hand slides over what feels like a small box, but she is too short to close her fingers around it, so with the help of a stool from the dining room, the box is now in her hands, and she is back on the floor.

From the window, Sasha sees Grandpa in the courtyard, pulling the yellow bursts of dandelions out of a bed of radishes, as she holds the box like a stone weighing on her palms, something she already knows she shouldn't have taken down from its deliberate hiding place. Something that ought to have stayed out of sight where it belonged, where someone placed it not to be found. But it is too late. It is in her hands now, claiming its space with sudden urgency, deliberate and jarring.

She lowers herself onto the stool and peers out the window again, as if looking away would make the box in her hands vanish back into its shelter on the top shelf of the armoire. Grandpa has pulled out the last dandelion and is now cranking the rusty handle of the courtyard well, waiting for the bucket to creak its way up from the echoey darkness into daylight. A watering can is waiting at his feet, ready to be carried to the bed of carrots and beets. Sasha pulls up the lid of the box. Inside is a book-size square wrapped in the kind of cloth Grandma used to make cottage cheese. Inside the cloth, after she untangles it, is a piece of cardboard bent in two, held by a rubber band. Someone has made an effort to disguise what is inside, trying to hide it not only from an outsider accidentally stumbling onto it but also from himself.

She weighs the folder on her palm, as if its heft could determine its importance, as if the act of staring at its brown cover could reveal what is contained inside. Behind the window, Grandpa is lugging a watering can in one hand and a bucket in the other, his shoulders stooping under their weight, his knees nearly buckling. She didn't know he was so old. Or did he suddenly get old because Grandma is no longer here to fill him with reasons to go on, reasons beyond the garden with its watering and weeding?

The rubber band around the folder crumbles under her fingers, but the creased cardboard doesn't spring open, kept folded for years. How many years—five, fifteen, twenty? How long has this box been sitting on the top shelf of the armoire, away from anyone's reach?

Sasha doesn't want to wedge herself between the past and present again; she doesn't want to become complicit in another secret. But with the empty box in her hand, she knows she already has.

She straightens the crease and tries to massage away the years of storage with her fingers. The inside feels about a centimeter thick. She thinks of the storage space above the kitchen where years ago she found Kolya's journal, of its cramped interior that smelled of dust and old shoes and that held so many secrets. She closes her eyes and sees the magazines with poetry by the writers no longer recognized by the state, recipes for dishes whose ingredients have long vanished from their store shelves, hats—the objects of frivolity and luxury— that women gave up wearing decades ago. She thinks of the small things that made up their life here: Mama helping Grandma shred heads of cabbage, then pouring salt over the crunchy layers that were stuffed into a barrel until the slivers of thick leaves reached the brim; of Grandma singing as she knitted another sweater or another pair of mittens; of Mama sorting strawberries and currants before she poured them into copper bowls to make jam; of the life Sasha so deliberately left to be an actress. And now the question stares her in the face: Was it worth it? Have her performances and her acting changed anything or anyone? Have they brought back the forbidden writers, or the forgotten foods, or even women's hats that all those years before the Great Terror had kept her grandmother elegant and young?

Inside the folder is an envelope, long and narrow, with foreign stamps and red-and-blue airmail stripes around the edges. It is not at all like one of the Russian envelopes, plain and square. It is addressed to her grandparents, in a handwriting that is definitely Russian in the way it effortlessly loops the letters together, the way they taught them cursive writing in first grade, through hard work, repetition, and shame. On the other side is the return address that makes the blood drain from her veins: Nikolai Kuzmin, 41 Grand Street, New York, USA. A letter from Kolya.

The stamp on the envelope is a washed-out blot of black ink, the post date dissolved, impossible to make out. The top of the envelope is neatly cut open with a knife, the way Grandpa opens all mail, and Sasha yanks out the folded pages, the date glaring from the top right corner: 15 of April, 1956. Twelve years ago.

40

*My dearest mamochka, papochka, Galochka, and Sashenka
(whom I've never met but who should now be thirteen).*

For a second, she raises her eyes and looks at Grandma's dress hanging
in the armoire, its little white stars beginning to twirl in a wild dance
before her eyes, together with the whole room. I am now twenty-five,
she wants to scream to him. I have lived my entire life with your paintings and your journal; with your disdain for the lies of our motherland; with your story of Nadia and the war, which to a large extent
has defined my life. I have lived with your memory but without you,
because you were dead. You were the first to leave us, before Mama,
before Grandma, maybe even before Sima, who died in this house in
1942. You were our conscience, our truth. Just like Theater is for me.
So why did you not return after the war? Why weren't you here to give
me guidance, to protect me from floggings and old neighbors' gossip,
to stand in for my father? Why did you abandon me?

As tears blur her vision, she sniffles them away and continues
reading.

*It took me so long to write because I was afraid to send you a letter
from the United States. For all these years, I've been torn apart by
not being able to contact you, to tell you that I am alive and well*

because of what we hear about Stalin and his terror. I've heard that a letter from the West could land someone in prison, and I didn't want this to happen to any of you, so I decided to keep silent, as difficult and heart-wrenching as it was. But after Stalin's death, and particularly after Khrushchev's speech, things seem to be different, so I'm hoping this letter will reach you and cause you no harm.

I sent you my journal from the Leningrad Front, with a soldier who was demobilized and going back home to Ivanovo. Did you get it? I only received one letter from you, addressed to the Leningrad Front, where you wrote about Sashenka's birth and Sima's death in 1942, only a few weeks apart. I cried, tears of joy and tears of sorrow. I was lucky to survive when so many others didn't. All these years since the war ended, eleven endless years, every day I fought with myself not to tell you I was alive, not to write to you, to send you a telegram, to call. It was a struggle, and I had to remind myself that I couldn't selfishly announce what I wanted you to know because it would hurt you, and that was the last thing I wanted to do. I wanted so much to be with you, but I couldn't be there. I miss all of you terribly; I miss the dusty road that led to our house, the brown oilskin of the river, the smell of pirozhki Mamochka always baked for my birthday. And I couldn't write to you; I couldn't even tell you how much I missed you all.

If you're reading these lines, please know that all I think about is you, my dearest mamochka and papochka, you Galochka, and Sashenka, whom I've never met but who so often comes to me in my dreams. She is always little, four or five, in a navy-blue dress and canvas shoes rubbed with chalk to make them whiter, the way I remember Galochka was dressed for our family photograph when she was that age.

Sasha looks up from the letter and takes a breath. What was true only a few minutes earlier—Grandma's fresh grave dug by the same two drunks with veiny faces who have dug every grave she can remember, the cotton dress that still holds her smell, Grandpa watering and weeding as if this routine would erase this last week from his memory and grant him peace—is no longer real. Reality seems to have shifted, the past and the present bleeding into each other, the straight timeline crumpling into an accordion of chaos, making everything muddled and disorderly, something Mama would have hated. But she is no longer here to tell Sasha how unruly all of this is or how much she abhors this bedlam.

Sasha looks down at the boards of the floor, scuffed almost white by their feet, by the intertwined lives now all happening at once. She sees her five-year-old mother in a navy dress, a picture she remembers from Grandma's photo album. Did Sasha also have a dress like this, with a white sailor's collar stretched over her shoulders, complete with the canvas shoes rubbed with chalk? She begins to feel the weight of its thick, heavy cotton on her arms. Was it her mother's dress or Sasha's? She lifts her eyes and through the window she sees Kolya standing by the apple tree, in round glasses that make his features even softer, trying to reach an apple dangling on the highest branch, laughing at his own clumsiness when the branch he is holding slips out of his hand and whips him in the face. As images flood her consciousness, the present and the past jostle for space, crowding the room like pieces of furniture from her childhood, bending and breaking the paths of their lives she has always assumed to be linear. She stares down at the letter in her hands, at her and her mother's names written twelve years ago with such fierce urgency somewhere on the other side of the world.

When the Leningrad Front moved west, I moved with it. So much death had passed before my eyes by then that I couldn't comprehend how my soul could still take more in. I was almost numb, and yet we had to keep walking, pulling our cannons and machine guns and carrying our backpacks filled with rations, ammunition, and unsent letters home. I walked and pulled cannons, like everyone around me. As the Germans retreated, they mined the roads, and we had to move carefully, inching forward. In my mind, I can still see an armored vehicle twisted into a tangle of metal parts, bodies of soldiers blasted out of the truck. A wounded cow baying by the side of the road, the image of a burning building reflected in its eyes. I still see a dog running across a charred field, a human bone in its mouth.

Somehow I survived the worst two years of the war, the Leningrad Front, and then I almost didn't survive. One foolish misstep got me captured, although it should have cost me my life. Would it be better to have been killed than captured by the Germans? After being a soldier, would it be better to be dead or be a prisoner of war, with the big letters SU—Soviet Union—painted on the back of my military coat in indelible white paint? We were marched west, hundreds of prisoners, in our torn boots and uniforms infested with lice, until we arrived in a prison camp somewhere in Germany. It was as bad as you can imagine: yellow drinking water with stains of machine oil, dysentery, rotten turnips, routine beatings with a gun barrel, and yet I only grasped at one thing, life. I would have never known, even after three years at the front, how fiercely we claw for life, even life in a German prison camp.

We escaped just before the camp was liberated in April of 1945, those of us who were still alive, everyone ecstatic and free, no longer prisoners of war. We were ready to go back home. Or were we? There were fifty-six nationalities in the camp, but I only made friends with two men. Yura was from Pinsk and slept on the bunk below mine. He was captured just as I was, on a reconnaissance mission, stalking through the woods right into the enemy position. My other friend from the bunk above was John from Saint Petersburg, America, who was captured in Normandy. Saint Petersburg, can you imagine? We were born on different sides of the world and yet our cities had the same name. He taught me some English, and I taught him some Russian, so he called me Nick and I called him Vanya. Yura didn't trust him, accusing him of being a capitalist spy. But one look at John's face—freckles and a gap between his front teeth—made me laugh off Yura's warning, despite Yura being a veteran and having served in the Finnish War.

Yura told me stories about that war, about him witnessing how our prisoners were exchanged for captured Finns. He saw them marching in columns toward each other, the Finns reaching their comrades first, embracing and kissing them. When our captured soldiers reached our side, Yura and thirty or so other soldiers were ordered to encircle and escort them to a nearby barrack behind rows of barbed wire. One of the released soldiers tried to embrace Yura, who fought off the soldier's hug as if he were contaminated. The lieutenant's command was clear. "Freeze!" he yelled. "One step and we'll shoot." Those prisoners of war, so happy to be back on their home soil, were now our enemies. We all knew what Stalin said: "Soviet soldiers do not surrender. There are no prisoners of war. There are only traitors."

There were no trials. There were days of interrogation, all ending in the same verdict. They were all declared traitors for having been captured and were given six years in labor camps in Vorkuta.

So was I ready to go home? Yura was, despite what he witnessed in 1940. He was ready to see his family in Pinsk, silent about a possible Vorkuta camp diversion. The end of the war was in the air: we knew it when the guards deserted during the night and those of us who could escape, escaped. A day later, the US troops liberated the camp, although there weren't many of us left to liberate. "So what are you going to do?" Yura asked as we stood in the field, our former barracks still in sight. I didn't answer right away, and he became impatient. "Don't you want to go home and live in a great country?" he asked, looking over the forest, where the sun was rising. "The country that won the world war?"

I thought of all of you. I thought of Nadia, wishing I were as sure as Yura, as clearheaded and free of doubt. "I want to live in a normal country, not a great one," I said. "A country that doesn't kill its own." Yura just shrugged, saluted us goodbye, and started walking east. I wish I felt as optimistic as he did, as certain about the future.

I couldn't go east, not yet. For a few weeks, John and I stayed with the American division that liberated our camp, pulling bodies out of shallow graves, then moving north from Bavaria toward Berlin. The west, despite the magnitude of its colossal ruin, lay powerful and calm, like a large, sleeping lion. By the time we reached Berlin, Germany had surrendered. "Come with me to the States," said John, who by then—from our conversations in two broken languages and from my drawings—knew about all of you, my art studies, and Nadia. "If you go back, they'll kill you. You're talented, and maybe someday you'll be famous and rich," he said and smiled, a naive smile showing the gap between his front teeth.

So clearheaded, so simple, so American. I was already in the west—beyond our borders that were soon to close shut and be guarded day and night again—having paid with four years of hell for a one-way ticket out of my motherland's murderous embrace. But in my mind I saw all of you, even Sashenka; I saw our Ivanovo house, and my Leningrad art classroom, and Nadia on the Palace Bridge, her yellow hat bobbing in the waves.

In 1941, after Nadia's arrest, I went to the prison on Liteyny Prospekt and stood in line with hundreds of others looking for their loved ones—a useless act brought on by overpowering guilt. When my turn came, a woman behind a glass window ran her hand down the long list of names until her finger slowed down and froze. "Without the right of correspondence," she muttered and looked up, *calling the next person in line. I only learned later what this meant: Nadia didn't have the right of correspondence because she had already been executed.*

We remained in Berlin for a few days, or was it weeks? It was a strange time, almost surreal, pulsing with energy that radiated from the law-abiding Americans, the mild-mannered British, and from my compatriots, who drove too fast on the broken streets and shouted about their victories in the loud, arrogant voices of winners. I walked around the city with my pad and pencil, soaking in this air of impossible unity, albeit short-lived, of buds of the future unfolding before my eyes. And then one morning, John charged into the room where I slept, dropped his backpack by his feet, and yelled that I should get up and catch the plane with refugees leaving for America. I had only a few seconds to make the decision that has haunted me ever since.

Now you know everything there is to know. I live in New York. I never got married. I've been without you all for sixteen years, and I can wait no longer. Please forgive me for leaving you after the war, for not coming back. I was young and selfish, obsessed with my art, blinded by freedom and terrified of what the state would do to me for allowing myself to be captured and held as a prisoner of war. I want you to know that John was right, and I've become a little famous. But no amount of fame or money can take away the fact that I am an ocean and a half away from you.

With kisses for everyone, until we are all together again,
Yours forever,
Kolya

41

Sasha lowers the pages onto her lap and sits there. How long? She doesn't know. Images roll before her eyes, things that happened after this letter had already been written and delivered. As she was memorizing her lines for her high school's acting club, as the fire they'd made in the forest was licking at the snow and Andrei was handing the shell to Marik, as she was standing on the platform by the train bound for Moscow, this letter was already in this house, received and stashed away by her grandfather. Was it ever answered? Sasha can't conceive of Grandma, who had been waiting for Kolya until the day she died, running to the gate every time it creaked, not answering this letter. She can't imagine her not getting on a train to Moscow, with the letter in her purse; not taking a taxi straight to the Lubyanka KGB Headquarters and demanding—in a leaden voice Sasha heard only once—an immediate visa to see her son in the United States.

The bang of the front door plucks her out of her trance, and she knows it is Grandpa coming back, having finished his watering and weeding. She hears him stomp his feet on the doormat; she hears him wheeze and lumber toward where she is sitting, in front of the open door of the armoire, with his son's letter, plucked out of darkness, in her lap.

For a few seconds he takes it all in, and she watches his jaw tighten and his nostrils flare as if he were taking a deep breath.

She rises from the stool and thrusts the letter into his face.

"Did you at least have the decency to write back?"

He doesn't answer, but she sees his eyes darken, despite a sudden ray of sun that slants through the window from the courtyard.

"What are you doing in my room?" he roars.

"You know what I'm doing in your room," she says in a voice she has never dared use in this house before. "You know what I'm doing, and you know what I'm holding in my hand." She realizes this is the first time in her life that she has ever confronted him, a thought that surprisingly doesn't make her knees wobble because she is no longer afraid of him. "Answer me!" she demands, knowing she is the only one left to whom he must now answer.

His face has stiffened, a ripple of hard wrinkles, like bark on an old oak. He turns his head away from her, clamps his hand into a fist. His fingers are old and gnarled, joints swollen with arthritis, and there is dirt under his fingernails. "My son was a traitor," he says, spitting the last word out as if he were spitting out poison.

His words are hardly a revelation. This is what Sasha expected to hear, but she knows this is only the beginning of their battle.

"You had no right," he sputters. "Who gave you the right?"

Sasha leans toward him, the pages with Kolya's handwriting in her hand like a weapon. "Did you have the courage to tell Grandma about this letter?" she demands, although she already knows the answer.

He is silent, and she is livid, sparks of rage spewing in her throat. "Did you tell her that her son was alive?" she shouts.

"This"—he stabs his index finger at the letter—"would have killed her."

"This?" She lifts the letter. "This would have killed her?" she yells. "This?" She shakes the letter, a piece of damning evidence that sprang to light twelve years too late. "This would have given her a reason to live! She waited for this letter her whole life. For this piece of paper. For proof that Kolya was alive."

Her grandfather grips the bedpost behind him, leans on it, and sits down, his hand clutching at his chest. A terrible thought rises in her mind: if he died here, right in front of her, it wouldn't even make her cry. It wouldn't make her feel anything.

"I did write back," he says, his voice muffled, as if it came from an empty barrel. "I wrote back that we were ashamed of him. I wrote that he was a coward. That we no longer have a son."

"You wrote *we*?" she says. "You wrote *we*, without ever showing the letter to Grandma?" In her mind, Sasha can see her grandfather carefully inscribing the foreign address in Latin letters, sealing the envelope by spitting on the glue and holding it with two fingers, as though it were a worm.

"You know nothing about the war," he growls. "You know nothing and have no right to judge me. He should have died like a soldier. Instead, my son was a traitor."

"You're right. I only know about the war from what Kolya wrote in his journal. And from what Mama told me. But that was enough for me to know he was not a traitor. Enough to know that he was a hero in a country that betrayed him."

"We fought, we lost millions, but we won," he says, the old fire sparkling in his eyes once again. "We saved the world. Soviet Russia, the first socialist state, under the leadership of Stalin, saved the entire world."

There is nothing Sasha can say to this. It's useless to tell him that Stalin killed as many millions of their own people as Hitler did, that their motherland is nothing but a colossal mountain of lies. Her Bolshevik grandfather, ardent in his self-righteousness, will remain here until the end of his days, tending to his radishes and apple trees, dusting the branches of black currants with DDT, cranking the handle of the well, leafing through the four pages of *Pravda*. Fossilized like an ant in a piece of Baltic amber. Sasha finds perverse satisfaction with the image she has conjured up in her mind—her grandpa as a relic—but she can see he isn't yet ready to fossilize and give up his power. His nostrils flare, and he draws in breath as he used to do before he flogged her.

"You're nothing but an arrogant fool," he thunders. "You think you know things, but you don't. You think you're like one of those pundits who live in the capital and see the truth." He straightens his spine, pulls his shoulders back. "The truth is that you know nothing. You're blind, just like your mother. You don't see that all these years, you've been pining for a murderer. A man who killed his own father."

His words strike her with the stinging force of nettles whipped across her face, and now it is Sasha's turn to grab the bedpost. The day of the fire flashes in her memory, the figure of Andrei crouched in front of the smoldering heap of wood that used to be his house, a smell of wet ash hanging in the air.

"Everyone knows that his father was nothing but a drunken convict. A man who threw a Molotov cocktail through the window of his house to trap his wife inside. That was his way to get back at her for all those times she dragged him back home, his shirt stained with vomit and his pants soaked with piss. All those bystanders, the crowd that watched, think they know the truth, but what they saw was what became the official story. I was in the garden, and I saw what really happened. I saw it all."

Sasha lowers herself onto the other end of the bed. They are both sitting now, facing each other.

"I knew Andrei wanted to kill his father, even before the roof cratered and the house collapsed. I saw him with my own eyes. I saw him pick up a rock big enough to crush through his drunken father's skull. But the thug saw what his son was up to. He smashed a bottle in his hand against the fence; then he turned toward the crowd. One of the neighbors yelled at him to drop the bottle. Instead he shouted back a squall of curses and took a few wobbly steps. That was when he lost his balance and fell." Her grandfather pauses, takes a breath, stares into space in front of him. "It would've been so easy if he'd died right then.

The son rushed forward and squatted over him, to see what he was hoping to see. The drunk's face was bloodied from the fall, but he opened one eye and looked up as if waiting for the verdict. His hand was still holding the bottle, a bloody circle on his shirt, but it was only a minor wound. Not deep enough to kill him. I could see that from where I stood, and his son could, too."

Sasha draws a deep breath and runs her palm over her cheeks as if to sweep away the words her grandfather is pressing upon her, rubbing into her face.

"There was still a rock in Andrei's hand, and I saw him linger. Maybe he imagined what should've been that miscreant's death. Maybe he imagined yanking his father to his feet so that he would tumble straight into the flames. It would be like flinging him directly into hell. But that didn't happen. What happened was that with his back to the crowd, Andrei closed his fingers around his father's hand with the broken bottle and drove the jagged glass deep under his ribs. The father gasped, but the two of us were the only ones to hear it."

Sasha almost gasps, too, but stifles a groan in the depth of her throat. Grandpa's words metamorphose into images in her mind, rushing before her eyes like frames of a film she would rather not see. Scenes of what Andrei had told her over the years and what he hadn't told her, what he couldn't tell her. She thinks of how his face cringed into a mask of hatred when he spoke about his father after the fire, when he spat out his father's camp stories, almost as if he had to purge them out of his system. She thinks of their walk to the Neva when Andrei admitted he had done something that his father-in-law could send him to prison for. Something that was too late to confess to her, too late to mend. She thinks of the wife Andrei did not choose. Now it all begins to make sense. Like colors in a kaleidoscope, with one turn of Grandpa's hand, Andrei's cryptic stories and his refusal to explain anything have snapped together, arranged into a pattern.

Sasha gets up and stuffs the pages of the letter into the envelope with foreign stamps. "I'm going back to Leningrad tomorrow," she says, walking to the door, heading for the exit from her Ivanovo life. She turns back one last time and sees a commander again—snow-haired, rooted to this house, not nearly extinct—her grandfather, who has fought his last battle and won.

Past Kolya's paintings on the walls, past Grandma's holiday tea-cups in the sideboard, she flees to the room she used to share with her mother, where she kneels by her suitcase and carefully fits the letter into the zipper compartment on the bottom. It will stay there in dark safety until she arrives home, to her Leningrad apartment, where she will expose it to the milky light streaming through the windows, the light Kolya painted so well, where she will decide what to do about the two secrets revealed today: her uncle's letter from America and the truth just forced upon her.

42

She stares at the card Andrei gave her, at his name printed in bold official letters, Andrei Stepanovich Gordeev. Would anything be different now if he had told her what really happened on the day of the fire, what transpired later between him and his father-in-law? Would her knowing the truth have brought them closer together or torn them even further apart? Andrei and Kolya, the two names ingrained in her heart, the two Ivanovo revelations that now seem inherently connected. She rereads the handwritten pages of the letter several times until she, too, begins to question Kolya's decision not to go home, until she begins to hate herself because this doubt diminishes her, makes her just like Grandpa, cruel and small-minded. What is it in Kolya's letter that brings this doubt to the surface, makes it unfold like the petals of a poisonous flower? Why wasn't his love for Nadia strong enough to make him return to look for her, not to give up after just one trip to the Liteyny prison? Why did it take the word of only one bureaucrat to end his search?

Andrei's name stares back at her from the card, constricting her heart, making her wonder if what she feels for him is a disease, a stubborn virus she has been unable to clear from her system. Is that what has been feeding her toxic doubts about Kolya? Is that why she keeps returning to the question of how he could be in America, instead of searching for Nadia in the wastelands of their country? On a scale with love on one side and the Gulag on the other, shouldn't love always outweigh fear? Shouldn't love outweigh everything?

She lifts the receiver and dials Andrei's number.

~

The car he sends for her flies along Nevsky Prospekt and then turns off toward the Smolny. It is a black Volga, the preferred apparatchik vehicle, a car that smells of gasoline and old leather. Borya, the chauffeur, who is close to his pension age, occasionally glances at Sasha in the rearview mirror, his broad face collapsing into a cascade of wrinkles when he smiles.

"Where do I know you from?" he finally asks.

The recent Gorky television production of *The Philistines*, probably, rather than the latest addition to the theater repertoire, *The Shadow* by Evgeny Schwartz, another play recently decreed as destined for closure by the Ministry of Culture.

"Yes, yes, the Gorky play." Borya nods enthusiastically. "You were the merchant's wife, the one who had an affair." She nods. She is always the one who has an affair, or who is unkind to her stepchildren, or who is morally bankrupt in so many other ways. She is a character actress: a villain, or a bully, or a miser, or a simpleton. From Borya's eyes in the rearview mirror, she can see he is completely satisfied with her character's moral failings.

Why, in all these years, did Andrei tell her nothing about what he had done? Was he paralyzed by the fear of her judgment, embarrassed by the prospect of her condemnation? Did he think she would be harsh and unforgiving? She stares out at the tree-lined canal where a motorboat is plowing through gray water, overtaking Borya's car, its engine revving up unsettling questions in her head. Does she really know Andrei? Did she ever know him? Why does she doubt him so much? Why does she doubt Kolya?

As the motorboat speeds under a bridge and disappears behind a bend in the canal, her memory springs twenty years back, to Mama on a park bench, smiling at the pilot in uniform Sasha had hoped would become her father. For months, when she was seven, she rode on his shoulders around the courtyard, triumphant of her accomplishment, past the neighbors' envious glances, so certain that she had finally found a father, so sure that the thrill boiling inside her would never end. It did end, despite her stubborn, childish confidence in the future, despite the fact that she didn't doubt him at all, not even for a second.

Is this the reason she now lacks certainty in Andrei and Kolya, the two most important people left in her world?

Soon, the Smolny Cathedral sails into view, its pearly cupolas glinting softly against the sky. Next to it in the yellow buildings of Smolny resides the Leningrad Communist Party. The car bounces through the main gate and pulls along the driveway to the entrance. Borya waves for her to get out, and they face two soldiers standing guard at both sides of the door, both holding guns as big as the ones from the classic painting of *The Hunters at Rest* by Perov she saw at the Russian Museum. The soldiers' eyes stare into the distance, but when they see Borya, they silently step aside to let them in. She and Borya walk along a corridor that smells of fresh paint, toward a door with a black sign on the front, where Andrei's full name is etched into a metal plate. Borya knocks on the door, politely shakes her hand, and disappears.

In the few seconds before the door opens, Sasha tries to conjure up the person on the other side, the person she hasn't seen in almost two years, ever since he warned her that his ministry was closing her production of *An Ardent Heart*. The person whose dark secret is now lodged in her chest like a malignant lump. Although she cannot track his bureaucratic trajectory, she is almost certain he has been tracking her artistic one. Behind this door, she is certain that he watches over the entire city of Leningrad—shielded by a wall of bureaucracy everyone in the Theater can feel—controlling its exposure to culture, letting only those plays that won't harm fragile psyches pass through the gates of his censorship. Or is it her anger surfacing, gearing up to distract her from listening to what he is reluctant to say? Would she have learned the truth about his father's death from him rather than from her grandfather had she been ready to listen? Is she about to sabotage, again, the truth she can portray so well onstage?

As she hears the steps on the other side, Sasha takes a breath, trying to silence the pounding in her chest. Andrei opens the door and draws her inside, his arms carefully making their way around her shoulders, his breath a hot puff against her cheek. If anyone were watching them, they wouldn't detect even a glimmer of impropriety in this embrace, the warm greeting of two old friends. He kisses her on the cheek, holds her at arm's length, and peers at her, his hands still on her shoulders. They stand like this for at least a minute, studying each other for changes time may have carved into their faces, for signs that Ivanovo—with its field leading into the forest where their grass bed used to be, and its lilac bushes behind the fence where he stood waiting for her, and its unpaved roads covered with silky dust—is still there, gouged into their hearts.

His eyes have darkened since Sasha last saw him. They seem brown now instead of green; they swallow and trap the light instead of reflecting it; they are wary, guarded eyes. There are parentheses of wrinkles around his mouth, and the hair around his temples has turned gray, as though he has lived through a battle. The air between them is still cold, and neither of them wants to be the first to yield any emotional ground, to expose even a centimeter of vulnerability.

"It's genetic," Andrei says, catching her eye. "My father turned gray when he was only thirty-three, my mother told me." All Sasha remembers of his father's hair was wisps of white bristling from under a cap he never removed when he was outside.

The mention of his mother thaws the air, and he leads her toward the two armchairs that sit around a coffee table by a safe, an intimidating-looking cabinet of steel. *This is a perfect place for top official secrets,* Sasha thinks, imagining the inside of the safe stuffed with dissident files, plans for nuclear attacks on the West, and lists of books and plays that are to be banned. This is, she imagines, where Pasternak's *Doctor Zhivago* and the works of Solzhenitsyn are stacked in neat, forbidden piles, next to the names of film and theater directors whose productions have been pulled from screens and stages because of their insufficient patriotism or the lack of optimism in the lead characters' objectives.

"Do you want some cognac?" Andrei asks before he sits down. It is around four in the afternoon, and she rarely turns down cognac, especially official Party cognac that they never see in stores.

Out of the top drawer of his desk, he produces a small key, turns it in the lock, and the safe door opens noiselessly. Inside, where Sasha imagined dissident files and plans to obliterate the West, presides a round bottle of cognac surrounded by a coterie of small glasses. He fills two of them and raises his glass in a toast, the same honey-colored alcohol they drank in her apartment what seems like a century ago, when she felt happy and light-headed, when she thought their life together was finally about to begin.

"To another reunion," he says—*another reunion* is what their life seems to have come to—and he empties his glass in one gulp with the effortlessness of a regular drinker. Sasha sips the contents of her glass, as though she could fool anyone into thinking that she wasn't one. He pours again, and they drink, and from his quick pace, she knows he is waiting for her to explain why she is here, in this vast office, helping reduce the liquid contents of his Smolny safe.

"Three weeks ago, Grandma died."

She sees him scrunch his face and shut his eyes for a moment, as if her words have struck him on the head. His eyes are even darker when he opens them, as black as Grandpa's well.

"I didn't know," he says, "otherwise I would've helped with the funeral." This seems to be his main function in her life, arranging funerals for her family. "Are you all right?" he asks, although he knows that if she were all right, she wouldn't be sitting in an armchair across from him in the middle of the afternoon with a glass of cognac in her hand.

"Do you remember Kolya's journal?"

He nods. Of course, she knows he remembers.

"I found a letter from Kolya. From America. Dated 1956."

Andrei puts down his glass and straightens in his chair.

"He wasn't killed in the war, like we all thought. He made it to Berlin and then, instead of coming back home, he went in the other direction. He lives in New York now. Or at least he lived in New York twelve years ago."

Her sentences come out short and hesitant, almost reluctant, as if her mouth refuses to wrap around the strange words and validate them with sound.

For a few moments, Andrei is silent, processing the news, his face expressionless, a functionary's face. She doesn't know what is brewing behind this Party mask and its practiced lack of emotion. Is he going to tell her that having a relative abroad has now placed her into the category of traitors? That she is now an enemy of the people, just like all those arrested and sent to the camps?

"This is good news," he says after a minute of silence. "An even greater reason to celebrate."

Is this what he really thinks? Sasha gives him a squinted-eye look, hoping to see the cracks in the stone of his face, the openings into the human features under the mask. Should she believe that he is sincere? And is it possible that he is right?

Why has she doubted Kolya's intentions? Why did she blame him for not coming back to look after her, like a father would, or to search for Nadia? Why does she blame him that he was determined not to die, that he made a choice to avoid the fate of Uncle Seryozha, Uncle Volya, Nadia's family, and millions of others? Why didn't she see Kolya's letter the way Grandma would've seen it—a triumph of life over death, a cause for celebration?

"I have no one else to tell this to," she says. "You are the only one left who knows about Kolya."

"Kolya and Marik, our two big secrets buried in Ivanovo. And here we are, in Leningrad, still stalked by them a half-life later." He pulls a pack of cigarettes out of his pocket and offers her one. "I often think about how we itch to run away from home and then keep searching for it for the rest of our lives."

He is right. Ivanovo, she knows, is tattooed onto her heart. But she also knows that if she hadn't left it to go to Moscow, they wouldn't be sitting here today, sharing their memories, talking about the transience of home. Sasha knows that Andrei knows this, too. Just as he knows that she knows. They are both poster children for *vranyo*, pretending that they live in a normal country, pretending that there is no fiery connection between them. Pretending he is simply helping out an old friend at a trying moment of her life, pouring her a few shots of cognac, offering a cigarette to calm her nerves. Nothing improper, nothing that the Party would frown upon.

"So what do I do with Kolya being alive?"

"What do you want to do?"

She knows what she wants. She wants him to still be alive, twelve years after the letter. She wants to talk to him, to hear his voice. She wants to ask him about growing up in Ivanovo, about his paintings, about the war and what it did to him. About the betrayal of their motherland. Not his betrayal of their motherland but their motherland's betrayal of him. She wants to see Mama through his eyes. She wants to ask him if he ever thinks of her, Sasha, the one he never met.

But she can't, of course, because he lives—if he is still alive—on the other side of the Atlantic Ocean, on the forbidden western side, behind a curtain that never lifts.

She looks at Andrei, who seems to be able to guess what she is thinking.

"To talk to him, is this what you want?"

Sasha nods and lifts her glass to acknowledge his insight.

"Life and fate, this is what it's all about," he says, quickly giving a snort of laughter at what he has just uttered. "There's a Russian novel, *Life and Fate*. It's as good as *War and Peace*, but it's one of those books that will never be published in this country. The author traveled with the Soviet Army all the way to Berlin, just like your uncle. So if Kolya were a writer and not a painter, this is what he would have written. Life and fate." Andrei gets up and walks over to the phone on his desk.

Sasha watches him from her chair, not knowing what he is about to do.

"Do you have Kolya's address in New York?"

She has Kolya's address, written in his own hand on an envelope stuffed into the inner pocket of her handbag. She unearths the envelope and hands it to Andrei, not sure what he plans to do with it, fearful that he could use it against him. Or, possibly, against her?

Andrei picks up the receiver and dials some numbers on his phone. "I need to be connected to Nicholas Kuzmin, 41 Grand Street, New York City, the United States. K-u-z-m-i-n," he spells to the operator. He is told to wait, she guesses, because he holds the receiver away from his ear, as if it were a weight. Sasha doesn't know if this is real or if it's a sick Party joke Andrei has learned in his job at the Smolny. They can barely place a call to Moscow, let alone the

West, so she is keeping her eyes on him, taking puffs on a cigarette, ensconced in her armchair, tired and tipsy and resigned to finish the cognac in her glass. She doesn't believe that it is possible to pick up a receiver and be connected to someone in New York. They all know there is an indestructible barrier that stops any attempts to make such calls. A thick curtain between them and the rest of the world that prohibits all communication. But as the minutes pass and these thoughts grind through her head with crushing slowness, it dawns on her that they are in the Smolny, the control center for the dreaded barrier. It dawns on her—something she should have realized much earlier—that the barrier may be standing right in front of her, a telephone clutched in his hand.

Andrei must hear something on the other end because the phone is now pressed to his ear. "Yes, go ahead," he says, walks over to where she sits, and hands her the receiver. "It's him," he says. "It's Kolya."

His words make no sense. Her uncle's name, the name of someone who has been dead her whole life, used with present-tense immediacy, stuns her senses and renders her mute. This is a Party office in Leningrad in 1968, and it can't be Kolya on the other end of the line, Kolya who has been missing in action since the war, who has been in limbo all this time, not listed among the dead or the living. The possibility of this unimaginable connection has warped the reality around them and emptied her of words. Andrei puts the phone into her hand, cradles his fingers around hers. "Talk to him," he says.

Sasha slowly lifts the receiver to her ear. "Hello," she mumbles, as if falling from a roof.

The voice on the other end is vulnerable, frightened. "Who is this?" he asks in the fragile tone Grandma used whenever there was a knock on the door of their Ivanovo house.

"It's eight in the morning there," Andrei whispers. "We woke him up."

"Uncle Kolya," she says, the words scraping out of her throat that suddenly feels parched. "It's me, Sasha. The one you never met." She doesn't recognize her own voice, a voice he has never heard.

There is silence peppered with static, and she presses the phone tighter to her ear, afraid to miss what he says next.

"Sasha, Galya's daughter?" he says finally, when her ear is numb from the pressure, when she looks at Andrei, desperately, pleading with her eyes for what she should do.

"Yes." She breathes in, not to be overtaken by rising tears, to be able to utter what she wants to say. "I found your letter in our Ivanovo house. Twelve years after you wrote it."

"Sashenka, wait . . ." She hears static again, the noises of fumbling, but now she is grateful for the pause, trying to sniffle away the tears, failing, rubbing them around her face with the palm of her hand. "This is so sudden . . . Please just give me a moment." She tries to imagine Kolya on the other side of the line, the other side of the world, in pajamas and slippers, fumbling for his glasses. "Where are you, Sashenka? Are you in New York? Where are you calling from? How were you able to leave?"

"No, Uncle Kolya, I'm in Leningrad. In a Party office, using an official phone. It's hard to explain." She is glad they are still talking about Party offices and phones and not about Grandma and Grandpa.

"I still don't understand. I never thought I would hear your voice. You weren't even born."

"Grandpa said he wrote back to you."

"I got his letter. I know he was the one who wrote it, not *mamochka*. He was so angry that I didn't return home or die." There is a pause, and she hears a sharp intake of breath. "What he didn't understand is that I did die." She can hear his voice break, and in her mind, she can see him crying into the crux of his arm, the way Grandma did when she needed to hide her tears.

She waits for Kolya to catch his breath. "Is he still alive? Is *Mamochka*?"

By the pause she takes to respond, Sasha can sense that he knows the answer. "Mama died in 1966. Grandma died two weeks ago, just before her name day. That's when I found your letter." She swipes at her eyes as Andrei's hand with a handkerchief comes into her line of vision. She is not sure if she hears the static echoes of her own sobs or Kolya's, on the other side of the world. "They are all gone," she manages to utter.

A minute passes, maybe several minutes, as she takes deep breaths to stop new tears from rising in her throat.

"Tell me about yourself, Sashenka," he says finally.

What should she tell him? What can she tell Mama's brother, whose story she knows as well as her own, her uncle who she always wished had been her father, a man who has been dead for as long as she has been alive and whose voice is now as close as if he were across the street, speaking to her from what can only be another life? "I'm an actress," she says, wiping her nose with Andrei's handkerchief. "I'm all grown-up."

There is more crackling, but she is able to make out his words through the static. "I feel like I abandoned all of you," says Kolya, a phrase that Sasha has often repeated in her mind, a thought that has woken her up at night. *I feel like I abandoned all of you* is what she often mumbles into the darkness at three or four in the morning. Mama and Grandma, Marik and Andrei and every soul in Ivanovo and Moscow who wished her well. This is the moment, with Kolya's guilt only a centimeter away from her own heart, when she knows what she should tell him. She swallows to steady her voice.

"Grandma never gave up hope that she would see you," she says. "To the end of her life, with every creak of the gate, she waited for you to return. Mama brought your war journal to Leningrad when she moved in with me. Your paintings still cover the walls of our

Ivanovo house. You have been with us every minute of our lives. We've never forgotten you," she says, and the more she tries to resist crying, the stronger the pressure pulses behind her eyes, the more her mouth trembles uncontrollably. She sees Mama perched on a stool in Leningrad, telling the story of the demented soldier who brought Kolya's war journal. She sees Grandma on the porch, her body leaning toward the gate she has just heard creaking open, her blue cotton dress as soft as her skin. She sees Nadia on the Palace Bridge, her face fallen, as if she has already glimpsed the future, looking down into the river at the yellow hat blown off by the wind. The three women who loved him, all gone. Sasha sees all this and weeps, and she can hear, through the static, that Kolya, all the way on the other side of the world, is weeping, too.

43

Sasha hangs up and stares at the gleaming phone that has just miraculously given her Kolya. Would Grandma and Mama still be here had Grandpa not hidden Kolya's letter away from them? Would they have died in peace knowing that Kolya was still alive?

She tries to imagine Kolya on that morning in Berlin, forced to make a split-second decision that defined his life. By crossing the border between East and West, he had entered a life from which there was no return. There is no connection between the two worlds, the old and the new, between the two lives, before and after the decision. There is no bridge, no road, not even a footpath. For Kolya, that decision meant death. Kolya died at that moment, and his life in the West is an afterlife.

"I need to go outside." She gets up. "To clear my head."

"I'll go with you," Andrei says. "I'll just walk by your side. We don't have to say anything."

What is going on behind the facade of his face? she wonders. Does his job require him to consider Kolya a traitor for making the decision not to return home, for questioning the sacred mercy of their motherland, for doubting the heroism and sacrifice of the war no one is allowed to doubt?

The little park in front of the Party building is filled with diffused light, and, as always in June, it is difficult to tell afternoon from night. Sasha doesn't know how long they spent in Andrei's office, how long she sat there staring at the phone after the call. It could be six in the evening, or it could be ten at night. They walk along the street toward the Neva, their silence matched by the unusual stillness of the city, interrupted only by gusts of wind from the river. It must be late, Sasha thinks, with most people home, windows lit by the pale light of white nights.

An occasional bus clangs by on the embankment as they cross the nearly empty street and lean on the brown granite banister. The light above the river is so white and thick that you feel you could hold it in your hand. With the baroque center of the city behind them, the view from here is rugged and industrial, necks of construction cranes hanging over the water, drawing long shadows onto its leaden surface with the sun sinking toward the Okhtinsky Bridge. This is the unbound time, the disconnected time, time that has lost its meaning, time where no time exists. Down below is the river—its surface rippling and sparkling in the sun, the image that Sasha knows is still burned into Kolya's brain—its enormity and depth an extension of life itself.

"So what do I do now?" she asks. This is a complicated question, but if it has an answer, her chances of finding it are better here, by the river, in this milky light, at this unknown time.

Andrei turns to her, and his eyes are dark green again, the eyes of their Ivanovo childhood. They are so close that she can no longer make out his whole face: his features have disintegrated and shifted, like she imagines in the Picasso portrait that she has never seen, the one Kolya described in his journal. They stay like this for what feels like several minutes—his chest rising when Sasha takes a breath, the two of them melded into one—their faces only centimeters away from each other, deconstructed and warped. What is she hoping for? That he will announce he is going to divorce his wife and quit his job so that he can be with an actress?

This thought breaks the magic of the moment, and they separate, his features assembling back to normal, his eyes turning brown again.

"I can do something for you that no one else can do," says Andrei, and from the deep place his voice emerges, she knows this is serious. "After all I've done to you, I hope you will accept this as a gift with no conditions." For a minute, he stares at the ripples of water below. "I know I hurt you, and we both know I can't undo what I did." His voice is hoarse, and she can see only one side of his face, a blue vein pulsing under his temple fringed with white hair. "But I can get you on a plane to see your uncle in America."

To go on a plane and see Kolya in America? Did he really say what Sasha thinks he said? She knows he can't be serious, or maybe she didn't hear him correctly, too busy staring at the blue vessel on his temple. Everyone knows that the two words, *go* and *America*, are as incompatible as *acting* and *lying*. No one can simply visit an uncle on the other side of the world, the Western, capitalist side. Even her mother, with her spotless record, wasn't allowed to go to Bulgaria to visit the medical students she had taught, despite receiving an official invitation to meet their parents in Sofia. After a stack of letters vouching for her character, after months of meetings and committees, her request was turned down because the visit was deemed unnecessary. And that was Bulgaria, their southern communist neighbor who believes in their shared shining future. No one Sasha knows has ever crossed over to the other half of the earth. They are all huddled here, on this side of the Iron Curtain, blissfully ignorant about the rest of the world, helplessly content.

Andrei must see the confusion in her face, because he doesn't press her for an answer. "Let's go somewhere we can sit down and talk," he says. "I know a place that's open late."

"And if you like it there, in America," he adds casually, as if in passing, as if what he is about to say amounts to nothing but a trifle, "you can do me a favor and never come back."

44

They are in Kavkazsky restaurant on Nevsky Prospekt, a few blocks from her theater, a hangout for actors to go after a performance. It stays open late; Andrei is right. At this hour it is nearly empty, unoccupied tables with white tablecloths, a couple of potted ficus trees scattered around the grand room, an air of withered luxury more suited to a town in a Chekhov story than the first proletarian city on earth. The scene is complete with a waiter, a disinterested look on his face and an oily stain on his black jacket sleeve. Like the rehearsal space in her theater, this dining room is windowless, and all the light comes from sconces between the tables, the coned light, the trapped light.

There are skewers of lamb and flattened halves of chicken *tabaka* on their plates, the food of Georgia; their glasses are filled with red wine to celebrate Kolya's newly discovered existence. The Georgian wine, despite their waiter's recommendation, tastes like syrupy compote made from a cheap port called *ink*. Nevertheless, it slides down her throat in harmony with the pomegranate sauce, making her head feel light and her body weightless, making her balance, for a little while at least, on the sweet, opaque edge between the harsh light of being sober and the blackness of being drunk. It is the edge where her love for Andrei begins to pulsate with such intensity that it nearly burns, her passion for him freed from its cage by the sweet Georgian wine, just the two of them in this empty restaurant where the present seems to run on a parallel course with the past.

Suddenly Andrei rises from his chair, leans across the table, and kisses her on the lips. It is a mature kiss, longer and more passionate than anything they exchanged in Ivanovo, deeper than the nervous kisses of the first night they spent in Suzdal, more melancholy than the blissful tumult of the few hours in her apartment before he suddenly announced he was married. It is a microcosm of every unfulfilled desire they have ever harbored for each other, the happiness they both know is no longer possible.

The waiter trudges in and looms by their table, forcing them to separate. He doesn't look at all embarrassed; on the contrary, he probably timed this moment to let them know that it is late and he wants to go home.

"We know it's late," Andrei says. "But we're not yet finished." His voice is not commanding, but there are distinct metallic notes in it. It is the voice Party leaders always have in textbooks, firm and assertive. "Why don't you clear away all this," he says and waves at the wreck of the breadbasket and plates and slips a bill into the waiter's pocket, "and bring us some good cognac. And something to chase it with."

A woman in an apron lumbers out of the kitchen and starts piling dirty dishes onto her forearm. A few minutes later, a bottle of cognac arrives, along with small plates of red beans spiced with tarragon and chicken in walnut sauce. He pours, and they drink. This day is ending with cognac, the same way it started. A few sips of alcohol in this empty restaurant remove the last bricks to the wall between them, loosen their muscles, untie their tongues. Sasha feels she may even be able to confront Andrei, tell him she knows the truth about his father's death.

As she weighs the glass of cognac in her hand, she feels words crowding in her head, demanding a release. Is it the alcohol that's prodding those words to break out of her mouth or the kiss she still can taste? Or is it Kolya's voice reaching from the other side, the voice of honesty and Grandma's softness? She doesn't know, but she hears herself begin to speak.

"My grandfather told me what happened on the day of the fire," she hears herself say. "What really happened." She watches Andrei's face tighten up as he leans back. "He was in the garden and saw it all. Your father was the one who set the fire. He didn't die from the fall." She pauses, as she paused before opening the box where Kolya's letter had been hidden. "You killed him."

Andrei balls his fists under his chin and stares down at the stained tablecloth. Does he see what she sees in her mind, the charred carcass of his house, his mother's grave? Does Sasha want him to admit his guilt? Does she want him to repent, to say anything at all? For what feels like several endless minutes, he stares at the tablecloth, and she stares at his face. When he finally looks up, his gaze has lightened. He remains silent a few minutes longer, but she can see that his face has softened, eyes lit with relief.

"I did what I'd wanted to do ever since my father returned from the camps. Ever since I remember." He speaks hastily, words rolling down his tongue, as if all these years he has been waiting for this moment to tell her his story. "As he stood there swaying and bragging about how she finally got what she deserved, all I could think of were those times when I tried to protect her from him. So just as the burning house crashed behind us, as I saw blood soaking his shirt, I knew exactly what I was going to do. For the first time, I knew I could be free of him." Andrei rubs his forehead, shielding his eyes with his palm. "I felt no guilt at that moment, no shame. But I must have felt shame because I drank for weeks. Every night when we returned from work, Vadim— my future father-in-law—set a bottle of vodka on the kitchen table. We drank from tea glasses, just the two of us."

Sasha remembers this from their talk in Ivanovo, when Andrei told her his father's camp stories. The two of them, he and his boss, *hozyaeva*, the masters of everything.

"I don't remember how long I stayed with Vadim and his family. I don't know how many times we left for work and came back together, how many bottles he set down on the table, how many times Natasha and her mother ladled soup into my bowl.

"What I do remember is that on one of those nights, I confessed to him what really happened. I told him I'd killed my father." Andrei props his forehead with his hand and looks down. "And he told me that I was a hero. That I did what I had to do, what he would have done, what any man would have done. That was when he gave me a promotion. He said the Party needed strong, determined men like me."

Andrei stops, presses his palms over his eyes, as if he wants to black out what he saw.

"With the promotion, they gave me an apartment, but I still went to dinner at Vadim's at least once a week, an invitation extended by his wife, without fail. And every time, without fail, I felt Natasha's liquid gaze on me, the heat emanating from her body when she stood close in the hallway to say goodbye. Why am I telling you all this? It doesn't change anything. It can't. Then one day she came to her father in tears and begged him to do anything to get me to marry her." He pauses. "That was when Vadim gave me a choice"—the word echoes in Sasha's head, in sync with her pulse—"a choice between a life of hard labor for murder and a life of privilege with his daughter."

For a minute, they are both silent. "But he knew that what you did was to avenge your mother's death," Sasha says quietly.

Andrei smirks. "At that point, who would have cared about this tiny detail? Not Vadim. Not the courts. Not anyone." He exhales loudly, as if he wants to rid his body of every detail of the story he has just told her. "This was the beginning of the end—not my first downfall and not my last."

In her mind, Sasha replays the day when she saw him crouched by the smoldering pile of wreckage that used to be his house. She didn't know then that everything had been already set in motion, that their lives had been already placed on tracks running in opposite directions.

Andrei stares down at the stains from the food and wine, his hand wiping away the invisible detritus from the tablecloth, as if he hoped to make it white and crisp again.

"When my father got back from the camps, he told me stories of what it was like, stories I refused to believe back then. Back in Ivanovo, I told you some of those stories. He said that among his fellow inmates were former Party members who had interrogated prisoners and carried out horrific verdicts. Now, in a kind of cosmic mockery, they found themselves incarcerated for the same crimes for which they had tortured and executed others. Later I thought of it as universal retribution. But what struck me most about his stories was that the victims' denouncers were not some foreign agents. The denouncers were their own neighbors and friends. Sometimes even their cousins, their own brothers and sisters."

Sasha thinks of Kolya's journal, of Kolya talking to the neighbor from Nadia's landing, of her suspicious, incriminating gaze from behind the door held by a chain. She thinks of the university secretary with nails bitten down to the skin, looking for Nadia's file, then finding it and telling him to leave, condemnation in her voice.

"Isn't it ironic," says Andrei, "that the executioner becomes the victim, and the victim becomes the executioner? Our system, if you think of it, is pure genius: executioners and victims are the same people. The engine of death has been in motion for decades, and no one is guilty, because everyone is guilty."

They sit looking at each other, not moving. It is so quiet in the room that Sasha can hear the buzzing of a neon lamp over the kitchen door.

"And you know what I'm wondering . . . ," Andrei says, glancing away from her, as if he is no longer able to look Sasha in the eye. "If I'd been born earlier, would I have also become an executioner, as my father-in-law insists? Would I have followed orders and murdered and tortured prisoners, as he did? Would I have shot a kneeling man in the back of his head?" He looks at her and squints. "It is a terrifying question. And if I'm willing to be honest, I don't know the answer. That's what really cripples me, what keeps me up at night." He pauses and leans back.

"Every day we make choices." His voice is thick, and his eyes are down. "Or at least, we think they are choices. I handed Marik that unexploded shell, a choice that killed him. Kolya decided not to return home, a choice that killed him, too, at least in the eyes of his family. You made a choice to go to Moscow." He pauses after *Moscow*, and she knows that of the three, this is the most consequential choice for him. "But there is one thing my father-in-law told me about choices that has always stayed with me: you either pull the trigger, or you kneel on the floor."

He straightens himself in his chair and then leans forward, as if to share another secret.

"That's why you have to go to America. You have to get out of here before it's too late, before the poison has seeped into your veins and you become just like the rest of us." He peers into her face for a few moments as Sasha shakes her head. "I know you think this could never happen to you, but with time, it does happen. It happens without you even knowing it. It happens to all of us." He props himself on his elbow and leans so close, she can feel his breath. "You were born in the wrong country, Sashenka. You're naive and uncompromising. You don't bend, and sooner or later, our motherland will break you. It breaks everyone."

She is not sure he is right, but she knows one thing: this is what her mother used to tell her, too. She wasn't as laconic, but she worried about Sasha's lack of self-censorship as much as she worried about all the other dangers.

Like a flash of lightning, an idea makes her heart lurch with hope. "Then let's go to America together," she says. "We will leave the past here. All the past, yours and mine. We will start over."

His face convulses into a grimace, and he shakes his head, as if what she has just said is a perfect example of her inability to bend. "I can't start over. I wish I could." For a moment, he closes his eyes, as though she didn't hear a word he said. "It's like when you try to carry a load that's too heavy. At first you manage to lift it, but after you've lugged it for a while, you can no longer carry it any farther. I know this feeling from when I unloaded freight trains. You try to carry the weight, you try to balance it and steady yourself, but it pushes you down further and further and it finally breaks your back. It's broken me, this load. It's too late for me to stop doing what I do. It's been too long." His hand rises to his throat, and his fingers fumble to undo the top two buttons of his shirt. "My back has been broken. I can no longer move forward. I'm now deep in this muck, up to my ears, drowning."

This late-night talk laced with wine and cognac, in this surreal, empty place, seems as close as they will ever get to their moment of truth, and Sasha has to try one last time. She needs to exhume her guilt of leaving Ivanovo for Moscow, surrender it to him.

"I know I'm naive, but this is our only chance. I left you at a terrible time. It is my fault that you've been drawn into this swamp, and I want to pull you out. Please. Let's leave together and start over."

She peers into his face, waiting. He doesn't say anything, but she can read the answer in his eyes. There is no light left there, no life. His silence is his answer. He hesitates, as if he were ready to say something, but it is only a hesitation, a bullet jammed in the throat of a gun.

Sasha has to turn away from the death of everything she sees in his eyes. Is this who she has been waiting for all these years, a man with dead eyes, a married Party functionary, a censor of her art?

"We should go," she says.

She gets up, and the waiter, with an expression of relief on his face, rushes to their table with a bill.

"I will arrange for you to go to America to see Kolya," Andrei says. He is back to being practical, back to arranging things, something he does so well. Does he think that his arrangement of this impossible trip, which Sasha knows involves breaking Party rules, is the deed that will redeem him? Does he think that sending her across the ocean will give him hope for atonement? The idea of going to America sounds surreal, but not any more surreal than hearing Kolya's voice on the phone a few hours ago, which now feels like a different life.

45

She wakes up at three in the morning and stares into the dark, the previous night—colossal, endless—immediately asserting itself in her mind, burning through the fog of sleep like the morning sun. The bitter taste of cognac still lingers in her mouth, little hammers of headache banging against the inside of her skull. The images rise impatiently, pushing against one another. Andrei's graying hair, a phone receiver pressed to her ear, a white tablecloth full of stains.

This is Sasha's final resolution, sealed by the darkness in her room: she will no longer allow herself to think about him. This time, at last, she will purge him like a deadly contagion; she will scoop him out, like Grandpa scoops dry their Ivanovo outhouse, bucket by bucket; she will rip him out of her heart, just as Masha tears out her love in *The Seagull*, by the roots.

She will no longer allow him to invade her mind. Instead, she will think about the place where Kolya lives, America. Sasha peers into the dusk, which has revealed the outlines of the table and the white panels of the door. Is it possible to conjure up something one knows nothing about? Here, on this side of the Iron Curtain, with no cracks to peek through, what do they know about America?

In the summer of 1959, her first summer in Moscow when she was admitted to study at the drama school, a miniature America sprouted up in Sokolniki Park outside the city, the American National

Exhibition that Sveta and Sasha waited three hours to enter. They had already read what Khrushchev said to the US president three weeks earlier, when the Expo opened. *In another seven years we will be on the same level as America. When we pass you along the way, we'll wave to you.* With the rest of the curious crowd, they gawked at the world they were promised in only seven years: cars laden with chrome, cameras that dispensed instant pictures, films that were not banned, stainless steel refrigerators, robot vacuums, and a machine that washed your dirty dishes in less than thirty minutes. They stared at a blonde woman modeling a dress, which Sveta considered for a minute and said she could sew one just like it, if only she could get her hands on three square meters of decent fabric. Sasha didn't know then that seven years later, just when they should have caught up with America, Sveta would lock herself in a hotel room in Kiev, where her theater was on tour, and pour down her throat a vial of drugs that were not supposed to exist in the healthy Soviet world.

But in 1959, with Sveta still alive, they stopped in each of the four model kitchens to watch a baking demonstration and then, when the American women in aprons, whether by accident or by design, turned their backs on their plates of finished little cakes called brownies, they grabbed as many as they could, like everyone else around them, and, their hands sticky with chocolate and sugar, raced to the next exhibit. Sveta's image rises before her eyes, her blonde hair in a long braid, her index finger raised didactically, as if she were admonishing Sasha with another scrap of wisdom about life in the theater. Sasha would call if Sveta were still alive to ask whether she remembered the America they saw nine years ago, to ask what Sasha should do about America today.

When we pass you along the way, we'll wave to you. Well, two years have passed since we were supposed to overtake America, and she hasn't seen one dishwasher or a single brownie. Is this what America looks like, that Expo? A model house for every model family, shelves filled with books that no one tries to censor, plays that no one decrees to ban?

Or is it a country where people sleep in cardboard boxes under bridges, as *Pravda* constantly reminds them? A place plagued by hurricanes and guns, where round-bellied capitalists in top hats, who glare from posters glued to newsstands, multiply their fortunes by exploiting men in chains? A place where human beings are disconnected and alone, stooped under the weight of questions that have no answers?

Is it really possible to cross to the other side? Is there a bridge between the two lives that seem to be so far apart, installed on opposite poles of the earth? Or are they—those living on this side—too burdened by their past and haunted by their memories: the physical and moral devastation of the Leningrad Front, of Nadia's disappearance, of Mama's scribbling spy reports on her professor? Is their past always going to hold them back, on this side of the Iron Curtain, wrapped— like babushkas in their kerchiefs—in their version of reality, always heroic and uplifting, always right, until they age and shrivel and become the grime of history? Or can she excise the images of this reality from her mind, rip them out of her heart, by the roots? Must Sasha clear her head of the past so that she can advance into the future?

She often sees Mama young, the way she looked in a photograph in Ivanovo before Sasha was born, her hair swept back in the style popular before the war, her smiling eyes still crinkled and ironic. This is how she now comes to Sasha in dreams, when she tries to hold fast to the diaphanous image of her mother in the first few moments of waking up. The mother she'd never known, the mother who still remembers Kolya in Ivanovo. Her mother, standing tall and straight, alone, outside time.

Maybe, after all, there is no solid demarcation between the living and the dead but rather a thin veil, more porous than they could know. Or maybe this thought is nothing but Sasha's pitiful attempt to soothe the wound of guilt, of not being next to her mother when her heart was failing, when she was lying in the hospital, most likely in the hallway, on a bed without sheets, frightened and alone. Maybe this thought is nothing but her feeble effort to alleviate the grief of allowing her mother to die. It still festers, this wound, spewing guilt. With time, will it dry up? Will this wishful thinking transport her mother solely into their memory, hers and Kolya's, where she will always be radiant and young, having achieved the impossible feat of slowing down the current of time?

Sasha thinks of Kolya's voice reaching over to her from the past, the voice of a man who won't, for her, remain forever young. A man she knows only from his paintings, his war journal, and his prewar photographs in the family album, a man who had in Sasha's mind, for so many years, replaced her father. A man who did cross over to another life, almost an afterlife, from which, back then, there was no return. Is there a chance that today may be the dawn of time when crossing to the other side will become possible, despite what Grandpa thinks? Possible with Andrei's help, which she is going to accept as the last arrangement he will make for her, the final manifestation of this corrosive, mutilated love.

~

On her way to the office of the administrative director, Sasha passes a sign for an upcoming meeting of her theater's Art Council. The sign announces the agenda: Why don't Communist Party members play more leading roles? She doesn't know if this question deserves a meeting-length discussion or if it is even a valid question that merits an answer, but she knows what she is going to say to Pavel Petrovich, their chief administrator, who presides over the daily machinery of her theater. She is going to tell him she is leaving.

His narrow features tense, gathering even closer around his nose. "You're leaving to go where?" he asks, peering at her from above his thin-rimmed glasses, his brow furrowed.

Sasha knows that the word *America* would explode in this stately office like a bomb, taking him and her and everyone else in the building with it, so she remains silent.

He gets up from his desk and paces to the wall and back, his hand hugging his sharp chin. "Alexandra Alexandrovna," he says, using a formal way to address her, something he has never done before. "You are our leading character actress," he says in a solemn voice, trying to maintain authority. "You are engaged in five performances. How do you expect us to function without you?" He turns to her from the wall. "Please enlighten me."

She has nothing to say to offer enlightenment. Instead, she says what she has wanted to say to him for months.

"You refused to allow me to go to the hospital when my mother was dying because I had a performance to deliver. Do you remember? You didn't let me travel to Ivanovo to my grandmother's funeral. It was more important that the shows kept running. The performance was more important than a human being. Theater was more important than life."

He stops before his desk and leans forward, his palms on the glass.

"This job has cost me dearly," she says, "and now I need to leave."

"And just how long do you plan to be away?" he asks, drilling into her face with one of his formidable stares that have extinguished scandals and severed careers. He is used to heartbreak and intrigue and all kinds of manipulation, having seen a great deal of drama, both onstage and off, in his twenty years of working in the theater, but Sasha can sense he knows that she is serious. His thick eyebrows have formed one line, and she notices that his left eyelid has begun to twitch.

"A couple of months, probably," she says in a tone he will perceive as nonchalant because she no longer cares. "I'm not sure yet." If she was honest, she would tell him that she is not sure of anything, except that she must leave. Leave Andrei here. Go where Kolya is.

He lowers himself into the chair and stares at the massive ink blotter no one has ever used. "You do realize that if you leave, we may not be able to offer you a position when you come to your senses and decide to return," he says.

She does realize this. She realizes that she is about to abandon her entire life, a life she has worked so hard to achieve. A life with the three pillars at its foundation: the graves in Leningrad and Ivanovo; her dusty blackhearted motherland; and the Theater, which in her six years of work here has grown into her big, dysfunctional family.

Abandoning all of them at once, she thinks, is the only way she will ever leave.

At the door, she turns, but not to bid him farewell. "By the way," she says, "you don't need an entire meeting to figure out why Party members rarely get leading roles. It's simple. They rarely have any talent."

~

She will stop to say goodbye to Lara and Slava, her former classmates, her fellow actors, her small *kompaniya* of friends. She will wish them happiness and luck in their lives in the theater. She will apologize to Lara for not protecting her from the assistant dean when they were students. She will thank her for listening to so many hours of rants about Andrei, about Marik, about insecurity and guilt; for being patient and quiet; for having survived to become Sasha's close friend.

Then Vladimir Ivanovich will hold her and kiss her on the head, as a father would his departing daughter. He will pour them a drink of whatever is stashed in his room for her upcoming trip, for crossing the ocean to the other side. It is like crossing the River Lethe, he will say, the river of oblivion, which runs between this life and the next. Its waters will make her forget the past, he will say. They will erase all memory of her present life.

46

She can't see Andrei as he stands in the check-in hall of Pulkovo Airport's international wing, concealing himself behind a column in the corner, away from the counter with the handwritten sign where the words NEW YORK are scribbled in the neat cursive loops of a top English student. But Sasha knows he is there. She can sense him. He watches her walk from the customs area, dragging her half-open suitcase, which has obviously been rummaged through, and he shakes his head in frustration. This was the one thing he failed to do, to give her name to the customs director. One thing he failed to do, but not the only thing. He clenches his jaw, but it is too late now. It is too late for so much. He watches her drag her suitcase away from the door, where she starts to fold the rumpled clothes and pack everything back into the bag. When she is done, Sasha looks around, sees the loopy handwritten sign, and joins the line for check-in. It is a short line, uncharacteristic of lines in this city: not many people travel to New York from Leningrad.

He sees a red passport in her hand, which, he knows, has just been issued and still smells of glue, a special external passport granting her permission to leave for the United States of America. Sasha knows he had to cash in some huge favors he had accumulated over the years in order to have that passport issued. He even got his father-in-law involved—he had to—although he knew Vadim smelled the truth, by the way his son-in-law begged. He had never asked for anything before, so the old man looked him in the eye and said, "This is for her, isn't it," which they both knew was not really a question. Andrei didn't nod or shake his head in denial. "Whoever this is for," he replied as impartially as he could muster, "I'm sending her away. Far away." "How far?" asked Vadim, a flare of suspicion in his eyes. "America," he said and turned to the wall, because the sound of that destination made him have to catch his breath. That was when the old man walked over to the internal office phone, lifted the receiver, and dialed a number that only he could dial. "A visa and a passport will be issued in her name," he said, his voice both a warning and a condemnation. "But if they investigate who authorized this, it will be you who takes the fall."

He is ready to take the fall. He has nothing to lose.

He watches Sasha heave her suitcase onto the scale; accept a boarding pass from the clerk, a woman with doughy forearms and henna-colored hair; fit it into her passport. A week ago, at her request, he called Kolya in New York with her flight number; he was surprised that her uncle still rounded his vowels the way they all did back in Ivanovo, a dialectal peculiarity. He watches the clerk peer at her as she is looking down, a stare of recognition. Of course people recognize her; she is an actress. She is wearing a navy dress with short sleeves and a narrow skirt, a pair of high-heeled shoes that make her legs look more muscled, like the legs of a ballerina. Her hair is the color of ash, the color of burn and ruin, and is pulled back into a ponytail; her bangs come down to her eyebrows; her eyes are big and gray, like frozen water on the winter canals. He can see her eyes as distinctly as if she were standing next to him. On her arm she is holding a beige raincoat, the one he knows, the raincoat she wore two months ago when she appeared on the threshold of his office, when she brought Kolya's letter to show him, when she thought there might still have been hope for the two of them. Or even hope for him alone.

He stands there behind the pillar, watching her walk toward the plane that will take her out of Russia, watching her leave, the same way he stood at the Ivanovo railway station when she was leaving for Moscow to study acting, the same way he stood at the cemetery at her mother's funeral—always an observer, almost a stalker, always watching her from the sidelines, perched on the periphery of her life.

47

Andrei's car is waiting outside the airport. He has just seen her pass through the glass door, gone through the passage to a life beyond the curtain. He gets into the front seat, next to Borya, leaning back into the familiar sweaty smell of old leather and gasoline. "To the office," he says and stares into the rusty lock of the glove compartment as Borya steps on the gas and turns the car around to go back to the city. Wordlessly, they drive past rows of newly erected apartments that his office has yet to allocate to the best workers of this factory or that school district.

"Is it the actress?" says Borya, a question he has earned the right to ask by six years of not asking too many questions. Andrei doesn't answer, and by not answering, by staring into the windshield, he acknowledges what Borya, who saw her get out of the taxi and enter the door of the small international wing, is asking. The actress, the airport, the final separation. All corroborated by his driver, who knows her from TV; all validated by the Aeroflot clerk who recognized her from one of her plays. They saw her leave, just as he did. They are witnesses. His feverish mind didn't make it up. She is now waiting to get on the plane, past the passport control, in the neutral zone between the countries' borders, unaffiliated with either land, free. She is free of him, finally. Ready to place the enormity of the Atlantic Ocean between them, as a confirmation. And is he free of her, as he has promised his father-in-law?

Borya pulls in front of the Smolny entrance and turns off the engine. Andrei opens the door and, with one foot on the pavement, fumbles in his pocket, takes out his silver lighter—the one shaped like a handgun, a birthday gift from his coworkers—and hands it to his driver. "Keep it," he says and nods Borya good night, sending him home.

The Smolny hallways are echoey; the offices behind the closed doors are empty, deserted for the night. In the whole building, he is alone. He unlocks the door to his office, creaks it open, and turns on the light. Everything is the same way he left it this afternoon, the same way he found it six years ago when he asked to be transferred to Leningrad to be close to her. All is the same except for one thing locked in the desk drawer, something small and weighty, something he placed there after the dacha talk with his father-in-law about all those enemies of the people murdered in NKVD cellars.

He sits at his desk, shakes a cigarette out of a pack, and rolls it between his fingers. The ashtray is full of cigarette butts he has smoked when he sat there for hours this afternoon, before the trip to the airport. He doesn't remember how long he sat there. His mind wandered, and his thoughts strayed, images rushing through his head, flooding, just as they are now, again. He sees their Ivanovo courtyard, a well with a creaky handle, chickens wading through the dust, the tar roof over the dump where he, Marik, and Sasha met after school. He sees the lilac bushes stretching their branches through the slats in the fence on the corner where he waited for her to return from a piano lesson. He sees the field where they lay among the tall grass, on the last day she came there before she left, rain falling in the distance, drawn toward the dark forest, like a heavy curtain.

He sits and smokes. His heart feels constricted, and he takes deep breaths of tobacco, inhaling as much as he can, filling his chest with cigarette smoke, as if it could ease the pressure of the cage around his heart. He thinks of his father lying on the ground in front of the burning house, watching him with one eye, of the rage compressing his chest.

He thinks of the forest in Ivanovo, the fire they made eleven years ago, the shell he placed into Marik's hand. The guilt he never admitted to anyone. Sasha was the only one who knew. He thinks of Sasha, of her love for him, of his love for her. Of her, Sasha, who is now on her way to another life, while he is still here, being sucked deeper and deeper into the vortex of the past.

He fumbles in the inner pocket of his jacket, wraps his fingers around a small key, and opens the desk drawer. The revolver glares with a matte finish tarnished by time. He won it from his father-in-law's NKVD friend on a bet, claiming he could down a glass of undiluted spirits twice as strong as vodka. It was May 9, 1965, the twentieth anniversary of Soviet victory over the Nazis, and they were all drinking at the dacha. The NKVD friend took his loss stoically, sliding the gun and a case with bullets across the table, although his jaw tightened and his Adam's apple silently gasped. "Cherish it," he said to Andrei in a dim voice. "This gun has a history."

Thanks to his father-in-law, he now knows that history, and looking at the revolver makes him consider the irony. He owns a gun that killed hundreds of his compatriots who had the misfortune of living during Russia's earlier, carnivorous times. Now, as his father-in-law often says, a rueful smile on his face, we live in vegetarian times, and the gun has been rendered useless. Or maybe it is simply on hiatus. With their motherland, where wars and revolutions happen with eerie regularity, one never knows. He glides his hand across the barrel, cold and a little rough; clicks the trigger; opens the case with bullets. They are pointed, made of brass. He pulls the hammer back and slides one in.

His wife will genuinely grieve, just as her mother and perhaps Vadim, who will be angered at seeing his daughter so devastated. And Sasha? She is gone from his life for good, vanished to the other side of the curtain. She is no longer here, within the confines of this reality. He has made sure of that.

A line from a poem floats to the surface of his mind: "Let's part tonight and end this madness." Mayakovsky, his favorite poet who has always been his lighthouse, his salvation. He scrunches his face and shakes his head. Mayakovsky, who ended up blowing his brains out. Some lighthouse. What a fucking joke.

He lifts the gun out of the drawer, weighs it on his palm. It feels too light to inflict such irreversible damage, too insignificantly small. He rubs the textured handle, presses the barrel against his temple, his forehead, his heart, as if trying to find a place most efficient for the bullet to inflict its ultimate damage, the place of certainty, the place of finality. He doesn't want to wake up in a hospital, with relatives and friends around his bed casting him pitying glances. How did Mayakovsky do it? he wonders. He read about it somewhere, but not, of course, in the Soviet papers where everyone is too optimistic, too busy building a bright future. Then he slides the gun in his mouth and pushes the end of the barrel against his upper palate. Is this only a rehearsal? He will know soon enough. He holds the gun there for a few moments, his tongue finding its way to wrap around it: a warm, wet life embracing its cold opposite. It tastes of metal, dust, and time. The savage time, the squandered time. The time about to end.

48

She is twelve thousand meters in the air, trying to clear her mind and focus on her imminent future. Or is she trying to understand her past? Every time she glances at the overhead television screen that shows the position of her Aeroflot flight, Kolya and America get closer. The miniature airplane on the screen is like a needle over the Atlantic, stitching the two hemispheres together with the thread of their route.

What is waiting for her there, on the other end of this thread? She tries to imagine a New York airport, but all she has at her disposal are images of airports in Tbilisi, Kiev, and Baku, where her theater company has recently been on tour. She tries to conjure up Kolya's face, but what rises before her eyes is the prewar photograph from their family album, of him in Grandpa's garden, holding a branch of an apple tree, laughing.

Beneath is a heavy blanket of clouds, a curtain flipped horizontally that sets them closer to the sun and obscures the earth below. The first rays of light are just beginning to leak from under the clouds as the sun rises above the curtain, a stage light that in only a few minutes will flood the cabin and make everything pink. She looks out as a stewardess, her hand glowing in the streak of light from the window, hands her a US customs form. Her newly minted passport for foreign travel is in her handbag, ready to oblige, and, leafing through a pocket dictionary, she writes the answers to the stern American immigration questions.

As the plane descends, it banks to the right and then the left, as if to show her from every perspective a new, other life waiting below. She looks down on the gray expanse of water held back by a barrier of stone rising higher than she has ever seen, spires etched against the sky, lit by the sun like a set for a play.

In her mind, Sasha sees herself handing the form and her passport to a border patrol agent in New York, someone who has the serious face of her theater's administrative director. "What are your reasons for leaving Russia?" the agent will ask. "What are you running away from?" In her broken English, she knows what she will tell him, the unpracticed words that don't require rehearsing. "From graves," she will say. "From pretending." He will listen carefully, even though he probably won't understand. "From shame," she will say. Then the agent will hand her passport back and fling open the metal gate into a new life.

In the waiting crowd, among hundreds of faces, she will immediately see Kolya. Although she has never met him, she will recognize him at once. Sasha is certain of this. It will only take her a second to make out Grandma's soft, round face. It will only take her a moment to see Mama's eyes.

He will wait for Sasha to approach and hold her in his embrace. "Sashenka," he will say, her name as soft as his cheek. "I'm so happy you've come." He will smell of their Ivanovo life: of summer dust and lilacs, of the wood-burning stove, of their evening tea with little crystal bowls of black currant jam. This is when Grandma will pour boiling water from a samovar into a good cup with a pattern of roses, a cup that has been waiting for him all these years since he left for the front. This is when Mama will open her arms and press Sasha into the pillows of her breasts, making sobs erupt from a deep well inside her, making tears run down her face and leave wet spots on her mother's dress with a red apple print she remembers so well. *Vsyo budet khorosho,* Mama will say, her voice like the tea with sugar in Kolya's cup. "All will be well," she'll say, healing her with the warmth of her embrace, and this time, despite her stubbornness and doubt, Sasha will believe her.

ACKNOWLEDGMENTS

These books provided an immersion into the times of the story in the novel:
Svetlana Alexievich. *Secondhand Time*, Penguin Random House, 2016
Nikolai Nikulin. *Memories of the War* (in Russian), Hermitage
Publishing, 2007
Antony Beevor and Luba Vinogradova. *A Writer at War: Vasily
Grossman with the Red Army, 1941–1945*, Pantheon Books, 2005
I am deeply grateful to my agent, Molly Friedrich, who shaped this
first novel and, with grace and humor, guided me through the minefield
of writing fiction. My gratitude also goes to my editor, Alicia Clancy,
whose exacting eye trimmed and enriched the story and who saw its
title hiding in plain sight.

My appreciation goes to my early readers Heather Carr, Zoe
Kharpertian, Liliane Gold, Nadia Carey, Mervyn Rothstein, and Rachel
Basch for their honesty and support. A special thank-you to Barbara
Jones for her invaluable suggestions of revisions.

This novel would not be possible without my sister, Marina, whose
stories about Ivanovo, Theater, and acting laid the foundation of this
story. I dedicate this book to her.

And finally, *spasibo* to my husband, Andy, who patiently read the
countless iterations of this novel, for his loving encouragement and
plainspoken advice.

DISCUSSION QUESTIONS

1. Do you think Sasha made the right choice leaving Andrei in his moment of tragedy to pursue her dreams of acting?
2. At the age of seven, Sasha heard Chekhov's *Three Sisters* on the radio, and it changed her life. Did you ever have a childhood experience that changed your life?
3. How did the war change Sasha's mother and uncle? How did it affect her grandmother and grandfather?
4. Grandpa is a true believer to the point that he disowned his own son. Why do you think he can't let go of his old ways of thinking? Can you imagine a situation where you would disown a loved one?
5. Sasha and Andrei are drawn together, again and again, despite their different views of life. Was there anything they could have done to make their relationship work?
6. Sasha's uncle's journal is a foundation of her beliefs. How did his experience shape her view of Soviet life? Would Sasha have followed the same path if she had not found his journal?
7. Against the landscape of Stalin's terror and postwar reality in Russia, do you think Sasha's mother needed to be so tough on her daughter?

8. How do you think Marik's death affected Sasha's life? Was she able to transform the guilt she carried after "the accident in the woods" into a positive force?

9. Andrei pulled many strings to help Sasha escape to America, risking his career and possibly his life. How do you think the story ends? Why is Andrei so drawn to Mayakovsky?

10. How do you envision Sasha's future in America?

11. The reality of war portrayed in Kolya's journal was not the reality Sasha learned in school. Do you think these dual realities exist in today's world?

ABOUT THE AUTHOR

Photo © 2015 Lauren Perlstein

Elena Gorokhova was born and raised in Leningrad, now Saint Petersburg, Russia. After graduating from Leningrad University, she moved to the United States, carrying one suitcase with twenty kilograms of what used to be her life. Elena is the author of two memoirs: *A Mountain of Crumbs* and *Russian Tattoo*. Her work has appeared in the *New York Times*, the *Daily Beast*, *New Jersey Monthly*, and the *Daily Telegraph*, as well as on NPR and BBC Radio and in a number of literary magazines. *A Train to Moscow* is Elena's first novel. She lives and teaches in New Jersey. For more information, visit www.elenagorokhova.com.